Unforgiven

To Vicky,
Love is Love is Love
so welcome it with open arms

RUTH CLAMPETT

all the best,

Unforgiven
Copyright © 2017 by Ruth Clampett
All Rights Reserved.

This book is a work of fiction. Names, characters, places and incidents are either products of the author's imagination or used fictitiously. Any resemblance to actual events, locales, or persons, living or dead, is entirely coincidental. No part of this publication can be reproduced or transmitted in any form or by any means, electronic or mechanical, without permission in writing from the author or publisher.

The author acknowledges the trademarked status and trademark owners of various products referenced in this work of fiction, which have been used without permission. The publication/use of these trademarks is not authorized, associated with, or sponsored by the trademark owners.

ISBN: 9781544068527

Cover Design:
Jada D'Lee

Cover Photograph/Graphics:
Fotolia and Adobe

Content Editor:
Angela Borda

Copy Editor:
Melissa of There For You Editing

Interior Formatting:
Christine Borgford of Type A Formatting

Summary

Would you live a lie to hold onto the one you love?

Dean and Jason are best friends, like brothers since boyhood, now architecture students and college roommates. They've always had each other's back, but when one walks in on the other with another man, everything changes. How do you explain to your best friend that he's the one you always wanted, that until now your life has been a lie?

Desperation and shame are two dirty words that run through Jason's veins. He carries the scars from a wayward priest who stole his innocence and left him shattered. Meanwhile for years he's watched Dean pursuing woman after woman as his own heart slowly breaks.

When their world blows apart, they learn the powerful bond between them has more fire than either understood. Can two broken souls find the light in their darkness and come together to make a whole, or will the sins of the past be forever unforgiven?

Love is Love is Love

To my beautiful and brave friends
that have stood tall and marched to the beat
of their own drum, no matter what it cost them.
You are my kind of heroes.

♥ ♥ ♥

Unforgiven

Dean .1

MY GAZE SCANS OVER OUR usual crowd holding plastic cups of beer or cheap wine, as the heavy bass of the music throbs through the dark room. With that promising feeling in the air of spring approaching a party sounded like a good idea tonight, but this one is quickly losing its charm.

Being an architecture student, this rambling, old stucco house with the original wood windows—many of them either broken or painted shut—makes me edgy. The worn hardwood floor planks on the first level sag in various spots and many of the walls slightly lean.

It's as if the house would just like to give up, and sink down into its foundation, never to be inhabited again if it weren't for the students who live here and infuse the house with the will to continue on. Still, in my dreams I'd love to tear it down and rebuild it in a cutting-edge, contemporary design.

I let out a long sigh as Cassie approaches and leans into me so her breasts skim my arm. Her sun-bleached hair is in a loose knot at the back of her head with tendrils trailing around her face, and she's wearing a tight, worn-out T-shirt with a picture of Einstein and the quote "Imagination is more important than knowledge" printed across the front. She's such a dichotomy to me; a brainy engineering student obsessed with providing energy through fusion technology, and equally obsessed with lots and lots of casual sex.

She gives me a wicked grin before leaning forward to drag her fingertips down my chest. Does she think I don't know what she wants? After a few beers, screwing her every way 'til Sunday seems like a good idea, but I always feel conflicted the next day. She's up for anything and so damn easy, and where's the challenge in that? I've enjoyed her talents many times, but it's getting old.

I'd always had a blueprint for my future life in my head, and my ex, Julie was a major part of that. So after she abandoned me, I didn't want to get attached to a girl and chance getting my heart broken again. Now if I'm going to hook-up, I like the sweet ones that aren't aggressive. Lately, though, none of the girls in our college crowd are appealing to me. Maybe I need a new scene. As lame as this party's been tonight, I'm ready to roll.

I turn to Keith. "Hey, where's Jason?"

He shrugs his shoulders. "He and Andrea's guy, Ramon were talking motorcycles last I saw him."

"Yeah, I think they went out to the garage to check out the bike he's rebuilding," Kirk adds in.

I smile over bike-obsessed Jason and anything that goes fast. When we were kids we used to race each other around the neighborhood on our BMXs. On Saturdays we'd ride over to Rand's Motorsports and look in the windows at the latest motorbikes.

He's always had the dream of having his own racing bike, but his mother goes uber-emotional at the mention of it. It's amazing he's not more of a wimp being such a momma's boy, but maybe being lifelong best buds with me has kept him just on the right side of badass.

I turn to Kirk. "Thanks, man. I'm outta here."

He nods, and Keith fist bumps me. "Later."

As I head out to the back patio, I see Cassie talking to another guy I don't recognize but she winks at me regardless. I turn away and roll my eyes.

The yard is dark as I walk toward the garage. I know I'm going to have to drag Jason away from this scene. I lay odds that he's stroking the bike like a bitch right now. Whatever he gets into he gets into hard, but I deal with his obsessions and he deals with mine. That's why we're best friends and perfect roommates.

Frankly I'm just glad he's not bringing that girl, Stacy, home. She was all over him earlier. Our walls are thin and word on the street is that she's way too loud in bed. I'm not up for that shit tonight.

The side door to the garage is cracked open just enough for me to step inside. The structure sags and leans like the rest of the old house. My gaze scans through the open space under the yellow light of the single bulb hanging from the ceiling. I see the bike—its chrome is polished like it'd just been shined—but there's no sign of Jason or Ramon.

I'm about to step back out of the garage when I hear a low moan, the sound so raw and hungry that my pulse speeds up. My eyes dart to the far wall where I spot Jason leaning against a wood post with his eyes wedged shut like he's in pain.

I start to step forward to see what's wrong, but stop when my gaze scans down. I realize in the next moment that Ramon is on his knees in front of Jason, whose jeans are pushed down to his thighs.

What the hell?

I'm so shocked I can't breathe and the next moan out of my best friend's mouth paralyzes me. *Is it what I think?* Watching Ramon's head bob, I hear rude sounds and my dark idea is confirmed. The next moment Jason's hands move down to Ramon's head, and instead of pushing the fucker away as I expect, he pulls him down harder over his dick.

"Ramon," he groans with a rough voice. It's a voice that says he wants more, not less, and it stuns me.

Ramon chokes. *No shit, fucker . . .* I've seen Jason naked and the guy is hung like a porn star.

So there I am paralyzed and watching Ramon do Jason and my mind is a pinball machine of crazy thoughts. There's no way Jason is gay. He's messed around with at least half of the hot girls in our year. Did someone slip him one of those weird drugs? That has to be it. My adrenaline fires up and I'm ready to go cage fighter on Ramon. I thought that guy was, according to his girl Andrea, *the Latin lover.*

My stomach turns as I watch Ramon's hands move over Jason's thighs before they slip between his legs. When Ramon lets out a moan louder than Jason's, I snap back to reality.

"Hey!" I yell out.

Jason's eyes fly open and Ramon turns while never letting Jason's cock out of his mouth. From this new side angle the girth of Jason's dick is even more impressive.

Jason's gaze darts down at Ramon, and then at me before he presses his hands over his forehead and rolls his eyes back. From his expression it's hard to tell if he's completely wasted. *What if he actually wants this guy to suck his cock? What the fuck?*

Ramon turns back and his head starts bobbing faster but now he moves his free hand down between his legs. *Is that bastard going to jerk off in front of me?*

Meanwhile Jason still hasn't pushed him away but instead his hips start rocking forward, forcing his hard dick down Ramon's throat. I feel all the blood rush between my legs and it makes me panic. If I get hard now, it will be the end of everything I thought I knew. My best friend is a stranger . . . and my cock is on the verge of being one too.

As my jeans tighten I give Jason another searing look and he serves it back. His eyes narrow as his hips rock harder. It feels like his penetrating gaze is a challenge.

Doesn't he know how this is fucking up my head? Does he even care? Or is this guy on his knees all that matters to him now?

Before I turn away he moans while glaring at me, and then he bites his lip. His stare cuts right through me . . . it's as if he wishes *I* was the one on my knees.

Screw you, Jason.

Has he secretly been wanting his cock in my mouth? Were all of our hot chick talks just for show? He knows I'm all about girls, and I thought he was the same.

Turning, I head out the door, and as I cross the threshold he cries out that choked sound I've heard before when he whacks off in his room. He's coming in that dude's mouth. Has he lost his mind? My fingers curl into tight fists as I storm across the lawn and head to my car.

Motherfucker can find his own ride home. On second thought he should just shack up with Ramon the cocksucker . . . because I can't handle my fury right now. He's always been the best friend I could trust with my life and my secrets. But what else can I conclude now other than Jason's life has been a lie and I'm apparently his beard. I feel completely betrayed, and I'm enraged to be part of his game.

I don't even remember the drive home, and the shots of whiskey, as evident from the drained shot glasses next to my bed . . . I remember even less. What really blows is that I'm drunk and spread across my bed and even all the booze can't wipe my mind clean of what I've seen. As I try to think about anything but Jason, my fucked up thoughts keep going back to him. Yet what haunts me most is the look in his eyes. It was something I'd never seen . . . like he was finally getting what he really wanted. *Could that be true?*

My balls tighten when I remember how into it Ramon was. That fucker is a linebacker on the football team and the last person I expected to see on his knees. I picture the look of drunken pleasure he had with Jason's cock between his lips.

I'm so shocked by all of it that I wonder. *Would it be different to have a guy suck you off?* Guys know what feels good and they're tougher. Jesus, Jason was fucking his mouth at the end and Ramon was taking it like a champ.

I feel the throbbing between my legs, and I don't have to look down to know my dick is rock hard from remembering the way Jason moaned with desire while our gazes locked. *What in the hell is happening to me?*

The haze of the whiskey is doing this, I reassure myself. I spit into my hand and make a tight fist around my cock. As I stroke myself I picture the way Jason rocked his hips and fisted Ramon's hair while glaring at me.

He wanted me to be the one going down on him. I could feel it in my bones.

Spreading my legs wider, I jerk myself faster to the rhythm of my pounding heart. Jason wanted me hard for him. *Well, you've got it now, buddy.*

My vision goes hot white as streams of come stripe my abs and chest. I keep pumping myself hard, pulling out every last feeling. With the final strokes, I picture Jason on his knees blowing *me*, and suddenly it's like I'm coming all over again . . . my cock jerking as I imagine his tongue sliding up my shaft.

"Jason," I repeat over and over until I pass out in a drunken stupor.

I have no idea what time it is when my eyes finally peel open. All the memories of the night before come crashing back into my consciousness, and I throw my arm over my eyes like a shield. I vaguely remember the images I jerked off to, and it freaks me out, but before I have a complete meltdown I decide to pass them off as a fucked up reaction from drunken shock. I mean who wouldn't flip out after what I saw last night?

Did Jason even come home? Or did he get on all fours for Ramon? Nothing should surprise me at this point.

A sensation comes over me and I realize it's like this weird hurt feeling. I feel left out and overlooked . . . as if Jason picked someone else on the schoolyard to play with.

Jason wasn't just my best friend growing up; for years we've dreamed of being partners in our own architectural firm. It started innocently enough, as one of those big ideas kids get, and then soon get over. But for us the idea just stuck, and we never wavered from our plan . . . even going to the same architecture program together for college.

The whole thing started over ten years ago when Dad overheard us talking about designing buildings together. He challenged us to come up with a unique house idea for he and Mom. We had so much fun working together on it that we just kept at it . . . asking virtually everyone we knew if we could design their dream home. We were obsessed and our ideas and drawings kept getting better.

But now realizing that Jason's been keeping secrets and lying to me, I've decided that feeling hurt from his betrayal is bullshit, and his fabrications just make me angry all over again. That's all it takes for the asshole side of me to come back with a vengeance.

I slowly slide off the side of the bed and will myself to get up. Pulling on my boxers, I walk through our apartment, looking for Jason. I'm going to punch him in his pretty face when I finally confront him.

His room is empty, as is the living room. I shake my head. Most likely, he slept curled up with Ramon. He's probably his little bitch now.

On the way to the bathroom, I start to imagine their morning sex . . . as much as I try not to. Maybe Jason is sucking off Ramon. I picture his wide mouth with Ramon's balls in them and my boxers start tenting.

I glance down at my crotch in disgust. *Damn traitor whore cock.* Fucker'll get hard at the idea of anything involving tongues and wet places.

Several minutes later I'm under the stream of hot water, my hand full of shower gel as I furiously jack off. I'm cursing myself with each stroke, but I can't chase the image of Ramon sucking off Jason out of my head. I come so hard against the tile wall of the shower that my knees almost buckle. *This shit has got to stop.*

I take a long time to dry off, especially between my legs where my cock is still acting confused. Is this a new thing? Me walking around half-mast and imagining what it would feel like to have a man's mouth on me?

I'm furious with Jason for screwing with my head like this. Did he really think so little of me that he couldn't be honest about what he was into? I thought we were like brothers, sharing all our secrets, but apparently not. As a result, I don't know which way is up anymore, and that is so not cool.

I'm half tempted to get on his laptop and see what kind of porn he's been jerking off to. I'm pretty sure it's not buxom babes.

My stomach growling, I secure the towel around my waist and head to the kitchen. After downing half the carton of milk I peel open a power bar and take a big bite while I search through the cupboards for something else to eat.

Hearing the front door unlock, I freeze in place. *Fucking great . . .* I've got a towel around my waist and a semi. I'm sure that's just what my gay ex-best friend wants to see.

I turn when he steps inside the door and my fury tampers seeing that Jason looks like complete shit. His skin has a green pallor and his eyes are red. He seems surprised to see me.

"Why'd you leave without me?" he asks as he shuts the door,

forgetting to lock it.

"Why do you think, asshole? You were pre-disposed."

Shoulders slumping, he casts his gaze downward. "I wouldn't have just left *you* there."

"Is that so? You look like shit, man. What the hell?"

He rubs his scalp hard and winces. "I passed out. I remember smoking some funky shit. I woke up on the lounge thing by the pool and walked home."

I arch my brow. *Is that how he's going to play this?* I'm still not sure he looked stoned to me when his lover boy was sucking him off.

"Really? Some funky shit? I thought you knew better than that, Jason. But I thought I knew a lot of things that maybe I don't."

Some of the green cast of his skin turns to red as he stares at me. His expression is defeated, like this event has completely floored him, and I guess I'm not surprised. Suddenly being gay must be a lot to handle.

His gaze moves down to my neck, over my shoulders and then across my chest before reaching the edge of my towel. He can't look any lower because I've moved against the kitchen counter so he can't see my stiff woody trying to make its way out of my towel. I try to will it soft, but now that he's staring at my hard nipples I can tell it's a lost cause.

What motherfucker? Are you thinking dirty thoughts as you stare at me? I feel a flush work its way down my chest. I imagine what it would be like for Jason to bite my nipples. I love it when chicks do that to me, but they never do it hard enough. I bet Jason would.

I'm losing my mind.

Shaking my head, I reach into the box of Wheaties, take a handful and shove it in my mouth.

"I'm going to go lie down," Jason says in a quiet voice. When he walks away I take a glance at his crotch, and sure enough, there's a noticeable bulge. I should probably follow him in there and fuck him raw just to screw with his head like he's screwed with mine. But I'm not a total asshole, and despite my hard-on, I'm definitely not into men. I decide to take another shower instead.

Jason. 2

AS SOON AS I STEP into my bedroom, I close my door and lean back against it. My breaths are coming in short gasps and my stomach is churning.

Damn it all. I was counting on Dean being in his room so I could slip into mine without a confrontation. I still can't believe how bad I fucked up last night. He probably hates me.

What was I thinking following Ramon into that garage? Deep down I knew he was going to try something, and honestly I was just worn out and worked up trying to push down all the sexual feelings I'm struggling with. I had no fight left in me.

I don't want to be gay. With every fiber of my being, I don't want to be an outcast, judged as a deviant by people who don't even know me. I've seen what happens to those guys. Our next-door neighbor where I grew up got taunted all the time, even though he pretty much kept to himself. It's not an easy life where I came from. Hell, my mom would probably disown me. I can still hear her voice in my head with her condemnations of "those sick homosexuals and their deviant ways" and her warnings to me about steering clear of them.

But even that can't change who I crave sexually . . . and most of all I crave Dean. I burn for him and with each passing month it gets harder to pretend that I don't.

Him standing there in the kitchen with only a towel around his waist was tantamount to torture. His body is my idea of perfection—broad, strong shoulders, muscled, tattooed arms and chest, and clearly defined abs. Fresh out of the shower, his smooth skin was still moist. I wanted to run my tongue across his chest and pull open that damn towel. But it was clear from the steely look in his eyes and the sharp set of his jawline, that if I even came close to touching him, he'd take me down hard.

Approaching my bed, I pull off all my clothes off except my boxers, and then flop down on the mattress. My mind reels as I try to figure out what to do. Dean didn't seem to buy my line about getting stoned and being so high I didn't know which way was up.

The only thing I know for sure is that he was disgusted by what he saw last night. I wasn't certain at first. In fact, I was shocked when I realized that he was watching what Ramon was doing to me, but I was also too far gone to stop it. I was in that desperate place, so close to coming, so turned on that I was going to implode if I didn't get off.

I think for a moment I was hoping that somehow he'd be turned on. Dean's pretty wild sexually and he's always horny, maybe he could just look at it as experimentation and then eventually I could coax him into experimenting, too.

He's always been one of the most open-minded of my circle. In high school he was friends with a couple of gay guys, even though most of his asshole friends taunted those guys when he wasn't around. I remember one was his lab partner and he thought he was really cool. So there's that.

But the longer I lie on my bed, the reality of what happened last night starts making me sick again and my stomach is churning and rolling. Dean was not only disgusted with what he witnessed, but he was also furious too before he stormed out of the garage. I remember the expression on Ramon's face after he rose off the floor.

"What the fuck was that about?" Ramon asked me as he adjusted his hard-on in his jeans. "Doesn't he know about you?"

"Know what?" I asked breathlessly, my heart pounding.

"That you like dudes."

I felt the blood drain from my face. "No. He has no idea."

Ramon shrugged. "Well he does now." Suddenly his expression darkened. "Hey, is he going to make trouble about this? I can't have that happen. I'll catch hell from my football team. No way. I need to finish up school and get out of this uptight place before I'm out of the closet."

In my stupor, I was impressed that he seemed to have a plan.

"Yeah, and then what?"

"Miami, babe. Have you ever been there? It's boys town."

Shaking my head, I looked down. That would never be me. But then I have to wonder. *What would be?*

When Ramon first started approaching me at parties I had no idea what he was up to. He was just suddenly interested in being friends and he seemed like a cool guy. But last week at one of the wilder parties, I was pretty drunk when he spotted me from across the room. I was leaning against a wall getting my bearings when Ramon approached me.

"What's up, dude?"

"Nothing. I'm buzzed," I slurred.

He leaned in closer to me and I noticed his broad shoulders and built arms straining against his T-shirt. He was so close to me that I could smell his cologne; a deep, spicy scent radiating off his dark, hot skin.

His gaze dropped down to my lips and it did something funny to me. Suddenly I sensed he was looking for something more from me. I just wasn't sure what.

"Hey, you want to get out of here?" He leaned in closer and I felt his hot breath on my neck. My skin was electrified.

"And do what?" I asked.

"I want to show you something," he replied. He stood taller and his intense gaze met mine as his knee nudged my thigh. "I think you'd like it."

I was drunk but not so drunk that his lusty gleam in his eyes wasn't computing. I glanced down at his bulge, and a corner of his mouth turned up when he looked down at mine.

Oh fuck. I was getting harder as he watched me. I was incredibly turned on, but scared shitless too.

"Whoa, you're a big boy aren't you?" He winked at me.

Damn, this guy is fearless.

"So what do you say? My car's right outside." He licked his lower lip as he waited for my reply.

Why had I never noticed how hot he was? Looking up, I scanned the crowd to see if anyone was watching us, and I noticed Dean about fifteen feet away. He was facing me but talking to some chick. It hit me that if I followed Ramon out he'd likely see me.

I started to panic. "Hey, man, I've got to take care of something. But another time, okay?"

Ramon all but smirked at me, taking one last bold glance at the situation in my jeans. "Sure, another time. Whenever you're ready."

I rushed upstairs and found the bathroom, locking the door while I tried to calm down, freaked out realizing how much I wanted to go with Ramon and find out exactly what he wanted from me.

Dean . 3

I DON'T THINK JASON COMES out of his room in the apartment for rest of the day. At one point I hear him upchucking in the bathroom and I leave some crackers and a can of 7Up in his room. It's a mothering thing to do but we've always helped each other out, and he sounds like hell.

I'll never forget that time in my junior year of high school where my parents were out of town for a few days for speaking engagements in Colorado. They figured my older brother and I were old and mature enough to take care of ourselves alone for a few days. It was awesome until I woke up one morning with a freaky high fever. I was half delirious when Jason let himself into the house wondering why I hadn't picked him up for school as usual. He looked alarmed when he found me covered with sweat and chanting weird stuff.

He tried to reach my parents but got their voicemail, so he Googled what to do for high fevers. I have vague memories of him taking my temperature, sponging my forehead to cool me off, and giving me Advil, while forcing me to drink lots of fluids. He never left for school, just stayed with me, hovering until my brother came home.

At that point I was getting worse, and after he took my temperature again he insisted that my brother take all of us to Urgent Care. Trent thought he was being dramatic, but Jason insisted. At that point my fever had spiked to 105 degrees. It was a damn good thing he refused to back down from Trent. I had contracted bacterial meningitis that left untreated could have caused a stroke or paralysis. Who knows how bad things would've gotten if he didn't care so much about me being okay.

So later that day as I check in on him, he's lying on top of his sheets in boxers with his body covered with sweat. *He must really be sick.*

I feel like an ass to admit it but his being sick makes me feel better. Maybe he was delirious last night and didn't know what he was doing. With relief surging through me I bring him a lukewarm, wet washcloth, Tylenol for his fever, and a bottle of water. He gives me a grateful look, and insists he doesn't need anything else before collapsing back on the bed.

Before I leave his room I notice that he still has our two architectural models on his dresser from a project at the end of our freshman year. The assignment was to design and make a model of a house inspired by your favorite architect. Of course Jason picked Richard Neutra, the Austrian architect who spent most of his notable career in California and is considered one of the most important modernist architects. Jason still talks about traveling to L.A. one day to see some of the homes he designed there.

I think just to spite him I picked the Spaniard Antoni Gaudi as my favorite, which was idiotic because that meant my model would have to be sculpted and embellished because his style was the opposite of Neutra's linear clean lines. Gaudi's work was organic irregular shapes, and fantastical. I remember the all-nighter before the models were due where Jason, despite being finished with his perfect model the day before, stayed up the entire night with me helping me recreate the tile mosaics swirling around the building with tiny bits of colored paper, glue, and tweezers.

He never even complained about it, just kept encouraging me. In the end he told me that I had the best model in the class. So I gave him the damn thing when we got our projects back, since it never would've been done in time without him.

Those were good times. I smile as I leave his room, closing the door quietly behind me.

Right while I'm trying to figure out what I want for dinner, Mom calls. My parents usually like to touch base with me weekly, even when they're traveling for Mom's motivational speaking engagements.

"Hey, Mom," I say, glad to connect with my folks.

"How's my boy?" she asks cheerfully. I'm the younger of her two sons but she speaks affectionately like this to both of us, even though we're far from being boys.

"Pretty good . . . busy with school work as usual. I thought it being our senior year they'd ease up a bit, but I think they want us to have a taste for how hard it will be in the working world."

"I'm sure it's challenging, but it will give you the confidence you'll need in your career. I'm proud of how hard you've worked."

"Thanks," I respond. I normally barely listen to Mom's 'positive thinking' mumbo jumbo, figuring it's straight out of one her motivational talks, but today it feels like I need some of her uplifting babble. "What's your latest lecture called again?" I ask randomly.

"How to be your best self," she says proudly. "That's what I'm talking about. I feel like you are achieving your best self, sweetheart, with your focus and drive."

I feel the heat of shame simmer through me, knowing what an ass I was to Jason last night. The logical side of me knows that he wasn't getting off with a guy just to piss me off. But I can't let go of how his lies have confused me. I also can't understand why what I saw turned me on.

"How's Jason?" Mom asks, as if she senses I was thinking about him, her affection for him clear in her tone. Jason has always had a soft spot for Mom with the way she always welcomed him in our home and treated him like one of her own. "Is he still playing on the team? I don't want him to re-injure himself."

"I think he's okay. He's playing but being very careful. He hasn't complained in a while about the pain."

"Good," she says with a sigh. "Did he ever read Dad's book, *Moving on After Loss*, that we sent him?"

"I think so," I lie. I'm pretty sure Jason never cracked the cover open. He doesn't like to examine his feelings too much.

"Is he happy . . . doing well overall?"

"He seems stressed, but there's a lot going on," I reply, keeping things vague.

"Well you let him know that I'm sending a big hug, and I hope to see you both soon."

That night I go back on my oath to avoid Cassie and go to her place for a 'movie' so I can purge all the gay stuff out of my system.

Sometimes when we get together we talk about trends in contemporary philosophy, a subject I considered minoring in, and no one can embrace a debate on that subject better than Cassie. One night we went on for hours arguing whether "x-phi" or experimental philosophy was the most significant force in the field. For someone expected to be a linear thinker, she always throws me curveballs. But she senses tonight isn't the night for mind-bending discussions.

I gotta hand it to the girl, she doesn't press me with idiotic questions as to why I'm so quiet and moody. She seems to understand the male psyche, rubbing my tense shoulders instead of trying to get me to talk.

We aren't much past the credits for the *Guardians of the Galaxy* DVD when she peels my shirt off and crawls onto my lap. Just minutes later my fly is undone, my jeans pushed open, and a condom rolled on. I lean back onto the pillows and watch her slowly ride me while I hold her large, heavy breasts in my hands and skim my thumbs over her nipples. I love watching my cock slide in and out of her. It's so damn hot.

I stay focused on Cassie and keep affirming in my head how much I like this . . . I like her riding me. I love her moans as her head sways back when I thrust into her deeper.

I like it all. I like that she's a she. It's what I've always wanted, and nothing's changed.

It's a relief when I feel my balls tighten, signaling that I'm about to come. I take over, my hands firm on her hips, pulling her down hard over me while she rubs her clit. I'm making all kinds of noise with my groans until a primal roar tears out of me. I'm fucking a girl and it's getting me off, and that's a damn good thing.

After we both catch our breaths and come down from our orgasms, we lie back against the headboard, and she lights a cigarette.

We're both quiet for a minute until she finally pipes up, "So how long have you and Jasie been friends?"

My brows arch up. She never seemed to pay much attention to Jason. Why would she ask about him now?

I look over as she takes a long drag on her cigarette and gives me a sideways glance.

Now that I think of it, it dawns on me that I never heard what happened after I left the party. I wonder if Cassie saw something with the Jason and Ramon situation. Clearing my throat, I try to sound casual and not as uptight as I suddenly feel.

"Since we were kids. He lived down the street from me, and we were always in some kind of trouble."

"I bet," she remarks with a sly smile. "Did you chase the little girls and pull their ponytails?"

"Nah, I was more the type to pull up their skirts."

She chuckles as she lets the smoke seep out between her lips. "So nothing's changed, huh?"

I shrug. "Not much."

"But Jasie didn't pull up the girls' skirts. Did he?"

Fuck. Does she know something? I need to defend his honor, now that I'm hopeful he isn't really gay.

I think about it for a minute remembering those wild days on Orange Drive. We were a team, a couple of horny kids, even studying my dad's collection of Playboy magazines down to the smallest details. I never saw a hint of anything gay with him.

Reaching over, I tug on a lock of her blonde hair. "He pulled their pony tails while I looked under their skirts."

"Yeah. So you've always been a team. I rarely see one of you without the other."

A fizz of anxiety flares in my chest. *What is she getting at?* "We're best friends. And your point is?"

She swings her legs over the side of the bed and gets up and stretches before turning toward the bathroom. "Nothing. Nothing at all."

I wish I believed her.

Several days pass and other than Jason being quiet and surly as opposed to an upbeat fucking chatterbox, things seem back to normal. Judging from the dirty clothes he left on the bathroom floor, he still wears boxers, not those gay little briefs, and he hasn't started highlighting his hair or some shit like that. My gaydar hasn't buzzed once.

Besides Jason's tutoring work, we're both carrying a heavy course load this semester and we've put in a lot of study hours. I'm glad no one warned me how tough the architecture program would be because I'm not sure I'd have stuck with it.

Jason is the one who first got me interested in buildings. Our teacher that year grew up in New York had an interest in architecture, and he let Jason and I look at his books of New York and Chicago skyscrapers which were the coolest things I'd ever seen—like a real life Gotham City.

After that Jason was always drawing buildings in the sketchbook he got for Christmas and he got me hooked too. Of course it's one thing to love coming up with ideas for houses and buildings, and another to get through linear programing, advanced calculus and statistics courses.

I wouldn't even have made it through our first year if Jason hadn't helped me. Math has never been my thing. Besides, I'm more interested in the constructing and building side of architecture.

He's not only smarter at math than me, but he has a real talent for this type of exacting design work. He was offered several scholarships in different architecture programs, but I have to believe that he chose Utah because it was the only decent architecture program I got into too.

Jason also has a fairly easy time with exams, and usually handles it all in stride, but even he seems worn down and edgy. Yet with this now being our final year there's every reason to push through the pain and finish.

Tuesday night I'm close to pulling an all-nighter when I slam my urban planning book closed and head to bed. I'm halfway down the hall to my room when I hear moaning in Jason's room. I stop and press my ear against his door.

From the slapping sound of skin against skin and his rhythm of moans I recognize that he's jerking off. This isn't new by any means, but he seems more into it than usual. He's chanting something I can't make out, and his breath is loud and almost gasping. What is he thinking about as he strokes himself? Is it Stacy in his bed, or Ramon on his knees deep-throating him?

My cock swells just listening to his moans of pleasure. The guy is really going at it. It makes me want to wrap my hand around my cock and rub one out right here in the hall. Just the thought of it reminds me of when we were in middle school. We jerked off watching porn together a bunch of times. It was dirty and exciting, but I never thought there was anything gay about it.

I seriously consider unzipping my fly and going at it, but then I realize that according to his grunts he's about to come.

Come on JJ, I whisper so low he can't hear it. "Let it go."

And apparently he does. Now I can hear the "Fuck, fuck, fuck!" he groans between gasps. Palming my painfully hard cock through my jeans, I imagine him shooting come all over his abs. If Ramon were here I bet the bastard would lick it off him.

I feel the fire move across my chest and up my neck as I imagine Ramon's tongue at work. I pull down the zipper of my fly so I can wrap my fingers around my hard dick.

Jason . 4

I'M TENSE ALL THE TIME now. My secrets are like carrying a monkey on my back and it's wearing me the fuck out.

Ramon has been pushing me to meet up with him, and according to the dirty messages he's leaving, I'm pretty clear what will happen if I do. I keep fighting my urge to see him, but that only spurs him on more, and it's getting harder and harder to turn him down. The guy clearly likes a challenge.

So tonight I turn off my phone, and hide in my room trying to study. Dean is in the living room and I wish I could join him. We're good study partners, but he hasn't really looked me in the eye without being pissed off since the thing with Ramon.

It's way past midnight when I finally slam my books shut and crawl in bed. The drag is that with all this shit going on in my head sleep eludes me. I toss and turn until I'm a bundle of nerves. I'm a tightly wound livewire and it's making me crazy.

Glancing over, I notice the unopened bottle of whiskey on my bookcase. I was going to bring it to Keith's birthday this weekend. Well, the hell with that . . . this is an emergency. I twist off the cap and take a big swig, letting the amber liquid burn its way down my throat. I immediately feel relief knowing the numbness will start setting in any minute. To insure that it does, I take several additional long draws on the bottle. My head is swimming by the time I settle back down on the bed.

What I really need is to get off, but it's a little risky with Dean just down the hall. I slowly run my fingers over the fly of my boxers as I listen for him. Other than the faint wail of Miles Davis, it's quiet in there. I picture him at the table, his broad shoulders hunched over as he rereads the pertinent sections of the study guide.

I've always liked watching him study. His intensity is sexy and I like the way he drags his fingers through his hair before letting it fall back over his forehead.

These feelings would be easier to ignore if Dean wasn't so damn good looking. He teases me about being a pretty boy that the girls love, but he's got that masculine vibe and body that's my ideal.

Even in high school he was taller and naturally more built than almost all the other guys. Now that he works out all the time he's off the charts. And he's got that crazy jawline, sharp cheekbones, and arched brows over steel grey eyes. I think he's so tough and intimidating on the outside that some girls shy away from him, but I know deep down he can be a softie. He just doesn't show it often, and so he comes off as a pissed-off asshole. But the thing about Dean is he's always had my back. He knows I get him and that means a lot to him.

As I picture him naked beside me, I grow stiff inside my boxers. I reach in and stroke myself, feeling the heat radiating off my cock, warming my fingers. I grow harder imagining Dean watching me jack off and stroking himself just the same before we start jacking each other.

This is a scenario I've imagined a thousand times. It started the summer of seventh grade when Dean's older brother, Travis, showed him how to find porn on the Internet. That was a game changer for both of us. I didn't have a computer, but Dean did, so he took pity on me, and before you know it we were spending time almost every day watching porn.

The first few times we just watched, and then when things got uncomfortable we'd each head off to separate bathrooms to take care of business. But the third time Dean was all worked up and blurted out that he wanted to keep watching while he got off and so I could leave if that squeaked me out.

It took everything I had not to jump up and down and fist-pump the air, but instead I stayed cool and low key. I assured him it wouldn't matter to me and that I'd just do the same. So despite how weird it sounds now, we became perfectly comfortable jacking off in front of each other.

The thing was that while we did it, his eyes would be glued to the screen watching, while all I wanted was for my hand to be the one wrapped around his dick.

The room swirls a little as I push my boxers off my hips and down my thighs. Now thanks to my sentimental journey, my cock is throbbing for attention. I coat my hand with lube and get to work, and damn does it feel good.

Spurred on by my Jonnie Walker haze, I start moaning and whispering dirty things since that shit only turns me on more. As the minutes pass, and the imagery in my head gets more graphic I'm close to getting off. My hand speeds, and I'm gasping for breath when I realize that the stereo is off and I hear footsteps down the hall. *Fuck.* The footsteps stop at my door just as I let out a long, desperate groan.

Dean is right outside my door probably listening to me getting off. Why is this making my lust shoot through the roof? I'm dying to know if he's turned on or disgusted. It's not like I have another guy in here and we both know what horny guys we are. I have no idea what he's thinking, but what I do know for sure is that he doesn't seem to be going anywhere.

The rebellious side of me decides to put on a show. If he's going to listen, I'm going to make it worth his while. I let out several long groans, but the thing that pushes me over the top is imagining it's his hand stroking me, and then all bets are off. I start howling, "fuck, fuck, fuck," as I come like a champ.

Dean. 5

DAMN. I NEED TO GET out of this hallway before he realizes I'm here. Once safe in my room, I quickly shed my clothes and get to work on my raging hard-on. But I'm no fool. I hear Jason's footsteps in the hall as he walks to the bathroom. To be safe I imagine he's got his ear pressed against my door as I stroke myself, so I'm quiet . . . using plenty of lube to keep my strokes smooth. The idea of him listening to me get off makes me harder as I choke back my groans.

I may be quiet, but if you could see the crazy shit going on in my head—images of my cock in places it's never been—just before I shoot a load of come, your gaydar would be howling.

I'm too drained after getting off so hard to even panic about what I'm imagining. *How gay is that?*

The good thing about living in denial is that as more days pass, it's like the gay thing with Jason was just a bad dream. I, for one, am all for pretending that it never happened. It's good to joke around with Jason again. I need things to be okay with my best bud.

There's a party at Keith's Saturday for his birthday and we agree to go, but late Friday nothing seems to be going on, so we order pizza. It's pretty much our mainstay, since we eat it about four times a week . . . not counting leftovers. It's also our *thing*—a running joke between us since whoever's turn it is to order gets to choose the toppings. Sometimes I'll do stuff to piss him off, like order artichokes, green olives, and that doughy, deep-dish crust that he hates.

He'll get me back the next time by ordering thin crust with no tomato sauce. Really? What the hell is a thin pizza with no sauce? I'll tell you what it is . . . a large, floppy cracker with melted cheese. Those nights you can bet I'll chase that pathetic pizza down with a beer or two.

After the messed up week I've had, I'm happy to park myself in front of the TV and do some gaming, so I fire up *World of Warcraft*.

Jason grabs a bag of Doritos and sits to the side, watching me play for a while, but his text alerts keep going off. With each text he seems to get more unsettled until he pops out of his chair and starts pacing the room.

I get a bad feeling but try to push it away.

I pause my game. "What, JJ?" I ask. "You wanna play?"

He shakes his head. "Nah, I think I need to get out. Maybe take a walk." His eyes are cast downward and my stomach sinks.

He's lying.

"A walk? When do you ever take a walk?" I challenge him.

"You don't know everything about me, asshole! I walk all the time," he lamely replies.

"Sure you do, Jason. Go have a walk, and maybe when you come back you can challenge me." I gesture to the screen where my game is still paused.

He nods and slips his phone in his jacket before hurrying out the front door.

I lift my thumb over my console to un-pause the game, but instead of pressing the button, I drop it down on the couch. My curiosity about where Jason is going and why he wouldn't tell me is consuming me. He never used to lie to me, and suddenly I don't know when to believe him or not. It's really screwing with my head.

I get off the couch and look out the window just as Jason hits the street heading east. A weird compulsion comes over me and I grab my jacket, wallet, and keys, and barrel out our door. When I get to the front landing I look in the distance, and in the dark I don't spot Jason at first, but then see him when he walks under a streetlight.

I start walking his way and rotate my baseball cap brim around from the back and pull it down just above my eyes. Luckily there are still enough people on the streets that even if he turned around I doubt that he'd notice me.

We've gone about a half a mile when he approaches a bar I've never been in. It's always looked like a dive, and about the last place I'd expect to see Jason, but maybe that's the point. He's just full of surprises this week. I've gotta wonder if I ever really knew him at all.

I stay back when he pauses several feet from the door and then pulls his cell phone out of his pocket. His shoulders slump and his head tips down as he put his phone away. Just seconds later I notice a built guy walking toward him. *Ramon.*

My whole body tenses as Jason lifts his head and their eyes meet. They don't say a word, but Ramon nods to the door and they slip inside.

Jason . 6

AS RAMON APPROACHES ME, THERE'S a moment where I have second thoughts. It's a wave of panic that makes me want to run the other direction. Meeting up with him tonight is just one more step down a road I may never come back from.

He nods a silent greeting and then opens the door to the bar. It's dark inside and I squint until my eyes readjust.

"What is this place?" I ask as he gestures toward an open booth.

He shrugs. "It's no place, but at least it's safe. No one here will recognize us."

"That's for sure," I agree as my gaze scans groups of middle-aged men, some still in work uniforms. From the looks of it, it feels like a working-class crowd.

A world-weary waitress approaches us. "What'll it be, fellas?"

"Two Buds and two shots of Jack," Ramon answers boldly without even asking me.

"You're pretty sure of yourself," I comment as she walks away.

Smiling, he leans back in the booth. "I don't know about that. Thanks for coming . . . I wasn't sure you would."

"I wasn't sure either."

"So what convinced you?"

"I don't know." I look down and dig my fingers into my knees.

He narrows his eyes at me. "I bet I know."

"Yeah?"

"You're horny."

I swallow hard. "True."

"Well, that's reason enough."

We're on our second round when I finally get the courage to ask Ramon how he knew that I wasn't straight.

He takes a swig of his beer and studies me. "You first blipped on my radar when Andrea told me that one of her besties had the hots for you, and when she finally got you to come home with her, you couldn't get it up."

I groan. "Who's her bestie?"

"Her name's Caroline. She's the curvy redhead that works part time at The Hot Spot."

I look off to the side. "Yeah, I remember her. That wasn't a good night."

Ramon nods. "Oh, I've been there. I'm curious . . . I always heard you were a player and made the rounds. But you asking who the girl was makes me assume that happened more than once."

I let out a long sigh. "Way more than once. I usually try to cover it with saying I've drunk too much. Most girls have been cool about it and kept it quiet."

"Well, Caroline's pretty chatty."

"Great," I growl.

"But it wasn't just that," Ramon says. "I've got a really strong vibe about you and your roommate, Dean. Are you guys fuck buddies?" He grins widely. "Please say yes. You two together would be hot."

"Dean? No! Remember, I told you he didn't know about me, and that's why he was so pissed off in the garage when he saw us."

Ramon's eyebrows shoot up. "I thought you were just covering for him. It looked to me more like jealous rage than anything else. Like another man was marking his territory."

"Nope. So your perception skills aren't perfect. Dean's straight and has zero interest in me that way."

"But you wish he did," Ramon states with a sympathetic gaze.

I glance down at my empty shot glass. "Yes," I whisper.

Reaching over, Ramon rests his hand on my shoulder. "I'm sorry, man. I've been in your shoes, and it sucks."

I nod without meeting his gaze.

"The best way to deal with it is to distract yourself." He slips his hand under the table and slowly runs his fingers from my knee up my thigh until his hand rests on my crotch. "I can be a real good distraction."

Taking a sharp breath, I lift my head up so I can scan the room to make sure no one is watching us. To my relief all I see are a bunch of backs since everyone is focused on the baseball game playing on the monitor above the bar.

"What kind of distraction?" I ask as his hand presses down where I'm already getting hard.

"The best kind. There's a reason they call me the Latin lover. Have you ever been kissed by a dude while he strokes your cock?"

"No," I lie, pushing back old memories that ended badly.

He gives me a gentle shove and gestures to slide out of the booth. "Well, let's go take care of that."

"But where can we go?"

"There's a half-empty parking lot out back and I'm parked in a dark corner."

Swallowing a deep breath, I slide out of the booth. I've got to get out of here before I'm fully hard and out of my mind with lust. I have a feeling that Ramon's groping hands and hot lips are the only way I'm going to get out of my head for a while tonight. I just want to *feel*, not think, even if it's just for a fleeting moment with a guy who's just a replacement for who I really want.

Dean . 7

WHEN I REALIZE THAT THE whole point of Jason's walk was to hook up with Ramon, a weird mix of fury, confusion, and nausea bubbles up inside of me, and I don't know what to do with myself. *So this is it*. This is the way it's going to be with the friend I thought I knew as well as I knew myself . . . my best friend since elementary school. He's a closet gay and a liar.

My legs feel like jelly and I mindlessly stumble over to the café across the street from the dive bar. The place is half empty and I sink into a small table in the corner that has a view of the bar's door.

As I spread my fingers over the linoleum tabletop I think of the gay guys that I've known in my life, once I was old enough to understand what gay was. A few have been friends, like Oscar who was my study partner in Honor's Chemistry. He was a great guy, really interesting and one of the few stand-outs from high school. I didn't have an issue with Oscar or any of those guys being gay, but this is different. Jason is my bro, the one guy who knows everything about me. Now as I realize that I don't know him at all, my whole life feels like a lie.

What about all the countless times he crashed at our house in high school, sleeping in the same bed as me? Other than being kicked a few times when he thrashed in his sleep, nothing ever happened. Sure he often woke up with some epic woodies, but who doesn't? It's not like he rubbed it up against me, or anything.

And what about all of our jack-off sessions? If he was gay all along why didn't he ever try anything with me? As far as I knew we were two horny straight boys getting off on porn . . . nothing strange about that.

An older waitress with her hair pulled tightly back approaches my table and I order a Coke. She lets out a huff and slips her pad back in her apron.

Yeah, lady, I'm a big spender. Got a problem with that?

When she returns with my drink I look up at her and point out the window. "Over there, across the street. It's a bar, right? What kind of a place is it?"

She nods as she looks out the window. "Jeb's place, Last Call? Yeah, it's a bar. They get an older crowd, guys from the industrial park and the union."

I glance up at the roofline noticing that the two ll's of the neon sign are burned out. "Just wondering. I'd never noticed it before."

She hands me the paper-wrapped straw for my drink and gives me a crooked smile. "It wouldn't be your kind of place. A good looking young man like you should be at those clubs near the university with all the cute girls."

I smile back at her. "Thanks for that. I'll definitely be heading that way next."

"You do that," she says as she leaves the check on my table and walks away.

I stare back at the bar's door and wonder why in the hell would two college boys with gay intentions go into a place full of straight old guys. The only thing that makes sense to me is that they don't want to be seen by people they know. Ramon, aka the Latin lover surely wouldn't want it getting out that he likes a hard cock in his mouth. As for Jason, maybe he'd follow Ramon anywhere to get sucked off like that again.

After tossing a few bucks on top of the check, I press my fingers hard against the table's surface. They're both spineless assholes and they deserve each other. I let out a long sigh. Now that I know what's what I may as well go home. But something keeps me stuck in that seat.

I fall into a trance watching the bar door. It rarely opens, so it's not like I'm entertained or anything. The waitress refills my Coke as I daydream remembering the summer before ninth grade when Jason rode his bike to my house late at night to tell me he'd had sex with his next door neighbor, Sue's, much older sister.

I was so jealous I could hardly take it, but I asked him for a play-by-play anyway and got a boner when he talked about the girl taking off her bra and letting him feel up her boobs right away. The way he described everything from the way it felt when he was in her pussy, to the way she pressed him to fuck her hard, he sounded more like a stud and not a fumbling kid. After that he was forever in my mind a sex-god.

It'd be another endless year and a half before I got Beverly Randall to drop her pants for me and spread those sweet legs wide. By that time Jason had screwed that older girl every way but Sunday.

He has those looks girls love: wavy, longish blonde hair, blue eyes and he's built. After he realized he was all that, he never had to go home to his hand again. The girls just threw themselves at him.

So how does one go from being a sex god with the ladies to having a big guy on his knees between your legs?

I've finished my Coke and am planning how to make a ninja exit from the café when I see the bar door swing wide open and Jason stumble out the door with Ramon right behind him. It looks like Jason may be ready to head home, but Ramon wraps his fingers around his wrist and drags him along until they head into the driveway that runs alongside the bar.

Pulling my cap down lower over my eyes, I jam my hands in my pockets before exiting the café and crossing the street. I stop right before the driveway and peek around the side of the building just as they walk into the large parking lot behind the bar. Once they round the corner they disappear from sight.

My heart is pounding as I slowly walk down the driveway. Stopping several times, I try to convince myself to turn around and head home, but I just fucking can't. The idea that I'm going to see that look on Jason's face again as he gets off is a freaky compulsion I can't shake.

When I reach the end of the driveway I position myself inside a long shadow and scan the lot, immediately spotting them in the corner, straight down from where I'm hiding. It's dark where they're lingering, but not so dark that I can't see what they're up to. They're leaning against the car talking. Jason looks tense but I can tell he also has a buzz on.

After a minute I decide to take off as it seems like nothing is going to happen. However a second later Ramon steps closer to Jason and starts kissing him while sliding his hand over Jason's crotch. He has a way of getting to the point, doesn't he?

Jason kisses him back, and before you know it they're all tangled up. Jason is tugging Ramon's hair with his free hand as Ramon's hand moves over him, squeezing and stroking.

When they finally break from their kiss fest, Jason leans back against the car and with hooded eyes looking down at where Ramon is rubbing him.

My fingers move down to my crotch, sliding over the worn denim where I'm fully hard now. My heart is pounding. I'm pretty sure their fun has just begun.

Is it wrong that I want to see things escalate? I'm wired on caffeine and sugar from the Coke. I'm craving some kind of epic payoff for all the time I spent staring at the closed door of the bar. That's not weird and gay, is it?

Ramon surprises me by letting go of Jason's package and undoing his own jeans. He whips out his hard cock and strokes it while Jason watches with wide eyes.

Ramon steps closer to Jason and takes his hand, then wraps it around his cock and proceeds to show how he wants to be stroked. He appears to be average in size so I can barely see his length once Jason has his large hand fisting him. As Jason pumps him, Ramon reaches over and undoes Jason's jeans, pulling out his enormous, hard cock.

My fingers stretch out of their own volition, as I imagine what it would be like to hold Jason's cock and feel it throb under my grip. Would he be harder for me than anyone else? Would he push me for more, and beg me to get down on my knees to get him off? Would I? Now that my mind is unraveling into crazy town I can barely breathe and my throbbing cock has taken on a life of its own.

In between more ravaged kissing, Ramon is pumping Jason's dick, all the movement between them frenetic and charged. I wonder who will come first. A moment later he has Jason pressed up against the car as he thrusts against him, his muscular ass clenching with each thrust.

What the hell? He can't be fucking him in that position. Yet the idea of their cocks rubbing together heats up my blood and makes my dick throb harder. Jason's head is thrown back with his eyes shut and his mouth slack as Ramon bites his neck or something. Meanwhile Ramon's hands are grabbing Jason's ass as he thrusts. By the look on my roomie's face, this shit must feel pretty damn good.

Fucking A.

I hear Jason cry out first before his eyes pop open and he looks down to see what's happening between them. Ramon is rutting wildly now and grunts as he gives one final thrust. His shoulders relax and he lets his head fall to the crook in Jason's neck.

I'm so wound up I feel like with a couple of jerks I could come. Regardless, I press my hand over my erection and will it to go down. I may be losing my mind but I'm not going to pull one out in the dark edge a parking lot, with two horny guys just yards away. I'm not that fucked up . . . yet.

I slowly take several steps backwards and then turn and uncomfortably walk toward the street. It's not easy when you're sporting a stiff boner the size of mine in your jeans. I've got to get the hell out of here before they lick the spunk off each other or whatever the hell they're going to do before Jason finally comes home. I'll lose it for sure if I have to see that shit.

Jason . 8

THE MINUTE RAMON PINS ME against his car I realize I'm seriously going to be man-handled and the idea makes my heart pound harder. Ramon is acting like an alpha and I'm feeling like his bitch. It freaks me out to realize that I'm being dominated, but turns me on even more.

My history of sex with girls has been that, other than my first, my neighbor's older sister, Audrey, I've always had to initiate everything. Even when a girl caught my interest, I was the one making the moves and I was always aware that I was much bigger and stronger than the women I held in my arms.

So to have this powerful guy, who's more built than me taking control, fucking my mouth with his tongue and grabbing my cock like he owned it, is everything I've wanted sexually and didn't know I needed.

He bites my lip hard while he thrusts his cock against mine, grabbing my ass so he controls our strokes. "I can't wait to fuck you," he growls in my ear and it's a miracle I don't lose it right then.

I'm imagining him bending me over when my lust can't hold off another second and I start coming, which then sets him off. He bites my shoulder as we get off. Letting out a guttural moan, I don't even care if anyone can hear us, let alone see what we've just done.

Ramon, who apparently is a biter, chews on my earlobe and hisses in my ear, "You're such a slut."

My breath catches and I can feel my cheeks burning even if it's too dark for him to see.

"I like that you're a slut," he murmurs while he runs his hand through my hair. Next thing I know his grip on my hair has tightened and he pushes me down. "Now I want you on your knees so you can clean me up."

"Here?" I ask, suddenly feeling panicked.

A darkness flashes through me and suddenly this isn't hot or sexy anymore as old memories flood back through me. Perhaps Ramon realizes that he's pushed me too hard, and he loosens his grip on my hair.

"If you're not into it, that's okay. I've got another T-shirt in my trunk. We can use mine to clean up."

As I nod mutely in reply, he pulls his shirt over his head and wipes himself off before handing me the soiled shirt. After cleaning up as best I can, I zip myself up.

When he's pulled the new shirt on he nods at me. "Get in, I'll give you a ride back to your place."

"It's okay. I want to walk," I reply.

"You sure?"

I nod.

He eyes me and takes a step closer. "You're really hot, you know?"

"Thanks, I-I guess," I stutter. "This is just new to me."

"Well then you're a natural."

"Do you really think I'm a slut?"

"Yeah, but coming from me that's the highest compliment. I meant what I said, Jase, I can't wait to fuck you."

Swallowing hard, I avert my gaze. This dude is so intense. I mean, I like directness, but I've never dealt with anyone like him.

"I d-d-don't know—" I start to stutter before he holds his hand up.

"Don't worry. No pressure. One step at a time, okay?"

"Okay, thanks."

As Ramon gets into his car, I slowly walk up the alley and turn back onto State Street to head to the apartment. I start wondering what I'm going to say to Dean about why I was gone so long. He was in a combative mood when I left. The last thing I want is for things to get worse between us.

Dean. 9

IT'S BEEN THIRTY MINUTES SINCE I left the gay dynamic duo in the parking lot of a dive bar. Part of me wishes I'd never followed Jason tonight, and another part of me is almost relieved that I've confirmed the truth about him.

Bottom line, my best friend is gay and leading a secret life I had no idea about. I end my spy session by beating off in the privacy of my own room as I picture crazy things in my head. I almost black out with the force of my orgasm and it fills me with fury that Jason is ruining me with my sudden obsession with him.

I just wish we could go back to the simple days when we compared what girls were hot and which were the nastiest in bed.

I've settled back down on the couch to play my game and have polished off a beer and shot of whiskey when our front door quietly opens up, temporarily filling the room with the fluorescent yellow-green of the hallway light.

"How was your walk?" I ask with an edge to my voice. I've decided to be a provocative asshole. I don't stop playing my game as I wait for Jason's response. The whole thing gives off the exact vibe that I want . . . essentially that I don't give a mother fuck about him and his "needs," but I won't be lied to.

"Good," he mumbles before stepping into the bathroom, and I hear the shower begin to run.

When he finally heads to his room, I call out for him, "Hey, come play me!"

"I'm tired. I'm gonna crash," he yells back.

"Don't be a drag. Get a beer and get your ass over here."

When he comes in the room he's wearing his drawstring PJ bottoms and no shirt, which is what he sleeps in every night, but tonight I see him differently. My gaze travels over his ripped abs and his pumped up shoulders, leading up to his face. With his full lips, classical features, and big blue eyes, he's so handsome he's almost too good looking. I guess I have to admit that if I were going to fuck a guy, he would be a viable choice.

As he studies the TV screen, he opens up a beer and takes a long swig. He wipes his mouth with the back of his hand, and I notice his lips are swollen and red.

Did he keep kissing his fuck-buddy, Ramon, or did he end their date sucking his cock for round two? My dick twitches at the thought of it.

Our eyes meet and it's clear he's still buzzed. I hand him the second console. "I'm gonna kick your ass."

"In your dreams," he mumbles as he sets his beer bottle on the coffee table, falls onto the couch, and then leans forward to focus on the game.

His reactions are slower than usual and in no time I'm kicking his sorry ass. After I've killed him about a dozen times he drops the console next to him and falls back against the couch cushions.

"Tired of getting your butt kicked?" I ask.

"You could say that." He nods as he watches me steer my spacecraft through an asteroid field. "Hey, is it true that James got in a car wreck?"

I nod. "Was texting his girlfriend and rear-ended an off-duty cop. He's so screwed."

"What a dumb bastard."

"I know, right? That's not going to look good on his application for law school. As it is, that chick talks to or texts him night and day."

Jason shakes his head. "She's such a clinger. I hate it when girls are like that."

I look over at him. *Apparently you also hate that girls don't have dicks.*

I can't help but play with him. "Speaking of girls, what's happening with Stacy? She looked like she was ready to serve herself up to you on a silver platter at that party."

Jason shrugs, and his cheeks start to color. "I've lost interest in her."

"Not good in bed? I hear she's a howler."

"I wouldn't know. She's just not my type."

Setting down my console, I turn to him. "And what type would that be?" *A linebacker with shoulders bigger than yours?*

"I don't know. Someone who knows what they want and just goes for it with no games."

I arch my brows as I turn to him. "Is that so. No games?" This from the fucker who's lying to his oldest and best friend about his sexual persuasion? *How ironic.* On top of which, it didn't slip my notice that he used the word "they" instead of "she."

He turns back to the TV screen, studying it like it's fascinating. "So are you still thinking about moving to Seattle after graduation?"

"I don't know. Why?"

"That's what I want to do, but if I don't get a job right away I may have to stay here for a while. And if you leave, I'll need to get another roommate."

"Really?" I feel a fury explode in my chest. So now that my best friend caught the gay train, he's ready to toss me out on the street.

Well, fuck that.

"Do you have someone lined up already?" I ask, trying to keep an even tone to my voice. If I rip him a new one now I won't get any important information out of him.

"No. No one lined up. But Andrea's guy, Ramon, was asking me the other day when I ran into him on campus."

If there was ever a specific occurrence of testosterone flooding a man's body, this is it. I feel like ripping off the roof before hunting down Ra-*cocksucking*-moan and beat the living crap out of him. He's already taking over my best friend's mind and now he's trying to oust me out of my own home.

He has no goddamned idea who he's dealing with.

Taking a deep breath, and willing myself to stay composed, I turn to him with wide eyes. "You mean Ramon, the world class pussy licker? Cassie said he went down on her and her friends all in one night last week."

Jason turns a little yellow-green, like the hallway light is perpetually shining on him.

"Ramon went down on Cassie?" he asks in a weak voice.

"Many times." Now that I'm seeing how much it's fucking with him, I decide to elaborate. "As a matter of fact, I tried to hook up with her today but she said Ramon was coming over this afternoon to do her and she had to get waxed first or something. I guess that guy is insatiable. I know I couldn't be as into that shit as he is. Could you?"

Jason looks crestfallen and he leans forward, his elbows digging into his knees. He shakes his head slowly. "No."

"I mean, I'd heard that guy will fuck anything that holds still long enough, but all that carpet munching? No. thank. you."

Jason's head drops and he examines the grain in the coffee table's surface like it's the most fascinating thing he's ever seen.

After pouring him a shot that's almost overflowing, I slide it toward him. "Here, take this. It helps blur the pictures in your mind."

He nods, and downs it without spilling a drop.

"I'm sorry I burst the bubble on your new roomie. I just think you should know what you're getting into if this place turns into pussy licking central." I pretend to shudder at the thought of it.

I can't believe I can be this big of an asshole. I also can't believe how much I enjoy watching him squirm.

Just then his phone goes off. He holds up the screen and scowls at it. When he taps on the surface his eyes grow wide and he uses his fingers to blow up whatever he's looking at.

"Who's texting you?" I ask.

"Ramon," he replies without taking his eyes off the screen.

"Well tell Mr. Pussy that he can't have my room yet." I snicker internally.

Jason looks up at me startled, like he's reminded what this guy is really about, and he begins furiously texting.

"What did he say?" I ask.

Jason answers while he's still typing like he's not thinking about what he's saying. "He sent a picture. He didn't say anything."

"A picture?" I hold my hand out toward him. "I wanna see."

Jason looks up at me, alarmed. "No."

"What do you mean, no?" I ask. "What the fuck is in that picture that you can't show your best friend?"

He pulls up his sagging PJ bottoms nervously. "It's a joke. You wouldn't get it."

"Try me." This time I reach toward him and almost have the phone when he pulls away.

"Fuck off," Jason growls as he gets up like he's going to his bedroom.

I don't know what comes over me, but I leap off the couch and tackle him, sending us both crashing to the floor. We hit the carpet with a giant thud.

"Mother fucker!" Jason cries out, twisting until he's on his back with me on top of him.

"Give me your fucking phone," I growl.

He fights me off while switching the phone from one hand to another. As I reach up, my entire weight presses down on him and he spreads his legs open so I sink between them. I immediately realize that he's sporting an epic hard-on, one that is trying to tango with my epic hard-on. I try to ignore the obvious as I strain to reach the hand holding the phone that is now extended far from us, due to his monkey-long arms.

He does some weird ninja move, and suddenly I'm under him and he's dodged my grasp once again.

"You're never going to get it," he taunts me.

"Fuck you, JJ," I say, gasping to catch my breath with his weight on me. His hard cock is rubbing against mine with every move, and every breath. The most fucked up part is that it feels good.

Too good.

Freaked out and unsure of my next move, I do the weirdest thing I can think of and I lick his chin with a loud slurp.

He yells out, "Asshole!" and when he goes to wipe his face I grab his phone. All it takes is a quick swipe of my thumb over the screen to reveal a picture of Ramon holding his hard dick and giving the *fuck me up the ass* goo-goo eyes.

It's more than I can take. "Holy hell," I moan.

Jason's head falls forward in defeat, landing in the crook of my neck. I can feel his hot, gasping breath and his lips against my skin. But even more vivid, I feel his throbbing hard-on pressed against mine. A second later he begins to rock his hips so we're doing the woody waltz.

What the motherfuck?

He grunts and thrusts against me even harder. Based on what I saw earlier, he likes this cock on cock action and as screwed-up as it is to admit . . . this shit feels better than I would've ever believed. My eyes roll back in my head every time his cock rubs up against mine.

I like how rough he is with me, I like his solid weight on me, and I even like the way he grits his teeth like I've pissed him off. All of it's freaking me out, but it's fucking hot. I must be drunk.

"Dean, you're so hard," he groans, before thrusting with more force.

"So are you, jackass," I hiss with my eyes wedged shut, the feeling of his dick rubbing against mine making me see stars in my head. It's so wrong and that just makes me grit my teeth and press against him harder.

He lets out a long moan and I look down to see the way he moves against me. He's so into it that there's an edge of desperation in the way he rubs against me.

He lifts up on his forearms and gives me a surprised and hopeful look as he thrusts. "Why are you hard, Dean? You like this, man?" He rocks his hips against me and I feel my balls tighten. "Does this feel good?"

I lie frozen as he grinds against me. Despite my immobility, I marvel at how huge I feel. My cock feels like a thick steel rod that's ready to penetrate anything to get off . . . even the tight ass of my best friend.

For one blinding moment I wonder what would happen if I

didn't stop him and let whatever this was leading to, happen. We're two friends just fucking around . . . experimenting. It wouldn't be the end of our friendship, or would it?

Jason. 10

I SWEAR FOR A MOMENT it feels like Dean is going to give into my advances and shit is going to get real. It's not exactly a completely irrational theory considering his dick is throbbing against mine. He's turned on, whether he can live with that fact or not, the evidence is about to bust through his jeans.

I desire him so powerfully. For a blinding moment every fantasy I've had about him now seems possible. I need to understand what it feels like to have his cock not just in my mouth, but taking my ass while I'm at his mercy. I want to kiss him in the shower enveloped in steam as our slick bodies slide against each other. I crave having him splayed out on a big bed looking at me with dark eyes and telling me all the things he wants me to do to him, and even better, all the things he plans to do to me. And then the next morning it would be perfect to wake up next to him.

God. I want all of those things more than anything else in the world. If only Dean wanted them too.

One undeniable fact is that he knows now that things are heating up in a very gay way with Ramon and me. I know he's jealous by nature. He used to go ape-shit if anyone even looked sideways at his ex, Julie, so the fact that he's territorial with me is fucking hot. He acts like he wants me all to himself. But does he want me all the ways I want him? I really need to know.

Dean . 11

SO THERE I AM STUNNED with my legs spread as my roommate lies on top of me, his hard cock jammed against mine. Suddenly Jason starts moaning and thrusting harder like this is suddenly okay, and it's not. When he leans over and molests my mouth with his, I almost bite his tongue.

"What the fuck?" I yell as a shot of adrenalin spurs me to shove him off of me with a burst of force.

He slams down on his side next to me, and his expression morphs to one of fury. "What?"

Curling my fingers into fists, I narrow my eyes. "What the hell are you doing? Stay the fuck off me! You may be gay, but I'm not!"

Jason glances down at my crotch where the expansive bulge of my hard-on is still obvious, and gives me a look with an arched brow. "Sure, Dean . . . whatever you say. *You* weren't into that *at all*."

I shove him farther away before pushing up onto my feet and glaring at him. I stumble down the hallway to my room, slam the door, and throw myself on my bed. My head pounds as I try to shut out the pictures in my head of Jason grinding against me with a hungry gleam in his eyes.

My fingers curl into fists as my frustration grows. Whatever the fuck is going on is going to ruin our friendship. Jason's always been like a brother to me and suddenly he's a stranger, and a lying, messed-up one at that.

I groan into the bedspread, pounding my fist against the pillow. Why the hell did this shit happen? Everything was cool and now I feel like our world is upside down. How are we going to face each other tomorrow?

I wake up hours later still in my clothes, my whole body tense as I roughly rub my hands over my face. As the light slowly grows brighter in my room, I run everything over and over in my mind until I've decided how I'm going to handle Jason.

Getting up and out of bed, I pull on my sweats. After using the bathroom and splashing water on my face, I head out the door for a run. As my feet pound the pavement and I catch my rhythm, I think about Jason with all the girls he's been with. He would chase after the hottest girls and skip from one to the other like he was tasting all the desserts at a Vegas buffet. Maybe he didn't find the flavor he was craving and maybe this gay thing is just a confused attempt to figure out what he's missing.

He never had a real thing with a girl like I had with Julie. I just figured it was because he was chasing skirts. Maybe he's searching for what he hasn't found and got lost along the way.

My tension lifts as I jog through the park. I bet that's it. This is some weird stage that Ramon literally sucked him into. He just needs a friend to set him straight.

As I approach our building I feel like my head is clear, and I decide to have a talk with him. We can't just pretend this shit didn't happen. Everything has gone too far.

I've just poured my coffee, when Jason charges out of his room with his hood pulled up over his hair and his head tucked down, making a straight line for the door.

"Hey," I call out. "Where are you going?"

He turns back to me, his eyes wide with surprise. "Out," he mumbles.

"I want to talk to you."

"Yeah?" He pauses long enough for his backpack to droop off his shoulder.

I pull a mug out of the cupboard, and fill it for him before sliding it across the counter. "Yeah, it's this thing you're going through."

He looks at me with a blank expression.

"You know, this weird ass experimenting thing." Grabbing the milk out of the fridge, I hand it to him.

He tentatively approaches the coffee and lets out a long sigh before pouring a stream of milk into the mug. "So if I'm experimenting, were you experimenting last night, too?"

"This isn't about me. I think you're going through some confusion and Ramon took advantage of that. You just haven't found a girl that you connect with."

"I've *connected* with plenty of girls." He gives me an irritated look.

"To fuck, yeah . . . but not one you like hanging with too. Until you find that, it's just easier to hang with your own kind."

He takes a slow sip of his coffee as he watches me.

I fold my arms over my chest. "Have you tried to figure out why you're suddenly into guys?"

Jason turns and stares out the window with a pained expression on his face. "I haven't figured out anything."

"Well, you're freaking me out, man. Hey, where are you going anyway?"

"The library. I'm way behind in two of my courses and I've got to kick some ass today."

I raise my eyebrows. "And that's all? You're going to study?"

He purses his lips. "What, now you're my mommy?"

"No, I'm your gaydar monitor. I'm going to get you back on track. Let's go out with Cassie and the girls tonight. Her high school friend, Nicola, is visiting this weekend. Remember her?"

He nods, but his expression is empty. "I told you, I've got to catch up."

"You can stop studying for a couple of hours, Jason."

"I'll think about it." He takes a couple swallows of the coffee, then pushes the mug toward me, before pulling his backpack up his shoulder.

"You're coming."

As he twists the doorknob he turns back to face me. "You know, Dean, maybe you should think about your own confusion. Judging from how turned on you were last night, you sure seemed to like me on top of you."

I feel the blood rushing up my neck, and my nostrils flair. "Fuck you, Jason."

"Is that an offer?" he says and then slips out the door, closing it firmly before I have a chance to reply.

"Asshole." I slam my mug down on the counter and what's left sloshes out onto the linoleum surface. I want to chase after him and pound him to a pulp. He's the one that fucking jumped me, rubbing his dick all over mine last night. I was hard out of shock, not because I was turned on.

As I head to the shower, I decide to go to the sports bar early. An afternoon of beer and football is just what I need to get this crap out of my head.

Hennigans is rowdy, and I yell at the big screen until I'm hoarse. I've lost track of how many beers I've had. It must be a lot because Keith forced me to eat a burger and wash it down with a Coke after I got a little wild during a botched field goal.

When Cassie saunters in with her girls I let out a satisfied sigh. She's the cure to my itch tonight and she looks pleased when I pull her onto my lap. She laughs as I stroke her thighs, slapping my hands when they push up too high.

"You really want all your buddies to see up my skirt?" she asks with wide eyes.

"No, that's just for me tonight," I slur, knowing how much I need to be inside of her . . . maybe for the wrong reasons, but I need her just the same.

She smiles as she wiggles her ass against me and I take a sharp breath. Cassie is my fix, my drug. "I want you, baby."

"Yeah? How bad?"

Feeling reckless, I lean back and slip her hand down to my crotch. She presses her fingers over my hard-on. "So bad," I whisper into her ear.

"Fuck, Dean." She wiggles her hips again.

I catch her earlobe between my teeth and tug gently. "Take me home," I whisper.

"Can't, Presley's parents are staying in my room this weekend."

I let out a low groan.

She winds her fingers into my hair and tugs. "Let's go to your place."

In my beer haze I try to remember if JJ was going to be at home tonight or not.

Sliding off my lap, she holds out her hand. "I'm driving. My car is in the lot."

She turns to Keith. "Can you give the girls a lift?"

He nods. "Sure."

Once home, I'm reminded from her reaction that she's never been at our place, I've always been at hers. Her eyes grow wide as her gaze scans the space.

"What's that about?" she asks pointing to the picture of a sofa taped to the back of our current junk sofa, and then another colorful printout taped to the wall, and others taped on almost every surface.

I shake my head laughing. "Jason did a bunch of drawings once with what he thinks our apartment should've looked like, being that we were architectural and design aficionados and all. Then he went online and picked out art and furniture he would have wanted if we had the big bucks. It's not like we're acquiring Rudolph Schindler's leather and chrome chairs anytime soon. We could barely afford this dump."

"Well yeah, you're students. What did he expect, the Taj Mahal?"

I smirk. "Exactly. So I started teasing him by printing pictures of stuff that fit his tastes, and then taping them on every surface."

"Oh, that's rich," she says as she walks up to one of the prints on the wall to examine it more closely.

"Yeah, well he used to tear them off and throw them away but then I'd immediately replace them with more outlandish things and he finally gave up. Now he pretends that he doesn't see them."

"That's a riot." Grinning, she settles down onto the couch.

"I know that secretly he loves it."

"You're so provocative," she whispers.

I wink back at her.

She pulls out the papers and bag of weed to roll a joint.

I watch her finish it like a pro, light it up, and inhale slow and deep. "You smoke a lot of pot, right? What's that about?"

She nods as she holds in her first drag, finally letting it out in a soft stream of smoke. "My mind is always buzzing with formulas and equations, and after a while it winds me up and makes me crazy. Weed and sex are the only things that take me out of my head so I can chill out once in a while."

I study her face as she passes me the joint. "Whatever works, right?"

She nods and leans back into the couch, her expression already more relaxed.

Unfortunately, the pot is not making me feel mellow, just more wound up, in a stoned half-out-of-my-mind way. Remembering the game earlier, I keep talking about the meaning of football until I realize that Cassie is naked and pressing herself against me.

"I want you," she says as I cup her tits in my hands. Somehow we end up with her straddling me on the couch and I've got my lips wrapped around one of her nipples, while my fingers pinch the other.

She exhibits amazing dexterity under the influence, as she moves over me. Meanwhile, I revel over my rediscovery of the miracle of tits under the influence of dope. I'm holding her breasts, while licking and kissing her nipples as she moans, and watching Cassie slowly lose her mind.

She crawls off my lap. "Wanna go to your bed?" she asks, licking her dry lips.

When I stand up and wobble, she giggles.

Stepping behind the couch, she bends over.

"Just take me here," she says. Her voice is low and sexy. "Come closer, handsome."

I undo my jeans as I approach her. Despite my haze I remember to reach into my pocket and pull out a condom. After tearing open the foil, I roll it down over my hard dick.

I'm fully sheathed and nudging my cock against her when I hear the sound of a key trying to open our front door.

"Damn," I grumble, lifting up as I try to figure out how to cover us up before the door opens.

She rocks back against me. "Don't stop, it's too late to hide. Maybe he won't even care."

I may be stoned, but I know she's wrong about JJ not caring. I don't even have time to argue when I hear the door close. Pressing my eyes shut, I lean back over her to still us both, my heart thundering in my chest. There are some muffled footsteps and then silence.

When nothing happens, I figure Jason went to his room so I slowly ease my hold on her, and as I do she starts pressing back against me.

"Come on," she whispers. "It's okay. He'll probably just hide in his room."

"You sure?" I guess I'm hoping she's right, but I can't believe she doesn't care about the risk of being exposed so completely. Maybe she's one of those exhibitionists that gets off at the idea of it.

I must be higher than I thought because instead of worrying about Jason seeing us fuck and getting her into my room, I focus on sliding my dick against where she's wet, slowly teasing her. She wiggles back in response and I finally ease my cock inside of her.

She takes a sharp breath. I look down and in my stoned haze I find the way my cock slides in and out of her completely fascinating. I marvel at the glisten of wetness, and take a sharp breath when I thrust and she clenches down tightly over me. I'm so stoned and focused that it feels like we are in our own world and Jason coming home has faded out of my mind.

But then the thud of something heavy hitting the floor makes Cassie jump.

I force myself to move my gaze from her round ass, up to the new addition to our scene—Jason and his tormented expression with his backpack down at his feet as he watches me touch her. At first glance he appears wounded, like I've betrayed him. There's a sad, defeated look in his eyes. But before I can feel bad about upsetting him, a fierce intensity burns across his features and he takes on a harsh expression of restrained fury.

I feel defensive realizing that this must be fucked up, but it's no worse than me seeing him with Ramon in that garage, and humping in that parking lot. Yes, this is in our place, but he knows I sleep with Cassie . . . Ramon was a big, fucking surprise. "What?" I ask, challenging him. I wonder how he feels having the tables turned. It stings thinking about what I've watched him do.

"Why are you doing this?" he asks waving his hand at us with a disgusted look.

I resent his tone. "Because this is what I want. You got a problem with that?"

"It's messed up you're screwing her in here and not your room. Besides you've got dubious taste," he mutters under his breath.

Cassie's head jerks up. "What the hell was that?"

Jason winks at her. "I told him he's got great taste." He turns and walks away but a minute later he comes back with the bottle of Jack Daniels and takes a slug right from the bottle as he leans against the living room wall. His eyes are wild and his cheeks red as he studies us. He takes another hit of Jack and then looks at me with a piercing gaze.

"So that's what you want . . . and that's how you fuck?" he growls, a sharp edge to his voice.

I don't like his mocking tone, and I grab Cassie's hips and pull her against me harder as I thrust.

"Yeah, are you taking notes or what?" I reply almost out of breath. My chest tightens as his eyes travel down to my cock as I thrust.

"Maybe," he says with a smirk.

Cassie moans as I start to fuck her with sharp thrusts. "Do you like to watch, Jasie?"

"Apparently," I answer for him. "He's still standing there, isn't he?"

She arches up enough that her breasts are fully exposed. "Does this turn you on?"

With the smoldering look on his face and bulge in his jeans it's clear how turned on he is. *Maybe he wants to screw Cassie.* I find the idea of it oddly encouraging and upsetting at the same time.

Jason palms his hard-on through his jeans roughly.

"Let me see," she says, biting her lower lip. "Show me how turned on you are."

He watches us with hooded eyes for another minute and when I grunt with a particularly hard thrust he takes one more swig of Jack and then leans over, setting the whiskey bottle on the floor. When he straightens he undoes his fly and eases his cock out.

"Hot damn," Cassie croons. "What is it with you two and your huge cocks?"

"Just lucky," Jason replies as he slowly strokes himself.

I can't take my eyes off his dick, so hard and ready for action. It makes my balls tighten, which then makes my head swim.

"Bring that thing over here," she instructs Jason.

I look at him and nod toward Cassie. "You want to fuck her?"

He shakes his head, but moves toward us anyway.

"Let me taste you, Jasie." Cassie's voice is low and seductive. Even though I encouraged this, now it's feeling a bit disturbing.

Stopping in front of her, he holds the thick head within reach of her mouth. Her tongue reaches out and licks it.

"Closer," she groans as she tips her head back.

A tremble rolls through me as I watch her open her lips wide, and he pushes his cock into her mouth. Even in my fuzzy state I can't believe this shit is happening. I hear her moan as she slowly sucks him in.

"Do it like you mean it," Jason commands with a rough voice that makes my dick harder.

Lifting her hand up, she wraps her fingers around the middle of his cock and then pulls him in farther. I've stopped mid-thrust as I watch her hand jerk over him while she sucks him in and out. I can't see everything but after a minute, just knowing how close he is to me, and that he's so turned on, is making me feel like my skin is burning.

When Cassie picks up the pace I start to thrust again, a new wave of arousal pumping through me. Jason is rocking his hips now and when I lift my gaze, his hooded eyes are only looking at me.

"Oh yeah, that feels good. You like it hard, don't you?" he says to me in a low, desperate voice.

I nod as I look into his eyes and I feel like I'm falling into his darkness.

There's a jumble of thoughts clouding my brain, including the burning urge to be fucking him instead of Cassie.

He's panting as his gaze pierces me. "Harder," he groans. "I want it hard."

Cassie doesn't know he's addressing me, so she gags with her next move.

Meanwhile my fingers dig into the soft flesh of her hips as I begin to pound her. It's all too much; we're both doing her and every kind of crazy hunger pulses between us.

As her fist blurs over him, he finally looks down and I can sense he's on his edge. He swallows hard just before his eyes roll back in his head. As he starts to come I can feel the waves of his pleasure, which then sets off my explosion.

"Oh fuck!" I yell, blinded by the intensity of my climax. I feel like my head's going to shoot off my shoulders. By the time I'm done thrusting my dick is numb.

When I open my eyes again, Jason is watching me and I notice the edge of his lips curl up, yet his eyes darken. He slowly steps back until his cock slides completely out of Cassie's mouth. He gives her a quiet smile as he tucks his cock into his jeans. Before he turns and walks out of the room, he reaches out and strokes her cheek with his fingers. "Thanks," he whispers. The next noise is the click of his bedroom door closing.

I glance down and Cassie looks spent. "You okay?" I inquire, rubbing my hand over her back.

She turns toward me with a content smile on her face. "That was so hot!"

"Yes, it was. And I gotta say, you act like you've done that before."
She grins. "Maybe I have."

I help lift her upright, and she stretches. "Nothing wrong with trying new things, Dean. I keep my options open. You should, too."

I nod, but remain silent. The idea of my options being open has never been more twisted and true.

Jason . 12

I COLLAPSE DOWN ON MY bed, still breathless from the wild scene I just left. I don't even know how to feel about it. Angry? Satiated? Confused? What I know for sure is that despite my bravado back in the living room, I feel like someone kicked me hard in the gut with a steel-toed boot. Watching Dean wanting and fucking someone else was like tearing off a piece of my heart.

It's never been clearer to me how messed up I am. The truth is I've been fucked up for way too long. I remember my junior high counselor calling my mom to talk to her about getting me into therapy. Mom politely told her that she was going to talk to my priest about starting up more sessions.

What a joke. Did she really have no idea that my *'sessions'* with Father Ryan are what screwed me up in the first place? Nothing like your priest forcing you to touch his private parts to turn your world upside down.

I've been a complete wreck inside, and damaged goods ever since. It's amazing I even made it through my teenage years when I remember how lost and hopeless I felt from the things he did to me. I lived each day desperately hoping for someone to turn to that I was confident would have the power to stop it. But my savior never came.

I've kept the truth from everyone, especially Dean. I just wanted to be a normal kid like him. I was terrified if I told him about my confusion over unnatural feelings toward other guys that he'd avoid me like the plague. Never mind telling him about my two years of being molested by my priest. That would freak anyone out. I mean what if Dean thought that I did something to encourage it?

There's a part of me, maybe the little boy who still lingers, that listens to the inner voice, making me feel like I should be punished for the feelings I have for men. Most guys who get molested by priests remain straight—maybe fucked up in other ways, but straight. They marry and have kids and try to get on with their lives.

So what is it about guys like me? Once the shock was over, I realized that my body seemed disconnected with my brain and my heart when it would react physically to what Father Ryan did to me. I was always terrified and confused when I walked through his door.

As I grew older I realized that I had feelings about guys that I knew were unnatural. I liked girls all right, but guys were who I'd think about in a sexual way. One guy in particular was always on my mind when I got into bed at night, making my dick instantly hard . . . Dean. It was always Dean. Anyone will tell you that the surest way for a gay guy to torture himself is to fall in love with a straight guy.

So here I am with a straight best friend I'm in love with, a strict Catholic mother, and I grew up in the conservative town of Boise, Idaho. To top it off I ended up attending University of Utah where being gay isn't shunned, but it isn't as openly cool as I'd hoped it'd be. After all, the school is in Salt Lake City, home base for the Mormons.

Fuck my life.

I couldn't see how my life could work out of the closet so I focused on girls, hoping I'd outgrow my confusion, and I tried to push the rest away. At least I'm not alone. Even football star Ramon feels like he has to pretend he's straight, and as a result he can't wait to move to Miami.

In some ways this is how my obsession with architecture started. For years I would have nightmares involving Father Ryan and I'd wake up with my pillow wet from crying, the sheets yanked off the bed, or having pissed myself.

I started to fear going to sleep at all because my nightmares chewed me up and spat me out. So my coping mechanism was to force myself awake during a bad scene, and then pull out my sketchbook to do drawings of building ideas.

I can see now that the appeal was born out of a desire to control my world. I'd even imagine the people inside the buildings I'd drawn, and they were all interesting and kind characters—no sick priests or homophobes . . . my very own utopia.

And here I am all these years later still trying to control my world and failing.

This tension and fighting with Dean is breaking me down, but now that I've screwed up and unintentionally put my sexuality in question for him and then provoked him during that three-way, I have to face facts. This friendship that has meant everything to me has been seriously damaged, and may never be the same.

Dean . 13

"SO THE RENT IS DUE by the third. You got it?" I ask, standing in Jason's doorway.

He glances up from his textbook. "I left it on the counter yesterday. Didn't you see it?"

Is the blank stare he gave me before he turned back to study supposed to mean complete disinterest or just that he's shut me out? I know that something is going on in that head of his. Things have been incredibly awkward between us again since the Cassie incident. I'm not sure what I expected to happen after that crazy scene, but it's getting to the point where I don't want to be at the apartment anymore.

"Can I ask you something?"

Lifting his gaze, he turns toward me. "What?"

"Are you mad about that thing with Cassie?" I can feel my cheeks getting red. This is messed up and awkward. We've never been this distant before.

"You mean that you were high and fucking a chick in our living room? That was quite a show."

"Well, I didn't mean to fuck her in there."

"Then why did you?"

"I don't know. I was high and I wasn't thinking. So you *are* pissed then."

"I suppose. You just were never an asshole like that before."

"Well, you've changed too, JJ."

Jason just stares at me silently.

"Didn't it count for something that Cassie sucked you off?"

"I didn't want her to blow me. I just did it so you could see what it's like to have to watch shit like that happening right in front of you. It kind of fucks with you, doesn't it?"

Does he not remember that I saw him getting sucked off by Ramon at the party? Was he really that out of it? If he only knew how much seeing his new sex-capades have fucked with me.

"I don't believe you. Why would you get off like that if you didn't like it? You seemed to be really into it."

Glaring at me he turns back to his desk. "I've got work to do."

As I stare at the back of his head, a sick feeling sinks to the pit of my stomach. *What's happened to us?* I wonder if things will ever be easy between us again.

The next day I meet up with Keith on campus for a study session.

"So what's up with Jason?" Keith asks as he hands me the book he borrowed. The study hall is crammed and everyone is talking.

"What do you mean?" I ask.

"I don't know. He just seems different. And suddenly he's hanging with Ramon all the time. Is he going to switch teams or something?"

My whole body tenses as my head jerks his way. "Switch teams?"

Keith nods his head. "Yeah, from tennis to football."

I feel a surge of relief to realize Keith doesn't know anything, and I answer with a light tone. "What? He doesn't even play football!"

"Ha! I know. I was joking, man. Like he could just decide to be on the football team anyway."

The tension settles and I force out a laugh. "Oh, I don't know. Maybe he's got secret skills and has been practicing behind our backs."

"And maybe I'll win a Nobel Prize."

I smirk at him. "Well both are about as implausible . . ."

"True that," he says.

"Hey, I'm not getting shit done here I think I'll head back to my place. You staying?"

"Yeah, but I'll catch up with you later."

I gather my stuff and give Keith a nod as I make my way toward the staircase. Deep in thought, I walk slowly back to the apartment, first across the wide walkway cutting through the straight-forward layout of our campus and then along the grid of streets that shape Salt Lake City. Everything feels wide open with the big sky and flat, simple landscape. My gaze scans the distant mountain ranges surrounding the city and knowing that I'll be leaving Salt Lake after graduation, I feel a little sad wondering if Jason and I will ever snowboard up there again. I've liked Salt Lake okay, despite the fact that I'd hoped there'd be more nightlife here, but what can you expect from the Mormon mecca of the world?

When I get back to the apartment I walk in to find Jason on the couch having some kind of emotional phone call with his voice low and mopey. As I close the door behind me I try to figure out who he's talking to, but as soon as he sees me he goes into his room and shuts the door.

I switch from the Lana del Rey playlist he was listening to, and put on Radiohead's "Fifteen Step" from their *In Rainbows* album. That's more my speed right now.

I think I heard him say "Becky" as he went to his room, but I can't be sure. I've noticed he's been talking to her more lately and I wonder what that's about. I can't imagine he'd willingly tell anyone that he's suddenly pitching for the other team, but Becky is probably the one person that wouldn't go ape-shit on him if he did tell her.

Becky is his girl bestie. She's a bookish, quirky, bossy broad and I have no idea why Jason likes to hang with her . . . maybe because she's the only girl who never tries to get him into bed. I asked Jason once if she'd ever had sex—since I'd never heard of her with a guy and he rolled his eyes at me.

Maybe she's gay and will now be his advocate as he flips his world upside down. That would be rich.

I know she's not part of my fan club. Jason told me once that she thinks I'm a jock asshole. Fine with me. She's a geeky bitch. If she encourages him on his sudden and confused path to homosexuality she's only going to make things worse.

Later I'm a quarter into the Seattle Seahawks and New Orleans Saints game, and Drew Brees is kicking some serious ass, when Jason sulks out of his room and opens the fridge, standing in front of it in a trance, like he's looking at one of the Seven Wonders of the World.

"Who was that on the phone?"

"Becky." He opens up a take-out box and smells the contents before closing it again and shoving it back inside.

"What'd she want?"

"Nothing."

"So you talked for over an hour about nothing?"

He gives me an exasperated glare. "Why do you care what we talked about?

I fold my arms over my chest. "Well you're not talking to me anymore so maybe it pisses me off that you're evidently telling her all your shit."

"Maybe if you weren't such an asshole all the time I'd talk to you."

"Pardon me for being an asshole. Excuse me if the fact that *surprise* you're suddenly gay, is a little hard for me to take."

"Yeah, you were *hard* all right when I was on top of you, man. And I'm not gay."

I mute the television, which is no small deal with Drew on a roll. "So you're a straight guy that likes to rub your hard-on against other guy's cocks. What is that? A straight-omo? A homo-aight?"

"I'm not a homo," he says with gritted teeth.

"So tell me, straight guy, what is Ramon to you?"

"A friend," he responds with a weak voice.

"A friend with benefits?"

He considers the idea for a moment and then shrugs. "Well, sort of. But just cause I've gotten drunk or stoned and let my guard down around him, doesn't mean I'm turning in my man card."

"Glad to hear it. So why don't you just stay the fuck away from him?"

"It's hard to explain how everything happened in the first place. But that's what I'm going to do from now on."

I'm suddenly overwhelmed with the urge to forgive Jason for all this gay shit so we can just go back to how we were. "Well, good," I say.

He stands there like he isn't sure what to do next.

I point to the T.V. "Hey, grab some beers, man, you gotta check out this game."

He nods and heads back to the fridge. When he returns he hands me my beer before plopping down on the couch. "What's the score?"

For a moment I feel good, this calm feeling that I haven't had around him in weeks. But as the game goes on and he calls out fouls and swigs his beer, my secure feeling starts to crumble. I can't put my finger on it but it just seems like he's putting on a show.

Jason. 14

DAMN. WHY DID I HAVE to lie and tell Dean I was keeping my man card? In the moment I knew he'd be relieved and happy to hear it, but in the big picture it was a weak-willed, jackass move. I just wanted things to feel like old times again. But there's no doubt that decision will blow up in my face.

He looks so happy that I'm taking the straight route and watching a game with him. As the evening progresses maybe I push it too far with the macho shit, but it feels good to step out of my head for a while and pretend to be someone else.

It's been a confusing day. Earlier, I was compelled to call Becky to get the point of view of someone I trust while explaining how my life was unraveling. She's the only person in my life who's known I'm attracted to guys. I'm sure that's the only reason she allows me to be a close friend of hers.

Meanwhile, it's always been a pain that she hates Dean. I'm not even sure why. She says he's an ass, yet knowing he's been my best friend all these years you would think she'd try a little harder. He's got more depth to him than she realizes.

I guess telling her on the phone that we've been fighting didn't help. It just gave her license to rail on him. She also warned me to be careful about Ramon. I don't think she liked the fact that he called me a slut. I guess I wouldn't like it if someone said that to her. The difference is that I *was* being a slut, and she wouldn't even know how to be one.

Dean. 15

AFTER JASON ANNOUNCED THAT HE was straightening himself out, so to speak, he swung so hard the other way that I didn't really appreciate the new Jason any more than the surprise gay one. That night was the birth of Jason the uber manly, man-whore.

Monday he tells me that the sophomore he's tutoring in calculus was hitting on him and he's not sure if he should nail her.

"Is she over eighteen and hot?" I ask.

He nods with a grin.

"Then what's the problem?"

"I need the green. If she gets clingy then I won't be able to keep tutoring her."

I arch my brow at him. "I'm sure you'll be able to manage that. You have my blessing."

He grins. "I'll let you know how it goes. I can't wait to peel those jeans off her. They're like a second damn skin."

Tuesday night he brings home a porn DVD with two buxom girls and a large black man. Even though I've got an exam the next day I watch it with him in support of his mission to be on the straight and narrow.

In between slugs of beer he makes rude comments about the guy's moves as he fucks the girls, like we're watching plays in a football game. It's a little over the top.

He comes home Thursday with a swagger and announces he just nailed the screamer, Stacy, three times in a row. I give him a grin and enthusiastic thumbs up but something just isn't sitting right with me. Could my reformed roomie be making this shit up to throw me off his trail?

That weekend we go to a party at the complex next to ours where a bunch of the communications majors live. It's a fact that a lot of the girls in the department are very fine. As soon as we arrive, Jason heads over to a group of hotties gathered near the fire pit. It's almost comical to watch their little circle part like the Red Sea to welcome him. He must be charming the panties off them the way their eyes twinkle in the firelight.

I turn away and shake my head. My roomie's bipolar behavior is wearing me out.

Keith steps up to me and hands me a beer before nodding to the fire pit. "Look at Jason go."

"Looks like it's his night."

Keith studies him for a minute. "He must really need to get laid. He's pouring it on thick, don't you think? He usually waits 'til the girls come to him."

"True." Taking a swig of my beer, I glance over at Jason who now has his arm around a petite brunette. *Pouring it on thick, indeed.*

At some point late in the evening Jason disappears and the party is too crowded for me to figure out who he may have left with. I assume it's the brunette and hope she's good in bed. We need every advantage in the game to keep him on the straight team. Despite all that, there's part of me that doesn't like the idea that he's with her. It almost feels like I'm jealous, but that's crazy.

I talk to a few girls half-heartedly but don't make any genuine effort to get laid. It's hard for me to put any enthusiasm into it when I'm so distracted with whatever Jason is up to. I head home around one and crash.

Hours later I hear him stumble into the apartment and I wedge my eyes open enough to see it's four fifteen on my alarm clock. I figure that's a good sign as I fall back into a deep sleep.

When I get up around ten, Jason is already up and gathering his tennis shit.

"Practice today?" I ask.

He nods. "I've gotta stay in shape. We have a tournament in two weeks."

He glances over at some books on the counter that he brought home from the library. "Hey, did you see that book I borrowed for you about that glass artist, Dale Chihuly? I remember you telling me that if we end up getting jobs in Seattle his glass museum is the first place you'd visit."

"Yeah, that was cool of you. Thanks."

"I flipped through it. I can see why you're so into his stuff. Maybe I'll go check the museum out with you."

I smile, liking that this conversation feels like the old days before Ramon became an issue, driving a massive wedge between us. "So where were you? I was looking for you before I left, but you were nowhere in sight. Did you end up with the little brunette from the party?" I plaster a fake smile on my face like I'm happy at the idea of it.

He looks over at me, confused. "Little brunette?"

"Isn't that the girl you hooked up with last night? I saw her draped all over you."

His eyes grow wide like the synapses have just connected. "Oh yeah. She was great. Really hot in bed."

"Awesome." But I have to think she couldn't have been so hot if he had trouble remembering her the next morning. *Did he end up with someone else last night?* I wonder for a second if he was with Ramon, but I push the idea out of my head.

Yet the idea festers so the next day after Jason leaves for his blueprint lab I snoop around on his computer. His emails seem innocent... nothing suspicious. But damn, if only the rest of his computer was innocent, too.

He's never bothered with a password locked computer and maybe he should've because all I have to do is open up his Internet to be assaulted with a picture of two guys full-on fucking. I let out a low groan.

"Dammit, Jason! What the hell?"

I double check the history hoping this could be an old post and he hasn't used the Internet for days. I know how unlikely that is, but what can I say? I'm a dreamer. Sure enough in between all the man porn I find a search for some building in New York he mentioned having to research last night for his project.

I take a deep breath and study his web history more carefully and it's a long list of rude names that indicate all the things that gay men do to each other: *CocksuckingBoys*, *BottomBoys* and *WellHungHoes*. My stomach starts to churn. In my low, booze-filled moments I may have gotten a stiffy imagining Jason getting sucked off, but these tight shots of hard cocks being shoved into assholes make me want to hurl. The next page I open is even worse.

If a guy tried sticking his tongue up my ass I'd beat the shit out of him. How in the fuck can Jason get off on this? I also find some disturbing sites with headlines like, *How Do I Know I'm Gay?* and *How to Prepare for My First Anal Sex*.

He's not getting better with this gay stuff . . . he's going ahead full steam. I feel kicked in the gut to know that he's a bigger liar than ever. I return the screen to the site I opened up to and shut it down, but as I stand up I have an unbelievable urge to hurl the display screen out the window.

As I pace through the apartment I dig deeper into my memories to see if I can find any scrap of something that would have indicated Jason was into guys. I roll my eyes thinking about his mom, Evelyn.

It's probably good he didn't show signs of this thing for guys or his mom probably would've killed him. She's hardcore Catholic and she's always at the church helping with stuff. She even had Jason be an altar boy when he was younger. Oh man, did I give him shit about it and that angelic-looking white robe thing he had to wear. He was miserable.

During high school he became really stressed because she'd made up her mind that he should be a priest. She even sent him to some weird camp that tried to indoctrinate him. All of her maneuvers wore him down until he was actually considering it, but I took care of that by constantly reminding him what he'd be missing as a priest. I mean, what the hell is the point of devoting your entire life to the church and not having sex anyway? That is just every kind of wrong. But his mom kept on him until he actually threatened to move to Vegas. He had a cousin there who worked in the casinos and had offered to him a place to stay while he finished high school.

That shut her up . . . no son of hers was going to live in Sin City.

I think about Mrs. Sorentino and wonder how she's going to handle it when he finally tells her where he's been sticking his dick.

Jason sticking his dick . . . his big, hard dick . . .

Hell, it's worth staying friends with him just so I can be there to see the look on her face. I never liked that woman. Her expression around me was usually like she'd just sucked on a lemon.

A moment later I wonder where Jason is sticking his big dick at this very moment, while I'm pacing up and down our hallway worried about what the hell is happening to our lives now that he is a serial liar. I'm sure this is traumatic for him but does he have any care at all at what this is doing to me? After all, he's been my sidekick for years. Everything is messed up now. My best bud is long gone and it stings.

Suddenly, I feel an overwhelming need to talk to another guy. I call the most macho guy I can think of, my brother Trent.

"Hey, little bro, what's shakin'?"

"Not much . . . well except I've got a question."

"Yeah?"

"Have you ever had a close friend, who you always thought was straight, suddenly become gay?"

There's a long silent pause. "Why do you ask?" he finally says with measured words.

"Well I have this friend—"

"A dude?"

"Yeah."

"I see. And he told you he's gay?"

"Not exactly. But the evidence is overwhelming. I've seen things."

"Is this really about you, bro? Are you trying to 'out' yourself to me?"

"Fuck no! How could you even ask that?"

"I always thought it was freaky how you and JJ would sleep in the same bed together. It was so damn gay. Is this about him?"

I pause. "Maybe."

"Right. Well, no surprises there. That guy seemed like he was straddling the line."

"He did? Why?"

"I don't know. I mean you were always telling me about all his conquests, but it was weird the way he looked at you."

"Like how?"

"Like he wanted to be the bottom to your top."

"Fuck, Trent!"

"Precisely. Has he tried to fuck you yet?"

I relive that moment where he'd pinned me down on the floor of the hallway with his hard dick thrusting against mine, but Trent is the last person I'd share that with. He'd taunt me for the rest of my life.

"No."

"Well keep your guard up, bro. If Jason is suddenly hot for dudes, I bet your tight ass is number one on his list. Lock your bedroom door at night. Hear me?"

I feel my face get hot at the visuals his words are putting in my head. "Whatever, Trent. I think you're wrong."

"Heed my words, Dean."

By the time evening rolls around I've turned all these emotions into one thing: rage. Rage toward Jason for putting me in this messed-up position. It's his fault I've stood in an alley watching two guys get off like some perverted old creeper. It's because of him that I wake up panting from dreaming that his lips are wrapped around my cock. I've never given a second thought to getting nasty with another guy, and suddenly it's on my mind all the time. This isn't how things were meant to be.

It just doesn't make sense. Did he hypnotize me while I was sleeping or something? Or maybe a shrink would say this is perfectly normal, that when a key figure in your life suddenly reveals themselves as a very different person than who you've intimately known, it's expected that you could begin to question everything, including your own values.

Whatever the hell is going on, what I know for sure is that the walls are closing in on me and I've got to get out of this place.

Grabbing my books, I storm out of the apartment, and head to the main library. Once I'm there I find that corner I like on the third floor and park myself at the table like I own it. I'm a big guy and so anyone who sits too close I glare at until they move. No one wants to fuck with me.

I return early the next morning and do the same set-up. The next day the guard comes by on the way to his coffee break and asks if I want a coffee too.

By Friday night the librarian is giving me the worried look since I've been there almost every waking hour this week. I glance at the table that I've reinforced with piles of books, creating a barricade around me. It suddenly occurs to me that maybe I need to chill out. I can't keep this up. Next thing I'll be taking sponge baths in the library bathroom with wads of wet paper towels. It's time to go home and face the music.

To my great surprise, Jason is home when I get there. I can't help but notice that he looks different. Instead of his regular jeans or cargo shorts he's wearing tight jeans. My eyes skim over his muscular thighs and I wonder how he even got those jeans up over all that muscle.

"Where've you been?" he asks halfheartedly, like he really doesn't care what my answer will be.

"At the library. Why, did you miss me?"

He side-eyes me and laughs. "Yeah, I missed you a lot, man. As a matter of fact, I missed you so much that I'm going out now to celebrate the fact that you've returned."

I really hate it when he's sarcastic. It makes me want to pound his face in. "Where you going?"

He pauses and gets a dark expression in his eyes. "To Darlene's."

"You gonna bang her?" I ask, my fists already clenching.

His lips curl up. "Hell yeah, I'm going to bang her 'til she screams." He turns and starts to walk out the door. "Later, man."

I'm so motherfucking done with his shit. I've sat on that hard-ass library chair all week wishing the gay fairy would get the hell out of our lives and explode in a fiery inferno so I could get my best friend back. Instead he has his gay tight jeans on so he can go bang gay, tight-ass Ramon. Well I'm over this shit.

O.V.E.R.

Stepping up behind him, I shove him hard against the wall. "Quit lying to me, bastard!"

He looks over his shoulder with a startled expression, turns, and shoves me back. "Hey! Get your hands the fuck off me!"

"You aren't going to Darlene's, are you?"

"Wh-what—" he starts to sputter before I press my fist into his shoulder until it's pinned to the wall.

I lean into him. "Are you?"

"How do you know where I'm going, asshole?"

"What's with these tight jeans? Who are you trying to get the goods from?"

"I told you . . . Darlene!"

Leaning in even closer until our faces are almost touching, I hiss in his ear. "Liar."

Jason is silent for a moment. I can see his chest expand with each ragged breath. "Why the hell are you saying I'm lying?"

I don't know why I'm getting off taunting him like this but my lips skim the edge of his ear with my next words. My voice is low and dark. "Because I spent some time on your computer, asshole."

Jason . 16

A LIGHTNING BOLT OF PANIC shoots through me and I can't breathe. *Why the hell didn't I delete my browser history?* However fucked up things felt between Dean and I is nothing compared to what's happening this very moment. This is tantamount to a live grenade being thrown into the middle of our friendship.

I'd be furious if I wasn't feeling so raw, like I've been stripped naked. Dean went into my room, opened my computer, and started searching through my files and history? It's a massive violation, and I'm never going to live this shit down. What would he do if I did that to him? He'd want to kill me.

Embarrassed and humiliated doesn't begin to describe how I'm feeling. I've been trolling gay porn for years online, but it wasn't until Ramon started coming onto me that I wanted to see exactly where I fell on the "gay" range. Even my best friend was sure I was straight until he learned about Ramon.

Ramon called me a slut and with the assortment of filthy sites Dean must've viewed, I'm sure he'd agree.

So now Dean has what he was looking for . . . proof that I was lying about wanting to straighten out. Now that he knows, what's he going to do about it? Can I take anymore of the fallout from disappointing him? Could things get any worse?

Panicked, I start sinking deep into my dark memories as the familiar heavy cloak of humiliation wraps around me. I'm prepared to fall to my knees and beg for Dean's forgiveness just as Father Ryan had me do all those years ago when I hadn't satisfied him. It's like I'm back in his locked study. I close my eyes and I can feel the wood floor under my knees and the scent of the Holy Oils used for sacrament as Father rests his hand on my bowed head and my terror sets in because I know what's coming. My inner voice is a quiet scream and my lips are trembling as I silently mouth the words I was forced to say.

Forgive me, Father, for I have sinned.

Dean. 17

HIS EYES DART TO MINE but otherwise Jason doesn't move. I watch the red spread across his neck and up his cheeks. "Fuck," he whispers before looking down.

"Fuck, indeed, my twisted friend." I step closer to him so that his shoulder is pressing into my chest. "So are you one of the *Well-Hung Hoes*? Or maybe a *Bottom-Boy*?"

"Don't." He holds up his hand and closes his eyes.

"Don't what? Don't tell you what I learned about preparing for anal sex. How you coat your fingers with lube before working them up some guy's ass to stretch him out. Or even better, how you were intrigued enough by the idea of anal fisting that you looked it up to understand how it's done."

He groans squeezing his eyes tighter.

"So unless Darlene is going to be shoving her fist up your ass tonight, I'm pretty sure you weren't heading out to bang her."

He whimpers, "Please Dean, just leave me alone."

"I don't know, Jason, the other night you didn't want me to leave you alone at all."

For some reason all of this shit is getting me worked up and to taunt him further I lean into him and press my hard cock against his hip.

He groans louder.

I slowly grind against him. "I know this is exciting you."

He nods and swallows hard.

"You want it."

He looks down where I've rubbed against him. "God help me, I do." He scrunches his face up like he's in pain.

I can feel my cock throb against his hip. "And I want to know why."

He shakes his head. "I don't know."

"And I also know you don't care how all of this has fucked with my head and confused me. All these years you never said a thing. Now I feel like everything between us has always been a lie."

He looks at me with his eyes wide and then blinks repeatedly. "No. Don't say that. Please don't say that. You've always been my best friend, Dean."

"You should've told me. You could've . . ."

His eyes dart down and his cheeks glow red again. His expression reminds me of when we were kids and he'd have to fess up for doing something wrong. "I was scared to tell you. I was afraid you'd hate me because of what I need."

"What you *need*? So that's it? You *need* guys now? You want cock?" I pull my hips back and thrust against him hard. My fury is barely contained.

"Dean . . ." he begs.

"And do you want me like that, too?"

He swallows hard and remains silent, but I can read the answer in his tortured expression.

I run my hands roughly over my face. "Well then."

He watches me with an anxious expression, waiting for my next move.

I clear the gravel out of my throat so I can speak. "Does the idea of being with me make you hard?"

"Yes," he whispers.

"Show me."

Gritting his teeth, he takes my hand and pushes it down over his cock. Even through his jeans it's obvious he's completely aroused.

"Well, feel that. You're very excited by this aren't you?"

"Yes. Are you ashamed of me, Dean?"

When my fingers tighten around him, he gasps. "I am."

His head drops and he's silent for a moment. But he focuses on where my fingers are still gripping him. I don't even know why they are. Maybe I'm fascinated by how steel hard and huge he is. My hand is getting hot as he throbs under my grip. When I slide my fist up and then back down he looks up at me with a weighted expression.

"I'm ashamed of myself. I'm so turned on right now and it's wrong. I'm fucked up. I know it," he says in a low voice.

"Have you always known it? We've been best friends for most of our lives. I haven't quite processed that you've switched teams when I didn't even see that coming."

"I don't know. Maybe I've always felt it. I've been confused for a long time."

"Damn, Jason." I shake my head.

Before I realize what's happening, my fingers suddenly lose grip on him and he sinks down to his knees. He presses his lips against my crotch and then gazes up at me with a searching expression. "Please don't hate me."

He's freaking me out with this shit.

"What in the fuck are you doing on your knees? Did you really just kiss my cock?" I leave out the part where I want him to do it again because that's just crazy.

"Can I show you, Dean?"

I narrow my eyes. "Show me how? By sucking me off?"

"Whatever you want. But yeah, I'll suck you off. You can close your eyes and pretend I'm someone else."

"Do you even understand how fucked up that is, man?"

His head drops.

"And isn't Ramon the one whose cock you should suck?"

"This isn't about Ramon. It's about you and me. I just thought that maybe it would help you understand . . . I swear I won't tell anyone."

"Would you stop fucking with my head?" I gasp.

"I'm sorry," he moans. He nuzzles his face right into my crotch and sighs. "Please, Dean, you're so hard. Please let me take care of you. I need this." His fingers reach up to my fly and I feel him slowly pull the zipper down. I don't stop him. I just watch him as my breath gets ragged.

It's scaring the hell out of me that I want to know how it feels with his lips wrapped around my dick.

When he pulls my cock free I can barely speak for the feeling of his warm hand gripping me. I look down just as his tongue gently laps the pre-come off the tip of my dick before pressing kisses over the swollen head. He lets out a raw moan and my cock throbs in response. The whole thing is surreal like I'm dreaming and will wake up any minute. I'm not sure I have it in me to stop him. So I don't.

I narrow my gaze as he stares up at me, his tongue swirling around the shaft. "Is this a tease, or are you going to let me fuck your mouth, like you fucked Ramon's?"

"Yes," he chokes out. His mouth opens wide as he sucks me in deep.

My eyes roll back. Damn, his mouth on me is something I couldn't have imagined. The wet heat, and the hopeful look in his eyes as he takes me deeper. This is my best friend, the one who knows me better than anyone, and he's got my dick in his mouth. *What the hell is happening to us?*

"Okay?" he asks as one of his hands slides around my hips and grabs my ass for better control.

I nod my head frantically. I can tell I'm not going to last long. This is sick and hot and tortured, but so fucking good. "Suck harder," I groan.

"Yes," he whispers under his breath while he works me into a frenzy.

I wind my fingers into his hair and start pulling him over me, not slowing down when he gags, just lost in the feeling of how he's taking everything I give.

This is so different than anything I've ever felt . . . so intense and desperate. I can feel how much he's getting off, too. Girls just blow you because they know you want it. This is much more. It's like a religious experience for JJ and I'm at his altar.

He's moaning as he sucks me and I feel the vibration course through my body.

The heat crawls over my chest and up my neck, until all I know in life is this feeling of uncontrolled lust as I take in his drunken, sublime expression while I fuck his mouth.

My heart is thundering, and I feel my control spiraling. My eyes press shut as I gasp for breath. "JJ, I'm gonna—"

Instead of pulling back he pulls me closer, his free hand grabbing my other ass cheek and securing me in his grip. My eyes open briefly, long enough to see his passionate gaze penetrate mine as I start to come.

"Fuck . . . fuck . . ." I gasp as my body seizes.

He moans loudly as I ride through my fierce climax and fill his mouth with my come until my thrusts slow to a rocking, and he finally eases my dick out of his mouth.

"Dean," he whispers, his hopeful expression more than I can take. He's still on his knees, and he gently strokes his hand up my thigh.

Chewing my lip, I avert my gaze. "Don't," I say as I try to back farther against the wall. The next moments hold a silence so weighted it's almost loud.

When I glance back at him his hopeful expression collapses into one of defeat as he sinks back down to the floor. I feel his head drop, his forehead pressing against my knees.

I'm starting to feel like I can't breathe. I carefully pull away from him, and then as steadily as I can, I walk to my room and firmly shut the door.

I collapse onto my back, spread-eagled on my bed, my jeans still loose around my hips. Part of me feels bad knowing that Jason must be freaking out . . . but I'm freaking out, too. I don't know how to process all of this. Even more shocking than finally hearing that my best friend wants me in a gay way is the shock of how much I got off on being gay with him.

He knows that I'm not a gay-hating asshole. I've had gay friends and had no issue, but they were out and there were no secrets or hidden agendas. Now I'm wondering if all the times we slept in the same bed, or jerked off to porn, that Jason was secretly horny for me. Just the idea of it is making me hard again. *Holy hell.*

I didn't think shit happened like this. I love fucking girls and then suddenly a switch turns on and now I want to fuck my best friend, too? *How is this possible? Am I bi? And if so, why the hell am I just feeling all this freaky stuff now?*

I swallow back the lump growing in my throat. I really need to talk to someone about all of this. Ironically, Jason is the one I talk to about everything . . . but I sure as hell can't now.

I take deep breaths to try to calm my racing heart. I've almost got a grip when there's a knock at my door.

A few seconds later Jason knocks again and then slowly opens the door. His expression is somber as our eyes meet.

"You okay?" he asks.

"Not really."

There's a heavy silence as his gaze drops to the floor.

"I just want to say I'm sorry, Dean. I feel so guilty for what just happened. I know it's not what you wanted."

If I wasn't so freaked out I'd man up and clarify that I did want it, but I can't admit that right now. Instead I look down, realizing that my jeans are still open and I lift my hips so I can pull them up and zip the fly.

His cheeks flush as he watches me lower my hips back onto the bed. "I wish none of this happened so we could just go back to where we were."

"But it did," I say. "Besides, Jason, you can't just live a lie, especially with me. We've always been brothers."

He looks up at me, crestfallen "Do you want me to move out?" he asks with a broken voice.

I feel the prickle of irritation. "Move out where? In with Ramon?"

"No!" he says, a little too forcefully.

I can't help it, but his quick response makes me feel a tiny bit better. "No, I don't want you to move, idiot."

His eyes grow wide and he nods, letting out a sigh of relief. "Okay, thanks. I'll just leave you alone then."

There's so much I want to say but can't. So when he turns and walks back out the door, I don't say a word.

Jason . 18

I'M NOT SURE I COULD hate myself anymore than I do at this moment. As if I haven't fucked myself up enough, now I've fucked up Dean too.

I feel like a creep and lousy all over so I decide to take a shower. Turning the water on extra hot, I take the pain as my punishment as it starts to burn my skin. I lean into the spray of water as I wonder if our friendship is salvageable. It hurts to even think that my dirty secret has pushed away the only person I've really cared about unconditionally—the only person I've loved so much that until tonight I've hidden my true self so I wouldn't lose him.

I scrub my scalded skin hard as I wince and then jerk the handle to cold to suffer the added shock to my system. I'm numb when I finally crawl out of the shower, and dry off enough to climb into bed.

Before I get under the covers I sit on the edge of the bed and open the second drawer of my nightstand, pulling out a book of prayers my mom gave me when I left for college. I flip through the pages until I find what I'm looking for. I take a deep breath and quietly whisper a prayer for sinners.

O Lord, Jesus Christ, Redeemer and Savior, forgive my sins, just as You forgave Peter's denial and those who crucified You. Count not my transgressions, but rather, my tears of repentance.

By the time I'm up in the morning Dean is gone. I remember him saying he had a study session so maybe that's where he is. I decide to clean the apartment as a gesture since he's letting me stay here despite how I've fucked everything up.

I start with the kitchen, which always aggravates me since the linoleum countertops are cracked and hard to clean. I try to ignore the busted handles on the cabinet where we keep our dishes and the silverware drawer. I vacuum the worn down beige carpet and even tackle the bathroom, which we clean only often enough to keep it from being gross.

But there's no doubt that this is the part of student life that I won't miss once I have a decent job and can afford a better place. The location and space in here has served Dean and I well, but the drab, busted up furniture and marked-up beige walls are depressing.

As I finish cleaning I still feel lousy about myself, but at least I tried to do something productive. I leave up all of Dean's print-outs that he has tacked up on every surface to taunt me about my obsession of what I wish our apartment looked like. I've made him think that they piss me off, but I actually love that he cares enough to come up with all of these crazy ideas.

In the late afternoon I'm just back from the gym when Ramon texts me about hooking up tonight.

Dude, my roommate left this morning for a funeral back at home. You can come over here tonight and I can finally get you naked.

I don't answer right away because my damn mind is spinning. Part of me wants to go to black out the memory of Dean pushing away from me with disgust after I gave him a blowjob. Maybe being with Ramon would help me forget. The other part of me knows that Dean is all I want. Just knowing how hard I got Dean, and how he got off, is making me wild. I'm fucked in the head.

I finally accept that I can't handle seeing him tonight. I text back, *This is such a drag but I'm feeling crappy,* I lie. *Must be something I ate.*

He responds immediately, *He's gone through Monday so if you're feeling better tomorrow, get your ass over here.*

Will do.

Setting my phone down, I let out a long sigh of relief but then the shame of lying starts to eat away at me. I live my life hiding so many secrets, especially from Dean, the person that matters most to me.

That sensation of shame takes me back to the time with my priest and the moment those memories strike, panic kicks in. I feel every muscle tighten and my breath shortens into gasps. Afraid I'm going to lose it, I try so hard to push the feelings away but the flame of panic burns hot and wild. It overtakes me until everything accelerates and it's as if I'm sitting in his study, my head dropped down and my cheeks ablaze with embarrassment.

Father Ryan used to tell me during our *sessions* that God made our bodies react the way they did so we could procreate. And thus when we weren't married and having sexual relations with our wife, we had to find another way to release the natural urges that overtook us. He told me that if he helped me release my "tension" I could then be a better young man, just as when I helped him release his "tension" he could be a better priest.

I can't remember if I thought he was lying when he first told me this in his locked study behind the sacristy as he parted his robe and reached into his pants and pulled out his hard dick, I just remembered being terrified that I'd get in trouble if I didn't obey him.

He calmly told me to touch him, and when I didn't comply he took my shaking hand and forced it over him. I wedged my eyes shut in horror, but when I heard his sharp breath—and I looked up and saw the sweat on his brow and his wide eyes—I understood how terribly wrong this was and nothing would right it. The way he used me that day led me not to just fear my priest, but God's retribution for what I'd done, regardless that it was against my will. Couldn't I have fought him off?

Right before he dismissed me, he swore me to secrecy. He warned that as long as I obeyed him no one would need to know how sick I was. The threat of public humiliation was clear and that paralyzed me. Did he somehow know or sense my yet undefined attraction to boys?

He unlocked the door, and as I stumbled through the sacristy I felt dirty and ashamed. That night was when my panic attacks and nightmares began, leaving me raw and unsteady throughout my days. Despite these collateral damages, his threats and my fear of being exposed were the reasons I returned when he summoned me two days later.

Dean . 19

WHEN I HIT MY TEENAGE years I became more aware of social and political issues outside my little world in Boise. With that awareness came some confusion as to why my liberal parents stayed in Boise when most of the people we knew were far more conservative than they were. Sure, I understood why they stayed when Grandma was still alive as my mom thought the sun rose and set on her, but once she passed, and with their line of work, they could have sold her house and moved us anywhere. We were still young and adaptable to a place that aligned more closely with their views.

So one evening at dinner I asked my parents why they stayed and my dad spoke up. "Maybe we're needed here to open up people's minds to other ways of thinking." My mom nodded with a big smile on her face.

Being at the height of my cynical phase of my teenage years, I rolled my eyes internally. My parents were so caught up in all their 'positive thinking' and 'change the world' crap that they actually believed this stuff.

So all these years later, it shouldn't have come as a surprise when Mom calls me to talk about Jason.

"Hi sweetheart," she says cheerfully.

I glance down at my watch. "Hey Mom, I'm trying to get to the gym before my afternoon class, so can we talk later?"

"Okay, when's a good time?"

She normally is spontaneous about calling so now I'm wondering what's up. "What's this about?"

"Well, Trent told me about your recent conversation regarding Jason."

My stomach drops. *Fucking Trent.* Didn't I tell him not to say anything? Recalling the conversation I realize that I don't think I did. *Damn.* "What about Jason?" I ask, playing it off, hoping that maybe this is about something else and Trent didn't out Jason. But I know I'm hopelessly grasping at straws.

"That he's gay." Her voice is serene, and I note that there's no hint of surprise in her tone.

"I shouldn't have said anything to Trent. I don't think Jason wants people to know, Mom."

"Oh poor boy, I can imagine how hard this is for him with his mother being the way she is. I know you have to go, but I just wanted to advise you that this undoubtedly is a very hard time for Jason and he's never needed you more."

I can feel the flush of embarrassment and shame spread across my skin since I've pretty much been a complete asshole since I found him in the garage with Ramon. "This has been very confusing for me, Mom."

"I'm sure it has, but imagine how this has been for him. He looks up to you like a brother, so whatever you can do to be compassionate and supportive would mean a lot. Please promise me that you'll be there for him."

Be there? Damn, I've been there for him but not in the ways she's suggesting. I'm sure she's not referring to me standing still when he drops down to his knees and unzips my fly.

"Um . . . okay," I mumble.

"Good, and when the time is right please tell Jason that we love him and support him in every way. If he needs his second Mom to talk to about anything I'm here for him."

I bite my tongue. I don't think Jason is ready to hear this stuff yet. He'd probably be horrified that he was outed like this.

"And we want you to know, Dean, that we love you, too . . . no matter if you're gay or straight or whatever. We're so proud of you."

What the hell? Do they think I'm gay now, too . . . like JJ and I are a package deal? "I'm not gay Mom, but thanks anyway for the support."

"Of course. Well, I won't keep you any longer but please let us know how things go."

"Will do."

Later that evening, I take a sharp breath as I pull up in front of the apartment building that Cassie lives in with her roommates. The conversation with my mom earlier freaked me out and so I'm relieved Cassie was free to see me tonight. She's the only one I can share this Jason shit-show with.

I debated the whole way over if I should tell her first about what happened with Jason last night, or if we should fuck first so I can get my mojo back and then the story will have a different perspective.

Settling on the latter, I grab the six-pack out of the backseat and take the stairs up two at a time.

"Hey handsome," she says when I pass through the door. She gives me a hug and I pull her closer so her softness presses against me. She feels different tonight. Maybe it's the loose shirt she's wearing made from some fuzzy fabric, or maybe it's the way she smells like cookies. It makes me want to cuddle with her, but that's not why I'm here.

"You smell good, like vanilla or something," I say as I take another deep whiff of her.

"Glad you like it—it's my new lotion," she replies as she pulls me down the hall toward her bedroom, only stopping to grab the bottle opener.

We settle on her bed, Cassie sitting cross-legged across from me as she takes the bottle of beer I've just opened for her. Her eyes narrow as she studies me. "You look tired. Everything all right?"

Her question makes me nervous. The thing is that in addition to Cassie being a highly-sexed, free spirit, she's also one of the most intuitive people I know. She's very observant and has one of those brains that's always computing.

I take a long swig of beer. "I'm fine," I lie.

"Everyone seems off this week. Rebecca was here crying last night because Ramon is giving her the cold shoulder."

I keep my mouth shut about what Ramon is really up to. He's not my problem tonight, so I ask a question to keep her on track. "Were they a couple? I thought they were just friends with benefits or something."

"Like us?" Cassie trails her fingers up my thigh.

"I suppose." I give her what feels like a half-hearted smile.

By the time we're finished with our first beer, it's taken some of the edge off my anxiety. After the second we're laughing about stupid stuff. I even take my T-shirt off after she accidently spills some beer down my front. Or maybe it wasn't accidental. Cassie is crafty like that.

She scrapes her fingernails down my bare chest. "You must hit the gym every day," she moans.

"Almost," I reply with pride. What man doesn't like to have his hard work appreciated?

"I know what you need to get you going," she whispers as she pushes me back against the pillows and then takes the near-empty bottle out of my hand.

"What's that?"

"A blowjob, big boy."

She crawls up over me like a wildcat, having no idea that the visions I'm having right now aren't Cassie's lips wrapped around my cock, but the look of raw lust on Jason's face while I fucked his mouth last night.

"Not so fast," I warn, knowing a blowjob from her would just make last night more vivid in my head. I need a distraction instead.

"Oh yeah?" she says, sitting up straight with a confused expression.

"I have other ideas." I finger the ends of her shirt and then slowly pull her top up and over her head. Sure enough, her glorious tits are bare, and judging from how her nipples are tightening, Cassie must be excited by this turn of events. She pulls her shoulders back, which make her tits even perkier.

When my cock twitches in response, I know stripping off her top was the right move to keep my mind where it should be. Jason is all hard lines and muscles. There's no way I can have confused thoughts about what's happening right now. Reaching out, I cup her heavy breasts in my hands.

She watches, squirming as I work my fingers over her nipples. "You're such a breast man. I love it," she says with a lazy smile.

"Mmmm," I moan, relieved that my dick is starting to react the more worked up she gets. I take her hard nipple between my teeth and then start to suck. She loves that shit and she eases back on the bed, taking me with her.

"So no blowjob?" she asks with a puzzled expression. We both know most guys would never turn down a blowjob.

I shake my head and release her nipple with a pop. "I'm gonna fuck you . . . I *need* to fuck you," I growl. I press my body against her while still working her tits. She's right, I'm a breast man and that's a good thing.

"Well then, I'm all yours," she replies breathlessly as she combs her fingers through my hair and spreads her legs wide.

We're still partially undressed as I settle over her. I start rocking my hips against her to get things going, but a little bell goes off in my head when I realize that I'm only about half-way there in the erection department.

Damn.

How can I fuck her with a semi? That's something you just can't fake.

As if she's read my signal, she starts pressing her crotch against me and between the way she's touching me and the dirty talk she's sharing in between ragged breaths, it's clear that Cassie is hungry for me to fill her. I need to amp up.

Squeezing my eyes shut, I fight back thoughts about Jason being under me instead of Cassie. I remember that night weeks ago when I was trying to get his phone and for a minute we were dry humping each other. You can bet my dick was cooperating that night. I was rock hard and burning for more. As I recall all those feelings I start rocking against Cassie and thankfully the front of my jeans tighten from my swelling hard-on.

By the time I'm fully lit, I'm pulling down her panties. I'm not willing to risk an idle moment in case my dick changes its mind.

She moans as I undo my fly and pull out my hard cock. Her expression is dark with desire while she watches me push off my jeans and roll the condom over my dick.

"You want this?" I ask with gritted teeth as I lean back over her and rub my cock against where she's wet.

"Hell yes. Fuck me already."

I thrust my hips and fill her up hard before she has time to ask twice.

And thus begins the curse of second thoughts and the shadow of homo desire. We go from zero to sixty until I'm pounding her harder than usual and she takes it like a champ, rocking her hips up to meet mine while her fingers dig into my ass.

My eyes are wedged shut as I imagine that it's Jason I'm fucking. But as if she's psychic or something, Cassie commands me to open my eyes and watch her. She writhes under me and sure enough I start to wilt, and panic sets in.

I lift up to my knees and grab her hand, then move it to her clit. "Here," I say breathlessly, "I want to watch you get yourself off."

She gives me a suspicious look for a second, but then she starts stroking herself with one hand while the other works her nipple. I watch and pick up fucking her again, while her raw moans are keeping things just hot enough that I can continue thrusting.

"Come on, baby," I pant. "You look so damn hot touching yourself while I fuck you."

"Oh Dean," she groans as her thighs start to tremble.

"I want you to come all over my cock," I moan. For a second I have an out-of-body experience like I'm floating above the scene watching me fuck her while she goes over the edge with a howl.

Letting out that low moan that signals the last wave of her orgasm, Cassie sinks down into the sheets and I realize that as much as I need it, I'm not going to come. I'm not even close. Instead I'm wilting again, so I pull out of her, and roll over onto my side.

"Damn, that was good," I say with a ragged breath.

There's an uncomfortable, silent pause that makes my palms start to sweat.

She props herself up on her elbow and slides her hand across my chest. "But you didn't even get off, Dean. Are you feeling okay?"

Closing my eyes, I try to imagine how I can get out of this. Talk about performance anxiety. I feel like my entire man-card was based on getting off tonight.

"Do you know how hot it was watching you get yourself off?" I ask, skimming my thumb over her jaw.

"Apparently not hot enough," she responds with a frown when she looks down and sees I'm not hard anymore.

"Ah, come on, Cassie," I moan. "It's been a rough week."

She scoots to the edge of the bed and grabs the bottle opener and proceeds to open two more bottles. When she hands one to me, I take a long swig and watch her take hers.

"Can we talk? Like really talk?" she asks, just when I'm starting to chill.

Every hair on my arms stands up. "Talk about what?"

"Is it me, or someone else?"

"What? Like who?" I ask, my lips suddenly parched and dry.

"I don't know for sure, but my girly intuition is telling me this has something to do with Jason. Did something happen after our three-way?"

Fuck.

Leave it to Cassie to be all intuitive and shit.

Turning, I stare out the window, like the most amazing thing is happening just outside.

"Dean?" she says with a coaxing tone.

I remain silent and swallow hard.

"You fucked him, didn't you?"

"God no!" I cry out, freaked out she thinks that.

She purses her lips together. "He wanted you to fuck him. Damn, he wanted it bad. That made the whole scene with the three of us even hotter."

'Well, I didn't fuck him," I say in a graveled voice.

"Then what?" she asks.

I turn and swing my legs over so they're hanging off the side of the bed and I'm not facing her. I can't watch her reaction when I finally admit the truth.

"He blew me."

She takes a sharp breath. "Wow. Okay then. You let him blow you. Did you like it?"

I don't answer but I feel the heat move up my chest and even feel the blood getting hot in the tips of my ears. I must look like the cat that ate the canary. Or the cat that got blown by the canary . . . and liked it . . . a lot.

Hell, I didn't just like it. I fucking loved it, and now the picture of him looking up at me with that sexy stare while his mouth is full of my hard cock is the filter I now look through for everything I see.

And there you go. I'm hard as a rock. *How absolutely gay is that?* Nubile goddess Cassie just spread her sweet thighs for me while I sucked on her perfect tits. I watched her come all over her fingers like a porn star, and instead I'm hot for my gay roommate who's on his knees begging me for more.

"You didn't *like* it," she whispers, "you *loved* it, didn't you, Dean?"

I swallow hard and nod.

"That's so fucking hot," she moans. "I want to watch."

"No!" I say a little too forcefully considering how cool she's been.

She flops down on her back. "See, I knew there was something naughty between you two. It's just taken you a while to catch on. That boy looks at you like you're dessert."

"You're tripping me with that talk," I say with a groan.

She rolls over to her stomach. "Why? Consider it a compliment. Jasie is hot as fuck. I can't even tell you how many girls I know swoon over him. Of course they have no idea he's gay. But the reality is that he *is* gay and he's into you."

She lets out a long sigh tinged with sadness.

"What?" I ask.

"And now he's finally got you under his spell. I'm going to miss this." She gestures between us. "I don't know if it was your super-sized cock, or what. But no one gets me off like you do."

"Gee thanks. But don't give up on me so quickly. I'm not gay. I'm just shocked about all of this. That's why I'm not myself . . . I don't know how to handle this change in my best friend."

"Right," she mutters, giving me a look like I'm incredibly naive. "When the shock wears off you'll be into girls again."

"Cassie . . ." I hope she can tell from my tone that she better leave it alone.

She gives me a wink. "Okay Dean. Sounds good to me. You know where to find me."

I'm sitting in my car outside our apartment trying to pull my shit together before I head inside. I'm really pissed off. I can't help it. I've never had this happen with a girl. What's next? Am I going to start jerking off to gay porn? I try to imagine it in my mind, and then frantically shake my head as if to knock the idea out of my brain.

If it was going to happen with anyone, at least it happened with Cassie. She was cool about it . . . almost too cool, now that I think about it. It's like she had always wondered about JJ and I. I've wondered about other guys I've known, the ones that were a little soft or effeminate. Hell, our suite mate our freshman year seemed into girls but he had a boner for Broadway musicals. That set my gaydar howling, but I didn't care one way or another, I just would wonder if he was going to come out with each year passing but never saw him switch sides, so I figured I was wrong.

But Jason? No way. He's always been a sports guy who likes watching cage fighting on cable. He even prefers the most brutal video games. But then I start replaying in my head the conversation that I had with my brother about JJ. He said something about the way Jason stared at me with lust and how he always wondered about him. And what about Mom who didn't seem the slightest bit surprised to hear that Jason is gay?

It's true that starting from our first days together, he spent as much time as possible with me. I always thought it was because his mom drove him nuts. She was a major case, after all. And we got along so well, so easily, that it just felt good to have him at my side.

We almost never disagreed, which makes this recent tension between us even more unnerving. I think back again to our teenage jack-off sessions and after the first few awkward times we did it in front of each other, it started to feel like the most natural thing in the world. Why was that? Although once he joked that I was lame at it and he should just show me how to do it right. I scoffed and warned him that if he touched my dick I'd have to punch him in his pretty face.

"I'm not pretty, asshole," he replied.

We ended up wrestling and I don't remember who won, just that we both ended up belly laughing.

And that's how it always was. Everything was easy; spending our free time together was just a given. It was one of the issues that got to my ex, too. She complained that it was hard to get any quality time with me alone since Jason was always with us.

I remember back in high school when his date, Rachel Simington told Jason that she wouldn't go our senior prom with him only two weeks before the event, I told my date, Katie that Jason was coming with us whether she liked it or not. She was pissed but immediately got one of her girlfriends to go with Jason and we went as a foursome.

Now that I think of it that was always the pattern. Girls fell hard for Jason but after a while they were usually the ones who dropped him. Did they see the gay thing firsthand before even his best friend did? Rachel Simington was one of the "racy" girls in our high school . . . did she figure JJ's secret "issue" out and dump him?

I feel a rush of adrenaline, and I need to start putting some of the pieces of this fucking puzzle together. Stepping out of my car, I slam the door hard, before marching up into our building.

Once inside, I find Jason in the living room, sitting slack on the couch with his legs stretched out wide and a beer in his hand. He's watching wrestling.

Of course he's watching wrestling . . . the gayest sport there is.

He turns and glances up at me with a nervous expression. "Hey," he says before looking down. When I don't answer, he turns back to the TV and slinks lower.

I open the fridge and pull out another beer, taking a long swig before dragging my hand over my wet mouth. I suddenly notice the kitchen looks like it got professionally cleaned. The living room looks straightened up, too. What's up with that? We're not slobs or anything, but this shit is over the top.

"Why's this place so clean?" I notice that one of the wrestlers has the other one pinned to the mat and they're both grunting. *Awesome.*

"Just felt like cleaning it," he answers.

"Wrestling is so gay," I say, nodding toward the TV. "Is that your favorite sport now?"

I cringe when the words leave my mouth. That was an asshole thing to say considering everything he must be going through.

He stays silent, but I notice he slides down another inch into the couch like he wishes he could disappear.

I'm overcome with the need for him to look me in the eye. No more of this wimpy stuff. That guy who sunk to his knees and begged to blow me . . . I don't know who that guy is, and I need to know why.

I walk over and stand next to the TV until he glances up at me. "Why did Rachel Simington bail on going to the prom with you?"

His eyes bug out. "Are you serious? Rachel Simington? That was a million years ago. Fuck her."

"Is that why?" I ask. "Did she bail because you wouldn't fuck her?"

He lets out a long sigh of defeat. "Well if you really need to know this—"

"I do," I interrupt.

He rubs his knuckles across his jaw and sighs. "I tried to screw her, more than once, but it didn't happen. And once everyone was scheming to get hotels rooms for after the prom she realized that if she went with me, we'd look hot together, but it wouldn't be the fuck fest she was counting on."

"You *tried*?" I say after taking a slug of beer to fortify myself. Rachel may not have been the most interesting girl but her body was hot as hell.

His cheekbones color. "She didn't do it for me, apparently."

"So even back then?" I say.

Nodding, he averts his gaze. "So where've you been?"

"With Cassie."

"At her place?" He seems bothered.

"Why do you care?" I ask.

He throws his head back and digs his fingers into the edge of the couch. "Did you fuck her?"

I glare at him. He has some goddamn nerve asking me that.

He's not backing down. "Did you get off? And did it make you feel better about things?"

"I couldn't get off," I reply angrily.

He blinks rapidly.

I step closer to him. I can feel my nostrils flare and my fingers tighten over my beer bottle. "You want to know why I couldn't get off?"

He nods but his eyes fix on my crotch for some reason and that just pisses me off more. Then, to insure that this conversation couldn't get any more fucked up, my cock starts to harden the longer he stares at me.

I clear my throat since it feels like it's full of gravel. "I couldn't get off because my head is screwed up thanks to you. This has never happened to me, asshole! I'm so fucked in the head, after you getting on your knees and blowing me, that I couldn't keep it up!"

Biting the corner of his lip, he rubs his palms over his knees. "Dean . . ."

My dick is trapped at a weird angle in my jeans and it's starting to hurt the harder I get, so I adjust myself while he watches. "So can you explain to me why I couldn't get hard enough for Cassie but I'm hard as a rock right now?"

"I d-d-don't know," he stutters, looking back at my crotch and taking a sharp breath.

I palm myself roughly, feeling a burning need surge through me. "You wanna *really* see how fucking hard I am?"

He sets his beer down on the coffee table. "I really don't think you want to do this, Dean."

I'm so damn mad. Every muscle in my arm is tight, and I'm aching to punch something. "Oh yeah, I do. I want you to see how confused you've made my dick." I unzip my fly and push my jeans open, then reach in and pull out my cock. It's fully hard now and I can feel Jason's piercing gaze on me as I slowly stroke it long and tight.

Jason takes a sharp breath. "Oh God," he moans.

"See that?" I say as I continue to stroke. "So the fucked up thing is that tonight my dick decided he didn't want to be between Cassie's legs, but in your mouth again instead. How fucked up is that?"

He leans back into the couch with a stunned expression, but I can see he's getting hard too, now. Of course he is. My cock is in my hands and it's a steel rod for him. This is probably his dream come true.

"You want me to get you off again?" he asks tentatively.

"What do you think, genius? You need to take care of this situation since this is your fault with how you've fucked with me."

"I don't know," he whispers.

"I know you want it. Don't you?" I taunt. I feel a wave of light-headedness, probably from all the blood in my body flooding my dick instead of my brain. I shove my jeans down and settle on the couch next to him.

He looks over at me and nods slowly, never taking his gaze off my cock.

I gesture to the floor right below where my legs are spread. "I want you on your knees."

Jason. 20

"I WANT YOU ON YOUR knees."

I close my eyes as Dean's command takes me back to around my thirteenth birthday, and my sessions with Father Ryan. He now summoned me almost every day after school, not just the bi-weekly sessions my mom had set up after tennis practice.

At that point we were about six weeks into our *sessions*. They always started with him inquiring about my classes and my socialization with the other boys at school. He would also ask me about my home life with mom, and how it was for me not having a father figure at home since my dad had walked out on us when I was young. These talks were excruciating for me; I wasn't a kid who spent a lot of time analyzing my feelings. I was the type that acted out shit instead. I guess that's how I ended up in these sessions in the first place.

Father Ryan was an imposing figure—tall, with an athletic build and dark hair that he kept very short. I had heard once that he was in his early forties but he seemed very fit which made him seem younger. His features were sharp, but they'd soften and his dark eyes would brighten when he was praising you. The opposite would happen, every feature looking more severe when he got angry.

I asked him once if he also did these sessions with other boys. He assured me that I'd helped him so much that I was all he needed. My stomach fell. He then rested his hand on my shoulder and said I was a very special young man and Jesus shines his light on special young men. I knew that he was making that shit up. Just as I knew that when he bought me video games, comic books, and my favorite stuff from the bakery down the street he thought he was making everything better. No amount of Jesus shining his light on me or cheese danishes could make this situation better.

And as it was the talking times got shorter and shorter, thus making more time for the "other" part of our sessions . . . the dirty, sinful part where he made me do things I didn't want to do.

On that hot afternoon, his study was stuffy and he seemed agitated when I closed the door behind me. He reminded me to lock it, and I did. He rubbed his hand across the top of his head and then told me that he was very tense so it was good we were meeting.

"Come here." He swiveled in his chair and pointed to the spot to the right beside his desk.

My mouth was dry and I swallowed hard. He glanced down at my slacks and I felt shame when I saw the gleam in his eyes as he reached for my fly. His face was flushed as he opened up my slacks and yanked them down so he could touch me.

No, no, no, my inner voice screamed.

I waited silently as he took several long breaths, his eyes hooded, staring at me with a lustful gaze. I turned away and thought about the picture I recently traced of the New York skyline filled with all the buildings I admired. I closed my eyes and imagined I was there as I focused on breathing so I wouldn't pass out with fear.

When he was done roughly handling me I prayed this session was over. My exposed skin burned with shame as if his touch had branded me. But my hope was extinguished when he cleared his throat and pointed to the floor.

"I want you on your knees."

Dean. 21

JASON GETS A GLAZED LOOK when I first tell him to get on his knees for me. He seems lost in a memory, and it makes me curious. But before I can ask what he's thinking about, he slides off the couch, and silently sinks down to the floor, and then crawls over until he's kneeling between my legs.

I make a show of stroking myself as he watches, his gaze fixed on my cock as I slowly run my fingers up and down the shaft and spread my legs open farther. I'm getting off on taunting him. I'm such a bastard.

"You like that I'm hard for you. Don't you?" I growl, my chest heaving with anticipation.

He nods, and I notice he drops his left hand down to grip himself.

I tip my head to the side so I can see what he's doing. "Go ahead," I say. "If you want to jerk while you blow me, be my guest. It's a fucking slut party tonight."

Jason remains kneeling while I slowly stroke, rocking my hips, my cock pushing up into my fist while my rhythm builds. I'm staring at him and he stares back, his eyes dark and stormy . . . his full lips in a straight line.

"What are you waiting for? I thought you wanted to suck me." I tip my cock his direction and pause, waiting to see if he can handle this.

He surprises me by approaching me slowly and not going straight for my cock. He bends toward me, and starts kissing and licking his way up my inner thighs. It's crazy sexy and making my blood boil. I feel the scratch of his stubble and his hot breath against my skin, and my dick grows impossibly harder. He spreads my legs farther the higher he gets, and my hand stops stroking when he runs his tongue over my balls.

"Oh damn," I moan as he keeps working me.

Next thing I know, he pushes my hand away and takes me in his mouth, sucking down my shaft while his fist slides up and down at my base. His face is flushed with pleasure and he's breathing in short gasps.

This time I'm ready for his hot mouth, not half-stunned like I was yesterday, and so I give myself up to the feeling completely, moaning and writhing at the perfection of his full lips on me. "Jesus, yes," I croon when he leans down and sucks on my balls again while his fist strokes up and down my shaft.

In this position I can't fuck his mouth completely, but I still rut up and watch his eyes water and grow wide when I hit deep in his throat. Reaching up, I place a hand on either side of his face so I can control his rhythm and he lets me lead him, pulling him deeper and deeper over my cock. He moans with such hunger for me that my cock throbs under his swirling tongue.

We're reaching a frenzied state when his hands suddenly drop down and I realize he's ripping his fly open. I like that he's at his edge just from sucking me off and I want to see the evidence of how turned on he is.

I can tell the moment his cock is free and his hand grips it. His eyes roll back and the muscles in his arms flex as his hand speeds up.

"I wanna watch," I groan, forgetting my own pleasure to see him finally getting his. He bites his lip, gasping for each breath as he stares at me. His eyes are wild with desire and his cheeks are flushed. I look down and watch how rough he is with his raging hard-on. I'd think he was punishing himself if he didn't look so out of his mind with lust.

I watch a moment longer, realizing he's about to get off. "That's so fucking hot," I moan before I fall back on the couch and fist my dick and arch a brow at him. He takes the hint and practically swallows my dick as his hand continues pumping himself.

"Yes, fuck yes," I groan as he goes down again, sucking me in even deeper. All I can do is lie back and watch this man turn me inside out. My mouth is slack and my eyes tearing up to feel my orgasm building to something I've never known. My thighs start shaking and with his final suck I start to blow, the feeling so powerful the room goes hot white and I let go, hoping my heart doesn't explode in the sheer force of it.

I have the vague notion of JJ practically swallowing me and then crying out, spazzing in jerky moves as he comes, too. *Holy hell.*

What the fuck was that?

It was the sexiest thing ever, and I'm drunk with it.

I finally start to focus again but I'm still gasping for breath. And when I look down I realize that he's slowly licking my abs. I feel so raw and wild that it doesn't even faze me.

As much as it guts me, I have to admit to myself that I liked all of this . . . him sucking me off gets me going more than I can believe. Last night was shocking and intense, but tonight I was able to stay inside my body and I fucking loved it. I start wondering when we can do it again. This doesn't mean I'm gay. Maybe I'm just choosing to be open-minded. My fury that I felt when I stormed home from Cassie's is a distant memory.

Jason sits up and our gazes meet. He looks worried as he waits for my reaction.

Between all the beer and the come-down from the fiercest climax of my life, I feel like I'm drugged and suddenly not only is my anger diffused, but I want to know more. "Damn JJ, where'd you learn to do that?"

His eyes cloud over like they did before we started up. "It's a long story I don't think you want to hear," he whispers.

"I swear, JJ, you've got a magic mouth. You should brand your skills. Whoever taught you that shit sure knows what they were doing."

He pushes back a smile. "You mean you liked it?"

"What do you think? I mean, don't get me wrong, I'm still fucked in the head, but damn, I've never come that hard."

He doesn't seem to take the compliment, instead focusing on my "fucked in the head" comment. He twists his hands together and his eyes narrow.

"What?" I ask. I don't like how troubled he looks.

"I don't know how to read what you're saying, Dean. You're fucked in the head but you liked it anyway?"

I shrug. "I guess, yeah, you could put it that way."

"But I don't want to make things any worse for you than I already have . . . but if you liked what we just did, does this mean you're willing to do more with me? Would you let me do that to you again?" He glances down nervously, but when his gaze meets mine and I can tell he's hopeful.

"I'm not gay, man, so I could never be 'out and proud,' but I'd be willing to do this again as long as you never tell anyone."

"So you'd be *willing* to let me blow you, but nothing else. Why would you even want to? I mean, what's the point of that?"

I shrug. "To release tension? Imagine how less stressed out we'd be. And we're comfortable with each other. Besides, that was by far the best blow job I've ever had and I'm greedy."

For a minute he stares at me silently. I don't know what I said that freaked him out so much, but he looks spooked.

"What?" I ask.

"Release tension? But I'm gay, Dean," he whispers. "That's not enough for me, and I'd want to explore these feelings between us."

"Explore feelings?" I say with a grimace. "I don't want to explore any feelings, I just want to get off like that . . . like I'm on fire."

He appears to be hurt or something, but this stuff is too complicated for me to figure out, especially when I'm still drunk with bliss. He shakes his head, looking wrecked.

What the hell?

I clear my throat. "Yeah, I get it . . . I'm not gay so I can't give you enough of what you need. So I guess what you're saying is that this *isn't* what you need, so we shouldn't do this again." I immediately feel crappy about it, but I'm on a downward roll so I continue. "Okay, look . . . I'm doing the best I can dealing with your gay thing. I'll try to be less of an ass but you've gotta start being honest with me. Okay?"

Maybe my little speech was too much. With a grim expression, he nods and silently gets up and heads to his room, quietly shutting the door.

I sit for a minute trying to figure out what that was about. He just walked away without a final word, and shut me out right when we're finally getting real and having an honest conversation about all this. What a chicken-shit thing to do.

Rising, I pull myself together and then go to his room. I don't bother knocking on the door, I just push it open and approach the bed where he's lying on his stomach his face buried in his pillow.

"Go away," he moans.

"What's going on, man?"

"I don't want to talk about it."

"Is this about when I asked you how you learned to do this? You looked spooked. Are you going to tell me what that was about? Or are we still fucking around with lies and cover-ups?"

Sighing, he meets my gaze, "You really want to know, Dean? I'm not sure you can handle it."

"What the fuck? Of course I can handle it. Let me guess, it was that guy, Phillip. He always seemed to have a thing for you. Is that who made you gay?"

He lets out a long, sorry sigh. "No, it wasn't Phillip."

"Who then?"

There's a weighted pause, like he's trying to decide whether to tell me or not. It must be pretty bad.

He looks down right before he speaks. "My priest, Father Ryan."

I blink hard, flattened with his confession. His priest? *Oh hell no.* My mind is reeling with the extent of how fucked up that is in every way. Going closer, I sit on the end of the bed and turn toward him.

"No bullshit, right?"

"No. I wouldn't make that up. I swear."

"Christ, Jason. That is so fucked up. When was this?"

"It started when I was in sixth grade and went on for almost two years."

I feel the fury burn across my skin. "Sixth fucking grade? So the fucker molested you."

"He did, and I didn't fight him off. So that shows you how fucked up I was."

It guts me to know Jason has been carrying this shit around with him. I can't even imagine how he coped. No wonder he's such a damn mess.

"And you kept that a secret . . . all these years?"

He shrugs. "What choice did I have? My mom thought the sun rose and set on Father Ryan, and you were the only person in my life keeping me sane. If I'd told you and you rejected me, I really didn't think I'd be able to keep going on."

"Damn."

He nods his head and turns on his side away from me.

"I wish I'd known. I would've kicked his ass."

"You would've done that for me?" he whispers.

"Fuck yes." I flex my fingers into fists. Feeling a tremor from the bed, I look back at Jason and his shoulders are shaking. I scoot down on the bed until I'm next to him. "JJ, what's going on? Are you crying?"

He doesn't respond but his shoulders are still shaking and he curls down into himself. Damn, I bet he's crying, and that never happens. I can't let him suffer anymore than he already has. Instinctively I want to listen and comfort him in whatever way helps.

Settling down behind him, I put my hand on his shoulder. "You're freaking me out, man. Why are you crying?"

His voice cracks when he finally speaks. "I don't want to talk about it."

"Well to hell with that," I murmur as I pull on his shoulder until he's flat on his back so I can see his face, now wet with tears. "You need to talk, and I need to hear."

"I can't," he gasps in between sobs. "I'm so ashamed of what I did."

"It's what *he* did to you, JJ. Not what *you* did. You can't blame yourself for this."

He bravely looks up at me, the pain vivid in his eyes. "But I didn't fight him off and I allowed it to happen, Dean. Well, most of it . . . until he wanted more than I could handle."

I pause for a moment. I need to keep him talking and if I freak out on him it will only damage him more. "Okay, first of all you were scared and he had authority over you, and maybe you would've ended up gay, even if that didn't happen, but still you being gay doesn't make it okay. He was your priest for fucks sake and he took advantage of you. And you were just a kid."

Those words seem to calm him a little and his shoulders stop shaking. He nods. "I was young and scared. I was already in trouble with my anger issues, and he knew exactly how to manipulate me."

"How often did this happen?" I hold my breath, hoping it was just a handful of times. Those two years that Jason went to Catholic boy's school we mainly just hung out on the weekends, although we called each other with stupid jokes and stuff during the week.

"It happened a lot." He wedges his eyes shut.

"Horny bastard," I curse under my breath.

"You have no idea," he sighs. "He was a master manipulator. If Mom hadn't lost her job, who knows how long it would've gone on."

"What do you mean?"

"When she lost her job at the accounting place she didn't have tuition money and Father Ryan told her he'd work out a scholarship arrangement for me. That's what pushed me over the edge. I knew if that happened I'd belong to him completely, so I used the situation to insist I go back to public school. I was unrelenting and she finally agreed."

"So you were free of him then?"

"Well, I'd see him at mass on Sunday obviously, but I was out the door as soon as it was over. I stopped taking communion and confessing but the fear always lingered that I'd get pulled into his web again somehow. Honestly the greatest relief about moving here with you and getting out of that damn town was knowing I'd never have to get on my knees for him again."

His shoulders start shaking once more and he presses his hands over his eyes.

"Hey," I murmur as I pull him closer and wrap my arms around him, wanting to calm him. "It's okay, it's okay."

He takes a long, ragged breath. "You aren't disgusted by all of this?" he asks, his voice raw and vulnerable.

"I'm disgusted by him, but not by you. I'm just so fucking sorry that you had to go through this alone."

I can feel his body relax and he rests his head on my shoulder. I slowly stroke his arm as his breathing starts to regulate. The most surprising thing is that me holding and comforting him doesn't feel weird. He's always been like my brother, and now that I have some understanding of the hell he's been dealing with I want to help him.

He sighs. "I can't even tell you how badly I've wanted to tell you about this but I was too afraid."

"You should've told me. I'm not that big of an asshole," I tease him.

"But then my secret would be your burden to carry, and it sucks when you can't do anything about it anyway."

"But still . . ."

"Besides, don't you think finding out that I'm into men was enough to handle for one semester?"

"Well, it hasn't been smooth but now we're managing that one okay, don't you think?"

"I guess."

"And look, I'm trying to be the friend you need. I'm holding you so I can comfort you. That's definitely not asshole behavior."

"I like this," he sighs, nudging closer. "But this experimenting thing you implied earlier . . ."

"Where we get each other off?" I ask. "If that wasn't me being open minded, I don't know what is. Besides you rejected that idea."

"I told you—" he whispers.

"I know, I know . . . you need *more*."

"I do. Do you understand?"

I pause, wondering if I do understand. It used to be fine when we were just two friends jerking off. *Can't we just be two friends jerking each other off? See how open minded I am?*

"So it means we'll each do our own thing, and our friendship is still intact?"

"Yeah," he says softly.

"See, I'm trying to understand," I admit.

"Thank you." His gaze is somber.

Is this really what he wants? I wait another moment and then when he stays quiet I know we're done for tonight.

"Okay, I think we both need to crash." I slowly slide away from him and ease myself off his bed. I stretch my arms up before walking toward the door. "But if you ever change your mind and want to experiment some more, you know where to find me."

He gives me a quiet smile, and I smile back before I head out the door.

Jason . 22

LONG AFTER DEAN LEAVES MY room I can still feel his arms around me and smell his scent, like trees and crisp morning air, natural and clean. He listened to my nightmare story and he held me. *He fucking held me.* Nobody has ever done that for me before.

When he said he wanted to kick Father's Ryan's ass, I felt a powerful surge of warmth knowing that he would've had my back with his fierce rage and instinct to protect me. His reaction was more than I ever would've hoped for.

Wrapping his powerful arms around me, his heart was thundering in his chest, as my cheek pressed against him. I could've stayed in his arms forever, and I desperately wish I knew he'd hold me like that again. But no matter what, I feel like we crossed a bridge tonight. I think his learning some of my past has given him more sympathy for why I felt forced to hide who I really was for so many years.

I love that man so damn much, my heart aches for the want of him. I don't know if it was the liquor talking, but Dean saying that he's willing to up our relationship to friends with benefits is so fucking tempting. I'm hungry to have my hands all over him, to watch him get hard just for me.

I took the most perverse pleasure in knowing that he couldn't keep it up for Cassie tonight because he was thinking of me . . . *me*! Now that I've seen that desperate look in his eyes as he watches me suck his cock, I have no idea how any other man will truly satisfy me. I'd do anything to have him, but it has to be more than fucking around because if it isn't the whole package, I don't think my heart will survive.

When Dean commanded that I get on my knees, it took me right back to the first time Father Ryan said the same thing to me. It stung because I never want anything about Dean to remind me of that fucked-up situation I was trapped in so many years ago.

But now telling him about Father Ryan has brought it all back to me in a vivid way. The memories are dark and dank, like the farthest corner of a basement in a decrepit old house. My shame is from my compliance. The fact that I didn't fight off his abuse is a shadow that has followed me everywhere. His actions splintered my soul and I may never be whole again.

Maybe if Father Ryan just kept our *sessions* to verbally provoking me, my pride could've remained intact. However, once that line was crossed when he began sexually using me, I realized that he could violate me in countless ways. I was nothing more than his toy to play with and abuse.

I'll never forget the day when he uttered those words: "I want you on your knees." His expression was troubled, and I sensed anguish. But I also saw hunger in his beady eyes, and my fear of him reached a new level. And now I'm reliving it in my head all over again.

At first I was hoping I didn't hear him right. I stood with my mouth gaping, and my stomach falling. Then he gestured sharply to a spot on the floor, and defeated I sunk down, the wood feeling hard and unforgiving against my knees.

He made quick work of making me understand what he wanted. I looked up at him with wide eyes, blinking. It's not that I didn't know about oral sex. I did, but the idea of doing that to him sickened me so that bile was crawling up my throat.

I was frozen, trying to desperately think of how to get out of him using me for his sick pleasure. "I'm not feeling well," I whispered, begging.

His brows knit together and his jaw locked as he ground his teeth. "You need to obey," he growled.

"But I don't want to do *that*."

He grabbed a section of my hair and I winced as he jerked me closer.

My eyes glazed over from the pain screaming from my scalp as his fingers tightened. Not understanding how things had gone from bad to worse, my eyes glazed with tears as the violation began. And that is when the last light shining on my youth burned out, leaving my innocence in darkness.

After, I rushed out of his office, through the sacristy, and just made it to the bathroom in time to vomit violently, over and over. My stomach finally empty, I scrubbed my hands, and face, even washing my mouth out with the foam from the liquid soap. But no amount of burning water and soap could wash away how dirty I'd feel from that moment on, my lips and throat sore from what he'd made me do.

I battle with myself inwardly to pull out of this memory that can make me self-destruct. I remind myself that Dean's words may have been the same as Father Ryan's but everything else was different . . . completely different. For one, I wanted Dean desperately. I would've let him do anything he wanted to me, and I took absolute pleasure in watching him writhe under my attention.

He was brave enough to be honest and say how turned on he was when we were together. Hearing those words made hope flare in my heart, but knowing he has his limits, I have to be satisfied for now that he seems willing to accept who I am without judgment. That's a big step from where I thought we stood even yesterday.

As desperate as I am to have another taste of him, I have to give Dean space while I keep myself distracted with feeble options to satiate my growing hunger . . . namely online porn and other men. Actually, Ramon isn't a feeble choice, he's powerful and confident and a damn good kisser. There's nothing wrong with us using each other to scratch an itch. Is there?

Dean. 23

I WAKE UP WITH A hard-on and thoughts of Jason and his full lips and warm mouth. I run memories of last night through my head and despite remembering most of it through a beer-drenched haze, I know that I felt things I'd never felt before, and for some reason in the reality of this new day, I'm fine with it. Hell, I'm more than fine with it . . . I'm lying here realizing that now that I've surrendered to raw lust and being worshipped, I don't want to let it go. Stretching my arms over my head, I stare at my hard dick wondering if Jason's awake and if he'd appreciate a visitor for a mutual jack-off session.

Still I can't forget that he said he needs "more," whatever that is. We already live together and are best friends. Maybe it's kissing and giving each other goo-goo eyes that would make us "enough" for him, but I'm not sure I could handle that.

By the time I shower and wander to the kitchen for breakfast, Jason's already left for his morning class. I don't see him the rest of the day and I can't help but wonder how he's doing.

It's almost midnight when he lets himself in the apartment and drops his keys on the counter. I look up from the TV. "Where've you been?"

"I got together with Ramon," he says casually, but then his gaze fixes on mine to judge how I take the news.

I don't like it one bit but I try not to show it. "Yeah, what'd you do?" I ask, trying to sound casual even though my throat is tight.

He shrugs. "Had a few drinks."

I swallow hard, feeling very uncomfortable that he drank and made himself vulnerable. "Did you get off?"

He nods and then turns to pour himself a glass of water.

"How?"

"Seriously?" he asks, his eyes wide, and his head tipped to the side.

"Yeah, did he blow you again?"

Jason let's out a labored breath. "I'm not going to give you a play-by-play, Dean. Just take my word that I got off."

I scowl. "And Jason . . . is he '*more*' for you? I mean like what he does for you, gives you."

"No," he whispers.

His response pisses me off. He can go mess around with Ramon and get off even though he's missing this illusive "more" bullshit, but he won't with me. *What am I chopped liver?* My fingers tighten into fists. "Why not?"

"Because to be that I'd have to *want* more from him, and I don't."

We both pause and stare at each other for what feels like minutes. I don't like him fucking around with other guys, so I'm going keep wearing him down until I understand what "more" has to be.

Turning off the kitchen light, he heads to his room. "Goodnight, Dean."

I want to ask him to stay up with me a little longer, but I can't find the words.

Jason . 24

I DON'T KNOW WHAT TO make of all of this, but Dean is acting like a jilted girlfriend. I thought we'd agreed to step back and do our own thing. But as I get ready to meet up with Ramon again the next night, he starts with the fifty questions.

"Where are you guys going?" he asks as I check my phone before heading out.

"A gay bar on the East side of town Ramon was telling me about. Ramon says he wants to dance."

"I bet that's not all he wants to do," he grumbles.

"You're welcome to come to the bar with us," I offer knowing there's no way in hell that he would.

"And watch him man-handle you? No thanks." He makes a sour face. I'm surprised that's all he protests about when I know a gay bar is way out of his comfort zone.

"So what are you doing tonight?" I ask.

"Haven't decided yet, but if I'm not here when you get home you'll know I figured it out."

I nod. "Later."

While Ramon and I are standing at the Lucky Boy bar I notice he's studying my face.

"What's up?" I ask.

"You look different."

"Bad different, or good?" He's making me nervous the more he stares at me.

"Kind of far away looking. Something heavy on your mind?" he asks as he hands me my beer.

"Just some stuff going on with Dean."

"Is he still being an ass? Or did he finally realize you're the hottest thing around?" He gives me that dimpled smile.

"Maybe a little of both," I respond before taking a swig of my beer.

He arches his brow. "Really? Well, tell him to back off, he had his chance. Now you're mine to claim."

I push my hair off my forehead and narrow my eyes as our weighted gazes challenge each other. "I'm not looking to get claimed."

He winks at me. He's so damn cocky. "Don't knock it 'til you've tried it."

He shows me around the club since he seems pretty familiar with it.

"Have you ever seen someone you know here?" I ask. I've never been around this many gay people at once.

He shakes his head. "I've seen a few guys I thought I recognized from campus, but they seemed cool. Nothing I worried about."

We've just finished off our second beer when he pulls me out to the dance floor. I've always thought of myself as a pretty good dancer, but I'm nothing next to Ramon, who halfway into the first song has everyone looking at him like he's man candy. He's working it, too, and must've been expecting that attention because he picked me up in the tightest jeans I've seen him in yet, and a dark grey T-shirt that fits him like a second skin. He's a good-looking guy, his dark complexion smoked caramel, and smooth. Our coloring is completely opposite—I'm a sandy blond, waves of my thick hair fall almost to my shoulders, while his dense black hair is short and slicked back. That's not the only difference between us. His bravado and confidence is a sharp contrast to my uncertainty of how to handle myself in this new world I'm stepping into.

Watching him dance, I can't help but be turned on. He undulates his hips to the music, rolling his shoulders like the music is moving through him. The guy behind him keeps checking out his tight, round ass, while the couple next to us seem fascinated with how built his arms are and how his muscles flex under the lights.

The third song is slow and sexy. Stepping up close he leans toward me, his full lips grazing the edge of my ear. "I like the way you move," he says. Tipping his head down, he presses his forehead against mine, and I shiver when I feel his hot breath on my neck. "Come on, dance *with* me," he whispers low and sexy.

My pulse speeds as he places his hand on my lower back possessively and pulls me closer. Then when his hips roll, he guides me so I shadow his movements, and to my surprise our bodies move in synchronicity like we've always danced together.

Now we're really attracting attention, and I can feel the hard, hungry stares of men who know what they want. After all, it's why they're here tonight. It's intense but exciting at the same time. My cock is excited too, and each time he slides his leg between my thighs I get harder.

A lot more people are watching us now so this is starting to feel like spectator sex when with the next move, he grinds against me. *Oh damn.* I'm painfully hard as a result. Dean flashes in my head, and I'm glad he stayed at home. I'm pretty sure Ramon practically doing me on the dance floor wouldn't fly with him.

What stings is that I'd so much rather it was Dean grinding against me, than my Latin lover. Ramon must sense my mind wandering because he suddenly cups his hands over my ass, and pulls me against him. He ups the game to something close to fucking with clothes on. His dick is rock hard, further proof that this is no longer just dancing.

He glides his hands away from my ass and up my back, finally combing his fingers through my hair. Pulling me into a passionate kiss, he sways against me in our lustful rhythm. I'm lightheaded from how aroused he's making me feel. My heartbeat is in sync with the club music's driving bass beat, and the dark walls, nooks, and corners throughout the space give a sexy mysterious vibe. I sense that you can get into a lot of trouble, the hot-nasty kind of trouble, in a place like this.

We've just parted from a long tongue-tangling kiss when I feel another man come up from behind me and dance close enough to rock his pelvis against my ass. Before I can whip my head around and see what the hell is going on, Ramon yanks me away and navigates me off the dance floor, which is now packed with hot, writhing bodies. Just seeing all the groping, desperate kissing and grinding is making me wild.

For the first time in my life, I'm present in the world that I've always yearned to be part of. I'm joined by dozens of hot men who not only don't care that I'm gay, they celebrate that I am. I'm high off the very idea that I'm with my people . . . I finally belong.

When we're off the dance floor, Ramon pulls me down a dark hallway that leads to the restrooms. We're halfway between the men and women's rooms when he stops, pins me against the wall, and wildly runs his hands over my abs and chest while kissing me between breathless moans. With each kiss he presses his dick against me harder, and now his hands are roaming along my crotch, grabbing my throbbing cock possessively.

"You're so damn big," he moans.

"You like that?" I ask in a rough voice, knowing already that he does.

"So fucking much." He nods to the women's room door just past us. "When that opens up I'm taking you in there."

"The women's room?" I ask.

"There are no women here. That's the fuck room, and believe me, babe, I want to fuck you."

My skin prickles uncomfortably.

"You're not going to fuck me in a woman's bathroom," I argue, knowing that it's a woman's room is not the only reason, but he doesn't need to know everything.

"Well, I'd let you fuck me, handsome, but it'd take too long to prepare me since you're hung like a horse."

"Sorry," I lie.

"Never be sorry for that." Just then the door opens, and two men with flushed faces tumble out to the hall. He slides us past them into the bathroom and locks the door. "There's other fun we can still have," he says, sliding his tongue back into my mouth as he rams me against the door.

Moments later both of our jeans are open and pushed down our thighs. I watch him tear open a foil packet of lube and then liberally coat his hand. When he leans against me and wraps his fist tightly around our two cocks, my head falls back with pleasure.

His hand starts to slowly pump us, and I look down to see our dicks rubbing against each other as he jerks us, joined together by his grip. My balls tighten almost immediately for the hot sensation of his hand taking care of us both at once, his tight grip making me harder and in no time ready to blow.

With his free hand he gropes under my shirt up my abs to my pecs, and then pinches my nipple hard. "You can get a body like this with tennis?" he groans against my neck as he pinches me again, noticing how it makes my dick throb.

"It's a power sport," I groan.

"Then what am I doing getting knocked around in fucking football? Maybe I'll change sports."

I reach around and grab his fine ass, my eyes rolling back as his grip moves faster over our slick cocks.

"Are you ready for me to make you come?" he asks breathlessly.

"Do it, man. I need it bad," I groan as my head sways from the dizzy high of raw pleasure. I close my eyes and Dean drifts into my mind. What if I was in his arms instead, and not in some women's bathroom/creepy sex room? "Oh, yeah," I cry out imagining Dean's hand jerking us together while he's got me pressed against his bedroom wall.

"You are such a dirty slut, Jason. A real whore." His hand is a blur now and I can tell his orgasm is going to be fierce.

I'm panting and spiraling, my body a tight coil of want and need until I can't hold on another second and I explode. Since he teased and taunted me, calling me a dirty slut, I feel vindicated as I shoot come all over his washboard abs and his grey T-shirt. My big cock has fire-power. That'll get him for calling me names.

Drunk with satisfaction, I'm in a post-bliss haze so I don't remember much about us cleaning up. When we step back into the hall we find two different couples waiting for the "fuck" room. Ramon calls out to the first pair, a handsome black guy, and his beefy red-headed partner, "It's all yours. Don't do anything we wouldn't do."

The redhead snorts and follows his mate inside.

Dean. 25

I'M RESTLESS AS FUCK ALL night. Scott calls to see if I want to go to a party at his old-roommate's. I take a pass. I'm not in the mood to be around a lot of drunk people tonight. I'd rather be alone and drunk . . . that's how shitty my mood is.

After the first two shots of whiskey, I decide to look up gay porn on my computer. This is all for research, of course, so I can be super supportive of my best friend.

Some of the crap I see makes me want to bleach my eyes. I mean who wants to look at a close-up shot of some dude's hairy asshole right before it gets filled? That would not be me. You can't unsee that shit, but as I keep searching I find a few things that I can tolerate. Mainly videos where the two guys don't look gay, and as they fuck or suck they have a surprised expression on their faces as if they can't figure out how they ended up in this situation. These are the videos I can relate to.

I will say that with a few that I refresh and watch over and over again, they definitely look like they're enjoying themselves. While this research is going on I may be hard, but I'm trying not to pay attention to that, because that would really be gay.

But all bets are off when I come to a video where the guy getting fucked looks just like Jason. This guy is his total doppelganger. It's uncanny, and I even freeze the frame so I can study him carefully and make sure it isn't him after all. I know that thought is completely illogical but Jason has been full of surprises lately.

It would be especially super weird if the guy fucking him looks like me, but of course he's darker skinned than I am, and not as tall.

Apparently, the universe showed me this video so that I could get pissed off again about Jason being with Ramon tonight.

As I refresh the video, I rig my laptop so that I can lean my copy of *Sport's Illustrated* over half the screen thus blocking out the Ramon lookalike, the Don Juan of cocksucking.

I down another shot and then pull off my boxers . . . it's time to take my research to a higher level. Stretching out across my bed, I watch my laptop with an intensity that feels like it could crack the screen. Man, look at that ass on the Jason-not-Jason guy in the video. It's almost as perfect as the real Jason's ass. I wish I could crop out the other guy completely as his dark hands knead Jason-not-Jason's firm butt and then parts his cheeks. A second later his dark sheathed cock drills him and Jason-not-Jason lets out a moan to wake the dead.

"Hell yeah," I groan as I fist my cock. But fuck my life . . . just then I hear the key in the front door lock, footsteps, and then the bathroom door closing. Good thing I left my bedroom door open so I'd be on alert. I snap my laptop shut without even bookmarking the best porn page of the night. I scowl, but there was really no choice in the matter. I'm pretty sure what I was just doing wasn't the "more" my real Jason was asking for.

I flop back against my pillow and stroke myself while listening to the shower running and wonder why he's showering this late. Suddenly I hear the bathroom door open, and I realize that there's no time to pull my boxers back on or close my door. His footsteps are just down the hall. I decide not to pull the sheet up over me because that would just look weird. Instead I grab my still-hard cock, and begin stroking it again. The set-up of a horny young guy jacking off on his bed while his roommate is out is so ordinary, he'd just have to believe it was real and that there's no master plan on my part.

For a second I think Jason is going to walk by my door without even looking inside. I should've left the damn overhead light on. He's almost passed, when he suddenly glances over and comes to an abrupt halt. His eyes grow wide as he watches my fist move up and down my cock.

"What are you doing?" His gaze darts around nervously like he thinks I've got someone hiding in my room.

"What do you think I'm doing? I'm working off some tension." My hand slows down but I don't stop. *Why should I?*

His cheeks get red. "Well don't let me interrupt you."

"I'm still jacking off, aren't I?" I reach down and cup my balls with my hand and then start stroking again. "Hey, remember when we used to do this together?"

He swallows hard as his gaze moves down to my cock. "Yeah, I remember."

"Good times, right?"

He nods. I notice him sway a bit. I bet Ramon liquored him up good.

I gesture to my laptop. "I could put on some porn and you could come over here and join me. It'd be like the good ol' days."

Arching his brow at me, he crosses his arms. "I don't think that'd be a good idea, Dean."

"Why not? I won't touch you or anything."

He shakes his head and takes a step away from the door. It pisses me off.

"Is this about Ramon? It is, isn't it? How was the gay bar?"

"Good. I had no idea there were so many gay men in this town."

"Awesome," I say with a frown. "Did Ramon dance like he wanted to?"

"Yeah, and the way that dude dances, all eyes were on him. He really knows how to move. He's like the Hispanic Justin Timberlake."

I can feel my blood pressure rising. "And you were dancing with him, right?"

"Well, yeah."

"And then what?" I let go of my dick and prop myself up on my elbows.

He shrugs. "The usual stuff."

"He sucked your cock?" I can't hide the jealous tone in my voice. All I know is that I feel crazy at the idea of Ramon sucking him off.

"No. Hey, I think I'm going to head to bed." He takes a step farther down the hall and I lose it.

"So did he fuck you?" I yell out. I feel this enormous pressure in my head that makes me want to punch something.

Jason takes several steps backward until he's framed in the door again. His eyes are wild with irritation. "What the hell is wrong with you?"

Realizing that I'm not going to get anything out of him unless I get my shit together, I take a deep breath. "I just want to make sure he doesn't hurt you. I don't trust that guy."

He tips his head as he studies me. "Well, you don't have to worry. He didn't hurt me *or* fuck me. Okay?"

I sigh. "Okay." My erection is no longer fierce, and my cock is resting across my abdomen. "Can I ask you something?"

"What?"

"Have you *ever* been fucked?"

His eyes narrow as his gaze moves over my body, including my confused dick, and then my laptop, before resting on my face. His expression is somber, and I wonder if I don't want to hear what he has to say.

"Once. I was fucked once, a long time ago, and not by my priest. And it wasn't a great experience so I'm not in a big hurry to do it again. So that's one less thing for you to worry about. Okay?"

"Did it hurt or something?"

He lets out an exasperated breath. "Dean, why are you asking all this stuff?"

"I just want to understand what you've been through."

His expression softens.

"You know, I think I would have liked it a lot more if it had been with the right person."

"Like someone you trusted? Someone who would care that it's good for you too."

He nods and arches his brow. "Are you saying all of this stuff because you want to fuck me?"

"Would you want me to?"

His cheekbones are flushed and he's biting his bottom lip.

"I'd let you do anything you want to me, but you'd have to be sure it's what you want."

Something about his words tugs at my heart. Like he'd sacrifice his own pleasure to make sure I had mine. Jason's always been like that with me, but I've never really understood the depth of what he's willing to do to make me happy. I shake my head at him. "You're really something, you know."

He scoffs.

I give him a stern look. "I mean it."

"What started all of this tonight? First I walk in on you having sex with yourself . . . then you grill me about having sex with Ramon . . . and then you suggest we have sex." He rakes his fingers through his hair. "You're making me crazy, dude. How much did you drink anyway?"

"Enough to loosen up and let my mind go places it normally doesn't."

His eyes light up. "I'll say."

"Hey, I'm really curious now. Will you let me fuck you? I promise I'll follow what you want and take it slow."

"Oh Jesus. Are you serious? So more experimenting, huh?"

"I think it'll help me understand more about you."

"You know when I said I needed more, this isn't exactly what I meant. Don't get me wrong, the idea of you fucking me is making me hard as hell, but it'll just complicate things even more."

"It doesn't have to complicate things. Is it really so crazy to just want to make each other feel good?" I pause for a moment. "Come on, JJ."

Lifting myself off the bed, I slowly approach him. As I get closer, I press my naked body into him so he's up against the doorjamb, then I boldly rub my palm over his hard cock that's trapped in his pajama bottoms.

I take a sharp breath because I'm shocked I'm even suggesting fucking my best friend. This is crazy, but feeling myself against him and imagining him naked under me is turning me on like a rocket with a sparking fuse.

He stands frozen, every part of him perfectly still, and then he gasps for air. "Please, Dean, please tell me you aren't toying with me."

I press my face into his neck. "I'm not toying with you, man. I don't know what's happening to me, but I have all these confusing feelings and my curiosity is through the roof. I've been so damn restless lately, and suddenly I have a feeling that if I turn a corner, I might find myself right where I need to be."

Jason slides his arm along my lower back and curves his fingers around my side, then pulls me closer. "Don't make me hope for something, and then crush me. I wouldn't be able to take it. Our friendship means everything to me. It's why I'm still standing and fighting for a future, when for a long time I wasn't sure if I deserved one."

I pull my head back so we can be face to face. It guts me to see so much pain in his eyes. Why the hell didn't I see all of this before? He's my best friend, dammit. I should have known he was hurting.

He shakes his head. "I can't lose you, Dean. I can't. Tread carefully, man." His eyes are glazed like he's fighting back tears.

I take his hand and guide him into my room. "You aren't going to lose me. Maybe this whole thing of me learning your secrets happened to bring us closer."

"I want that," he whispers, and then more softly he murmurs, "I want *you*."

Jason . 26

WHAT THE HELL IS HAPPENING?

I'm in some kind of weird, alternative-universe where Dean wants to fuck me, and he's undressing me while my hands tremble at my sides. I swore I wouldn't do this . . . I forced myself to go out with Ramon to get my mind off Dean, and now here he is, gloriously naked, his hard-on pressed against my stomach as he slowly circles my nipples with his fingers.

My head falls back as I groan. It comes from somewhere deep inside, and it's loud and raw and so fucking needy. This man is damn fine . . . all of him—from his rugged, handsome face, and wide, powerful shoulders to his narrow waist, and his ripped abs. I glance down at his huge, pulsing cock and study it, wondering how it'll ever fit inside my ass. At least I've seen on videos how guys prepare themselves for sex. Hopefully Dean will be patient about me needing that.

Dean takes his time easing my waistband down my thighs until my cock springs free. Licking his lips, he has a drunken look of lust in his heated expression.

I step out of my pajama bottoms and stand tall, my shoulders pulled back and my muscles flexed. I want his first view of me naked and aroused, that's just for *his* pleasure, to excite the hell out of him.

Groaning, he fists my cock. "Look at you, man . . . you're a fucking god. Just looking at you is making me so damn hard."

"Right back at you," I say in a ragged voice. He better get me horizontal soon or I may pass out from the head rush.

"Get on the bed," he groans. He takes the bottle of lube and hands it to me. "Show me what you do."

I quickly coat my fingers and then slide them down between my legs. "I have to prep myself." I lie back on the bed and slowly slide one finger and then two between my ass cheeks.

"Does it hurt?" he asks, his eyes wide as he studies my every move. I rock into myself, a rhythm building.

"No, I like it, I'm just careful. You can't rush this."

He nods. "I don't want to hurt you."

My heart tugs. He's holding my trust in his hands. This is risky business for me but I'm reckless and desperate with want for him.

He crawls over so he's kneeling inside the open V of my spread legs. Rising up, he places his big hands on top of my knees and eases my legs apart even wider.

Meanwhile my flushed cock bobs excitedly. I hand him the bottle of lube after he's rolled on a condom. "Here, coat your dick really well."

He snaps open the bottle and carefully slathers it on from base to tip. His eyes are dark as his hips start to rock, pushing his slick cock into his fist. "Are you ready?" he asks in a choked whisper.

He leans in and rubs the head of his cock along the apex of my legs. I'm already panting for breath.

"Ready?" he asks again, this time more urgently.

I nod, but I'm nervous, and judging from the look of concern on his face, he must see the fear in my eyes. Lifting up on his knees, he runs his large hand along my bent leg. "Why don't you flip over, and then I'll fuck you. I read that can be easier for newbies."

"You read up on how to fuck me?" I ask with a crooked grin as I get on all fours and press my chest into the mattress, my legs spread so my body is as open for him as it can be.

"I'm a detail man, you know that, JJ." He lets out a long sigh as he rubs his hands along my back and circles my ass. I feel him crawl up close to me so that his thighs press against my backside. I'm so aware of my throbbing dick trapped under me, and how his heavy cock is now slowly sliding along my ass crack.

His breath sharpens the deeper he glides up and down. "You okay?" he asks, his open palm resting on my lower back.

"Yeah," I gasp. "But I need you inside of me. Please, I'm ready

I swear."

He leans low over me, and whispers in my ear, "I may not last long. I'm already on my edge."

I look over my shoulder, and sure enough his face is completely flushed as he moves his hand holding his cock, positions it at my entrance, and then pushes forward until his tip starts to penetrate me.

I let out a low moan as I stretch open for him, and then rock my hips slightly so he slowly eases farther inside. He takes me a slow inch at a time, always checking on me with a tender, yet desperate expression. I keep nodding so he knows I'm okay.

"Oh my God, oh my God," he groans when he's finally fully seated inside of me. "You're so damn tight."

"Too tight?" I ask nervously, gasping for breath.

"Are you kidding? My cock is in love with your ass."

He becomes silent, and I feel his forehead rest against my back and he pulls away until his cock is barely inside of me, and then he slowly, powerfully, fills me again.

I'm delirious with the feeling of him filling me so completely. We've always been deeply connected, but now we're literally joined and it's not just a physical euphoria that's making me fly, it's the emotional connection, too. I've always loved this man, and now he's making love to me. He might argue with the words "making love" but it's beyond words . . . love is what he's showing me, and *loved* is how he's making me feel.

His hand runs up my back and his fingers squeeze my shoulder as he slowly moves in and out. Each time he reaches my limit of how much of him my body can fit, he pauses and then nudges just a bit more. It's making me crazy and I moan and gasp for air each time.

"Am I making you feel good, JJ? 'Cause this is blowing my mind," he growls.

"Oh God, yes," I groan, as I surrender completely.

I'm desperate to reach under me and jerk my throbbing cock but his weight and size is pressing me down deep into the mattress so I linger on the edge of an epic climax while he slowly, sweetly tortures me in the best way.

Then without warning he pulls out completely and backs away, inching across the mattress, and I feel like my heart is suddenly heavy as lead, it's weight about to sink me so far down I won't know how to get up. I shut my eyes tightly, not ready for whatever made Dean decide he couldn't fuck me anymore as I still lie open and completely vulnerable for him.

But a moment later his fingers comb through my hair and his hand grabs my bicep and pulls gently. "Hey, open your eyes and roll over. I want to be looking at you when I make you come." His voice is husky and incredibly sexy, as if he didn't already have me so close to my edge . . . as if there needed to be one more way I can lose my mind over him. If he keeps talking to me in that voice I may come from his words alone.

Suddenly I'm alive again, and I quickly twist around in the sheets to face him. The way he's staring at me is intense and all consuming. Maybe this is the *"more"* I needed . . . for him to look at me like I'm all he wants, not *just* enough to satisfy him, but *more* than enough . . . more than anyone else.

I feel a lazy smile break out on my face as he spreads me open, and pushes my knees back.

"You ready to get fucked some more?" he asks. And I'd think he was joking but he looks deadly serious. "Because I really need to finish what we've started. I've never . . ." He bites his lip as he leans over me and rests a hand on my inner thigh. "Nothing's ever felt this good, JJ. Nothing."

I nod, every part of my skin tingling, every molecule in my body wanting him to fill me in every way. "You can fuck me harder, you know," I say with a raspy voice. "I promise I won't break."

He clenches his jaw and I see the veins on his neck protruding. "You'd like that, really?" he asks tentatively, like he wants to make sure I'm not just saying that for him.

"Yeah, I'd really like it. Fuck me hard, Dean. Take what you want from me. That's what I need. I *need* you."

His ability to be gentle, but then take my cue to give me more, elevates him so far above that camp counselor that fucked me my first time, they can't even be compared. And his sheer physicality, muscular strength and size, puts him in an entirely different class. His muscles are sharply defined as he supports his weight with ease and begins to tease me.

Dean bends until he's over me, and licks his way across my shoulder and up my neck as I pant. I can feel his hard cock slide against mine, then he rocks his hips back, lifts up to his knees, and prepares to mount me.

He eases in like he's always belonged inside of me, and once he's seated fully he's less careful as he thrusts, building his rhythm and hitting that place inside of me that makes my eyes roll back and my toes curl until he's fucking me with hard, desperate strokes. His eyes darken as he lets out a long primal moan.

"Oh, man, you're making me feel so damn good," I groan.

He has no idea how long I've dreamt of this and prayed for some unexpected turn of events to make him realize that I was the one he should be with, not the women who couldn't hold his interest, couldn't love him with an understanding of the boy he'd been and the magnificent man he'd become.

"You okay, JJ?" he asks, his face flushed and his eyes wild.

I nod frantically as I rake my fingers down his back.

He's thrusting like he's about to come and going so deep that he's hitting that place inside of me that brings on a fireball of pleasure. I slide my hand between us and wrap my fingers around my cock and start stroking in rhythm to his thrusts. I'm panting and unraveling, certain that I've clawed and crawled up to the precipice of the orgasm of my life.

"Dean, Dean," I moan. "I can't hold back anymore, I'm—"

And before I can finish my thought, he's batted my hand away and his hand has replaced mine. "Come on, JJ, give it to me," he whispers huskily as his hand jacking me starts to blur.

My come hits my chest first, then starts striping across my torso, and I'm flying so high I may never come down. All the while Dean keeps fucking me, edging me on until he can't hold on either.

"JJ, oh fuck, I can't . . ." he cries out before he arches back like a

Greek god, all cut abs and muscular power.

Watching and feeling him go off, and knowing that I've taken him there, is the most amazing feeling.

"Yeah, yeah," I chant encouraging him on as he lets out a long, strangled moan.

After his final surge, he collapses on top of me, panting.

"Holy hell," he gasps. "What have I been missing? That was unbelievable."

I'm happily trapped underneath him and despite his size, I don't want him to move. I just want him to be mine a little longer. I brush my hand along his side and when he doesn't flinch I rub his back in long strokes. My body is electrified, and I'm so fucking happy.

"That was amazing, Dean," I murmur, kissing the top of his head.

He finally lifts his head off my shoulder. "You okay, my man?" he asks.

"More than okay, Dean. Way more."

He grins and carefully rolls off me to his side, and I roll too, so my front is against his back.

"Holy hell, that was intense. I had no idea it could be like that," he says in between deep breaths.

I lightly graze his shoulder with my fingertips. "Are you okay?"

He nods.

He lies silently while we both catch our breaths and calm down. Meanwhile, I slowly rub his back over and over. As far as I can tell he seems to be okay being here with me like this, which gives me hope that he won't freak out.

He finally clears his throat to speak. "I'd be open to doing that again if you want to."

My chest tightens and I bite back my smile. "Yeah, I'd consider it after some recovery time. You're fucking huge, dude."

He sighs. "I suppose that's a bad thing in this circumstance."

I can feel his shoulders droop and I lean in closer. "The thing is, you let me prepare and you took me slow until I adjusted, so you made it great. And then when you full-on fucked me hard . . . damn, I swear your cock is everything."

"Yeah?" His shoulders pull back again.

"Oh yeah. So fucking hot."

"You better stop with that 'cause I'll get hard again and you aren't ready for round two. I'm going to jump in the shower, okay?"

"Sure."

As he gets up I memorize every part of his perfect body as he moves away from me. He returns just a few minutes later, a towel wrapped around his waist, and his hair still wet. I want to dry him off and then bring him back to bed.

He lets out a lion-like yawn. "I'm gonna crash."

"Do you want me to sleep in here?" I ask, trying to regulate the sound of my voice so I don't sound desperate.

"Nah, I think I'm good."

"Okay." I feel so awkward. Just minutes ago my body and soul were wide open for him, and now it feels like we're back to status quo. I get out of bed and gather my clothes. "So, see you in the morning?"

His eyes cloud over. "Jason . . ."

"Yes?"

He looks down, deep in thought, but then doesn't reply.

I keep walking to the door, and then before I pass through I glance back at him one more time.

"Goodnight, Dean."

Dean . 27

I SUPPOSE I SHOULD'VE LET Jason stay with me tonight but I couldn't. I really need some space to process what just happened, and I'm afraid that if I did let him sleep with me, I'd keep trying to fuck him again, and he made it clear that even his strong body has its limits.

I loosen my towel, letting it drop to the floor, and flop down on my bed, stretching out spread-eagled on top of the sheets. I feel almost out of my body, since fucking Jason was so mind blowing. I can't figure out why it was so different than fucking a girl, but it's a wild revelation . . . taking him was the most amazing physical experience of my life.

All I can think about is when can we do it again.

I'm such a beast.

How is this going to work? We go on as usual in public and then once we're home alone the game changes? We only have a matter of months left until we graduate, and we've both applied to several firms in Seattle, but that doesn't change the fact that our future is uncertain. We may end up with jobs in different cities or states.

Maybe this is just my last college hurrah. Yeah, to wrap up the four years, why not start fucking your best friend and roommate? Talk about going out with a bang. We'd have to stop this bromance once we're out of school and possibly living in different cities, wouldn't we? Maybe it'll be out of my system by then.

Of course, Jason's situation is different since he *is* gay, but that doesn't mean he'd want me to be in his bed forever. He'll eventually want a guy who's really gay . . . not situationally gay like me.

That's it!

I let out a long sigh of relief. I'm *situationally* gay, only fucking my roommate because we both want to, but I'm not fucking other guys. No way would I fuck other guys. For some reason this label makes me feel a little better.

Jason, on the other hand isn't situational; he likes men and I'm guessing he wants a real boyfriend, not a horny best friend that's all man when he leaves his bed.

I close my eyes, the exhaustion of epic sex pulling me into the black void of sleep. I smile feeling weirdly content—as if the screwy, mismatched puzzle I just put together can work until we get our fill of each other. Who knows for how long, but carpe fucking diem. I want this and I'm going to have it.

The next morning I wake up sublimely rested and content, and hungry as hell. Remembering that I got some groceries this week, I pull on my boxers and go to the kitchen to dig up some food. Jason is already there wearing old gym shorts and drinking coffee while he plays a game on his phone. When he looks up at me I can see a smile in his eyes. His hair is crazy rumpled, he has a sleepy expression, and he's rocking a serious stubble. He looks like he had a wild night. *Yeah, I wonder why?* I chuckle to myself.

"Hey," he says.

"Hey. How'd you sleep?"

"All right. You?"

"Like a rock . . . or more like a boulder. I feel awesome." Rolling my shoulders back, I stretch. "How are you doing? Are you sore?"

"Yeah, but it was worth it." Blushing, he casts his gaze downward.

"Glad to hear it." The last thing I want is for him to be hurting so that he regrets what we did.

I start pulling stuff out of the fridge, and I take out the frying pan. "I'm going to make us breakfast," I announce. "We need refueling after last night."

Jason grins. "Can I help?"

"No, I've got this."

I fry the bacon first and then scramble eggs. Jason's quiet but he's abandoned his game on his phone, and he's watching me cook. I stack up the toast and when our plates are piled high I carry them over to the sitting area. We eat on the coffee table more than anywhere else since we're usually watching TV.

Jason turns on the game but turns the sound down. "So what's on your agenda today?" he asks.

"I'm thinking of hitting the gym before I head over to the blueprint lab. The plans for my group project are all jacked up so I have to get that sorted today. What about you?"

He shrugs. "Pretty much the same. Tennis practice and then to the library to see if they've got my book in yet . . . the one on post-modernism."

Jason loves post-modernism, and it's grown on me, too. We've always talked about one day having our own small architectural firm together, so it's a good thing our tastes align. You need to have a joined vision, no bullshit hybrid architecture.

Jason's done sketches of our dream company offices and I teased him about making my office bigger than his. He even went on the internet and showed me the minimalist furniture he thought would be cool.

As my dad always says, if you're going to dream, you may as well dream big.

My gaze wanders around our shabby rental apartment, which came furnished. The crappy couch we're sitting on has seen better days, and the coffee table has burn marks on top and a wobbly leg. I have no doubt that once we have money we'll never live like this again.

"What's up for tonight?" he inquires, setting his plate back down and patting his stomach.

"Steve's having a party, remember?" I remind him.

He turns sideways toward me and puts his feet up on the couch. "Right. What time are we leaving?"

"Nine?" I ask. Suddenly I get a bad feeling when I think about Jason and I walking in together. "Hey, you know how things will be at the party . . . right?"

He scrunches up his face. "What does that mean?"

"It means I'm not holding your hand or anything."

He snickers, but I think I see hurt in his eyes. "Yeah, just like nothing ever happened. We're just two guys who happen to be roommates."

"Exactly! Besides it's not like you're 'out' or anything. And no one needs to know what we do in the privacy of our man cave."

"What we do?" he asks.

"Yeah, that we're fucking." I nod and rub my hand through my hair.

He seems confused. "You said fucking, not fucked. Does that mean you still want to do it again as long as you don't have to hold my hand in public?"

"Well, sure. Don't you?"

He lets out a huff. "You're a piece of work, Dean."

I set my plate down and turn toward him, putting my feet on the couch. Then I push one foot closer and skim his. "So *you* don't want to?" I slide my foot farther between his legs and then pull my foot back so it grazes his inner calf. "Didn't I take good care of you last night?"

I'm such a teasing asshole, but damn it's fun to see him come undone.

His cheeks are pink, and he's looking completely flustered. "Quit screwing with me. You feed me a big breakfast and then you want to hump me? Didn't I tell you my ass is sore?"

"Calm down, Juliet. I'm not going to impale you with my big boner now. If you're nice to me, maybe later." Giving him a cocky grin, I wink.

His eyes grow wide. "Screw you, Romeo!" he sputters with a laugh. "How 'bout I fuck you right now and we'll see how you like it."

I shake my head dramatically. "No way. I'm a topper all the way. You aren't going to drill this ass."

He huffs. "We'll see about that."

I look over at the TV . . . not that I could give a shit about whatever game is playing. This game with Jason is far more interesting. "So last night you mentioned you've been fucked one time before. Who was it with?" My nerves flare after the words leave my mouth, and I wonder. *What if it's one of our friends . . . someone I know? Can I handle it?*

He digs his fingers into his hair and roughly moves his hands back and forth, making it an even crazier mess. "Well hell, I may as well share *all* of my screwed-up stories. No point holding back now," he mumbles.

"Yeah." I nod encouragingly.

"He was my counselor at bible camp. His name was Bryce."

Fucking camp counselor? I feel like my head is suddenly on fire and my mind spins as I remember Jason going to bible camp one summer. "Was that the time before our junior year when your mom was pushing you toward the priesthood?"

He nods with a pained expression.

"Where is that guy, Bryce, now?"

"I have no idea. Why? What difference does it make?"

I clench my fists. "Because I want to track down the motherfucker and beat the crap out of him."

He lets out a sigh. "Well, I don't know about that. This was different than Father Ryan. It was completely consensual and yeah, he was my counselor, but he was only three years older than me. The fact that he was lousy at fucking is a different issue. He was as clueless and awkward as me."

"Your mother and her fucking determination to make you a priest," I growl.

"You don't know the half of it. The camp thing started when she found my stash of porn magazines under my mattress."

"I didn't know you had a porn collection. Why didn't you share it with me? I sure as hell shared mine with you!" Now I'm pissed at him.

He gives me a measured gaze. "It was gay porn, Dean."

"Oh," I whisper. *Holy shit.* I blink rapidly. "Where'd you get the gay porn? I wouldn't have known how to get my hands on that when I was in high school."

"Father Ryan gave it to me." His expression is weary as he waits for me to compute what I've told him so far.

"Why would that monster give you gay porn?" My stomach is churning.

"He had made up his mind that he was going to fuck me, and I refused. Just the idea of it scared the shit out of me. So he kept trying to manipulate me different ways . . . bribing, coaxing, being extra attentive with me. I guess he thought when I saw the pictures of how straightforward it was, how all these men were doing it, that I would relent."

"Damn. And that was when you were how old?"

"At that point fourteen. And the thing is, if you study those pictures, the guys bottoming usually have a grimace on their face which only made me more determined not to do it. So I hid the magazines away and held my ground. Then some months after I got away from him I started up with Audrey, after she paid me to help her move into her apartment."

"Yeah, I remember her. I've been wondering about that actually, because the stories you told me back then made me think you were having crazy good sex."

"I was, and she taught me a lot. But the part I didn't tell you is that she would make me hard, but I could never come until I closed my eyes and imagined she was someone else."

"A guy?" I ask, not wanting to know who he was thinking of.

He nods. "So late at night I pulled out those old magazines and started studying them, trying to figure out what was going on in my head. And pretty soon when I couldn't open them and not end up jacking off, I had my answer. I knew that I was gay."

"How could I have not picked up on any of this?"

He lets out a long sigh. "Look, I didn't want to be gay, so I hid all that away just as much to hide it from myself as I did it to hide it from you."

"So back to your mom and camp . . ." I say, waving my hand in the air.

"Yeah, when she found the porn she went through the roof, and I know she wanted to send me back to Father Ryan. Lucky for me he was out of town conducting a retreat or something. So I'm not sure how she did it, but she found this camp that takes 'confused' boys and with the power of Jesus and prayer, their deviant thoughts are exorcised out of them. A week later I was shipped off for four weeks."

"I remember that. I was a junior counselor at sports camp that summer."

"And I bet your kids weren't perverts and deviants."

"Oh, I'm not sure about that. There was one kid in our group named Wally, who was constantly touching himself and jacking off in his sleeping bag. He used to flirt with the middle-aged women who served our food. I can only imagine what that one's like now."

Jason makes a sour face. "Gross."

"So how did things happen with your counselor? That's about as taboo as things get at camp."

"All of the staffs' job was to keep us busy so we were distracted in between our prayer sessions where we'd pray to be delivered from the devil that was polluting our thoughts and giving us unnatural urges."

"Nice," I hiss.

"Yeah, like I wasn't already hard enough on myself. So from the beginning I noticed that Bryce paid me special attention, often giving me the best positions in our games, and eating next to me at meals.

"We'd talk a lot in the afternoons when he'd have me help put equipment away. He told me that he was in college studying theology, and when he was done he was going to enter the priesthood. I kind of admired that he seemed so resolute in what he wanted when my head was such a ball of confusion.

"I asked him how he'd deal with not having sex. I'd been taught a lot of dogma from Father Ryan about urges and knew that no matter what no man could easily walk away from desire that can boil inside of you until your insides burn.

"He told me that righteous prayer would heal him from anything. I didn't believe him, but I wanted to."

I watch Jason's expressions carefully as he shares this story, and it stirs up all of the raw hurt again—not just that I didn't know all of this about my best friend, but that he'd suffered through the confusion and angst of his teen years in a much more profound way than anyone could imagine.

"So I take it he stopped praying while you were around making him crazy."

"Well for sure, I was a hopeless case but you're right, praying stopped working for him. It all started one night, near the end of my first week. It was a hot and muggy evening and hard to sleep. I heard something around midnight and looked up and saw him silently gesturing to me from the door of the cabin. I followed him outside and he had me grab my shoes and slip them on. I followed him wordlessly, and I realized that we were walking toward the lake. When we got there, he sat down on a landing by the dock and patted the spot next to him to join him.

"Everything felt kind-of dreamlike . . . the moon reflecting on the water, the harmony of crickets chirping in the distance, and silver clouds slowly moving through the night sky. I knew this was forbidden, sneaking out late at night. I was only in my boxers and hiking boots and with my counselor who was looking at me in a way he hadn't before.

"After a silent few minutes where we just gazed at the lake he started talking. He told me that he knew why I was here at camp, that I had inappropriate thoughts about men and an interest in pornography that needed to be purged from my heart and body. I didn't argue with him. There was no point.

"But then I looked down just as he rested his hand on my knee. He shared with me that he was struggling with his own thoughts and so he understood what I was going through. I felt his hand move up my thigh and pause, then he swallowed hard. 'I wish . . .' he said quietly, then shut his eyes and shook his head.

"My dick was fully hard at this point and I was shaking inside wondering if his hand was going to slide up farther. But instead he stood up and announced we should go swimming. As he pulled off his clothes, I removed my boots and then slid off my boxers, revealing my big boner. When his gaze fixed on my cock his mouth gaped open and he looked like he was going to pass out. I didn't get to see if he was hard because he rushed into the water. Well, you can imagine the rest . . ."

"He fucked you in the lake?" I ask, thinking about lake slime and mosquitoes. It didn't sound hot to me at all.

"No, not that night. We were just splashing around and shit, relieved to finally be cooling off, but then he swam close to me and started groping me, and he took my cock in his hand."

"And the high and mighty fall," I groan.

"It was kind of sweet, he was so damn earnest. And although I wasn't really attracted to him—he was pale and scrawny, nothing like the men in my porn magazines—he made me feel good."

"Sweet? Huh," I say.

"He started kissing me, and moaning, and then next thing I know we are jacking each other under the water. I don't think he'd done a lot of messing around, if any, so it was choppy and awkward, but he made up for it in enthusiasm. He moaned and grinded against me, kissing me over and over, telling me how much he wanted me. We were out there until dawn. I barely got back in my sleeping bag before people started waking up."

"And so it began?" I ask, wanting but not wanting to hear the rest.

"Yeah, finding private time at a camp is next to impossible but he was determined. There was sloppy kissing and hand jobs in the equipment shed, and he gave me a blow job when I'd returned to my cabin mid-day pretending I wasn't feeling well. It was kind of sad really, because the more we did, the more desperate he was for it, and also the more he must've realized that he could never be a priest. It's all he'd ever wanted, and so his sexual urges took away his dreams. I've wondered a number of times what happened with him."

"Well, let's just hope he didn't become a priest anyway," I reply with a grim frown. "We all know how well that works out."

Jason nods, his expression blank like his mind is far, far away.

I wait silently. I have to hear the end of the story because until last night, Jason hadn't wanted to get penetrated again. I'm sure Ramon has asked for it, and who knows who else has. He finally speaks up again.

"It took a lot of planning for us to have full-on sex. We needed lube, and there isn't a lot of that at a Catholic camp for perverted boys. Plus, being novices, we had no idea how long full-on sex would take, and so we needed to make sure we were guaranteed enough alone time. We finally agreed to meet by the lake at midnight on my final night at the camp.

"My heart was beating hard as I snuck out of the cabin and hurried down the path to the lake. He was already there when I arrived, pacing and nervously twisting his hands. When he finally saw me, I've never seen anyone look so relieved. Within seconds he had his tongue down my throat and my shorts pushed down."

"Horny fucker," I mumble. I already hated this guy.

"Yeah, he was kind of wild that night . . . frantically kissing me and jacking me, all the while asking forgiveness for what he was about to do, forgiveness for his sins. That didn't make me feel great. I wasn't even fully hard. It's like what we were about to do was something disgusting and dirty. I got enough of that kind of thinking from my mom and the church, I didn't need it from my first gay lover."

"Why'd you go through with it then?" I ask.

He shrugs. "Burning curiosity, and a part of me just wanted to get it over with. I had to know what it was like if this was going to be in my future life. Of course none of those were the right reasons.

"Next thing you know I'm bent over a big log with my legs spread apart, while he practically poured lube down my crack. It was like my ass was in an oil slick and it got everywhere. He was so worked up at that point that he just stuck his dick between my cheeks and shoved hard, missing my opening entirely. He did that two more times before he finally aimed right."

I screw up my face now that I know that anal sex requires stretching and preparation for it not to hurt like a motherfucker. "Damn," I say not hiding the anger in my voice.

"Yeah, even though he was on the small side, I was so tense that my ass constricted, so when he pounded me I felt like I was being torn in half. His fingers were slippery from lube so he couldn't grab hold of me, he just wildly thrusted and less than a minute later it was over."

"For fuck's sake!" I punch the couch cushion.

"Oh, it gets better. After he pulled . . . no, let me say this right, after he *slipped* out of me, he fell to his knees and started praying for forgiveness and I'm pretty sure it wasn't forgiveness from me. I waited for a minute to see if he'd get up and at least tend to me, but he was too busy losing his shit over his filthy, gay sex. I pulled up my shorts and walked away, never looking back. After returning to camp, I got in the shower and did the best I could washing off what remained of him and the lube.

"The next day he must have gone into hiding when we were packing up the buses and saying good-bye. I never saw or spoke to him again."

"Well that wasn't a hard act to follow. I know I did better than he did," I tease.

Jason gazes at me with a burning intensity. "Honestly, I'd stopped hoping that full-on sex could be great. And last night you changed all that for me."

"Glad to be of service." I give him a smug grin, but then I let it slide from my lips. "But seriously, man, I'm really sorry that was your first time. That sucks."

"Live and learn," he says with a sigh. "I think I'm more of a realist now. I may never have the life I'd once dreamt of, but I can hopefully have great moments like last night. Sometimes it's better not to wish for too much."

His philosophy, although it may be realistic, makes me sad. He's a great guy and unbelievably appealing. Why shouldn't he be able to have it all?

We spend the rest of the morning watching some of the game before we both head out for our days.

Jason . 28

IT'S JUST PAST NINE P.M. when I grab my keys off the kitchen counter so we can drive to the party. "Who's going to be there?" I ask as we pull out of the driveway.

"The usual people." Dean sighs and already sounds bored. There aren't many people who can hold his attention long. It's part of what draws me to him . . . I'm the one he never got tired of and he's the same for me.

But when we arrive at the party we're pulled in different directions. I have an overwhelming need to be by his side but I have to keep stopping myself. Keeping up appearances is the theme of this damn evening. I can't touch him, wait for his intense gaze to sizzle over me, or whisper in his ear that I want him to fuck me again.

He's not my lover who will slide his hand over my shoulder and pull me closer while we talk to our friends. He's now my secret.

My best secret.

I make my way to the kitchen and down a shot, and then another. My face instantly feels warm, and as the booze unfurls through me I feel myself relax bit by bit.

The house is crowded already. I can't remember how many people live in this place, but it looks like each of them invited a whole party's worth. Every room has thick air, clusters of warm bodies, and pot smoke that is wafting in from the back patio. Suddenly someone behind me tugs on my jeans belt loop and pulls me toward them.

"Where've you been? I haven't see you around," mews Stacy. She's got two girls with her and they all give a vibe like they're looking for trouble.

"Hey ladies," I say with a fake smile. "What's up?"

Stacy steps closer to me. "We were looking for hot guys, and suddenly, here you are!"

"But there's only one of me, and three of you. Does that mean you plan to share?"

"Hardly." She waggles her finger at her two friends.

More people join us, and among the jumble of bodies coming and going, more shots are passed out and I grab one. I know I'm going too fast but I really need to be numb tonight. All I really want is to be back at our place with Dean.

I follow Brian out to the back porch to take a hit off his joint. When I notice Ramon talking to some guy on the other side of the porch I slink back inside. I don't want to risk Dean seeing Ramon hitting me up. Our track record with Ramon setting him off has not been good.

Somehow, I end up in the living room in the middle of the couch with girls all around me. So of course it's just after Stacy has planted herself on my lap that Dean shows himself.

Stacy, who's high as a kite, wiggles on my lap and keeps attempting to unbutton my shirt while I try to stop her. From the corner of my eye, I see the same forest green color that Dean was wearing. Turning his direction, I discover he's glowering at me.

I roll my eyes and shake my head slightly hoping he understands that I don't want this.

His gaze is intense but he doesn't move, just watches sloppy Stacy groping me, while getting louder by the minute. She's gravely testing my thinly veiled tolerance for idiotic women.

When I finally peel her off my lap I look up, and Dean is gone.

Great . . . fucking great.

A minute later I'm up on unsteady feet, and suddenly the music seems louder. The heavy bass pounds like it's beating inside of my body. My mouth is parched, and I smack my numb lips as my gaze scans the room. I push my way outside hoping that's where Dean went, and once out there I take gulps of air in an attempt to clear the fuzz out of my mind.

I feel someone squeezing my shoulder. When I turn, I can't hide my disappointment that it's Ramon.

"Well, that's not the greeting I was hoping for," he half teases.

"Sorry, I'm just feeling off," I lamely explain.

He studies my face. "Yeah, you look off. Too much too fast?"

Nodding, I wipe my hand over my forehead.

He steps away for a minute and comes back with a bottle of water. "Here, drink up."

"Thanks." The cool water feels unbelievably good sliding down my throat and I finish half the bottle before I take a break. I smile at him realizing that Ramon may be all about the sex, but he's always seemed like a good guy to me.

There's a loud laugh behind us and Ramon looks over my shoulder, and I let my gaze roam over him as I try to figure out why I'm not feeling any electricity for him right now . . . and not just because I'm coming down from getting high too fast.

He's wearing one of those thin sweaters that clings against his skin and his shoulders have never looked beefier, nor his arms as pumped. Did he just finish a workout? Because his caramel-colored skin is glowing like he did. His jeans seem custom made to fit his powerful thighs and ample ass. If he were in the Lucky Boy Bar right now he'd have men prowling all around him.

But even with all that goodness, I'm still not feeling any attraction amping up my lust factor tonight. Instead I'm concerned about Dean and wondering if what he saw with Stacy and the girls is going to shift him away from me again.

Ramon leans into me. "Hey, I just heard about a place we should check out soon."

"Yeah, what's that?" I ask, pretending to be interested.

"It's a gay sex club on the edge of town. My friend told me that they have a special deal for students over 18."

My brows knit together. "What happens there?"

"Anything and everything you can imagine," he answers with a wicked grin.

My mind starts spinning, various frames of gay porn that I've seen or watched, flashing through my head. I feel my knees get weak. "I don't know . . . I'm not sure I'm ready for that. You know?"

He shrugs. "You don't have to do anything if you don't want. You can just watch. But no pressure. I'll send you the link to their website. Keep it in mind and let me know when you're up for trying something new."

I soon part from Ramon determined to find Dean. I'm glad my head is starting to clear. The blur of color and movement, and the loud discordant music is no longer making me sway. I push my way through the rooms but don't spot Dean until I step out of the dining room into the downstairs hallway. In the shadows I see Dean kissing some chick he's got pressed up against the wall. It's a punch in the gut and for a moment I can't breathe.

I feel my mouth go slack and my eyes bug out as I back up a few feet. This isn't just kissing, this is mouth fucking, the final step before you drag your partner into bed. He slides his hand up from her waist to cup her breast over her top. I can hear her soft moan, and I grit my teeth.

I know this is fucked up but as I watch them go at it what burns me most is that he's never even come close to kissing me. *And why the hell not?* He can put his dick all the way up my ass, but he can't press his lips against mine? I clench my fists.

Kissing is about connecting, it's emotional. It's claiming someone as yours. I must not be his at all, even though last night I fooled myself into thinking that I was. Maybe this girl is his now, whomever the hell she is.

I look at him groping her and notice that her boobs seem small and that irks me, too. If he's going for girls why not one with big tits and curves to get him as far away from guys as possible?

Oh for fuck's sake, are they ever going to take a break? I'm waiting for a moment when his tongue isn't down her throat to tell him I'm leaving. I'm classy like that, not the asshole he was when he stormed out of the garage when Ramon was blowing me. He just left me high and dry so that I had to walk home.

Ironically, it's the girl who finally opens her eyes and notices me gawking at them. Pulling away from the kiss, she tugs at Dean's arm and then gestures toward me.

He rolls his eyes. "What?" he barks.

I jingle my car keys. "I'm not feeling great. I've gotta get home."

"Okay. See you," he mutters before turning back to the girl.

I know I should move on, but I don't seem able to. "Aren't you coming with me?"

"I'm busy," he growls. I notice his whole body is tense.

"Are you going to fuck her?"

The girl lets out a sharp gasp and he snaps his head toward me. Fury burns in his eyes. "You asshole! Get the hell out of here!"

We share a long, weighted stare before I turn away and stomp out of the hall. By the time I'm outside next to my car door, my hands are trembling so bad I can't focus. I crawl into the car and lean my forehead on the steering wheel. My heart is pounding and as much as I want to get the hell out of here, I'm sure as hell not calm enough to drive.

Regret starts to settle over me.

Are you going to fuck her?

Did I really say that? I must be losing my damn mind. I shouldn't have come to this party. Didn't I realize that something like this could happen? Dean is still into girls and that make-out scene in the hall makes me think that no matter what happened between us last night, women are still where his allegiance lies. He's not mine . . . he'll never be mine. Wrapping my arms over my stomach, I curl forward and wedge my eyes shut, trying to hold back my stupid tears.

Suddenly, the passenger door snaps open. The car dips with the weight of his body and then he pulls the door shut hard enough to make the car shake.

I close my eyes then turn slightly and peek at him with my one barely open eye. His gaze is fixed forward and his hands are in tight fists pressed against his thighs.

"Start the car, Jason," he growls.

"You're leaving the party?" I ask, in an uneasy voice. "What about your girl?"

"Drive, damn it," he barks.

I fall silent and flip the key in the ignition. We're quiet, with him seething and silent, the entire drive home.

Once back in the apartment, he walks straight into his room and closes the door. I press my hands against the doorframe, then rest my cheek against the cool wood. "I'm sorry, Dean," I say, hopefully loud enough for him to hear. "I'm really sorry." Then when he remains silent on the other side of the door, I turn and enter my bedroom.

I pace back and forth a few times, desperately trying to sort out what is going on. Am I going to fuck up Dean and our friendship as I drag him through all my drama? He was perfectly fine until that night he walked in on Ramon and I. He doesn't want to be gay. I shouldn't even be touching him, let alone writhing and panting under him as he fucks me.

I'm a monster, no better than Father Ryan, seducing him so that I can have my desperate fantasies realized. The room fades darker and starts to morph into a scene from my memories as I fall to my knees and the pious chant comes back to me just as the tremor of a panic attack tightens around my lungs.

Forgive me, Father, for I have sinned.

My hands begin to tremble and my heart races because it's as if I can feel Father Ryan standing next to me, angrily peering down at me with a grimace of disgust.

It was late afternoon on a school day, and a classmate and I had been discovered groping in a stall of the boys bathroom after tennis practice. Father Ryan personally came to yank me from the scene and administer my discipline. He was wild with barely restrained anger as he dragged me back to the sacristy and into his adjoining study. Once inside, he slammed the door and locked it.

"Do you understand what you've done?" he hissed.

I'd never seen him so mad and it terrified me.

"You've shamed me, and shamed our church. You take an innocent boy into the bathroom stall and put your hands on him?" His voice got louder and angrier. "You have sinned gravely. Do you have so little restraint?"

My head fell down, my chin rested on my chest. I didn't even think to challenge him, demanding to know why what I had done was a sin, and what he's done to me isn't. I also didn't bother to tell him that Beckett was the one who lured me into the bathroom and shoved his hands down my pants. I was glad he did. It was the first I'd been kissed by a boy, and I liked it.

"I'm sorry Father. I'm really sorry," I said softly, trying to calm him down.

Father was gripping the edge of his desk and his knuckles were white. "You must be punished . . . yes, punished and purged of your sins," he chanted as he stepped away from the desk and circled me. Grabbing the back of my collar, he jerked me upward. He pointed to the desk, and from this angle I could look up and see how red his face was, and the darkness in his eyes.

"Be prepared to take your punishment. You'll beg for forgiveness following."

Terrified, I approached the edge of the desk, and he put his hand on my upper back, and pressed hard until I folded down, my chest slamming down to the desktop. He yanked down my pants and I thought I was going to pass out.

He stepped up behind me. "Say it!" he barked.

"Forgive me, Father, for I have sinned."

When Father Ryan smacked me with his palm I jolted forward. The sting was sharp, and the humiliation acute.

"You've shamed me," he repeated in a low, dangerous voice.

He smacked me again hard, and my eyes blinked closed as I swallowed the pain. This time he rubbed his hand where he'd hit me.

"Tell me you want this punishment," he said.

"I want it," I replied without hesitation.

"You regret your sinful ways?"

I didn't answer, but nodded my head.

He hit me again. "What am I going to do with you, son?"

"Guide me, Father," I said, trying to placate him.

I felt his hands on my ass again, but this time it felt different as he lingered. My body seized with fear.

I heard the rustle of his robes opening.

No, no, no.

I'd put up with all of his needs but I couldn't do this. This would surely be my undoing.

"You know it's a sin to corrupt other boys. You're mine, Jason . . . my responsibility, and I won't tolerate your sinful behavior."

He rubbed his hand where my ass stung the most. "You must submit to me and learn to obey my teachings," he said in a strained voice.

My whole body started shaking. I felt like I was going to pass out.

"No!" I cried out. "No!"

"Quiet!" he roared as he prepared to mount me.

"No!" I begged, twisting around and falling to my knees.

For a moment he paused, like he was considering how to restrain and fuck me, but then he angrily grabbed a handful of my hair and yanked me forward as he forced his way into my mouth.

This was not *'relieving tension.'* This wasn't my priest speaking softly to me while stroking my face, telling me what a good son I was. Each angry thrust hitting the back of my throat was a violation. I shed tears of regret as he used me, and profound fury that I didn't fight him off and report him the very first time he was alone with me. With this final act he had ruined me and I'd never be the same.

I took my punishment and was coldly dismissed, but despite his demands, summoning me over and over during the next few weeks, that was the last time I entered Father Ryan's study.

Still on my knees, I pull myself out of the memory, and press my hands over my face. Father broke me, and now I taint the ones I love. I picture the look of fury on Dean's face tonight, and my remorse for all the things I've done to him overwhelms me.

"Please forgive me, Dean, for I have sinned," I say softly, trembling.

"Sinned?"

His voice shocks me, and I look over to see him standing in my doorway with his hands jammed down in his pockets.

"How long have you been there?" I ask, my eyes trained on the floor. Shifting off my knees, I sit down.

He sinks down until he's sitting cross-legged in the doorway. "Long enough. Hey, man, you're freaking me out. What is up with you?"

I rub my hands roughly over my face. "I don't know . . . all this shit from the past is coming back and messing with me."

"The shit with your pervert priest?"

"Yeah. It all started when you learned what was going with Ramon and me, and that I'd been lying to you all this time. It brought up all my self-loathing and shame."

"Maybe you should talk to someone about that. That situation with your priest would screw anyone up."

"You mean like talk to a shrink?"

He nods.

"But that would just make it feel more real again. I want it out of my mind, and out of my life."

"So what was that stuff you were mumbling about me forgiving you for your sins? Is there something else I need to know?"

"These tortured memories are my punishment, Dean. This is my penance for desperately wanting more from you. You're a straight man, and I'm corrupting you. I've gotten in the way of your relationships because I was always around . . . constantly needing your companionship. If it weren't for Julie getting sick of me being so close to you, you'd probably be happily living with her and not dealing with my crazy shit."

He shakes his head with a frustrated expression. "So now you're taking on not just screwing up your own life, but mine, too? Do you hear how crazy that is? We all make our own choices, JJ. You aren't my priest and you're not making me do anything that I don't want to do."

"Like making out with that girl at the party?" I can't even look at him to see his reaction.

"Okay, I get why that upset you. And yeah, I may have done it because I was pissed off when I saw Stacy crawling all over you. But that was a real asshole thing to do . . . to call out asking if I was going to fuck her."

I drop my head. "I know. I felt bad right after I said it."

Rising, he walks over to me and extends his hand to help me up. "We're a couple of idiots. Come on, you need to shut your big brain off. I think it's time for bed."

"I'm really fucked up, Dean," I mutter, noting my bitter tone. I'm so drained that I stand limply, too spent to move.

"Join the club, my man," he says with a sigh.

He helps me pull my shirt over my head and then eases my jeans down while I grasp his shoulder with my free hand. It feels good to be taken care of.

And since apparently I've regressed to being a five year old again, I ask him if he can stay with me until I fall asleep. He removes all of his clothes except his boxers and flops down on the bed next to me.

Stretched out on the bed, I look over at Dean to see if I can figure out what he's thinking. He's staring at me with a similar look.

"Hey, Dean," I whisper.

"Yeah, JJ?"

"You want to know what the real reason is that I got riled up about you kissing that girl?"

"Hey, I thought we were past all that," he says with a groan.

"You were kissing her." I whisper, pressing my head into the pillow.

"And?" he asks sounding frustrated.

"You've never kissed me, Dean . . . even when you fucked me. Even when I worshipped your cock with my mouth, you've never kissed me."

"Seriously?" he asks, in a teasing tone. "Man, it's just not something we'd do."

"Well, I wish we did."

He lies silent.

"I know that stuff makes you uncomfortable, but will you kiss me on my birthday? That would be the best present ever."

"Okay, Jason. I'll do that for sure."

Dean. 29

JASON ASKED ME TO STAY with him until he falls asleep, but here I am, still lying next to him and he's been out for a while. I watch his chest rise and fall and his long eyelashes flutter through his REM movements. I can only imagine how dark his dreams are.

On the other hand, I've never felt more wide-awake. My pulse feels like electrical surges shooting through my body as my mind feverishly tries to process everything I've learned about Jason the last couple of months. I'm ashamed now at what an ass I was with him when I first found out that he was sneaking around with Ramon. My rage was all about how he'd betrayed our friendship by lying to me all this time.

But now that I know about his molesting priest, humiliation by his mother, and fucked up sexual encounters, the anger has dissipated to be replaced by the sad ache of heartbreak for the person closest to me in my life. Jason has always stood up for me and been by my side, through the good and the bad, and now I need to do the same for him.

Tonight when I saw Stacy on his lap, rubbing herself all over him, I saw red. I know I'm jealous by nature, but my rage was primal—almost blinding. I wanted to grab her by the hair and drag her off his lap and down to the floor like a friggin' caveman. In that moment I felt crazy and capable of anything. So when I forced myself to walk away and regroup, it hit me like a ton of bricks. My jealousy was not because some girl was hitting on my best friend. I was jealous because she was trying to seduce my man, and he belongs to *me*.

My body jolts as that thought settles in. So now I'm bi, and what? Am I in love with my best friend? This is feeling like a lot more than just some sexual experimentation. *Holy hell*. What is happening to me, to us?

Feeling flushed, I press my hands over my face, and try to regulate my breathing. If I lose my shit over this, it's only going to hurt JJ more. Look at how he lost it when he saw me revenge-kissing that girl I couldn't have cared less about. I don't even remember her name. Yet I'll never forget the look on his face as he watched us. It was rough. I should've never fucked with him like that.

I hear a sharp gasp and I turn to see an agonized look on Jason's face, and then a pained grimace as his fingers suddenly straighten and move like he's trying to push something in his sleep. A gurgled cry works its way out of his throat and he shakes his head.

I reach out, taking hold of his arm and gently shake it. "Jason, you're having a bad dream. Wake up."

His eyes remain tightly shut and another cry escapes through his moving lips.

I lift myself up on my elbow and lean into him. Placing my hand on his chest, I jostle him harder. "Jason, wake up!"

His eyes start to blink open, and I see fear in their depths.

"What?" he mumbles.

"You were dreaming, buddy. It's okay. I'm here."

He shuts his eyes tightly. "A dream? It was bad . . . so real."

I rub slow circles across his chest. "I know, but you're okay. Do you want to talk about it?"

"No." When he opens his eyes, they grow wide as he gazes at me. "Hey, didn't you go to your own bed? You're still here."

I give him a soft smile. "I was watching you sleep."

He gazes at me for several long seconds and then smiles back and touches my arm. "Will you still stay?"

"Sure." I run my fingers up his neck, along his jaw, and then across his cheek, before kissing him high on his forehead.

He sighs. "You kissed me."

"And it's not even your birthday," I reply with a grin.

"But on my birthday it has to be a real kiss," he insists.

"So now you're getting bossy about it? Do you mean a kiss like this?" I softly press my lips over his and give him the lightest of kisses before pulling away. The weird thing is that it doesn't feel weird. It just makes me want to kiss him again.

"Hardly," he scoffs.

"Okay, I'll try again. Maybe this time I can do it to your satisfaction." Shifting closer to him, I cup my hand along his jaw and turn him toward me. This time his lips are parted when our lips meet and he kisses me back, his kiss soft and urgent as my tongue brushes against his. I want more but I can't help but tease him by pulling back again.

"Better?" My gaze shifts down his torso where I notice he's already hard.

He shrugs. "A little bit. But I was really expecting more tongue action. And I'm not getting the part where you're pressing against me. I was really counting on some of that."

"Well, I'll remember all that when it's your birthday. Thanks for walking me through it, so to speak."

He bites his lip, which is already flushed a bronzed shade of pink. "I think it'd really be better if we worked it out now, you know? It has to be just right on my birthday. Think of this as the dress rehearsal."

"Or maybe the undressed rehearsal, as it were. So you want my weight on you? You can handle that?"

"Yeah, you're a big guy, but so am I."

He has such a goofy smile that I can't believe this is the guy who looked like his world was ending while he slept. It feels so damn good to know I've turned this moment around for him, and I'm pretty sure it's only going to get better because he's not the only one tenting his boxers.

I lift up and shift over, then slowly settle my body over his, and his legs spread apart. We pause for a moment, adjusting to each other and taking in the hot thrill of our hard cocks pressed together.

"So more tongue?" I ask with a wink.

He nods, as he waits for me.

I lean over and start at his ear, circling the rim with my tongue and then biting his lobe gently before sliding inside and then along the edge of his ear.

"Oh God," he moans, his cock throbbing underneath me.

I then trace along his jaw, feather kisses down his neck, and then lick my way back up. I scrape his jaw with my teeth, finally lingering over his lips before lightly running my tongue across them and back.

"Dean . . ." he groans.

I'm so worked up I'm afraid I'm going to lose it by the time I start the actual kiss. I remember Julie telling me once that some girls said Jason was the best kisser they'd ever had, and now I know why. The moment our lips meet he pulls me against him and it's like an erotic dance beginning with a rhythm and pulse of its own. His fingers are in my hair, and he moans in my mouth as our tongues tease each other, while our lips nibbling, grinding, and sucking, languidly do what they do best.

I slide one hand behind his head so I can hold him, tipping his head back when I need to suck on his neck, tipping it forward when I need more of his kisses. His sugar-sweet lips are sex, liquid lust, and heat sparking a fire in my chest that sizzles straight down to my groin.

He starts thrusting his hips up against mine, our cocks throbbing with need to be manhandled. He pushes me up enough so that he can kiss down my neck and then suck on my nipples. I swear to God, he's making me see stars.

"Was that the kiss you wanted?" I gasp as I watch him move to my other nipple, lightly biting it while looking up at me with lust-filled eyes.

"Oh yeah," he sighs. "The only thing that would make it better is if you fucked me while you were kissing me."

My cock throbs so hard I'm willing it to calm down. "You want that now?" I'm trying not to sound like I'm begging. "I mean, aren't you still too sore?"

"Now," he insists, yanking on my boxers.

I help him push them down, then I rise on my knees to pull off his. He gestures to the nightstand and I stretch far enough to yank the drawer open and grab a condom and the bottle of lube.

He coats his fingers and slips them down between his legs, all without breaking our intense gaze.

I glance down where his fingers are sliding slowly into him, and I study his movements.

"Can I?" I ask.

His eyes are still sleepy, but that wakes him up. "Yes, please," he answers as his free hand grabs the lube and hands it to me.

After my fingers are coated, I slide my index finger along his crack and then circle his opening before slowly pushing it inside of him. He's hot and tight as I watch for his reactions. He's lit up by what feels like a blend of raw lust and pure joy. Jason is so happy that the feeling spills over into me.

I keep kissing him while my finger, and then two fingers, fuck him . . . my lips pressing against his temples, his chiseled cheekbones, and his swollen lips. I'm keeping it light because once I start fucking him I know it's going to be crazy passionate. I'm craving that feeling of being buried deep inside of him with the hunger that's taken over me.

"Okay," he whispers, nodding.

"You sure?"

"Oh yeah. Very sure."

He watches with hooded eyes as I spread his legs apart farther, then roll down the condom and lube my cock. I'm as careful penetrating him as the first time, pushing in slowly as our gazes dart down to where I'm entering him, then to each other, and then back again.

He lets out the sexiest moan I've ever heard when I've finally filled him. Reaching up for me, he releases a deep breath. "You know, this is on my bucket list."

I'm pulsing inside of him, more than ready to starting moving to fuck him, but I've got to know. "Fucking and kissing at the same time is on your bucket list?"

He shakes his head. "No, *you* fucking me while passionately kissing me is on my bucket list."

Lowering myself over him, I growl with pleasure as I take his face in my hands and embrace him, our lips melting together while I pull my hips back and slowly start to thrust.

"Check it off your list, baby."

I suddenly startle. *Baby?* Did I just call JJ *baby* while my cock was in his ass? What in holy hell is happening to me? And who would've thought that I'd love it so damn much?

Jason. 30

IT WAS SO GOOD THE first time, but this . . . this . . .

Dean giving me all of himself—his cock, his kisses, his tenderness—and his powerful desire has me breathless. He seems to have no hesitation, and the idea that we are unencumbered by second thoughts and labels is freeing. We're not merely two men, nor a gay man and a bi, we're lovers, implying all the unrestraint and freedom that two people joining can be.

I'm not sure if it's because I'm in love with him, or because he truly has the sexiest lips, but his kissing skills are unbelievable, epic really. I would guess he'd say that I've inspired him, but it's more than that. His kisses consume me, each one an emotional surrender as his cock fills me again and again. When I wave the white flag after a particularly toe-curling kiss, accompanied by his powerful thrusts, I find the next one even more intense.

"Am I making you feel good?" he asks between pants, sharply thrusting while tugging on my hair. He's figured out how to angle himself so he hits that spot inside of me that makes me crazy. I couldn't have imagined anything could feel this good.

"I'm so close, Dean," I gasp. "So close."

He pulls me tight to his body. "Hold on, I'm going to roll us over." Next thing I know, he's on the bottom, while I'm on top, his cock deeper inside me than ever. He reaches for the lube and coats his right hand.

"I want you to ride me, JJ. We'll come together." He grasps my cock in his slick fist and starts pumping me.

"Oh hell yes," I groan, picturing times I've watched porn with the guys receiving on top.

It takes a moment for me to find my rhythm, but once I do I'm in control, fucking him as I roll my hips and lift up and then rock back over his huge, hard length.

"It's like *I'm* fucking you," I gasp.

He swallows hard, his expression strained. "You're so deep over me, JJ. Go on . . . fuck me harder. You're going to make me come, baby." His breath is ragged now, and I can feel his cock swelling and throbbing inside of me.

His hand on my shaft is a blur, taking long, firm strokes while gripping me tight, just how I like it.

I feel my balls tighten. I'm almost there. "Dean . . ." I cry out spurred on by his desperate moans.

Suddenly he reaches around with his free hand and grabs my ass cheek and then pulls me down hard over him again and again.

"That's right, baby, fuck me hard. You're so damn tight," he groans, rocking his hips up to thrust even deeper.

"And you're so damn big," I gasp, taking all of him, feeling how close he is. A moment later he explodes inside of me, setting off my climax.

"Oh fuck yeah!" I cry out at the force of it, my body practically convulsing.

This time I'm the one to collapse onto his chest, but before I settle my head into the crook of his neck, I lean in to kiss him as Dean shudders through his final wave of orgasm. It's a sweet, sexy kiss, drunk with satisfaction, my lips telling him how much I love him without saying a single word.

When I finally lift off him and sink to his side, he gives me one more kiss and pulls the sheet up to our chests. Sleep settles over us so gently that it's almost like I'd never woken, but dreamt of Dean instead.

Dean. 31

AS I GRAB OUR MAIL and head upstairs to our apartment, it occurs to me that the last few weeks have been some of the happiest of my life. Until a couple of months ago, Jason and my relationship was the easiest, best one I'd known. He made me laugh, and made me think. He was always behind me, everything from being my campaign manager when I ran for office in high school, to standing up and fighting for me when a girl I'd once dated wrongly accused me of shame-slutting her anonymously on social media. He was the one friend I could always depend on . . . the one friend I never got bored of.

Well believe me, when you wake up with your cock in Jason's mouth and his hot, dirty kisses when you return from class, your appreciation for your best friend expands ten-fold. Hell, the last time he blew me I let him tease my prostrate with his fingers, which not only made me come like a wild man, but left me wanting even more. So now "friend" isn't an adequate word for what this man means to me in my life. He's simply *mine*.

When I get up to the apartment he's playing Mortal Combat, and judging from his body language he's really into it. I try to get his attention to ask him if he wants to do the Park City trip for the weekend of Spring Break, but he's just nodding and essentially ignoring me. Sitting down next to him, I run my hand over the denim covering his thighs, and he bats my hand away.

"Park City, JJ?" I ask, teasing him.

He juts the console toward the screen. "Game, Dean," he mutters.

Challenge on. I'm determined to get his attention just because it seems all but impossible right now.

I slide off the couch and crawl until I'm in between his legs. Reaching up, I run a hand up either side of his inner thighs and back down. The video game suddenly is paused.

"What are you doing?" he asks with a rough voice.

"Seeing how fast I can get you hard." I look up in time to see his cheeks flush.

"Can you wait until the game is done?"

"No." I start kissing my way up his inner thighs, spreading his legs wider as I go. I have a plan.

He sets the console down and leans back into the couch and watches me. I look up and see the beginning outline of his growing erection in his jeans and I'm encouraged. I slowly run my fingers along the denim bulge and he moans. Next I press my lips along his growing length, hoping the heat of my lips gets him hot. I want him excited as I am, but even more, I want to please him.

"What inspired this?" he finally asks, his hips instinctively starting to rock, his cheeks bright red.

"I was sitting in my advanced Urban Planning class and all of a sudden I had an overwhelming urge to have your cock in my mouth. So I hurried home to follow through with that idea. Would you mind if I try sucking your dick, or in other classier words, blow you?"

Throwing his head back, he laughs, and then sobers and meets my gaze. "Are you fucking with me, Dean? You're not gay so you don't *give* blow jobs, you receive them."

"Well there's always an opportunity to try something new. You've got an impressive cock. Can you blame me for wanting to have it in my mouth? Are you going to take it out or what?" I point to what's obviously happening in his jeans. "It really looks like it wants to be let out."

He shakes his head and undoes his fly, then lifts his hips so he can slide his jeans and boxers down. His cock is hard, and it stands up straight and waves at me. I'm tempted to wave back.

My heart is already speeding as I reach out and wrap my fingers around him. "How do you like it?" I ask as I rub the head over my lips.

His expression is lustful as he watches me. "How do I like my blow jobs?"

"Yeah," I answer as I lightly tease the head of his cock with my tongue.

"You could start by putting it in your mouth," he says dryly as I continue to tease him.

"Anything else?"

"I'm not that fussy, man. You can moan the national anthem over my cock and it'll still be perfect because it's *you* blowing me." He gives me a grin as he rocks his hips up so his cock passes across my lips to make his point.

I feel my face heat up. It kills me how this guy always makes me feel like I'm something special . . . so much better than anyone else he could be with. I wonder if he knows how hot that makes me? How it only makes me want to fuck him more.

"Good to know," I say with a wink, and then swirl my tongue down his shaft as I suck him in deep.

Jason's hips lift right off the couch and his eyes bug out as he watches me. "Oh, fuck. Oh, oh . . ."

Even though my mouth is stretched wide around his cock I still manage to smile. I guess I shouldn't be surprised that I'm good at going down on him. After all, I'm a guy that knows what feels good and I pay attention to his reactions. I know Jason better than anyone else in the world.

For instance, right now I learn that JJ goes a little crazy when I roll his balls in my mouth, and I also learn that he lied when he said he wouldn't mind humming. He squints his eyes with a stern expression when I hum the *Star Wars* theme while trying to swallow him, and call his cock a lightsaber of love. I think a little humor can be good in sex, don't you? Apparently, Jason takes his blowjobs really seriously.

But man, when I moan that hungry desperate moan as I suck him deep, he starts to tremble and watch me with wild eyes before groaning, "So fucking good. Please, baby, please . . ."

"Please what?" I tease.

"Oh God, make me come," he begs.

And I deliver. He's practically levitating off the couch as I use all my skills to make him come like a wildman and I surprise myself by swallowing everything he gives me. Turns out that I like everything about Jason, even how he tastes.

He's still panting as he blinks at me wide-eyed. "Was that really the first time you've ever done that?" Jason asks.

"Yes," I say smugly. I can tell that my inexperience wasn't a hindrance.

"Well damn, you're a natural. That's by far the best I've ever had."

"Good to hear!" I grin widely. "So you're telling me you wouldn't mind me doing it again sometime?"

"Wouldn't mind? I'll beg for it, baby."

"Good. I liked it. Too. And I love your cock, so that won't be the last one from me."

He grins blissfully while lying spread out on the couch, his jeans still down around his ankles, and his head thrown back against the couch cushion when I get up to get us two sodas.

"Are you going to resume your game?" I ask as I pop my can open.

"What game?" he replies, blinking his dreamy eyes. His expression has never been softer.

I chuckle. "I was that good, huh?"

He nods lazily. "Epic." He sighs happily. "Just for that I'm going to let you order that weird Hawaiian pizza tonight. That's the bizarre one you like with the ham and pineapple, right?" He scrunches his face up in disgust.

"Yes it is! Score!" I say, as I fist-pump the air. "Thick crust, too."

He gazes up at me dreamily. "Sure, whatever you want."

I grin and then remember I'd left the mail on the counter, so I get up to check it for my cell phone bill I've been having problems with. He slowly sits up and then stands to pull up his jeans.

I'm two pieces of mail in when one official looking letter jumps out at me. I turn toward him. "Hey, JJ, what's this letter from a law firm? You suing someone or something?"

He scoffs and reaches out his hand. "Hardly. Let me see it."

I watch him slowly open the letter, and when he starts reading and cups his hand over his mouth, I go over and join him on the couch.

His fingers tighten along the edges of the paper and it seems like he's reading it a second time while shaking his head slowly. His brows are furrowed and his eyes appear strained.

"What?" I ask, my stomach falling. I have no idea what this could be but I can tell already it's really bad.

The letter slips out of his fingers to the floor and he curls over, covering his face with his hands.

Scooting closer, I extend my arm over his shoulder. "What is it?"

"They want to meet with me, and they're willing to come all the way to Salt Lake City and do the meeting in one of their associate's offices. It's a class action suit regarding the actions of Father Ryan Morrison on behalf of the numerous boys he allegedly abused. They're taking on the Catholic church."

"Oh damn," I curse as I watch him start to inwardly collapse. "They're taking on the church? How do you take on the Catholic church?" My tone is full of restrained fury.

"How did they find me? Am I am on some fucking list or something. How did they know?" He's gasping for air and his eyes are wild.

I pull him toward me until his head is resting on my chest.

His body is starting to heave and I'm scared. I'm not sure he can handle any of this right now. I have no idea what I can do to help him, but I do what I can in the moment and hold him tighter.

"Why now? Why does this have to be now? I can't handle it," he rasps in a broken voice.

"You're not alone, Jason. I'm with you, man. I'll be with you no matter what you decide to do . . . whatever you can handle."

And that is when the first of his many tears start to fall.

Jason . 32

NUMEROUS.

That single word has ripped me apart. I'm not the only one he destroyed with his abuse. The sick motherfucker preyed on boys he had authority over, boys he convinced to keep a dirty secret that would start rotting their souls from the inside out.

One brave boy refused to stay a victim and stepped forward to stop the cycle. I'm full of shame that boy wasn't me. I'm a grown man that can't even show the world who he is. I'm not brave . . . I'm the worst kind of coward.

Dean is rubbing his hand up and down my back, and judging from his frightened expression right before I folded into him, I know he's seriously worried about me.

"What do they want you to do?" he asks in a gentle tone.

"A preliminary meeting to determine if I'm a good candidate for the case."

"Are you going to do it?"

"What's the point?" I ask. "The minute they figure out I'm gay I won't be taken seriously. Hell, they'll probably try to turn it that I seduced him."

"I really doubt that, but you won't know if you don't talk to them. What that monster did to you was mental and physical abuse. He needs to get his comeuppance. How do you fire a priest anyway? He should be in jail."

"I read an article once. Priests who commit serious offenses aren't fired, they're moved to another parish."

"Where they can do it again," Dean growls.

"Exactly," I agree, rubbing my hands over my tear-streaked face.

Dean rests his hand on my shoulder. "Promise me that you'll seriously think about following through with the lawyer's meeting. I'll go with you."

"I've been trying to come to terms with who I am, and I just want to forget about my past, so I can find some peace in my life."

"I get it, JJ, really I do. But as far as I can tell, those memories seem to be rising out of you with a vengeance, not fading away. Maybe facing the demon is the answer to get past it."

I let out a long, sorry sigh, and Dean rubs his fingers across my tight shoulders. We stay like that silently for a long time while I slowly calm at his touch.

"Hey, Dean?"

"Yeah?"

"Can we go to the movies tonight? Not one of those deep thinking films you like but something stupid and mindless. And then maybe grab some beers?"

"Like a date?" he teases.

The corners of my mouth turn up a little. "Yeah, sure, a date, but you don't need to bring me flowers or anything."

"You can bring me some though." He winks at me playfully. I'm grateful he's going along with lightening the mood. I need to have something good to look forward to.

Pulling out my phone, I start tapping the keys.

"What are you doing?"

"A search to find out where I can get you a Venus Fly Trap. That'd be really romantic, don't you think?" I hold back my laugh as he rolls his eyes.

Dean snorts. "On second thought, no flowers . . . just shower and shave, and bring *you*."

Dean. 33

SOMETIMES I LITERALLY STOP IN my tracks wondering who I am now. Two months ago I was easily rolling along with Jason and I being best buds as always. There was never a reason to question anything about who we were to each other . . . we just were. Then suddenly, he pulled the rug out from under me and I was full of rage, feeling like I'd been living in a lie with the person closest to me in the world. And now the pendulum has swung so far in the other direction I'm completely stunned. I'm not just kissing and holding my best friend, but I'm fucking him and I like it a lot. The whole crazy cycle has my head spinning.

But today what I feel is protective—fiercely protective. I want to rip the throat out of that damn priest for the way he damaged JJ. And although Jason doesn't want to face lawyers and the hell of those two years with that monster, I think he has to. He needs to defend himself in the way he couldn't at that young, vulnerable age. He needs to take his power back. I really believe that only then will he find peace in his life.

I meant what I said to him. I'm going to be by his side through this. But more than that I'm going to make him believe that he's strong enough to fight.

Earlier when he asked me to take him out tonight, we joked about it being a date, and I bristled inside. Taking another man on what feels like a girly 'date' is way too gay for me. But I can swallow that down tonight and go along with it. He needs me and I'm going to come through for him.

"You ready?" I ask, knocking on his bedroom door. In fairness,

I hogged the shower before he got a chance so naturally I'm ready before him.

When he opens the door, I take half a step back. He looks like he put more effort into getting ready for tonight than he usually does. He's got a blue button-down shirt on that matches his eyes, and his good jeans. He's also shaved which makes his skin smooth, a big contrast to the stubble he's usually rocking. He's so damn hot I'm flustered.

"You shaved," I mumble.

Reaching over, he pats my cheek. "So did you. No razor burn when we make out later."

I arch my brow. "Is that so?"

"Yup. So what are we seeing?"

"How about that new movie, *Trainwreck*?"

He scrunches up his nose. "That's a chick flick."

"It is?"

"Yeah, even though it doesn't sound like one. Isn't there a Marvel Comics movie playing? They put one out like every few months."

We head out and settle on the latest Bourne movie at the local movie cineplex. When the theater goes dark he keeps trying to hold my hand, and although I'm pretty sure he's just screwing with me, I keep batting his hand away. I finally huff, stand up, and move over a seat, taking the tub of popcorn with me.

He looks over at me exasperated, and I give him a 'what the fuck' look. If he wants to blow me in a dark movie theater I'll consider it, but holding hands . . . no way. After he finally motions that he's giving up, I return to his seat and offer the tub of popcorn as a peace offering. If that isn't being affectionate, I don't know what is.

Afterwards, we head over to Joe's Place but it's packed, so we decide to do the drive-thru for burgers and pick up a twelve pack of Rolling Rock, then head home.

Once parked on the couch with *Saturday Night Live* on, it feels just like old times, except we don't discuss the girls we're interested in. Instead we're like two happy sloths stretched out on the couch, laughing at the comedy sketches.

When the show is almost over, Jason slides over next to me and rests his head on my shoulder. "Thanks for this," he murmurs, releasing a sigh.

I turn toward him, thinking that this wasn't any different than the hundred of nights we've spent doing about the same. The difference tonight was that we made a bigger deal of it, showering, and shaving first. "No biggie, man," I say with a shrug.

"It really got my mind off things."

Reaching over, I take his hand and wind my fingers through his. "That was my intent."

He stares at our hands intertwined for several long seconds and I wonder what he's thinking. But when he turns toward me, his eyes are glazed and his lips are pressed tightly together. I sense that he wants to say something to me but can't.

"It's okay," I whisper, putting my free hand on his thigh.

He reaches up and gently combs his fingers through my hair before pulling my face toward his. When he kisses me it's tender, almost tentative at first, but it's sexy too. Since he's incredibly hot, when he starts up with me like this I'm swept to my aroused state so fast I can barely catch my breath. I lean back into the couch and pull him closer as his lips slowly melt mine.

We spend the next minutes, hours . . . hell I don't know how long, lying on the couch, touching and kissing, pressing our bodies together so our hard cocks align. I run my fingers over his biceps and his abs and all the places where his muscles are sharply defined. I'm still processing how much his masculine body turns me on. But we don't do more, and I don't push it. This is about something else.

Should I be scared that it feels like he's falling in love with me? I don't know if this thing is to be short lived—a fling that ends when school does, and our circumstances change so we go back to just being friends. I've always imagined myself married one day with a few kids, but now that idea feels more abstract and less firmly rooted in my psyche. I'm pretty sure I could still be attracted to women when not being distracted by Jason, but what if I'm not?

And what if I'm falling in love with him too? What then?

Jason . 34

DEAN WANTS ME TO BE tough and meet with the lawyers, and how can I say no to him when he's been everything to me lately? I feel like I'm holding my breath all the time waiting for him to wake up and remember that he's not gay and move on. But then another day passes and I figure I'm going to take as much as I can get, even if it kills me when he finally gets tired of having me in his bed.

My only regret is that when he's done with 'experimenting' or whatever this is to him, I don't think I can handle just being friends again. Now that I know what it's like kissing him, sleeping next to his warm body, and getting fucked by him, I don't think I can give that up and see him with his girlfriends or future wife. That would rip my heart out.

I should've known that it was all too good to be true. Two more amazing weeks have passed when I run into Ramon on campus and he drops the bomb on me.

"So Dean's old girlfriend Julie is moving back here, huh?"

I can tell by the way he's watching me that he's counting on a big reaction, and I'm not going to give it to him.

"Really?" I reply nonchalantly. "Dean didn't mention that."

"Yeah, Andrea says she got a job at the university in communications."

"Cool." I nod, while hoping the panic that's roaring through me isn't outwardly visible.

"Maybe they'll get back together."

"Maybe. Time will tell," I reply, sounding vague. If I don't get him off this subject I'm going to lose it. "So what have you been up to?" I give him a forced grin so he gets my drift.

"Well since you kept turning me down, I've spent a lot of time at the dance club. I've met some great guys there. You know, you have an open invitation if you ever want to go back . . . or to the sex club I told you about. I haven't been there yet. I was hoping to go with you."

I nod, and as I do I'm wondering if I did go out with Ramon again how Dean would be about it. Maybe if Julie's back he won't care.

That night Dean returns to our apartment late. When he stumbles through our door he's sweaty and wearing his gym clothes.

I'm sitting at the table pretending to study, and act like I haven't been on the edge of a panic attack about what's going on.

I look up at him while he drops his stuff to the floor. "Hey, where've you been?"

"At the gym. Remember I told you last night that I was working out after classes today?"

"Did you tell me while you were fucking me, or after? Because the way you fucked me was pretty much all I remember about last night."

His eyes narrow as he studies me. "You okay?"

"Sure, great." I look back down at my textbook, and slowly turn the page I'm pretending to read. "So I hear Julie's moving back here." I don't look up to see his expression but the silence is pretty weighty.

"Yeah, she texted me last week. Guess she got a job here."

"Were you going to mention that?"

"It didn't occur to me. What's the big deal anyway?"

"Uh, I don't know. Maybe it's not a big deal but you sure lost it back when she moved, and when I tried to comfort you to calm you down, I told you that it probably wasn't forever and you'd likely end up back together. And you said you'd take her back in a second. So, I guess you're right . . . from where I sit, her coming back isn't a big deal at all."

"Jason," he says with a warning tone.

I want to tell him, *She left you and you're mine now. She doesn't get another chance.* But how can I say that? It's not my life to live, not my decision, and the fact that he didn't tell me she was coming back makes me feel pretty damn insecure.

He pulls out the other chair at the table. "JJ, that conversation we had when she left feels like a million years ago. I don't even know her anymore, and she sure as hell doesn't know me." He cocks his brow at me like to say. *Have you forgotten that you're the one I'm fucking?*

"Besides, why are you worrying about it? We're probably not getting jobs here, and we'll be moving away if not immediately, hopefully soon."

"Are you going to see her?" I ask, my hands under the table grabbing my knees so he doesn't see that they're shaking.

He shrugs. "Probably."

"Are you going to fuck her?"

His face turns red so fast that I wonder for a second if he's having a stroke or something. He's so mad even his eyes look red.

"Are you really asking me that, asshole?"

"Well, are you?" I'm beyond helping myself by shutting the fuck up. I'm too crazed with jealousy.

Folding his arms over his chest, he grits his teeth. *"Probably* not."

Probably?

I jump out of my chair so fast it falls over backward. Grabbing my jacket, I head to the door.

"Where are you going?" he barks.

"For a walk," I snap back as I comb the counter for my keys.

"To hook up with Ramon?" His fists are clenched like he's going to punch me.

"Probably not," I say before yanking the door open, and slamming it loudly behind me.

Dean. 35

THE LAST TIME JASON TOOK a "walk" at night it ended up being the walk of shame as he all but fucked that asshole in a dive bar parking lot. So he has a helluva lot of nerve to walk out on me and think I'm not going to be really pissed off.

If the idiot had just kept his shit together we could have talked about Julie and calmly discussed how we felt about it. I knew her coming back was going to upset him. So I was holding off telling him as long as I could. I can see now that was a mistake.

It takes everything I have to not trail him. Instead, I kick my gym bag across the apartment and watch the water seep out of the bag after the impact cracks open the plastic bottle stuffed inside. I get in the shower and don't get out until I'm done cursing.

After I dry off and pull on my clean clothes, I head to the kitchen to find my phone, and call the asshole. If he's with Ramon, I swear, it'll be the end of this 'relationship' he claims means 'everything to him.'

I press his number, still cursing under my breath, when I hear his ringtone in the living room. I look up and see Jason sitting in the chair across from the couch. He looks like an angry statue until he lifts up his phone and rejects the call.

"How long have you been there?" I ask.

"A while."

"Did you know you're an asshole?"

He shrugs. "Yeah. Did you know you're one, too?"

I grab a beer out of the fridge and take my time opening it, and down a long swig before I address him again.

"Did you try to reach Ramon?" I ask, because if he did, I swear I'm done with him.

He shakes his head. "No. I walked around the block a few times."

I take a sharp breath, relieved that he at least had the common sense not to do anything dramatic. Walking it off was a much better choice.

"So are you really going to run out of here like a baby every time things don't go exactly how you want them to?"

He sits silently for a while and I can tell he's simmering.

He rolls his eyes and then glares at me. "So are you going to tell me about the 'love of your life' returning next time, so I'm spared of hearing about it on the street?"

I go sit down on the couch and rub my hands together. "Look, yes I came unglued when she left. I don't handle change well . . . as you know." I give him a pointed look.

His gaze drops to the floor. I would think he'd remember that fact when he looks back on what an ass I was when I first saw him with Ramon.

"So yeah, I freaked out. It meant letting go of a plan I'd had for my future that I finally had to face wasn't going to happen. But you also know that things hadn't been good with her and I for a while, and as long as she was living here neither of us was brave enough to break it off."

His eyes light up with recognition and he slowly nods.

"So yeah, there was talking about possibly getting back together once we'd taken a clean break from each other, but in my gut I knew we were just saying that. I knew that with distance we'd just grow further apart. And we did . . . or at least I did."

"If you knew all that, why didn't you just tell me she was coming back, Dean?"

It's hard to see the pain etched across his face, knowing I put it there. My instincts are to protect him, not to tear him down.

Leaning forward, I hold his intense gaze with mine. "Look, JJ, you've been dealing with a lot here, and I know better than anyone what it's doing to you. I was worried this would be one more weight on you, maybe one more thing when stacked up would just be too much."

He roughly rubs his hands over his face. "Well, you're right about that. It did feel like too much. I don't want to be a pain in your ass, but I need you, Dean. Right now you're the only reason I'm barely keeping my shit together."

"Come on, man. Not the only reason . . ."

He gives me a lopsided grin. "Okay, that was a little dramatic. But you know what I'm saying."

Standing up, I hold my arms open. "Come here."

He gets off the couch and as he steps up to me he practically falls into my arms. I wrap myself around him and hold on tight. "You know I need you too."

"No you don't. Don't just say that to make me feel better." He buries his face into my shoulder.

"You think I'm lying? Why do you think I don't need you?"

He lifts his head and stares at me with this gaze that feels like admiration. "Because . . . you're *Dean*."

"And you're *Jason*. Remember before your injury, back when you were winning your tennis tournaments and I used to tell you that you're a superstar?"

His eyes have a faraway look and he nods, a sad smile breaking across his face.

"Well, you're still a superstar. You are to me."

He blinks at me with wide eyes and I can feel his body slack a bit so I hold him tighter.

He places his hand over my heart and his gaze drops. "Dean, I . . ." He pauses.

I know what he's going to say and I'm not ready to hear it . . . not now. So I do what I've been wanting to since I pulled him into my arms. I cup his jaw with my hand and tip his head up so my lips have perfect access to his. And when we meet it's liquid fire, an unrestrained passion built up during our fight that's finally let loose. He opens up to me and groans as my mouth takes his, roughly fueled by raw desire.

I kiss him again and again, all tongues and teeth, moans and sighs, my hand sliding down his back until I can grab his ass and hold on, while I slide my thigh between his and slowly rock my erection against him.

"Take me . . . I need it," he gasps.

I reach around and find the edge of his shirt and tug it up his back and over his head. I then yank mine off as fast as I can so I can pull him back into my arms and revel in his sculpted chest against mine. "Oh fuck, yeah," I groan.

I start leading him down the hall, me stepping forward pushing him, and Jason walking backward following my lead. I take us into his room because there's something so satisfying when I fuck him in his bed, on his sheets. For those moments as he begs me to fuck him harder, it feels like every part of him belongs to me.

Before we've come to a stop I'm opening his fly, and once I've got him against the bed, I jerk his jeans down.

He's already panting. "Fuck me, Dean."

I nod, swallowing hard as I take his erection in my hand and squeeze. I'm about to command him to get on the bed, when I suddenly pause. The idea comes to me that me dominating isn't helping JJ, it's what he's always had from other men. He needs to learn how to be in control in all areas of his life, especially in bed. I push down my fear as I realize what I'm going to say.

I take his hand and press it over my throbbing cock still trapped in my jeans. "Tonight I want to change things up."

His brows knit together and he narrows his eyes. "Change, how?"

I pull him tight against me and roll my hips into him as I press my lips to his ear. "I want *you* to fuck me."

"What?" he asks, pulling back. "Why?"

Leaning closer, I run my tongue around the rim of his ear. "I *need* you to take me. I want to feel your cock inside of me. I've been thinking about it . . . a lot."

He looks flustered, his cheeks a dark pink. "But what if I hurt you? It would kill me if I did."

"I know you'll take care of me," I say, giving him a confident look like I know he can handle this.

Honestly, I'm scared out of my mind of what his huge dick will do to me, but I instinctively know that if Jason can do this it's going to help him. He needs to learn he can be in control in bed.

I push my jeans off while he silently stares at me, and once I'm naked I start stroking my cock. "See how turned on I am at the thought of it?"

He swallows, then coughs nervously as he gestures to the bed. "Oh God, this is really going to happen. Lie down, so I can get you ready."

I feel exposed as I spread myself open. He fumbles in the bedside table drawer until he pulls out the lube and a condom. Crawling up beside me, he looks down at me with a serious expression. "Are you sure, Dean? Really sure?"

I nod. "Can't you tell how much I want this?"

His face flushes more. "Oh fuck. I hope I survive this."

"You will," I assure him.

Since he's already played with my ass a few times, it's not shocking when his lubed up finger slides inside of me. I focus on staying relaxed as he slowly works me. But when he adds a second finger it ups the game and I start panting, partially out of fear, but also because I like the full sensation.

While he works the two fingers he leans over and runs his tongue up my shaft and then across my chest, licking and sucking on one nipple and then the other. After a few more passes over my cock, I'm rocking my hips up to meet his mouth.

"I need to try three fingers now, baby," he moans in my ear. "I need you to relax, okay?"

I nod mutely.

He goes super slow, but once he's in I don't want slow, I want more. It's like my skin is on fire from his heat and I need his cock like I need my next breath. He goes deeper and my eyes roll back in my head. He's also panting now as he pumps his fingers and sucks my cock into his mouth.

"More," I groan. "Come on, JJ, fuck me. I'm going to lose it if you don't do it now."

He pulls his fingers out and sits up straight. "Roll over," he commands, his voice gruff.

My cock throbs. I like this, all of it . . . especially how he seems to be getting stronger the longer we go on.

I position myself like he was positioned the first time, and he tells me to press my chest into the mattress so my ass angles up. Rubbing his hand over my back, he lets out a sharp breath. My eyes are closed as I hear the tear of the condom foil and then the lube bottle snapping open. My heart is thundering knowing he's about to take me . . . make me his.

He leans down and brushes his lips against my ass, and kisses the sensitive skin before his hands spread my ass cheeks open. When he speaks to me his voice is tight. "I'm going to fuck you, and I don't want to lose control, but I want this so fucking much."

In that moment I realize I'm not just doing this to help Jason . . . I need it, too. The feelings that are surging through me are confusing, but I want him to fuck me until I don't know anything but the sensation of him filling me. I loved the feeling when I was on top that we were two powerful bodies joined as one, and now our circle of power will be complete. I gulp back my emotion, my voice trembling. "Lose control. I just need this from you. Please . . ."

And before I've finished my thought I feel his cock pressed against my entrance and for a second it's surreal, but then I focus on staying relaxed as I settle myself lower so my ass is even more open to him.

"That's right, baby," he says in a low, sexy voice as he starts to push his way in. He goes slow, giving me time to adjust and breathe. Just when I think I can't take another inch he pauses, and I sense his thighs against my ass. I feel so full and connected with him that lust surges through me.

"Oh my God," he groans.

Glancing back over my shoulder, I see that JJ's eyes are wild and his face flushed. He looks drugged—high as a kite—and he lets out a long moan.

He still isn't moving, and I need him to, desperately.

"Are you okay?" I ask, pushing my ass up to urge him on.

"I'm holding on, man. I feel like I'm going to explode already. This feels a million times better than I ever dreamt it would be."

I grin and rest my turned head on my arm. "Okay, but if you don't fuck me soon . . ."

And with that he slowly pulls back and then thrusts into me with enough force to take my breath away.

"Is that how you want it?" he asks, between gritted teeth.

"Yeahhhh," I groan.

He continues to thrust, holding himself upright with his strong arms, and with each stroke I can feel his rhythm and confidence building. His strength and power is such a turn on and submitting to him is electrifying. "You feel so fucking good, Dean."

"So do you," I say with a gasp.

A minute later he lowers himself so he's curled over my body as he fucks me. I feel his tongue trace up my spine and then he bites me lightly at the crook of my neck, then harder as his thrusts get more frantic. I'm panting, my eyes roll to the back of my head and my whole body is sizzling. I can tell he's right on the edge and with each deep thrust rubbing up against that crazy place inside of me, I'm on my edge, too.

"You're making me crazy," I growl at him.

His fingers work into my hair and tighten and then he jerks my head sideways and bites my neck again. He's frantic now, his cock drilling me as he chants in my ear, "You're mine, baby . . . you're *mine*."

He bears down harder, each thrust going deeper, my cock throbbing as my balls tighten until I can't see straight.

The next thing I know I'm exploding as my release comes in tidal waves, and he rides right along with me, his body lifting up while he comes as he cries out my name.

A silent minute passes. "Holy hell," he finally whispers. He's spread over me and catching his breath. I'm speechless; not able to do much more than blink and breathe.

When he carefully pulls out and we finally roll apart, we end up on our sides facing each other. He gazes at me pensively as he traces his fingers down my chest. His expression shifts to something almost stern. "You're mine, Dean Whitley."

I nod my head slowly and sigh contentedly. "I'm yours."

Jason. 36

I NEVER DREAMT THAT DEAN would want me to fuck him, let alone so soon in our 'new relationship.' But when he got on the bed and laid open for me I felt like I'd won the lottery.

The thing I'd never allowed myself to dream, is how much I'd love fucking him. If I had, I would've gone mad with my want and need to have him under me. Now that I've experienced him it's everything. He was tight and hot, all muscle and man, and he needed me to fuck him as much as I needed him to let me take him. I may never recover from the sheer perfection of that first time.

We're having sex all the time now, two amped-up, horny-as-hell guys trying everything we can think of and more. I straddle him on the couch when he's trying to study. He shoves my plate aside and bends me over the table when I'm trying to eat. There's no drama or wondering what the neighbors think. There's just the two of us, experiencing everything we can together in this new relationship we're navigating.

Our wild fucking, ravaged tongue kissing, all-consuming blowjobs, dirty groping, and raw intimacy is going great. It's shitty real life that wants to drag things down. Dean said a few days ago that Julie texted and said she's going to be here in a two weeks and he didn't reply. Meanwhile he's been pushing me to meet with the lawyers about Father Ryan.

After yet another conversation about it, he wore me down. So when he pulled out his phone and dialed the number on the letter, I took the phone from him with a shaky hand and made the appointment. His hand was on my shoulder the whole time I spoke with the lawyer.

"When's the appointment? Did you say Friday?" he asks after I hang up.

"Yeah, the twenty-fifth at four p.m."

And for a moment I'm able to set my anxiety aside and realize that means that Dean is going to be dealing with me on the edge over this meeting and Julie coming back, all at the same time. It's going to be a rough time for him too. They say bad things come in threes . . . what next?

"Okay, four p.m.," Dean says, punching it into his phone.

My brows knit together. "Why?"

He looks up at me and blinks. "I'm going with you."

"Really?"

"I told you I'd be by your side for this, JJ. I meant it."

The weighted gaze we share gives me strength. And in that moment I believe that if Dean's with me, I can get through anything.

I keep wondering if the conversation will come up about us going public as a couple. With so little time left here at school, there's no point to stir everything up but if we do figure out a way to live in the same city I won't want us to be a secret anymore. My guess is Dean won't be okay with that. His plan for our future relationship-wise is probably very different than mine. I try to push those thoughts away because they only torture me and I want to make the best of whatever time we have left like this.

Work-wise we've both had interest for entry-level positions from firms in Seattle where development is booming. I'm willing to take anything I can get if I can be near Dean.

Dean . 37

FOR THE LAST TWO WEEKS I've been nervous about JJ's lawyer meeting, so this morning as I wake up and remember where we're going this afternoon I'm almost relieved. At least we can get this legal shit over with and hopefully go on with our lives.

Jason is still asleep, his full lips so damn kissable, as his chest slowly rises and falls, and the waves of his hair fall over onto his pillow. I lightly skim my fingertips over the contours of his face. Why does he have to be so handsome and hot on top of everything else?

He blinks his eyes open, and lets out a big yawn. "What're you doing?" he asks.

"Waking you up. Why do you have to be so damn good looking?"

He shrugs, then gives me a lazy smile. "Look who's talking? You look like one of those swimsuit models . . . the ruggedly handsome, built ones with the big package."

He holds his arm out and I slide over and settle down next to him.

I have to check myself as soon as I'm close to him. This guy makes my desire amp up from zero to sixty in seconds when he starts touching me. I don't even care if I'm late for class or any other real life bullshit. My time in bed with JJ has become my obsession.

What's even stranger is the fact that's he's a guy and I'm regularly fucking him, and that doesn't give me pause anymore. It's stunning how right it feels, like the most natural thing that I'm now tongue-kissing my best friend and sucking his cock.

At night we drag each other into bed, horny as hell, and wake up just as horny, grabbing each other's morning wood. But this morning

I have to convince myself to lay off since Jason must be stressed about today's lawyer meeting, even though I'm still all stirred up inside.

As we've grown closer I've gotten bolder, resting my hand over his crotch as we watch TV just so I can feel him swell under my touch. He never bats my hand away, just watches me with hooded eyes as I explore the feel and taste of him. Every part of him is so sensitive, and once I get started it's only a minute or so before his eyes are glazed and he's groaning as he throbs in my grip.

As we lie together silently, I feel his body start to tense and I need to know why. I'm assuming it's the meeting later, but I want to make sure. "Are you okay?" I whisper, resting my hand on his chest and slowly rubbing circles over his smooth skin.

"I'm just worried and I have to ask . . . are you going to get tired of me, of this?" he wonders aloud with a shaky voice.

"What?" I ask, completely lost as to how the conversation took this turn.

"When Julie comes, or maybe even another woman, is that where you see your future?"

Oh damn . . . we were feeling so fine. Why did he bring that up now?

His voice is thin, and as fragile as fine glass . . . like he could shatter any moment.

I pull him close to me. "Don't start fabricating bullshit situations. I'm with you now. That's what matters, okay?"

He slowly nods and rests his head on my chest.

"I know you don't like dramatic declarations, Dean, and I'm feeling emotional. You might not want to hear this, but I love what we have here. I've always wanted this with you."

"Dramatic declarations? Are you telling me you've been watching those soap operas again, JJ?"

He doesn't answer at first but rolls on his side. Eventually he whispers, "I'm sorry. But I meant what I said."

"Hey, don't turn away from me. I love what we have here, too."

"You do?"

"Don't start acting clueless now, JJ. If you can't tell how much

I'm into this than I'm doing something wrong."

He lets out a contented sigh. "No. You always do everything just right."

Jason . 38

I DIDN'T PLAN ON TELLING Dean that I loved him yet, but I was so swept away in the moment that I said something close. He was holding and soothing me. In that perfect moment of bliss the words fell out of my mouth before I could take them back.

There was an awkward moment where he teased me, but then he shared his truth with no embellishment. Dean Whitley said he loves what we have between us. Did he mean the brotherly kind of love? I hope not since the things we've done to each other are so fucking intimate . . . so *not* brotherly.

The most complete I've ever felt in my life was when he gave me what I'd asked for, spreading my legs wide and fucking me slow and deep while kissing me tenderly. That is what I'll always picture in my head when I think of what *making love* means.

Maybe he really does love me the way I crave to be loved. Maybe one day he'll say he loves not just what we have here, but that he's in love with *me,* too.

At three-thirty he meets me at our apartment for the drive to the lawyer's. Giving me a grave look he nods encouragingly. "You ready?"

Casting my eyes down at the floor, I fight to get my bearings. How can I possibly be ready? I'm terrified of facing the raw memories that robbed me of my self-respect, and made me feel worthless and weak.

If I'd been stronger I would've figured a way to get away from Father Ryan. My shame for not fighting him off when he touched me has defined and nearly ruined me. Now I have Dean, a real man, in my bed who touches me with no shame between us, and I just want to be whole for him. I want to be the man he deserves.

I nod at Dean, blinking to shield the fear in my eyes. "I'm ready."

He pulls me into a tight hug. It's quiet but it says so much about the man he is and the man I want to be. When we part I slowly follow him out to his car.

The road is a blur as I gaze out the passenger window. I grip the door handle trying to keep the memories that have been creeping into my mind as this day approached away.

When I close my eyes, my recollections take me to Father Ryan's study behind the sacristy, the falling sun casting colors as it shines through the stained glass windows. That afternoon was two weeks before our final meeting, and I can picture Father's angry face because he's lost all patience with me.

I'm sitting on the stiff wooden chair in front of his desk with my head bowed.

"Do you think you've properly served me, son?" His eyes narrow as he stares at me. "I've been exceedingly generous and patient with you."

I point to the open porn magazine he's just shown me. "But . . . I-I-I . . . don't want to do th-that . . ." I stutter.

"Do what? Touch and experience each other's flesh? When we dispel our filthy thoughts and urges by serving each other and relieving built-up stress, its God's will."

I shake my head but don't dare say a word.

"You doubt me? If it makes us feel so good to clear our minds and have such a profound release, how can it not be God's will?"

I look up at him and for the first time I wonder if he's actually crazy, not just a boy-obsessed pervert. "Do you truly think that?" I ask carefully, trying not to sound belligerent.

"Of course I do." He reaches over and picks up the magazine and then pulls it toward him. Licking the pad of his thumb, he proceeds to slowly turn the pages with a dark gleam in his eyes. "Do you look at these magazines that I've given you when you're alone?"

I think of the hard-core gay porn magazines he's given me that are currently shoved deep under my mattress for safe keeping. "Yes, I look at them," I whisper, immediately regretting my confession.

His nostrils flare. "And when you look at them do you touch yourself?"

I nod, my gaze dropping to the floor.

"The men in these magazines are helping each other, like I want to help you. Can you see that? Look how satisfied they are." He holds one of the magazine spreads up.

I notice his pupils are blown out as I nod, my mouth dry.

He parts his robe and undoes his fly. "Imagine how good it would feel if I were behind you, filling you, satisfying both of us."

I swallow hard, my fear paralyzing me.

He gestures to the desk. "I want you to lower your pants and bend over the desk so I can show you."

Clasping my hand over my mouth, I try to force the bile back down my throat. I frantically shake my head.

"Do you defy me?"

Suddenly there's a gentle knock on the door. "Father Ryan, Father Bertrand from Saint Augustine is here to see you."

His eyes widen and he takes a sharp breath before clearing his throat. "Thank you, Mrs. Tagliani, please have him wait for me in the nave. I'll be just a minute." He stands and adjusts himself before zipping his fly back up.

I can tell from his angry scowl that he's not pleased at all with this turn of events, but knowing I have this reprieve makes me feel like I can breathe again.

He quickly instructs me how to slip out the back once he's exited the sacristy, and then his eyes narrow and darken.

"We'll continue this *discussion* later."

Dean . 39

JASON MAY BE SILENT AS I drive, but his expression is tormented, like the bad noise in his head is especially loud. It's at times like these that I don't know what I can do for him . . . all I know is that I can't imagine what that asshole did to his head that kept him coming back.

His hand has been clutching the door handle so tightly that his knuckles are white, but he suddenly releases his grip and starts twisting his two hands together in his lap.

"Maybe we shouldn't do this," he says in a voice so low I barely hear it.

"You're just talking to some lawyers, and they've come all the way from Boise. Remember, it's not like you're facing that priest or anything," I say gently.

"It feels like I'm facing him. And it reminds me how scared I was of him, scared of his anger and disapproval."

I blow a rush of air out of my mouth. "Damn, he really had you by the balls, didn't he?"

"Literally," he whispers. "He used to tell me that since my father was not part of my life that I was brought to him so he could be my *spiritual* father. He made me believe that pleasing him was key to our relationship."

I grit my teeth as I watch him fall silent and look back out the car window.

After parking the car, we wander into the building lobby and find the elevator. I notice when we step inside he looks pale and drawn. I hope he's going to make it through this without losing it. Checking in with the receptionist, we sit down in the reception area and I pick up a *Time* Magazine and mindlessly flip through it. Jason goes up to the desk and asks for the bathroom key.

I watch him go back into the hallway until he's out of sight. When a couple of minutes pass, I start tapping my foot. After another few minutes I stand up and drop my magazine on the coffee table before approaching the receptionist with the curly auburn hair and friendly face.

"I'll be right back," I say, giving her a knowing look.

She nods and I see compassion in her gaze.

When I approach the locked men's room door I knock on it gently. "Hey, JJ, you okay?" I wait but don't hear anything.

I knock louder and press my ear against the door. I think I hear water running.

I'm about to pound on the door when he cracks it open. His face is dripping with water.

Narrowing my eyes, I study his drawn features. "Are you okay?"

"I was feeling like I couldn't breathe," he says. "I splashed water on my face."

His gaze meets mine, but then drops to the floor as he wipes his face with a paper towel. "I'm not sure I can do this."

Oh no, I'm not going to let him back out now.

"You can, Jason. I know you can. You're one of the strongest people I know."

He shakes his head slowly. "No I'm not. Not when it comes to this."

I firmly grip his shoulder. "I'm going to be right next to you. So let me be strong for the both of us. I'm not going to let you give up. I want you to fight, man . . . fight what that fucker did to you. Let's take the bastard down."

When his gaze travels back up I finally see determination in his eyes.

I hold my arm out. "Come on."

He slams the wadded up paper towel into the trash and steps up next to me so I can slide my arm over his shoulders.

As soon as we return to the waiting room, the receptionist nods to another woman wearing a navy jacket and slacks who comes around to get us. We're following her down a long hallway when she turns back to face us. "Would you like water, or perhaps coffee?"

"Water would be good, thanks," I reply and then wave at Jason. "For both of us."

She leads us to a double door that opens to a small conference room with a large landscape painting hanging on the wall. A stocky man in a suit, with gray hair and wire-rimmed glasses approaches us. "Mr. Sorentino?" he asks, not sure which one of us belongs to the name.

I push Jason forward a few inches. "This is Jason. I'm Dean. Dean Whitley."

"Theodore Jacobson," he replies as he shakes both of our hands. "You can call me Ted."

He introduces us to two members of his team. A younger woman in a suit with her hair pulled back named Allison, and a tall lanky guy with a trimmed beard named George.

The lawyer's eyes connect with Jason's. "It would be best if we interview you alone, Mr. Sorentino."

Jason shakes his head and takes a step back before grabbing my arm. "I can't do this," he whispers to me but I'm sure Ted can hear.

"He needs me here," I warn.

"Are you a relative?" he asks. Jason looks over at me, panicked, and there's a long, weighted moment as I ponder my response that will give me the chance to stay with him.

Swallowing hard, I make up my mind. "I'm his boyfriend," I state, pulling my shoulders back and taking JJ's hand in mine and squeezing it.

As soon as the words leave my mouth a righteous feeling comes over me. It feels good to not be afraid of what that word means.

Jason's head snaps toward me, his eyes wide with wonder, and I hope he senses those weren't just words I'm saying to appease the lawyers; it's a feeling and it's real. He *is* who I want to be with and not just in bed. He's been my "person" since I was a boy, but now we belong to each other in every way.

Jason turns back to the lawyer and steps closer to me. "Please . . . let him stay."

I can hear the pain in his voice and my fingers tighten over his so we can't be separated.

The lawyer nods and gestures to where we can sit.

Right after we settle down in the chairs, Jason blurts out, "Um, so, I'm gay."

The legal team just stares at him for a moment until Ted responds, "Yes?"

JJ bites the edge of his thumb and scoots forward in his chair. "So I'm pretty sure I won't help your case. Won't people say that I wanted what he did to me?"

Ted clears his throat and his warm eyes suddenly look very serious. "Whether you're gay or straight isn't a factor here, Jason. We've already identified a number of boys that Father Ryan abused. You all were victimized, and regardless of the color of your skin, your social class, or your sexual preference, he used his position to commit unspeakable offenses and he must not just be stopped, but he and the church need to pay for the harm that young boys like you suffered through. That suffering must be acknowledged."

I find myself nodding at the lawyer's proclamation as I think of how much JJ has suffered. That fucker needs to pay and I'm going to do whatever I can to make sure it happens.

Jason . 40

BOYFRIEND. DEAN SAID HE WAS my boyfriend. Despite that I'm sitting in the pit of hell, feeling incredibly scared as I'm about to reveal my worst humiliation, everything stings less suddenly because of that word. Now I see my life as the time before Dean declared himself as my *boyfriend* outside our bed, and now after when there is a gilded frame around my life with him making everything infinitely more beautiful.

I glance over at him, his jaw tight with anger. I feel this tidal wave of love wash over me and for a moment all the other shit of this day fades away. Sighing, I look at his lips, so full and kissable even when he's grimacing like he is right now. I want to pull my fingers through his thick shiny hair so badly that I have to press my hands down tightly over my thighs to control my impulses. He's so fucking desirable, my *boyfriend,* Dean.

I'm completely lost in him, until I notice someone in the background talking and the word "victimized" is thrown out there and it's cold water in my face. What they're describing is like someone ran into my car, or stole my laptop, when what actually happened is that my soul was crushed and nothing—even a massive pile of money—can repair and gloss over what that loss of dignity did to me.

Moments later my legal rights are explained, a recorder is turned on, and despite their gentle reassurances, the questions start coming steady and sure.

"What was the situation that allowed you to have private time with Father Ryan? How old were you when the first inappropriate advances or touching occurred? How often were you alone with him during this period?

Did he touch your genitals? Did he make you perform oral sex? Did he sodomize you?"

The list of questions seemed to go on and on, and the more detail he asks for the more exhausted I get. It's weird because they seem energized by my answers. Maybe I'm the jackpot of sordid stories of depravity.

After what feels like hours, I get so tired that I lie my head down on the conference table and close my eyes. I hear Dean speak up. "Would you mind if we take five? I think he needs a break."

"Of course," I hear murmured. I reach out for Dean's hand, and when he takes it I whisper, "Thank you."

He slowly rubs large circles over my back. "JJ, you're doing great. I think you've given them even more than they'd hoped for."

I open one eye and look up at him. "Really? They haven't even heard the half of it."

"Damn, JJ. That fucker was stealth. Look how many boys he screwed with before anyone stepped forward."

I let out a defeated sigh, while my cheek still rests on the table. "It's the church . . . it's supposed to be sacred, right? And he became the ultimate father figure, always acting like my feelings were important. He built me up before he started tearing me down. I'm sure he did the same with all the other boys."

Dean's strong hands move up to my neck, and he massages me hard, working to release some of the tension frozen there. Closing my eyes, I fall into the feeling.

But it's like the floodgates have flung open and now I can't seem to shut the memories out and everything gets confused. With my eyes closed, Dean's touch reminds me of Father Ryan rubbing my neck. He used to do that when I got tense and upset.

It all comes back to me in a giant surge, the dark wood and dim light of his study during my first talks with the father, his soothing voice asking me about my struggles at school . . . telling me how smart and strong I was, how much better I was than the other boys who taunted me.

When I'd tell him about the things that upset me the most he'd rub my neck and run his hands through my hair, massaging my scalp. It felt so good even though I knew there was something not right about it.

The shift happened so gradually that I wasn't as alarmed as I should've been. Next thing I knew he was asking me what I thought about girls, and if the thought of them excited me. I was flustered and not sure how to answer, my cheeks burning in embarrassment. He then asked if I was aroused when we talked about physical attraction and touching someone else's naked flesh. I blinked at him, speechless, and that was the moment my world split apart.

I'll never forget the darkness in his beady eyes as he stared hungrily at me. I felt dirty and depraved. If I'd only known that this was just the beginning of my spiral into his maniacal control.

"JJ?" Dean whispers, pulling me out of my dark memory. "They're back. Are you ready to talk more?"

I nod silently.

When they start up to finish the rest of the interview, I'm so numb that I can barely give lucid answers. Ted seems to realize that I've reached the limit of what I can handle and he starts to wrap up. I sink back into the leather chair with my eyes closed and watch Dean take over, asking specific questions about next steps and what all this will mean for me. It's all grey noise to me at this point; there's nothing left in me to be logical or analytical. I just want all the light and noise to go away.

I open one eye when I suddenly hear a woman's voice, and sure enough, Allison is holding up some papers and a brochure. She's focusing on Dean since he's the only one of us still paying attention. "This is a support group called S.N.A.P., Survivor's Network of those Abused by Priests. People we've worked with find it very helpful. Here's also a list of therapists in the area who are equipped to deal with this issue. If Jason decides to move forward with us, we can look at fronting the expense of a therapist for what his student insurance doesn't cover."

"Okay, thanks," Dean replies as he gathers the papers up.

Ted speaks up. "Most people need time to think about what they want to do. This is a very serious decision. We'll contact you in two weeks to see how you're feeling about all of it. Of course, feel free to call us sooner with any questions or concerns."

Dean is silent as we leave the offices, and all the way down the elevator, but once we get in the car he clears his throat. "You know, JJ, I think therapy could be a really good thing for you right now."

"So now you think I'm crazy?" I snap, sounding like an asshole when Dean doesn't deserve that.

He takes a deep breath. "No. I just think this is more than most people are equipped to deal with. Talking with an expert could help."

"But that's the thing, isn't it?" I groan. "I don't want to keep talking and thinking about it. The flashbacks and memories are the worst they've ever been. Why in the hell would I want to make it even more vivid in my memory than it already is?"

"JJ, you have to face it to get past it," he warns.

Suddenly, I have an overwhelming urge to throw myself out of his damn car. I start rocking back and forth. "I feel like I'm going crazy, Dean. What if I'm never going to be okay?"

Dean . 41

I'M NOT GOING TO LIE. Jason is scaring the hell out of me. He keeps quietly mumbling and rocking back and forth the whole ride home. I almost regret taking him to that meeting. They say hindsight is twenty-twenty, and maybe it was too much for him.

"JJ, you're freaking me out," I finally say when I realize the rocking isn't slowing down.

"Why don't you pull over and I'll get out," he mumbles.

"Get out? And then what?" I ask, trying not to lose my patience.

"I'll walk home."

"Oh, for fuck's sake. You're not walking home." I glance over at him and he's still rocking and now his face is in his hands.

Reaching out, I squeeze his shoulder. "Take some deep breaths, man. This was rough, but it's not always going to gut you like today did."

"How do you know? Maybe it'll be worse."

"I won't let it be worse." I lock my jaw as I stare straight ahead at the road.

He lets out a ragged sigh.

"What?" I ask.

"Why are you here? Right now. With me. Is this a pity thing? Because lately I'm pathetic enough to be pitied."

"Get over yourself. I'm with you because you've been my best friend forever and I'd never abandon you when you were going through serious shit like this."

He doesn't respond, just rubs his hands over his face.

Whatever I'm saying isn't helping so I try another tactic. "Besides,

I can't stop thinking about your mouth on my dick, or the way it feels when I'm fucking you. What we have going is good and maybe it's selfish but I don't want to lose it. So no . . . pity doesn't factor into it."

He lets out a sharp laugh. "What does factor? How great a fuck I am?"

"Well sure, that's one of the attractions. It's also because there's no one else on earth I feel more comfortable with, who gets me like you do."

We remain silent the rest of the drive, but at least he uncovers his face, sits up, and looks out the window. After parking, I start walking toward the stairs and he stops and jams his hands in his back pockets.

"Hey, I need to shake some of this off me. I'm going to take a walk."

I arch a brow at him. "A walk?" *Here we go again with the damn walks.*

"No. It's not like that . . . I'm not going to meet anyone. I'm just going to walk, I swear."

I study him as his eyes dart around nervously. "Do you have your phone?"

He nods.

"And you'll call me if you need me to get you?"

"Christ, Dean, I'm not jumping off a bridge or anything."

"You better not. All right, go ahead and walk but I expect you back by dinner. It's my turn to order the Chinese."

He looks completely drained, but he smirks anyway. "Okay, Mom."

Jason . 42

WHEN I START OUT DOWN our street I have no idea where I'm going to walk to, just that I want to rush away from anything that reminds me of how I'm suffocating with self-loathing and fear that things are only going to get worse.

Thankfully with each footstep forward, and each block passed, I feel the heavy weight start to lift bit by bit until I no longer feel like I'm sinking. Part of what buoys me are my impressions of Dean the last few days . . . his determination for me to talk to the lawyers so I can get some grip, no matter how weak, on the sheer wrongness of my abuse, and then his steadfastness in holding me up when my emotions took me down. He's turned out to be my champion, instead of my harshest critic.

I realize after walking aimlessly for so long that I've ended up in an unfamiliar neighborhood, but I'm surprisingly okay with that. It makes me wonder about what life could be once Dean and I get jobs and move away to start our new life, hopefully together.

As I pass each home and apartment complex I try to imagine where we'd end up and how it could be different than our years of only being roomies. We could even have a one bedroom since that would be all that we need.

When I reach the corner after a block of small houses, I decide to take a right and up ahead, on South Temple Street, I see the grand Madeleine Cathedral. We learned in class that the Romanesque structure was built near the turn of the 20th century and the design is classic and heavily detailed. Slowing my gait a bit, I take in the intricate architectural detail, sandstone surface, and tall spires with gargoyles.

It looks like it's weathered these many decades just fine.

When I'm finally in front of it, I find my legs moving without my prompting, bringing me toward the dramatic front entrance. Curling my hand around the smooth brass handle of the tall, carved door, I pull on it. It smoothly opens up, spilling light from the outside onto the dark oak floors.

I pause for a moment and then step inside the vestibule. The silence reminds me of my altar boy days where we were instructed to be silent more often than we were allowed to talk.

I keep walking until I'm in the nave, and I lower myself onto a pew as I gaze up at the altar in the sanctuary. Colors are scattered around me from the late afternoon sun beaming through the stained glass windows. I take a deep breath, and then another, a calm feeling settling over me as I remember the early days at our church, when being there gave me a sense of community. It had been just Mom and me, so our time at St. Thomas brought me around families with dads and loads of siblings. It was both envy inspiring, and fascinating.

I remember helping big-hearted Mrs. Fortuno at the bake sales, and how she rewarded me with her amazing Italian cookies and pastries. I was also chosen to be the special helper by my *Bible* class teacher, Miss Rambosa, who I had a boyish crush on. She was pretty with long, wavy hair that I'd always wanted to touch even though I didn't dare. Church was a happy place for me, until I got older and caught Father Ryan's attention, and then it wasn't.

Dean didn't know it, but he became my sanctuary once Father Ryan's abuse started. We hung out playing video games and raced our bikes all over the neighborhood, burning off my fear and fury during the golden hours we were together.

Returning my focus to the present, I fold my hands in prayer and press the edges of my palms onto the top of the pew in front of me, lowering my head until it meets my hands. I take a deep breath and try to focus on the feelings of solace that church once gave me.

I think of Dean, and I whisper a prayer of thanks to God for bringing him into my life. Taking a deep breath, I imagine him back at the house waiting for me. Could I really be that bad of a person if someone like him is by my side?

My mom used to read prayers to me every night and one of my favorites, The Prayer of Aspiration, comes back to me, and I whisper it into my folded hands, hoping God is listening.

I have broken out of my prison, but I am still not free.

I have been comforted in weakness, yet I have too little strength.

I have experienced the warmth and depth of human friendship, but I am not fulfilled.

I seek, I give, I possess and yet I yearn

It is You I seek, O Lord, my unlosable friend forever.

Fill me up, Lord—complete me—

I will be restless . . . until I rest in You.

For a brief moment a sense of profound peace settles over me, but then my ears prick as I hear slow footsteps down the aisle. I burrow my face farther into my hands and take deep breaths.

The footsteps stop and I slowly lift my head up. A priest with a full head of silver hair and kind eyes nods toward me before smiling. "Are you all right, young man?"

I've seen a priest smile like that before and it was a mask hiding the devil inside him.

Remaining silent, I stare at his clerical, white collar, and then my gaze travels up to his expression that is shifting to one of concern. "I sense you're suffering. Would you like to talk?"

I feel my eyes grow wide and I blink nervously. Even though he doesn't look anything like Father Ryan, the bile is still rising into my throat and my heart is starting to race.

He stands silently for a moment observing me, and then takes a step closer a places his hand on my shoulder. In a calm, gentle voice he asks, "Would you like to confess?"

Panic bites into me like fangs and the venom races through my veins as I jerk away from his touch. A moment later I rise from the pew, rushing to the opposite side of the bench and up the aisle. I begin to run by the time I reach the vestibule and I shove the cathedral door open so hard that the brass handle hits the outside wall.

Stumbling down the front stairs, I hit the sidewalk running at full speed, having no idea where I'm heading, just a fierce instinct to flee from a danger I can't comprehend. Every one of my footsteps pounding the pavement confirms that I need to run fast from what scares me most.

It's a good thing I had years of sprinting practice playing tennis and I'm several blocks away before I even slow down to a jog. By now the sun has fallen and the shadows are long as they darken into night. Everything becomes menacing, every foreign sound makes my heart pound harder.

I have a vague sense that I'm losing my grip on reality, like I've stumbled into a horror film and the demons are about to descend over me. Every street I pass confuses me more until I finally slow down and realize I'm in an industrial area of old factory buildings and fenced-in work yards. As I turn around and around trying to figure out where I am I feel my phone vibrate in my pocket. Digging it out, I see that Dean has called three times.

With a shaky finger, I touch the screen to return his call. He jumps in before I can say his name.

"Jason, have you walked the entire city or something? Why haven't you answered my calls? What are you doing?"

"I don't know," I reply with a shudder.

There's a long, weighted pause. "You don't know?"

I can hear the concern in his voice.

"Dean," I whisper.

"Where are you, Jason? I'm going to come get you."

"I don't know."

"Fuck! You're outside, right?"

I nod but don't speak. His voice is the only thing grounding me.

"Listen to me . . . if you're outside, walk to a corner and tell me the names of the two street signs."

"Okay."

In the distance I see a corner and I numbly move toward it. It's almost completely dark now.

"Traction and Grand," I mumble before trying to lick my lips, but my mouth is completely dry.

"Traction and Grand? Where the fuck is that?"

"I don't know . . . some industrial area."

"Oh Jesus. I'll Mapquest it. You'll wait for me, right?"

I drop down until I'm sitting on the curb and I rub my face with my hands.

"Jason, damn it!" he calls out. "You'll wait for me, promise me."

"I promise."

"I'm on my way."

Dean. 43

I GRIP MY PHONE TIGHTLY as I type in the information and wait for the map to download. Why the hell did I let him go off? I knew something like this could happen. Firing up the engine, I gun my car out of the parking lot as I focus on the directions bleating out of my phone.

My heart is pounding furiously and I try to calm down. If I go off right now it will only make things worse for Jason. He needs me with my shit together since apparently he's lost his.

It only takes about fifteen minutes to find the intersection Jason indicated. It's so dark that at first I don't see him before I realize that there's a figure hunched over on the curb. Pulling over I put the car in park, but leave the engine running.

I jump out and rush over to him, leaning over and grasping one of his shoulders. "JJ, what happened to you?"

He keeps looking down and just shakes his head mutely.

Yanking open the passenger door, I pull on his arm. "Come on, get in the car."

Once he's inside and I'm back in the driver's seat, I turn to him. "Where did you go that freaked you out so badly? Did something happen?"

"I went into Madeleine Cathedral," he whispers.

I press my lips together. A Catholic church is about the last place on Earth he needs to be going right now. "Damn JJ, why would you go there of all places?"

He grasps his knees tightly to stop his hands from shaking. "It's hard to explain. But when I stumbled upon it, I had the most overwhelming feeling to go inside and try to remember the earlier happy days I had at St. Joseph's."

"Okay . . ." I reply warily. "And then what?"

"I was feeling okay, but then a priest approached me as I was praying in the pews. I must've looked unsettled and I guess he was trying to help me, but when he touched my shoulder I freaked and ran out of the church."

Glancing over at him, I discover that his eyes look wild as he gazes straight ahead. His reaction sounds like a PTSD response, and it's no wonder. Reaching over, I place my hand over his. "Well, you're safe now and we'll be home soon."

Home. I realize it sounds weird that I suddenly referred to our apartment as *home*, but now that we have become more than best friends the word seemed to fit where it didn't quite before.

Once inside, he collapses onto the couch and I realize that he's shivering. So I pull a blanket off my bed and wrap it over his shoulder, then get him a shot of whiskey before I take one as well. He shudders after he throws it back, but then immediately asks me for another and I comply.

I ask if he wants me to heat up what's left of the Chinese food I ordered while he was out getting lost and he shakes his head.

"You need sleep," I offer.

He nods.

Leading him into my bedroom I slowly undress him while he wobbles, unsteady on his feet. I need him close tonight. After lowering him onto the bed I slide the blankets over him. Quickly taking off my clothes I join him, pulling him close to me so his head is resting on my chest. This is how we fall asleep, and as the hours pass we wind our limbs together until we're almost one.

Jason . 44

IT'S LATE MORNING WHEN I wake up with Dean slowly stroking my back. His voice is warm and comforting. I can't think of anything more soothing and it gives me hope that today will be a better day.

"JJ, you've got to wake up and eat something. You must be starving."

I blink my eyes open and take him in—all messy hair and stubble along his sharply defined jaw. My heart swells as he studies my expression like he's making sure I'm all right. I love everything about this man.

Right then I determine that today I'm going to push all of yesterday's crap away and just focus on being completely in the here and now with my boyfriend, like we were before I got that letter from the lawyers.

He nods toward the bedside table. "Look, I brought you some coffee, juice, and a bagel. Eat it."

I let out a laugh. "Yes, sir."

He settles next to me on the bed, with his back against the headboard. Reaching for his coffee tumbler, he takes a long sip.

"Aren't you eating?" I ask before downing half the glass of juice and taking a big bite of the bagel.

"Already ate a while ago. I asked you if I could bring you anything then but you were gone to the world."

I rub the sleep out of my eyes. "I was so fucking tired."

"Well then, I'm glad you slept so much." Smiling at me, he runs his fingers through my hair. "I'm going to take a shower . . . it won't take long. Do you need anything else right now?"

"No, I'm good." I give him a smile so he knows I'm okay, and that today's going to be different. "Thanks, Dean."

He grins widely. "Sure."

While Dean is showering I keep my mind focused on the good stuff, like how he's stood by me through all this crap. I start wondering what it would be like if we took a vacation together, going someplace where we didn't know anyone and could just be together freely with no restraint.

He's not in the bathroom for long, and when he returns he refills my coffee before settling back on the bed.

I turn to gaze at him as I trail my fingers down his arm. "Why are you so good to me?"

He shrugs. "I don't know. You're all right I guess." He bites back a smile. "You're easy on the eyes, too."

"I bet it's the hot sex, isn't it?" I narrow my eyes at him with an exaggerated sexy look.

He rolls his eyes. "Yeah, I brought you a bagel because you're so good in bed."

Smirking, I take the last bite of the bagel. "See, I knew that's why. I bet you're expecting an after-breakfast blow job."

"Ha!" he huffs. "If that's how it works, you'll get breakfast in bed every day."

"I'm that good!" I tease.

"You've got talent, JJ. No need to brag about it. But can we change the subject? My cock is waking up, convinced that it's going to be in your mouth soon, and I'm not up for walking around with a stiffie all day."

"Let me see," I whisper. I look down at his gym shorts and sure enough that nylon fabric is perfectly sculpted around his big, hard dick. He lifts his T-shirt up a couple of inches so the outline of his erection is in full view.

"Damn, Dean."

"There's something about you. I just think about anything sexual with you and I'm instantly rock hard." Reaching down, he grips his shaft over the shorts and takes a deep breath.

"Does that feel good?" I ask, my morning wood starting to tent the sheet up.

He swallows hard as he nods and strokes himself slowly.

After pushing his hand away, I feel my way up his shaft from base to tip and then down again. "Take your shorts off, Dean," I say, my voice husky from the leftover sleepiness.

"Maybe we shouldn't do this? You had a rough day yesterday."

"Yeah, but this makes it better," I grumble. "Take your shirt off, too."

He gives me a long look, but then yanks his shirt over his head and slides down on the bed to pull off his shorts. His cock springs up, and the sight of him makes my mouth water.

"So fucking sexy," I gasp as I slide my fingers around his shaft and squeeze.

He pulls me closer, so I lean into him and start to suck his nipple while I stroke him.

He lets out a low, raw groan. "Fuck, yeah."

"You like that?" I rise up and take his other nipple between my teeth.

"I like everything you do to me."

"I'm glad, 'cause it's the same for me."

"Speaking of which . . ." He reaches down and palms my hard-on that's lifting the bedsheet. "Wanna sixty-nine again? That was so hot."

I shake my head while I suck on his nipple harder. "No, baby, this is about you." I need him to know how much he means to me, so I start kissing my way across his abs while I cup his balls in my hand, massaging them.

Taking time to pleasure every inch of him, I circle my tongue around his belly button and scrape my teeth along his hipbone before leaving a trail of kisses down to the base of his cock. I don't just want him to understand that he's everything to me, I *need* him to know he's all I'll ever want.

He's already writhing under me and it makes me feel great.

"Please," he moans as my teasing continues. "I need your mouth on me."

"Like this?" I whisper, barely skimming my lips over his cockhead.

He lifts his head and gazes at me intensely. "Stop torturing me."

"You're going to have to be patient," I say as I push my sheet off and crawl over him, settling down on top of him until our chests meet and our hard cocks rub together. He spreads his legs apart so I can settle down between them. I cradle his face in my hands as I gaze down into his eyes. He returns it with an intense stare as his chest rises and falls under me, his hips rocking so that friction builds.

I kiss him lightly at first, but when his hands grab my ass, my tongue slips into his mouth and our kiss amps up so fast for a moment I don't even know where I am. All I know is that the most gorgeous man is under me doing all kinds of dirty things, like sliding his finger between my cheeks and teasing my hole.

"I'll need to fuck you if you don't blow me soon," he warns, his voice tense and gruff.

Sliding off him, I reach over and pull the bottle of lube out of the drawer. "Just for that you're getting finger fucked while I blow you."

As I snap open the bottle and start lubing him up, he growls as he folds his arms behind his head so he can watch me. "When did you get to be such a dirty boy, JJ?"

I lube my finger and gently ease it inside of him. "Maybe I always was one, just waiting for you to come around so we could be dirty together." I look down and watch as I pump my finger in and out of him. His cock throbs and bobs over his abs each time I push inside of him. I curl my finger and he lets out a raw groan.

"Oh fuck, that's it. Right there."

I stroke the spot again while leaning over, and lick his cock from base to tip. "Do you think I'm a slut?" I ask, not even sure where that question came from. I plunge my finger into him with more force and suck the head of his cock so he lifts his hips right off the bed.

"Fuckkkkk."

"Well?" I demand.

Letting out a tense laugh, he pushes my head down so his cock fills my mouth. "Yeah, you're a filthy slut," he growls between pants and then he grins. "Suck harder, slut."

Even though I've prompted all of this, there's something about his words and the way he's pushed me down over him that sets me off. I'm not even being careful as I finger fuck him but he doesn't seem to mind. I've sent him to a wild place and I don't think he's coming down until he gets off.

With two fingers now inside of him, and my other hand pumping the base of his dick while my mouth gets fucked, I start to actually feel dirty. It's as if I was just branded with the word filthy slut, and it's jumbled up my mind and emotions so I try to just focus on getting him off.

His fingers wind into my hair and tighten, jerking me down faster, and I close my eyes and let him take me.

"Oh that fucking mouth of yours is making me crazy. I'm gonna explode if you keep sucking me like that." He's panting and his chest and face are flushed.

I moan around his stiff cock and it throbs in response. "Give it to me," I demand before swallowing him in deep.

A minute later he curses loudly as his cock jerks and then shudders violently while his come fills my mouth.

I swallow everything as he rides it out, then tries to catch his breath.

"Jesus, JJ, that was crazy hot."

Settling down, I'm at his side feeling his heart pound as he wraps his arms around me. "Good," I whisper. "I wanted to make you feel great."

He strokes me. "Want me to return the favor?"

"No thanks. Actually, can we just lie here a bit? I want you to keep holding me."

"Sure," he says as he pulls me into a hug and closes his eyes.

We lie silently in each other's arms long enough that I'm pretty sure Dean is falling back asleep when I gently shake him. "Didn't you say you had a project meeting before lunch with your group?"

He sits up. "Damn, my mind went blank after that epic orgasm. Thanks for reminding me." Sliding off the bed, he pulls on his clothes and glances at the clock. "I better jump in the shower. I still have enough time."

I cock my head. "Hey was that our doorbell?" We fall silent to listen. This time we both hear the ring.

"Yeah. Maybe it's our landlord. He said something about picking up the rent checks in person today since he's going out of town. I'll get it."

"Thanks. Let me know when you're out of the bathroom."

He nods and steps out of his room, closing the door behind him.

Dean. 45

I'M IN A BLISSFUL HAZE as I shuffle to our front door. *Damn.* JJ is giving me the best sex of my life. I'm pretty sure I'll never be able to give him up.

I shake my head realizing that the thought of sticking with him as his lover and boyfriend long term doesn't even freak me out anymore.

Unlocking the door, I pull it open, but as soon as I see her face my blissful feeling is gone.

"Julie!" I'm sure my expression reveals how startled I am as I nervously run my fingers through my messed-up hair. I can only imagine what I look like to her, all freshly sexed-up and unshaved.

She looks bewildered the longer we stand there until she finally speaks. "Well, that's a strange greeting. Hello to you, too. Aren't you going to ask me in?"

I jerk the door open wider. "Oh damn! Yes, of course. You just surprised me. Come in."

I'm so used to Jason's height now that I'm strangely surprised by Julie's petite frame. She barely reaches past my chin. Her long, blonde hair is swept smoothly over her shoulders, and she looks perfectly put together as she always did. Her wide brown eyes study me.

"You got my texts, didn't you?" Her gaze looks confused or maybe irritated.

"The one about you moving back? Oh yeah, and there was one about a dinner." My expression gets sheepish. "I forgot to answer that one . . . sorry about that. There's so much going on."

When she steps inside my gaze follows her and I feel shitty that the apartment is such a mess. Jason and I just threw stuff down when we got home last night. I start to move some of the most obvious stuff, like taking my plate from the Chinese dinner to the kitchen.

"So you still live with Jason?" she asks, noticing his tennis stuff.

"Yup." I try to sound low-key but the mention of Jason freaks me out. He's in my bedroom right now with no idea of what's happening out here.

"Does he have a girlfriend yet?" She's trying to sound nonchalant but I can hear a faint tone of irritation in her voice.

"Nope," I answer.

Holy hell . . . if she only knew what's really going on.

She focuses back on me. "Well, it's good to see you. Can I have a hug?"

"Sure." I gingerly wrap my arms around her and give her a quick squeeze. She smells good and memories come flooding back to me. She looks good, too. I'm glad to see she's taken care of herself but despite all the positives I'm surprised that I'm not feeling excited to see her again. There's someone else on my mind and he's just down the hall.

When I pull away I give her a thumbs up. "Hey, congrats for scoring a job already. You're the first person I know that has. That's a big fucking deal."

Her smile grows wide. "Thanks, Dean. I'm very excited about it. And I know you'll be surprised to hear it, but I'm really happy I'm coming back. I've missed it here . . . and I've missed you."

Oh damn. What the hell do I say to that? I've missed you too? I sure did when she first left, but now I hardly ever even think of her. "Me too," I lie and then immediately feel shitty about it.

"So is Jason on campus at one of the design labs?"

My stomach starts churning. "Um . . . actually, no. He had a late night last night and he slept in. He's probably still asleep."

She purses her lips. "Well, I'd like to say hi to him. I know we didn't always get along but I want to have a fresh start with everyone here. Can you see if he's awake so I can say hi?"

Damn! Julie knows which room is my bedroom and to get Jason I'd have to go in there. After a moment of panic I realize that if I get her to sit down by the TV she won't see what door I open to get JJ. I make a quick scan of the living room area to make sure there aren't any random condom wrappers lying around and then point to the armchair. "Here, have a seat and I'll go see if he's up."

She nods and sits down, setting her purse down on the floor.

Rubbing my sweaty palms down my shorts, I head down the short hall. Quietly opening the door to my room, I slip inside and shut the door quickly behind me.

Jason has his boxers pulled up and is sitting on the edge of the bed with a startled expression. "What's going on out there?" he asks.

I wave my arm toward the door and I can feel my eyes bugging out. "It's Julie."

"She's in our apartment? She's here?" he asks in a hoarse whisper. All the color instantly drains from his face.

I nod frantically. "Yes. And she wants to say hi to you."

His eyes grow wide. "Say hi? But she hates my guts."

I rake my fingers through my hair over and over but I can't get a grip. "Some crap about wanting to have a fresh start."

"Fuck no. I don't want any fresh start with her. I want her to go back to wherever. Why the fuck is she still here?" He jabs his hand toward the door.

"I don't know. Just come out and say hi and I'll get her to leave." Opening my drawer, I throw a pair of clean jeans and a newer T-shirt at him . . . one Julie wouldn't have seen.

I figure Jason's going to refuse, but he stands and starts to get dressed. I'm guessing he wants to see for himself what she's really about. For a moment, I wonder if he's going to do something crazy like out us, but then I stop myself knowing he wouldn't do that to me.

He zips the fly and nods at me with a dour look like he's going for a root canal or something. "Let's get this bullshit over with."

I feel nauseous as I pull the door open.

"Hey, look who I found," I say with a false casual tone as I gesture back to JJ.

His hands are jammed in the jean's pockets and he keeps a distance. "Hey Julie."

Smiling, she quickly stands up. "Hey, Jason. How've you been?"

He shrugs. "Pretty good. Busy with school and stuff. You know how it is."

She nods. "I do. And Dean says you don't have a girlfriend. But knowing you I'm sure you're still having lots of fun." She winks at him.

What the fuck is she up to commenting about stuff like this with Jason? To make it even stranger I feel a weird sense of jealousy at what she's implying.

Jason rubs his hand over his stubble-covered jaw and then glances over at me, then back to her. "Oh yeah, don't worry about me. I'm having some serious fun."

"Great!" Julie says. She used to refer to JJ as a man-whore, so I don't buy her enthusiasm for his proclamation one bit.

I clear my throat nervously. I'm not sure how much of this I can take.

Jason scowls at me. "Hey, didn't you say you had a meeting with your project group about now?"

"Damn! Yes, thanks for reminding me." I glance over to Julie with an expectant look. "I should go."

Disappointment briefly clouds her happy expression. "Sure, okay. But you're coming to dinner tonight, right?"

"Dinner?"

"Remember, that was one of the texts I sent. It's at Marinello's at seven."

I look over at Jason. "Can Jason come, too?"

Julie looks perplexed. "Well the reservations are for 8 and we have 4 couples, but I'm sure if I call they can add a chair and make it nine." We all know she's being polite; at least Julie is classy that way.

Jason narrows his eyes. "No, that's okay. I already have plans," he says, directing his focus on me. "But thanks anyway."

Her expression brightens up again. "Okay then, well another time for sure."

I let her out the door, mumbling about seeing her later, and once the door is closed, I shut my eyes tightly and press my forehead to the door.

Fuck.

Fuck.

Fuck.

When I step back toward Jason he's giving me a frosty look I've never seen before as he slowly pulls my T-shirt over his head and hands it to me. He follows by doing the same with my jeans. "Have fun tonight," he says with an acidic tone before turning and walking toward his room.

Following him, I reach out and grip his shoulder. "Jason—"

He shakes me free. "Don't touch me, asshole."

"What the fuck?"

He turns back to me. "I knew you'd never tell her about us, but going with her to a 'couples' dinner' and then inviting me along? Do you even know how fucked up that is? If this is how this is going to play out now that she's back, I'm over and out."

I slap my hand hard on the wall next to his head. "Damn, JJ! That isn't fair. She just fucking showed up here with no warning and threw me off-guard."

"Well if you'd dealt with her goddamned texts this wouldn't have happened. You could've declined the dinner when she first texted you about it."

My head falls to my chest as I try to think about what to say. I know he's right and I feel like shit about it.

"We'd talked about going to the movies tonight, Dean. But I guess you forgot all about that."

"We'll go tomorrow night," I respond with a frantic tone. "It'll be another 'date night' okay?"

His eyes are empty, completely dead of any expression or feeling. "Don't fucking bother. Looks like you've got a *real* date tonight."

He turns on his heel and is in his bedroom with the door locked before I can even register what's just happened.

I gently rattle the handle and lean into the door. "Come on, Jason, let's talk about this. Please."

Despite my repeated pleas, all I get back is a profound silence. I glance down at my watch and realize I'm already ten minutes late for our team meeting. Feeling like complete shit knowing Jason is still upset, I slip on my shoes, grab my backpack, and head out the door.

Jason . 46

WHEN I SINK DOWN ON my bed I feel like I can't breathe and that my insides are collapsing. The feelings are intensified because I can still smell Dean's scent in the sheets and see his imprint in the loosely gathered blankets, the ravaged archeological site of yesterday's sex-filled morning. Dean's sudden absence after our intimacy and reunion with his ex is torturing me.

I have brief moments where I tell myself to see reason. Dean surely didn't know Julie would just show up at our place. Hell, he was fucking my mouth just minutes before she rang the bell. He was surprised and not thinking as he reacted to her. If he had been thinking, he would've made an excuse for not being able to go to the "couple's" dinner and he sure as hell wouldn't have tried to include me.

But a moment later my reasonable thoughts drift away like vapor into a dry breeze. He welcomed her into our place and treated me like nothing more than a roommate. Julie with the cute figure and adoring starburst eyes—Julie who left him, dumping him like refuse on the side of the road, and now she wants him back. I'm pretty sure I'm going to be the one left at the side of the road this time.

Maybe all of this experimenting Dean's been doing started because he felt sorry for me once he realized that I'd wanted him forever. He's a good guy and has always looked out for me, whether at a lawyer's office or when I was desperate to taste, kiss, and get fucked by him. But was any of it what he truly wanted? Yes, he's gotten into it, but if it can't be part of his life plan eventually he'll be walking away from what we have.

After lying motionless for God knows how long, and letting my mind go to all the dark places, I decide to get my ass up and take a shower before I flip out. The apartment is starting to stifle me and I'm sure I don't want to be here when Dean gets back. As it is, my memories of all my intimate times with him are shadows following me as I wander from room to room. I sorely wish I had someone to talk to about my terror of losing him and I think about texting Ramon to see if he's free, but he's not the right one to discuss my love problems with. I have no one. Dean was all I had . . . the only one who knows all my truths. What will I do without him?

Gathering up my laptop, I head to my favorite cloistered spot in the library where I'm shielded from everyone and everything. My original intent was to study for my upcoming Urban Planning exam to get my mind off things, but now that I've settled into my corner that's the furthest thing from my mind.

I open up my laptop and bring up the Google page. My dark mood knows no bounds and wraps around me tightly until I can barely breathe. Remembering Dean calling me a filthy slut and how that made me feel dirty even though I encouraged him, I do provocative searches, typing out "sexual deviant," "sexual humiliation" and "sexual abuse by priests." Each entry that I read is more unsettling than the last, but I can't seem to stop myself. If I'm unworthy of a man like Dean, maybe I should figure out the type of man I deserve, no matter how degrading. Maybe that is my destiny, my penance for submitting to my priest, for corrupting my straight best friend, for being so much less of the man I'd hoped to be.

Dean . 47

THAT AFTERNOON WHEN I RETURN to our apartment there's no sign of Jason. In some ways I'm relieved as I'm not sure I can handle how upset he is with me, but on the other hand, knowing he's in a fragile state I was hoping to see him and know he's all right. I've been worried since I rushed off to my team meeting.

Should I be surprised that he has no faith in me, thinking I'd abandon him as soon as Julie reappeared in my life? Does he not understand what our relationship means to me? He's under my skin now . . . possessing me. I've never had a raw hunger for anyone in my life like I have for him, and I wander through my days in a lust-filled haze remembering how I often wake up with his mouth on me, pleasuring and loving me. I get lost in memories of our midnight hours in bed as I fill his ass with my cock and watch him writhe under me. The fact that we've always been best friends and each other's greatest confidant makes it that much sweeter. Plain and simple, I've always loved being with him, just now it's in every way.

Around six I start feeling edgy and wonder if he's reached out to Ramon, who he all but abandoned once we let our protective guards down in our "new" relationship. He may be flipping out that I'm going to see Julie tonight, but *I* know that I'm not attracted to her anymore. She's as pretty as she ever was, but she isn't who I want . . . who I need.

But Jason can't say the same about Ramon. They were sucking each other's dicks just weeks ago, and if he gets together with him in his troubled state anything could happen. Ramon is a crafty bastard and makes no bones about going after what he wants.

I text Jason, trying to sound casual, but I get no reply. Frustrated,

I shower and shave and put on clean clothes, dressing a little nicer than usual considering the restaurant.

Right before I leave the apartment I try calling him but the phone goes right to voicemail. I'm half furious and half panicked, worried that he's not okay. But if he is okay and just pissed off and fucking with me, I swear I'm going to kick his ass.

The restaurant is close by, so after I walk over to Marinello's, I check my phone. *Nothing.* My fingers tighten over the case before I shove my phone back into my pocket.

The scene at the restaurant is immediately awkward. It's like a time machine has hurled me backward to the time before Julie decided to change schools and move away from her life here, and away from me.

Keith and Celia, Erik and Beth, and James and Alicia were the couples we sometimes hung out with. They all look as startled to see me there with Julie as I feel. But Julie circles the group enthusiastically hugging everyone, apparently thrilled "beyond belief" to see us all together again. My stomach tightens as old memories of one of our last arguments about her going away, comes back to me.

It was a weeknight in early spring and we'd just slept together, but even though we both got off I could tell she wasn't really into it.

"What's going on?" I asked, when she returned from using the bathroom.

Instead of sliding back into bed and curling up against me as she usually did, she pulled on her T-shirt and panties then sat on the edge of the mattress.

"What do you mean?" she countered, trying to deflect the obvious.

"You feel really far away." As I say the words my stomach starts to cramp, an unsettling fear rolling through me.

She shrugs. "I don't know. I've been thinking . . ."

"And . . ."

"Where is all of this going?" She waves over the bed like I'm supposed to know what she fucking means.

"All of what?" I can feel my eyebrows knit together. I hate it when she gets vague and needy.

She smooths out the sheets on either side of where she sits. "I don't know, Dean. Are we building toward a future, or just staying together because we're lazy?"

"You calling me lazy?" I say in my Al Pacino voice. I'm hoping some comic relief lightens this conversation up, because I sure as hell don't like where it's going.

She wrinkles her nose and then narrows her eyes. "I'm being serious here."

Fuck.

"Well, I don't know what to say. We just got off and we're almost done with mid-terms, so things are looking pretty damn good from my viewpoint."

She groans and flops back on the bed, her shirt pulling up, revealing the tops of her creamy soft thighs. For a minute I think about getting her off again to lighten her mood, but then she starts back in with the relationship talk.

"I'm not happy."

It's a punch in the gut, because this doesn't sound like her monthly emotional rant . . . it sounds like something more.

"You're. Not. Happy," I repeat with a staccato tone.

There's a long silent pause. "No. I'm not," she says sounding flat, and lifeless.

"Well, what would make you happy?" I make a mental checklist that I better buy her some flowers and take her on a "date" next weekend if I expect her to get past this shit.

"I think we need a change," she proclaims, sitting back up straight.

"Really?" I'm not liking the direction this is going.

"Yes, really," she clips. "I've decided to make a change. I'm going to do my final year at UC Davis."

"In California?" I ask, not hiding the disbelief in my voice. She sounds like she's already planned everything and has been accepted. I can't believe she did all this without talking to me first. "So you're just telling me this shit now?"

"This is a decision I had to make alone and there was no point upsetting you if it wasn't going to happen. I've told you before that they have a great Communications program, and there's a professor there that I've heard awesome things about. You know I haven't been too impressed with the program here."

"But what about us?"

"Exactly," she quips. "What about us? We've grown stagnant, Dean. You know it and I know it, and maybe this year away will be just what we need to know if we're meant to have a future together."

"Are you talking about a long-distance relationship? Because I'm not okay with that."

She turns back to me and rolls her eyes . . . actually rolls her fucking eyes. "It's the sex, isn't it? You and that big cock of yours can't wait for me, can you?"

"Wait? Wait for what? If you go to Cali, you aren't coming back and you know it." The fury burns up my neck, and I suddenly feel like there's a vice squeezing my head. "And yes, my big cock and I like to fuck often and there's nothing wrong with that. It just means I'm a man. I thought you liked getting fucked often, too."

I cringe as soon as the words leave my mouth. That was a dumbass thing to say. I watch her lips curl back as she sneers at me. "Gee, thanks for making me feel like your whore. I know. As soon as I leave you're going to feel free to chase tail with your horndog roommate, Jason. I can see it now . . . you'll probably put a scoreboard in the kitchen to see who wins for the most fucks."

"Stop it," I growl. "Leave JJ out of this. Besides, I don't deserve this crap. If you're going to leave, just fucking leave, and don't make this about me. It's all you, baby, and I won't forget that."

Jumping up, she pulls on her jeans and turns back to me. "Thanks for your support, Dean."

"Yeah, and thank *you* for nothing!" I yell as she grabs her shoes and socks and storms out my bedroom door.

Almost a week passed before we spoke again. In an effort to

sort-of make up we tried to make peace with each other, but it was never the same between us.

Those old memories now feel like a lifetime ago . . . a time I never want to live again. I sure as hell didn't like myself then.

I look up at this current-day bubbly Julie. Is she new and improved, or just even more jaded and demanding for what her future should hold?

When the hostess takes us to our table, Julie already has it planned where we all will sit and it's annoying me. Who the hell does she think she is to just come back here and expect everything from the past to click right into place, like this last year hasn't even happened? I work to suppress all my anger, but it still manages to seep through my cracks. Realizing that I buried down a lot of fury when she left, now all those feelings have the opportunity to see the light of day.

I down my first drink quickly and it takes the edge off so that I'm not just sitting here grimacing. I order a second one immediately and ignore the look Julie gives me. At this point I'm in emotional survivor mode. When she gets up to use the restroom I check my phone again. *Still nothing from JJ.* If ignoring me is some kind of shitty revenge on Jason's part, it's working. I'm tied up in knots.

Julie soon returns to the table and takes command of the conversation again as the girls ask her all kinds of questions about UC Davis and life in California. Was Julie always such an attention hog? I guess as I listen to her I come to the conclusion that she always was. Maybe it didn't bother me then, but now it does. Funny how a new relationship can shine a light on what wasn't working with your old one. Jason always wants to know more about me than I can imagine anyone would care about. But that's just who he is.

When the torture is finally over and the bill has been paid, we head to the exit and say our good-byes on the sidewalk in front of the restaurant. Julie grabs my hand and doesn't let go as she assures each couple that she'll see them soon. I'm losing my patience as she clings onto me, even though I've explained that I have to get home for my long night of "studying" ahead of me.

When the last pair walks away, she turns and places her hand flat against the center of my chest. The sense of propriety in her gesture doesn't sit well with me.

"Are you okay, Dean?" she asks.

"I'm fine, it's just I'm behind with my work, so if I could get going . . ." I take a step back but she pulls me forward.

"You seem so distant tonight," she says softly.

"What did you expect?"

Reaching up, she slides her fingers inside the top of my shirt skimming my skin just under my collarbone, then sliding slowly down the front of my shirt and stopping just above my belt. The feeling is foreign and doesn't excite like it would have back when we were a couple. If that doesn't tell me what I'm really about now, I don't know what will.

"Being here with you tonight has been intense for me," she says in a quiet voice as she lightly brushes her fingers along the edge of my jeans. "For a long time I've wondered how it would feel to see you again." She takes a sharp breath. "And I've got to say, I'm still so attracted to you."

"Julie . . ." I mumble, feeling incredibly awkward. It's frankly weird as hell to have her coming onto me like this, when at one point I would have dropped to my knees for her, and yet now I have none of those feelings left for her.

She steps closer so that I can smell her familiar scent, a subtle perfume that intoxicated me the first time I met her. "Can I come home with you?" she boldly asks.

In that moment I know I have to break her heart and despite what I would have thought leading up to this moment, I don't relish this at all. But it has to be done, there's no point giving her false hope since seeing her has only made it crystal clear to me that Jason is the only one I want in my bed, and in my heart.

For some reason my next thought is about my parents. They were always nice and welcoming to Julie when they'd come and visit me while traveling on their speaking tours, but they never warmed up to her like they did with Jason. I remembered several months after she left Dad telling me that they had never thought she was the right person for me. At the time, I thought he was just trying to make me feel better so I could get over her, but maybe not.

I pull her into my arms and hold her tight, almost feeling sad for the loss of what we thought we would be. Now she's just a memory, a series of pages in the scrapbook of my life.

She reaches up and starts trailing kisses along my jaw, and I lean in close to her as I slowly rub my hand over her back in a fatherly-like way. "Julie, I'm in a relationship."

She pulls away, takes a step back, and blinks several times, her doe-eyes wide with disbelief. "You are? No one told me about that."

I nod. Of course no one told her about *that*, because no one but Cassie knew. And Cassie may be a handful, but she's not one for gossip.

"Is it serious?" she asks, like that would make a difference.

"Very."

"But—" she protests, not giving up the game.

"I'm in love." I swallow hard, picturing Jason in my mind. "So in love."

Her expression falls and she doesn't even try to hide it.

"Wow. I'm kind of shocked. I thought you'd wait for me."

"I thought you wouldn't leave," I retort. "But you know what? Not to sound like an ass, but I'm glad you did, because otherwise this may have never happened."

Her expression sinks into sadness and she steps back. "Well, that's wonderful . . . you deserve that, Dean. I guess that's it then. Good to know. I guess you didn't think I was worth waiting for."

I wish she didn't always say what she's thinking because some of that stuff sucks to hear. It makes me reply defensively. Besides, what made her think I'd know she'd be returning?

"And apparently you didn't think I was worth staying for, so I think we're even."

She gives me a weak smile. "Point made. Well, I guess this is it then. Not how I hoped it would go, but that's life. Will you at least walk me to my car? I'm in the lot."

"Of course," I say as I slide my arm over her shoulders and pull her close in the way a supportive friend would. "Let's go."

Jason . 48

I WAIT TO RETURN TO the apartment until almost seven so I know Dean won't be there. He's on his way to be reunited with his ex, eating fancy Italian food while they plan their future together. I'm not bitter.
Not at all.
Damn Julie and her gall to come back after a year and claim her man. He's mine now, so she can go fuck herself.

Besides, she's always been so damn perfect: a great student, cute as hell, nice—at least most of the time—and from what Dean told me once, she's good in bed.

After grabbing a beer out of the fridge, I sink down on the couch while wondering if I should encourage him to go back to Julie if he seems to be vacillating just to test him. I take several long swigs of beer as I try to imagine our conversation about it. Maybe Dean would be relieved to be done with this closeted lifestyle he wasn't ever intending to live.

I could lie and tell him that after seeing him with Julie, it became clear to me that I need to be with a man who isn't straight and that doesn't just skirt around being bi or gay, but is okay about it. Maybe I should tell him that I've decided that I want to give it a go with Ramon . . . that he's a man who knows what he wants and he wants me. I need to work toward an open relationship, not this bullshit where we go to parties and ignore each other, acting like we can't wait to pick up some random girl to take home.

So that scenario will leave him free to be with Julie, who from the looks of it earlier, is ready and more than willing to pick up immediately where they left off a year ago. But what if the test fails and he agrees to go back with her? Then I've just screwed myself out of a chance to fight for him, and that would make me the biggest idiot of all time.

I get up to use the bathroom and as soon as I pass through the door the smell of my favorite aftershave of Dean's hits me. Despite my bravado with my latest scheming, I have to grab onto the edge of the sink to steady myself. Closing my eyes, I picture him getting ready to meet Julie: Dean naked in the shower, the water cascading over his muscular shoulders and sculpted chest, shaving after with just a towel around his waist, slapping the back of his neck with aftershave and running his hands down his chest to spread the earthy scent.

My desire and need for him is almost visceral, taking over my body and mind, giving me urges to do crazy things like tracking him down and begging him to choose me, or telling Julie to her face that we're lovers as I'm pretty sure that would put an end to everything.

I open my eyes and gaze in the mirror. What I see reflected back is a desperate man about to lose the only person who every truly mattered to him. Gasping for air, I splash cold water on my face while admonishing myself to get a damn grip.

When I'm done in the bathroom, I return to the couch. Collapsing back into the cushions, I let out a deep breath. There's no way I can just give Dean up.

I need liquid courage, and someone, anyone, to tell me what I can do to hold onto him.

Suddenly an idea hits me. I think of Becky, and although she isn't a fan of Dean's, when she hears how things have progressed and how much I love him, maybe she'll give me good advice. I hope so at least, since there's really no one else to turn to.

Her phone only rings twice before she picks up.

"Hey Jason. Good to hear from you."

"Becky," I say with a shaky voice. My eyes tear up I'm so relieved she answered.

Her tone immediately changes to one of concern. "What's the matter?"

"Is there any way you could meet me? I'm freaking out."

"Is this about Dean?"

"Yes-s-s," I stutter. "I really need—"

"Don't worry. Of course I'll meet you. I have a party to go to, but that can wait."

"Thank you," I say quietly. "Thank you so much."

"Just tell me where. I can be out of here in five minutes. I've already gotten ready for the party."

A crazy idea comes into my head but I can't fight off the impulse. "Let's meet at Hugo's on Third. Right across from Marinello's."

"See you soon," she replies.

I've got a table by the window and I'm nursing a beer when Becky approaches me. I almost don't recognize her. Normally she looks like she pulled on the only clean thing that was piled at the bottom of her closet, but tonight she has on a nice outfit and a little make-up.

"Hey," she says, giving me a warm hug before slipping into the chair across from me.

"Hi. Thanks so much for coming." I give her a smile. "You look good."

"Thanks. I'm trying to push myself to be more social."

"Well, you're off to a great start."

I wave the waitress over so Becky can order. She asks for one of those fruity blended drinks, but with no rum.

"So virgin?" the waitress asks.

Becky blushes and nods. As soon as the waitress walks away, she turns to me with a concerned expression. "So what's happening with Dean?"

Sighing, I gaze out the window. "We've been spending a lot of time together."

She seems confused. "But you've always spent a lot of time together."

I can feel my face flush hot as I nod. No point in not being honest with her.

"I'm talking about time in bed . . . together."

"I see." She stirs her drink with her colored straw. "Isn't that what you've always wanted? You've had a thing for him forever."

Nodding, I swallow the lump in my throat, realizing that statement couldn't be more true.

"So what's the problem?"

"You remember his girlfriend, Julie? The one who transferred away last year?"

"I remember you telling me about her. Wait, isn't she the pretty blonde that I met at your birthday party?"

"Yes, that's her."

"And I remember you were happy when she moved to California."

"She *was* in Cali, but unfortunately for me, she's back."

"What? No!"

"Yes. And Dean is with her right now at a reunion dinner."

"But—"

I turn toward the window and gesture widely. "And they're right across the street."

She glances up at me with a worried expression. "I've got to be honest with you . . . I don't think it's a good idea to be here right now."

I lean over the table and press my face in my hands. "I know, but I'm freaking out. I'm crazy for him, and I just can't lose him. Although I know Dean cares about me, and really seems into fucking me, what if I'm not enough to hold onto him? What if he can never come to terms letting people know that he's *with* me?"

She leans back in her chair, her eyes wide. "Wait a minute. He's fucked you? That's a lot more than two guys just messing around. Has he done it more than once?"

"A bunch of times. He even let me fuck him."

Her expression suddenly looks hopeful. "Well, that changes things. If he's doing all that with you, I can't imagine it's so simple to just go back to his ex. Have they been talking or making plans since she left?"

Her line of questioning is making me feel hopeful. "No. As a matter of fact, she texted him a couple of weeks ago about tonight, and he forgot to even get back to her. She had to show up at our apartment this morning to push him to come."

"Okay, that's saying something. And you guys have always had something special between you, even before the sex, so there's every chance that she's never going to satisfy him now. You must know how gorgeous you are . . . and you're a passionate guy with a heart of gold. Maybe he'll come around to being okay with being 'out' in the world. Just give him some time. Meanwhile, don't do anything stupid."

"I wish it were that simple," I sigh.

"Look, I've always been very aware of how you've felt about Dean. You're devoted to him."

My heart aches at her revelation. Devoted is the single word that best describes how I much I care about Dean.

Her expression looks a bit more hopeful.

"What are you thinking?" I ask her.

"That love is love is love," she says. "And I want to believe that true love conquers all."

The corners of my mouth turn up and realize it's the first time I've smiled since Julie showed up at our apartment. I place my free hand over Becky's and squeeze gently. "Thank you so much for meeting me."

I can see her smile in her eyes. "Of course. You'd do the same for me."

The conversation finally shifts off me, and Becky starts telling me about her promotion at the bookstore when the waitress interrupts us, and my gaze skims the view outside. I notice a small group of college-aged couples that I recognize walk out of Marinello's. The last couple to emerge are Dean and Julie . . . and they're holding hands.

I practically drop my beer and Becky quickly takes the bottle out of my hand, sets it on the table, and squeezes my fingers. "Jason, what's wrong?" She turns her focus on where my gaze is fixed and then a second later she gasps. "Oh, damn. That's them, isn't it?"

"Look at the happy couple," I say quietly, my voice breaking at the last word.

While still holding hands, they're sharing farewells with each of the other three couples. It's like an episode of that old show, *Friends*, but this isn't TV, it's my real life. When it's finally just the two of them left in front of the restaurant, she turns toward Dean and places her hand on his chest with a familiarity that I'd only imagine a current lover would do. She steps closer and they appear to be sharing words, and then suddenly he pulls her tightly into his arms.

"Damn," Becky says with a sigh. When I look over, her expression is deeply troubled, aligning with the hopelessness I'm drowning in.

When I see Julie kissing his perfect neck, undoubtedly smelling manly and fuckable Dean with that aphrodisiac cologne of his, I feel my beer, now a foaming acid, slowly working its way back up my throat.

"Do you see that?" I mumble. "Just like that, Becky. Just fucking like that." I'm suddenly so dizzy and numb that I'm feeling like I could pass out.

"Oh, JJ," she says with doe eyes, rubbing her hand up and down my forearm. "I'm so sorry." She looks back across the street and squints. "Where are they going?"

I bite back the bile as I watch Dean pull Julie close under his arm and walk them around the corner, presumably to the parking lot where her chariot awaits for them to ride off into the sunset together.

"Probably to her place so he can fuck her without his gay lover stirring up trouble."

"Maybe you should go confront him so he knows what you saw. You two are involved and he owes you an explanation. Everything needs to be out in the open . . . no secrets."

I look over at Becky, hoping she can see the panic in my expression. "No! If I confronted him right now I'd probably lose it completely. Do you understand how desperately I love him?"

She stares at me for what feels like forever and she reaches up and catches in her fingertips a tear that's started to slide down my cheek. "I do now," she whispers.

"I can't watch him go off with her. This is killing me."

"What are you going to do?" she asks, looking concerned.

"I can't go back to our place. I have to figure something out."

She nods just as her phone pings. She looks down to read the text, and then sighs and frowns before slipping her phone away.

"What?" I ask, gesturing to where she pocketed her phone.

"Nothing." She shrugs.

"You looked upset."

"It's my girlfriend, mad I'm not at the party yet. But don't worry . . . this is much more important. Why don't we go back to my place?"

If I go to Becky's I'll probably lose it completely. I need a fucking distraction. Ramon's face pops into my head.

I reach over and take her hand realizing that she's been my lifeline tonight. "Thanks, Becky, you're amazing . . . but please go to the party. I'll call my friend, Ramon. He'll look out for me. I bet he can help me forget all of this for a while."

"Are you sure?" she asks, her brows knitting together. "Call him. I'm not leaving until I know you won't be alone tonight."

I fish my phone out of my pocket and with trembling fingers I hit Ramon's number on my contact list. He answers after just two rings.

"Well, well, well . . . and here I thought you erased me from your call list."

"Sorry, I deserve that," I mumble. "There's been a lot going on."

"With your *straight* roommate? I warned you that would only lead to heartbreak."

"Well, you were right."

"I see. So how are you holding up?"

"Not very good. Look, I know you don't owe me anything. I've been a shit friend . . ."

"More like a neglectful lover . . . it's not like we were besties or anything. You know I still want your ass," he says.

"Can you go easy with that stuff?" My voice cracks.

"Hey, you sound like hell. Are things really that bad?"

"Yeah, really bad. I don't want to be alone right now."

"I was about to head out for the dance club. I guess I could pick you up as long as you promise to try to have a good time."

"I promise."

"Good boy, now where the hell are you?"

Right after I end the call, I turn to Becky and nudge her. "Call your friend and tell her you're on your way."

She studies my expression like she sees through my attempt to be stoic. "Are you sure?"

"Yes."

Sighing, Becky retrieves her phone then punches a text out before meeting my gaze. "Will you call me tomorrow and let me know how you're doing?"

I nod. "Thank you, Becky. I'm not sure what I would've done if you hadn't met up with me."

"I just wish we would've met somewhere else," she replies, gesturing to where we saw Dean hugging Julie.

"I probably would have ended up here one way or another. In my gut, I needed to see what would happen if he didn't know I was watching."

She frowns and then pushes my hair out of my eyes. "It would've have been better if you didn't see them together like that."

"No. I had been creating this fantasy of my future, and it's best I know that it was all smoke and mirrors. It's time to get real."

I'm trying so hard to sound strong when inside I'm completely crumbling.

We walk out of Hugo's together and she stays with me until Ramon pulls up out front. I give her a big hug and she whispers in my ear, "Take care, Jason You deserve to be happy."

"Who's the girl?" Ramon asks after I slide into the passenger seat and close the door.

"My friend, Becky. I met her my first semester here."

He glances over at me. "Hmm, and where's Dean tonight?"

"With his ex-girlfriend."

Ramon lets out a low whistle. "Well, I'm glad you called. I know how to get your mind off all that troubles you."

"Really?" I ask, wishing I could believe him. Nothing is going to shake the image of Dean holding Julie out of my head.

I remain silent, staring out the window, trying to get a hold on my emotions. Ramon turns on the radio to Macklemore to drown out the silence, and starts rapping along loudly until he finally pulls into the club parking lot.

"You ready to dance?" he asks with a grin.

"I'm gonna try."

"Hey, how much did you drink tonight?"

I shrug. "Not that much. Why?"

He fishes in his jacket pocket. "I've scored some Molly. The real thing . . . good shit. What do you say?"

"Ecstasy? I didn't think athletes did stuff like that."

He shrugs. "We're off season. Come on, it will get you completely out of your head. It's such a turn on." After carefully pulling one of the capsules out of the plastic bag, he sets it into my open hand. He then pulls out another and drops it in his mouth and chugs down half the bottle of water sitting in the car's console.

I don't even hesitate. I mean, at this point, what the fucking hell do I have to lose? I follow his example, and finish off what remains of the water as the capsule tumbles down my throat.

He tucks the bag away into the inside pocket of his jacket and opens his car door. "Come on, let's go inside and get this party started."

Dean . 49

AFTER JULIE BUCKLES HER SEATBELT and gives me a forlorn look, I close her car door and watch her drive off. Feeling a weird jumble of regret for what might have been, mixed with relief that I've manned up and told her we don't have a future, I know I did the right thing as I start the walk back to our apartment.

It's good to have this time alone to process all the drama of the last few days. I've never seen Jason so close to his edge and it's worried the hell out of me. I'm anxious to tell him about my conversation with Julie knowing it will give him relief, and hopefully encourage him to trust me.

It's important he understands that I'm choosing *him*. I still don't think of myself as gay, but I'm willing to accept that I'm bi, even if I'm not ready to share that with the world yet. Because that saying *Love is Love is Love* is true. What I've come to understand is that what I feel for Jason *is* love, and our sex life is an absolute expression of that love.

Maybe this is the only man I'll ever feel this way about, but I know it's built on years of being best friends. That closeness allowed us to be vulnerable with each other and explore something I never would've imagined. I don't need to overthink it and try to force myself into some kind of box just so society can pigeonhole me. We are simply Jason and Dean. . . . best friends that got physical, and fell in love.

The last block of my walk home I break into a jog, feeling anxious to see him and know he's okay. We haven't been able to talk since he locked his door on me this morning. I hope he's calmed down.

But when I get upstairs I can feel that he's not in the apartment before I've even fully stepped inside. The place echoes with a deafening silence, a haunting empty feeling.

"Jason," I call out, hoping I'm wrong and that he's here.

I slowly move from room to room as I swallow the quiet chill that surrounds me, confirming that he isn't asleep or moping somewhere. Meanwhile, I try to push down my feeling of panic. He wasn't of a right mind earlier, where the hell has he gone?

I open his bedroom door and I wonder if he still has that old-fashioned address book his mother had given him. He's always been paranoid about not having a hardcopy back-up of important contacts. Maybe that irritating friend of his, Becky, knows where he is and I need that damn book to get her phone number.

Scanning the tops of his dresser and desk, I don't find anything. So I open a few drawers and dig around. When I get to the middle dresser drawer I'm surprised what I find and it isn't his address book. Instead it's a small, framed picture of us at Lake Coeur d'Alene, in the northern part of Idaho.

We were about fifteen at the time and my parents had brought Jason along on our family vacation. In the photo, we're sporting dark tans, and big grins, with our arms thrown over each other's bare shoulders, the picturesque lake glimmering behind us.

I'll never forget that week. We had the best time water skiing and playing foosball at the local arcade. I remember how it felt as if we were in a carefree bubble of sunshine, like we'd always be fun, crazy kids just looking to have a good time. My fingers tighten over the frame as a feeling of longing presses down over me.

When I start to set the frame back in the drawer I notice a green and yellow lanyard lying on top of an old sweatshirt.

Lifting it up to look at it more closely, I realize that I made this for Jason the first time I had to go to summer camp without him because his mom couldn't afford it. *Why the hell did he keep these things all these years, even taking them with him to college?* I'm gutted as my fingers tighten over the woven strip of plastic laces. Maybe I've always meant more to Jason than I realized.

Yanking my phone out of my pocket, I tap his number. The call immediately goes to voicemail and I feel my entire body tense up before

I leave my message. "Where are you, JJ? Don't do this to me, and shut me out . . . I really need to know you're okay. I need to talk to you."

After I end the message I keep speaking to him in my mind, picturing him so close that I can reach out and touch him. I do one more sweep of his room for the phone book but it alludes me. How can I find him and tell him my truth?

Jason, you need to understand how real all of this is for me. Come on, baby, please, please come home.

Jason . 50

I DON'T FEEL ANY EFFECTS of the drug at first, as I settle into a seat at a small table near the edge of the dance floor. Ramon goes to buy us a couple of drinks. I just sit back and listen to the music, letting it surge through me as I slowly rock my head to the pounding beat. I have a sense that he's gone a long time but I've started to relax and ignore the random guys who are checking me out. As a result, I'm so chill and in the moment that it doesn't even bother me that I'm sitting here alone with guys circling me.

The memory of Dean going off with Julie to rekindle things still burns me, but now it's like there's a frosted glass wall between us, making his image and the memory of them holding each other become fuzzy.

I focus back on the music and it feels synched to my heartbeat, surging so hard I can feel it in my head. When Ramon returns to the table every color in the room starts to look brighter and my focus falls in and out of sharpness. Despite being disoriented, a feeling hits me like none of my earlier upsets matter. Life is so fucking beautiful. Leaning back into my chair, I grin.

As he sets the drinks down he glances at me. "You're already tripping, aren't you?"

"This place is awesome," I announce. "We can just be who we're meant to be here." I lean forward and spread my arms out like they are rays of sunshine and I am the sun.

His narrows his eyes. "How much beer did you say you'd drank?"

"More than a shot glass could hold, less than a pitcher full." I laugh but I'm not really sure why.

Chuckling, he rolls his eyes. "Whatever, dude. You must be super sensitive to Molly."

I survey the happy crowd and then look over at Ramon who is watching the action on the dance floor. I start to wonder if I've ever told him that his muscular body is hot and totally turns me on. I'm already hard, and he hasn't even touched me yet. All of a sudden I have a blinding urge to fuck him. It's like I can't live another day until I take him. Reaching over, I start stroking his thigh. "You wanna go into the girl's room?" I ask in an unsteady voice.

"Not yet, cowboy. What do you say we dance first?"

I pout like a kid who had his toy taken away. "You aren't even high?"

Reclining on the bar stool, he slowly drags his fingers through his hair. "Don't worry, I'm getting there."

I can feel my heart racing and I start to tap my fingers on the table before I reach over and stroke the side of his neck. I want to lick and bite him along the thick muscles that run down into his Superman shoulders. Ramon notices me chewing on my lip as I gaze at him.

He chuckles. "I should have warned you that Molly amps up the sex drive. Not like you ever needed any amping up."

"I'm so hard right now," I say breathlessly. "Here, slide your hand over here so you can feel it."

His hand gropes me. "Damn, maybe I should have only given you half."

"Don't say that. I feel a million times better than when I called you. This is just what I needed." I throw back a swallow of the strong drink he brought me.

He grabs me and pulls me to the dance floor. "Let's get moving and burn off some of this energy."

I love being on this dance floor full of man-loving men. I like the way they move, their alluring smell, the direct way they stare at each other. I want to dance across the floor and touch and grope every one of them, but Ramon keeps reeling me in so I grope and touch him instead. It's cool to feel so free, like anything is possible . . . every feeling I have is good, and there's nothing in my world to be ashamed of.

I notice men watching when I dance up behind Ramon and wrap my arm around his chest and then start grinding my hard cock against his perfect ass. I smile at the onlookers as I lean over and kiss Ramon just above his ear, while grinding against his ass even harder. They smile back with lustful gazes.

I'm going to dance and fuck Ramon, and then dance again, over and over all night long until I get my fill of his sizzling Latino hotness. He is perfect. Everything is perfect. Life is perfect.

Dean has become a ghost to me, now transparent by his lies about loving me as he slowly floats out of my subconscious.

Ramon shifts me around and a moment later we're stealing kisses like thieves, my tongue invading his soft lips and warm mouth, wanting to do the same to other parts of him. I slide my hand down to feel him up where his erection is straining against his black jeans.

He thrusts into my hand, and chants into my ear so I can hear him over the loud music, "Hey, why don't we try out that sex club and have some serious fun?"

"How far away is it?" I ask. Because if it's a long drive that won't work with my desperate needs that he's fired up in me.

"Ten maybe fifteen minutes," he says as he grabs my ass and pulls me close.

Despite my euphoric mood, I pause for a second. Going to a sex club is a big deal. But a second later I remember that Dean is off having his fun, why the hell shouldn't I?

He made his choice, didn't he? I look up at the disco ball and the starbursts of light that it showers over the crowd. It makes me feel optimistic for some reason. Or maybe I'm just really fucked up.

"So, what do you say?" Ramon asks as he pulls me hard against him and kisses my jaw.

"Hell yes, let's go."

He doesn't hesitate as he pulls me outside, perhaps worried that if he lingers I may change my mind. He wraps his arm around my lower back. "This is going to be such a turn on, you sexy beast. And don't worry, I'll take good care of you."

When we get into Ramon's car in the parking lot I start groping him before he even has time to buckle his seatbelt. "Wow, dude," he says with a gasp as I start to unzip his jeans. "Who knew that Molly would unleash the sex fiend in you?"

His words send a flame up my spine. I feel like suddenly I've learned to fly with absolutely no fear of crashing. The sensation makes me bold. "Isn't sex awesome?" I ask, feeling both horny and warm and fuzzy toward Ramon.

He laughs. "Super awesome," he teases.

This is such a weird, happy high. A feeling of freedom comes over me, making me want to embrace every urge and desire flashing through me.

"See, I knew you felt like I do about it. That's why I wanna suck your cock," I say as I skim my lips over his crotch.

He spreads his legs wider and drops his car keys in the console. "Go ahead and be my guest."

He's hard as hell as I zip open his fly, and pull him free of his briefs. My mind starts imagining beyond this moment. "If I blow you, will you let me fuck you later?"

"Maybe," he says with a gasp as I lick up and down his shaft. I'm suddenly fascinated with his dick, the shape of it, how rock-hard it is, and the way it throbs in my grip. I study and tend to it like it's the first cock I've ever man-handled. I trace circles with the tip of my tongue around the head and look up to see him gazing at me with glazed eyes, as he softly moans under each breath.

"You really like giving head," he murmurs as he combs his fingers through my hair and pulls me down over him.

I nod while I bob over him, but my mind can't help but drift back to Dean and how he was the first man I truly loved going down on. I feel a kick in the gut to realize that I will likely never give him head again. In that moment, my rainbow-blurred, drugged-out bliss darkens, a dark shadow casting over my high and I slow down.

Despite the feeling, I try to refocus, but Ramon seems to sense that I'm distracted and he pushes me up. "Hey, man, I'm buzzing hard and I want to get there. Let's finish this up at the club, okay?"

I drag the back of my hand across my wet mouth. "Sure. Yeah, let's get there and see what it's all about."

He pulls himself together and when we're on the road he glances over at me. "So did you check out the link to their website that I sent you?"

"The Man Cave? Yeah, I checked it out. Seems pretty wild."

"I know. And they let students over eighteen in for free for the first three visits. But we've got to play it really cool there, all right? They don't allow drugs or alcohol."

My eyes grow wide with surprise. "Why not? That kind of place seems like where you'd need a drink most."

Ramon shrugs. "I guess when people are drunk or high they can get unpredictable."

"What bullshit! Screw that," I respond right as he pulls into the parking lot.

He pats the right side of his upper chest. "But they don't have to know about everything we do. I've got a small flask in here. We can be sneaky bastards and take a shot before the party gets started." He winks at me.

I imagine the warmth sliding down my throat and spreading through my body. "Sounds like a plan."

As we walk toward the entrance I note how subtle the place is from the outside. I'm sure anyone driving by has no idea about all the kinky stuff going on inside.

In contrast, as we pass through the entrance I realize that the inside is nicer than I expected from the shitty website pictures. In my hazy high I look at everything from an architect's perspective. The lights are low and there's an industrial feeling, but the layout and design is hip. They've used corrugated metal, polished cement, and chrome accents throughout the space. It's pure industrial and male in its vibe. The seating area near the front desk has a black leather couch and chairs.

The guy behind the desk has jet-black hair threaded with silver, a beard, tattoo sleeves running up his arms, and a nose ring. He's wearing an etched, black nametag that says Billy. But despite his hard look, Billy's professional and gets right down to business. He has us show our IDs, fill out release forms, gives us our locker keys, several condoms each, and a map of the place before asking if we have any questions.

Luckily, I can focus and do what he asks of us without a problem and Ramon almost seems like his usual self so we don't set off any red flags.

"What's the dungeon?" I ask, pointing to an area mapped out in the far corner of the building. I don't remember seeing it on the website and it sounds creepy as hell, but I'm curious.

"That area is for our fetish customers, mainly BDSM." He points his finger and areas sectioned off within the larger space. "These are individual rooms that Dom's rent for privacy with their subs. They're equipped with restraints and various paddles, floggers, and such. This is the open area where others can observe various forms of bondage play, and over here subs are punished or humiliated by club members . . . all consensual of course. There's no extra charge to go into the dungeon unless you get a private room." He glances over to Ramon and gives him a wink.

Humiliated? A sick feeling flares up in my stomach, but at the same time I realize I'm getting aroused. Something about being humiliated doesn't just resonate with me . . . it's turning me on. I don't know if it's the Ecstasy high, or that I'm so stripped raw that I'm craving something to bring me down, but my compulsion to go into the dungeon is strong.

After a few more questions for Billy, Ramon pulls me by the arm away from the desk. "What is up with you, dude? I had no idea you were that kinky."

"Have you ever been a submissive?" I ask, noticing that his pupils are blown out and he keeps chewing on his bottom lip.

"No way. I'd be a dom for sure if I was into that shit, but I play football, man, and believe me I take and give enough pain there. I definitely wouldn't get off on it." He studies me with knitted brows and narrowed eyes. "Would you get off on it?"

"I don't know. Maybe it's what I need right now."

"Nah, I don't think so. Don't make decisions like that when you're flying on Molly. You'll regret it later."

I nod half-heartedly because in my gut I'm not sure I care about regrets tonight.

As instructed by Billy, we go to the lockers first to strip down, wrap the supplied towel around our waist, and slip on the shower shoes. My high feels like it's getting hazier. Before I start disrobing, I watch Ramon undress with fascination at his compact muscular body and caramel-colored skin. I step up behind him and trace my fingers over the lines of his back, trailing my touch down his spine to the edge of his towel. He shivers and leans back into me.

"Your body is amazing," I murmur, as I lean closer.

"I'm glad you think so, babe. 'Cause it's yours tonight . . . and you're mine." He grabs my hands and pulls them around him in a backwards hug. When he releases me, he turns my direction. "Hey, quit checking out my fine ass and strip down."

I'm starting to feel nervous as I pull my T-shirt over my head.

Ramon brings over two little cups with water from the cooler which we knock back before he sneaks them into his locker and refills them with shots of vodka. I'm dizzy for a minute after downing my oversized shot of rocket fuel, but once I get my bearings, the club suddenly takes on a new look. As Ramon grasps my hand and pulls me along, the place looks deviously dark and wild, like it's an exotic vampire lair or something equally wicked.

As we keep moving I note that all the walls are painted a matte black, and with the low lighting you really feel like you're in a cave . . . or maybe a den of iniquity. It's tripping me out.

It's still feeling surreal that I'm even here. Maybe my new life is about to become a dark adventure. I've never pictured myself as a gleeful gay guy soaring over a rainbow on a unicorn's back.

When we get into one of the front sections of the play area the first thing I notice is the long wall with holes cut into it. At the far end some guy is on his knees at a bench, with his face up to the hole. "What's he doing?" I ask Ramon.

"Damn, Jason. Don't you know anything about being gay? Those are glory holes. You go on the other side and stick your dick through so someone will suck you off."

"Really?" I wonder who thought up that idea. Judging from the number of holes it must be a popular thing.

A group of guys approach the area just as Ramon leans into me. "I'm going to try it. Watch and see what happens."

Wow. That didn't take him long. "Okay, sure," I reply as he rounds the corner around the wall and disappears.

One of the younger looking guys from the group is checking me out right as Ramon reappears pressed up against one of the glory holes. His cock protrudes out of the wall like one of those hunting plaques with only the animal's head attached. It's really freaky. Ramon is only semi-hard though, so that sight could be more exciting, but he's stroking himself so he's getting harder by the second.

The second guy in the group nudges the third guy and he steps up closer to the bench in front of Ramon. He replaces Ramon's hand with his own and then he starts jerking him. I wonder what Ramon is feeling to be touched like that by a stranger. We watch them go at it and before you know it the guy is on his knees, blowing Ramon, and the whole scene is dreamlike, a swirling jumble of images and impressions. Despite all the random club noises, I can hear Ramon's moans getting louder.

I lose my focus, finding myself distracted by the flow of other men through the space, each apparently looking for something they haven't found yet. It makes me want to see and experience more. I think back to the map of the club layout and wonder if any of these guys have been to the dungeon. My curiosity of what goes on in there starts to take all my focus, so I set out to wander through the dark halls to see what I can find.

Each new area I pass through seems like a lesson in the gay lifestyle. One door says Wet Room, which lights my imagination on fire.

The sauna room is a hot fog of sweaty, naked men, and in the next room there's an oversized bed and the orgy on top of it is a Rubik's cube of writhing bodies fitting together, all taking and giving whatever they can. It's blowing my mind. All of this makes me wonder the kind of man I'd be attracted to if Dean didn't still own me.

Finally ending up in the far corner of the building, I realize I've arrived at the dungeon. The door leading into the space is covered with black bars and I can feel my heart racing as I tentatively pull it open. Immediately seeing a row of private rooms with closed doors, I slowly walk to the end of the hall where I begin to see glimpses into the large open room I suspect is for open punishment.

As I approach the entry I see suspension bars hanging from the ceiling, a primitive looking wood contraption with head and hand locks, like something out of an old movie, and X crosses with restraints. One lean guy has his wrists shackled to the suspension bar and another taller man with thick biceps and a face that looks like it's seen battle is circling him, dragging a flogger against his bare skin.

"You disgust me," the big man hisses. His voice and words immediately take me back to my afternoons with Father Ryan. I almost turn and rush out of the room, but an invisible net holds me in place, hauntingly riveted to the man's expression as he taunts the submissive.

The sub's head is hanging down, humiliation etched across his features, yet he's aroused. Suddenly there's the crack of the flogger over bare skin and he flinches, his head dropping lower.

"Are you ashamed of yourself?" the dom asks.

The sub now dangling from the suspension bar nods. "I am."

"Well, what should we do about it?" His voice is haunting, as if there's nothing he could enjoy more than bringing the other guy to his knees.

As I watch I realize that I'm panting, not just because the sordid scene is electrifying me, but because I'm burning up and my heart is racing. A moment later I realize that I'm painfully aroused—possibly harder than I've ever been—from the idea of being shamed. I sway back and forth, knowing I need this badly . . . I'm wondering how it would feel to be bound and gagged, punished and then allowed release while I'm baptized in this dark place, where every man is worshiped or vilified, depending on what they desire. It all becomes very clear to me.

This may be just what I need.

While on the slippery slope between rational thought, and drug inspired insanity, I'm craving evil things. I'm surging with need to be punished for all my bad choices . . . for corrupting Dean, for every shaky step I took through the church's sacristy straight into the den of the devil, also known as Father Ryan.

Welcome to the deviant pleasure dome, gentlemen, and those of you who were once young boys robbed of your innocence. Here you'll be bestowed every dark pleasure and you'll pay for it dearly.

With those words booming in my head, I have a strong sense that my time is up and it's my turn to pay.

I tighten my towel around my waist, hoping to keep my arousal hidden, but I'm not even sure why I'm covering up. If I get my way I'll soon be naked, bound, and vulnerable. I move toward an employee who seems to be monitoring the room.

"Excuse me," I say, forcing him to look back at me instead of the guy being beaten. I nod toward the public humiliation platform. "I want to do that."

Folding his arms over his chest, he gives me a hard look. "Have you done this before?"

"No, but I've watch enough porn. I know what it's about."

"So you understand this is about accepting pain and being humiliated?"

I nod, trying to appear calm but my nerves are wreaking havoc inside of my body.

"It can get pretty rough . . . you sure that's what you want?" he asks again, giving me a way out.

"Very sure."

"Okay." He points to the different stations. "What's your pleasure?"

I point to a suspended piece of wood with one large hole in the middle, and two smaller ones on either side. I like it because it seems like the most uncomfortable and humiliating of the devices. That is what I deserve now.

"The pillory?" he asks.

"Is that what it's called?"

He nods. "It was used for punishment and public display back in the medieval times. See, after I lock you down, the dom will punish you, but it's an open forum for whoever wants to punish or humiliate you, too."

I nod. "I understand."

He studies me, a hard gaze moving over my face. "How old are you, kid?"

"Twenty-one, old enough to know what I want."

He shrugs. "All right. As long as you understand how intense this can get."

I swallow hard, pushing down my fear and give him a concise nod.

"Okay then, I'll be checking with you once it starts. When I ask about continuing, if you want to be released give me a firm yes or no. If you say yes, or you don't respond I'll release you and you're done."

I nod, but then wonder, *Will this be my undoing? And if it is, do I even care?* Maybe this is exactly how things are meant to be.

Dean . 51

I'M PACING BACK AND FORTH through the apartment when my phone rings. I grab it but my hope deflates when it's not Jason. Even though I don't recognize the number, I decide I better answer it anyway.

"Is this Dean? Jason's Dean?" the caller asks.

"Who's this?" I don't like how panicked this guy sounds.

"It's Ramon."

I let out a groan. "Oh, Ramon. Fucking great. What do you want?"

"You've got to go get Jason."

"Go get him? Where is he?"

"At a sex club called The Man Cave."

"Man Cave? What the fuck is he doing at a place like that, and how'd he get there?" I feel sick just at the idea of Jason being in a place like that.

"I took him, but then he took off for the dungeon. I had no idea he was into crazy shit like that, and when I couldn't convince him, I had to get out of there. That scene was freaking me out!"

My hands curl into tight fists. "You fucking took him to a sex club and left him there? I'm going to kick your ass."

"Go ahead and try. Regardless, this has to be dealt with right the fuck now. He's high as a kite. He had a bad reaction to the Molly and he's doing shit he's going to regret."

"You gave him Ecstasy?" I can't contain the fury in my voice.

"Don't rail on me, man. You're the one he saw across from Hugo's groping your ex. He was losing it, and needed to get out of his mind for a night."

"He saw me with her tonight?"

"He sure as fuck did. And to say that he didn't take it well is the understatement of the century."

My heart is pounding. My pulse is jagging in my neck. I have to get to Jason before something really bad happens.

Jason . 52

A LIFETIME HAS PASSED IN this self-imposed prison as the light slowly fades. My neck is aching, barely holding up my heavy head that's brimming with dark thoughts. But when the man asks if I want to be set free, I say no again and again.

With each sharp blow I die a little more, a brittle leaf tumbling and crumbling across a vast windblown field.

I am aimless, hopeless, soulless, and likely will not survive this degradation. My regrets tumble over me knowing I'll never hold or make love to Dean again. Never is fucking forever and I may as well be left here to die, locked down and stripped naked. Losing your one love is losing everything, and now I have nothing.

I feel hands sliding, grabbing, jerking my raw skin. I feel wetness, and hear ugly words before each strike. "Slut." "Whore." "Worthless trash." I deserve this censure . . . I'm fundamentally wrong and will never be right. Burning tears well in my hollow eyes, my lids flutter, and my pupils roll back into my head. All the colors fade to black, white, and grey.

I am nothing.

Dean. 53

WHEN I PULL UP TO the address Ramon gave me, I have to stop and recheck the number I wrote down. From the outside this place looks like some type of small manufacturing business or storage place. After I park, I hurry to the side entrance, and then as I approach the steel door Ramon described, I final see a small simple sign. "The Man Cave." This must be it. Obviously they don't want to draw too much attention to themselves in this conservative town.

The guy at the front desk eyes me as I approach. He's tall and built, with a beard, tattoos, and a compelling presence. Before he addresses me he turns to another man who's just stepped behind the check-in desk. "Hey, Randy, can you check on that kid in the dungeon? Mark said something may be off with him."

Holy fuck, are they talking about Jason? I sure as hell hope not, but judging from what Ramon said it's possible. Fear roars through me like a fierce storm. I have to get to him.

"Sure, man." The guy named Randy steps back out from behind the desk and heads down a dark hall.

The desk clerk looks at me and points up to the sign with all the services they offer. "First time?"

I shake my head firmly and press my fists on the counter. "Look, I need to get to the dungeon. An asshole friend of my boyfriend gave him Molly on top of booze, and he's having a bad reaction. I need to get him before something bad happens."

Narrowing his eyes, the guy steps back. "I don't want trouble."

I clench my fists tighter and can feel every muscle in my arms bulge. "There won't be trouble if you just tell me where the damn dungeon is. Then we're out of here."

Leaning over the counter, he points down the dark hall.

It takes everything I have to ignore whatever the fuck is going on in this crazy club as I storm through the place. As it is I can barely see since my eyes haven't adjusted yet to the almost non-existent light, which isn't helped by the black walls. What a freak show.

I have another surge of determination to kill or at least gravely injure Ramon for dragging Jason here when this was the worst possible place for him to be in his current state of mind. I mean, seriously . . . he's in a fucking dungeon being tortured or some crazy shit? This is beyond anything I've ever had to face.

My entire body is tense, and my hands curl into fists as I charge toward the door in the back covered with bars. Jerking the door open, I step inside. My gut feeling is that Jason isn't far from me now.

Once I'm inside the wide doorway I freeze in place. There's several weird contraptions that look like they can't be for anything good, but the one at the end takes my breath away because it has Jason prisoner.

The blood rushes out of my head so fast that I'm sure I'll black out. *What the fucking hell?* His neck and wrists are locked into some kind of primitive wood device.

His head is dropped down, and he's naked. From the looks of it, he's been beaten and has red stripes and patches marking his skin where he was hit. My gaze lifts up to notice a man standing behind him with a paddle and an angry expression.

"You're worthless, aren't you?" he barks at Jason as he pulls the paddle back.

My rage is so intense that I feel like I could kill this guy, or at the very least, seriously fuck him up. Right as I'm charged up to take on the asshole I hear Jason's faint voice.

"Yes," he replies weakly.

"Yes, what?" the asshole grows.

"Yes, sir."

Sir? The sharp snap of wood slapping his skin stuns me, and I rush forward. Screw beating the shit out of that guy. I can't take another moment of this. I need to get Jason out of this hell-hole.

"Stop," I yell loudly as he's swinging the paddle back to strike Jason again.

He turns to me with an irritated glare. "Stop? Who the hell are you?"

I notice Jason's head sinking lower, and I rush over.

"Who the hell do you think I am? I'm his boyfriend! And he's clearly fucked up on drugs right now. Are you fucking blind?" I roar.

He glances over at the guy wearing the club uniform and leaning against the wall who apparently observes everything. He's the one the guy at the front desk instructed to come back here to check things out. Why the fuck hasn't he stopped this? The guy nods at him so he lowers his raised arm, drops the paddle, and turns away, before walking out of the room.

When I step up behind Jason I see his legs are trembling and the raw marks on his skin are even worse than what I observed on his front. I also see something trailing down his lower back and the backs of his thighs. I try to suppress my gag reflex. *Did someone jerk off on him? More than one person? Oh God. No, just no.*

If I ever find out what motherfuckers did this to him, I will beat the crap out of them. I step to his front side wondering why he still hasn't seemed to react to my voice, even now that I'm right next to him. *How fucked up is he?* I lean in close to his ear.

"Jason . . ."

I hear a whimper and a soft moan but instead of turning his face toward me, his head drops lower.

"Jason, it's me, Dean." When he doesn't respond, I'm so freaked out that fear shoots up my spine. Is he overdosing or something?

I gently place a hand on either side of his head so I can lift him up a little and turn him my direction. When his gaze meets mine, part of me dies inside. His face is flushed and tear-streaked, and his eyes are completely blank. It's like how I'd imagine someone who had a lobotomy would look . . . lifeless and empty inside. I stop breathing. Although I know this is Jason, it's like he's no longer in his body.

Panicked, I turn to the jackass employee still leaning against the wall and observing us. "What the hell is wrong with you? Get him the fuck out of this thing!"

As the guy marches over I turn Jason's face up and around so the guy can see how fucked up he is. "Are you crazy? Look at his face!" He's so out of it that he doesn't react to my handling of him.

"Damn," he mutters, shaking his head as he jerks a key ring out of his pocket, quickly flips the lock, and pulls off the top part so Jason is no longer constrained.

I move to Jason's side and carefully lift his head out from where he'd been secured. He has raw abrasions around his neck. His hands are released next and when he's free from his bondage he starts to crumble. I slide my arm across his back and tighten my grip to hold him up. His head rolls back right before he goes limp in my arms.

I turn back to the guy, feeling a surge of adrenaline burn through me. "This is serious. I've got to get him to the emergency room." Grabbing a towel, I wrap it around his waist, then sweep one arm under his legs and carefully pick him up. "Fucking find his clothes and wallet and bring them outside. I need his ID . . . now!"

I have laser focus as I surge forward, holding my best friend and lover in my arms. Jason's a big guy so my muscles are screaming by the time I kick the front door open and rush through the parking lot, but all I can think of is saving him before he downslides further. What if he's permanently damaged from the drugs and other shit tonight? What if he's overdosing?

I have to half-prop him up along the side of the car and keep holding him, so I can click the lock and pull the passenger door open.

Once I've maneuvered him into the car I recline the seat as far back as possible for him, then fasten the seatbelt and pull the towel back over him. The guy runs up to the car with his hands full of Jason's clothes and his wallet.

"Hey," he calls out when he gets close enough to hand over the stuff. "Your friend looks worse."

My gaze drops down, and I see that Jason's streaked face is ghostly white and his wide, frightened eyes are unfocused. He looks like he's flipping out. Leaning over, I comb my fingers through his disheveled hair while I try to keep my shit together. The expression on my boyfriend's face is dark and distraught. It's as if he's traveled into a fucked up place that he may never come back from. I wedge my eyes shut for a second, holding back my rage for what's been done to him.

Is this what would become of Jason if he lost me? I'm not sure I could live with the guilt.

I gently run my fingertips along his jaw. "Hang on, JJ, we're on our way."

He blinks his eyes as if he's having trouble focusing on me. "No," he whispers before his head droops down again.

I swallow hard, feeling gutted as I turn on the ignition. I'll forever regret that I didn't handle the Julie situation right. It's wrong that Jason is bearing the brunt of the fall-out. I clear my throat, trying to push back my emotion. "We're going to the ER," I say into the silence as I lay my hand on his knee. "I'll be with you, making sure you get what you need to be okay."

The rest of our journey is a blur, from the frantic drive to the University Hospital, to the medical team strapping him on a gurney and rolling him away from me as a medic asks for information.

It infuriates me that I don't even know how much Molly he took, how much he drank, or what else he may have ingested. The worst part is warning them about all the markings on his body. I get the horrible impression that they think I'm responsible for all of this.

Some time after he's admitted into the ER, the doctor comes out to tell me that they're hydrating Jason and trying to stabilize his temperature. They also are testing his oxygen and blood levels. Once he's stable they'll keep him for observation a few more hours. It's going to be a long night but thank God he's here and not back at that club. Who knows what kind of shape he'd be in?

After endlessly pacing in the waiting room and then asking about fifty times, they finally let me see him. He's conscious and I notice that his eyes widen when he sees me before he sinks farther back against the pillow. I step up to the bed and run my fingers through his hair, smoothing it off his forehead.

"You scared the shit out of me, JJ." I stare at him plaintively. I can't help it. I'm just so damn glad he already looks a bit better.

He blinks and I'm not sure if he's really clear about what's going on.

"I've been in the waiting room making hell until they let me in to see you. What a bunch of stubborn fuckers."

He glances down, his gaze taking in the hospital bed.

I press my open hand over his forehead, and then against his cheek. He doesn't appear to be burning up anymore. Thank goodness for that.

His lack of verbal response just makes me want to keep talking. I walk over to the bag of fluid dangling from a rolling stand. "Can they turn this thing up or something so you can hurry up and get hydrated? I want to get you home."

He closes his eyes and I wait patiently for him to open them again. Did he fall asleep or something? But as I step closer I see tears trailing down his cheeks.

I run my fingers along his forearm. "Hey, JJ. Why are you crying?"

He silently shakes his head without opening his eyes.

Taking the edge of my sweatshirt, I gently wipe his cheeks then pull up a chair close to where his hand is lying still across the sheet. Sitting down, I reach out and wind my fingers through his. "Don't worry. You're going to be okay. I promise."

He slowly shakes his head before closing his eyes again.

It's like everything has collapsed around us, and all I can do is try to remember to breathe.

Jason . 54

WHEN MY EYES ARE CLOSED I'm pretty sure I've been buried alive, the heavy weight of loss pressing down on my chest. To make things a million times worse, Dean is here and I don't understand why. *Isn't he back with Julie now?* Tears work their way down my face no matter how hard I press my eyes shut to stop them.

I feel his gentle touch, his fingers in my hair, stroking my arm, his fingers woven through mine. Each gesture makes me ache as I know it may be my last. With my eyes closed he is a ghost hovering over me, and I pray that he'll visit me again in my dreams.

Flashes from last night haunt me, brought on by random triggers like a nearby patient moaning, or a nurse inspecting the abrasions on my wrists while checking my IV. But the memories aren't clear, like photographs that were left in the sun too long and faded, all the images becoming hard to define.

My time here has been endless, constant poking and prodding until I want to slug the next person who handles me but I'm boneless. There's a part of me that wants to give up. I'm so tired of Earth's gravity pulling me down when all I want to do is fly far away.

Dean. 55

WHILE I'M WAITING FOR JASON'S release papers I go get a cup of coffee to push back the exhaustion that's got me on the edge. I know they need to retest all his levels, but I also know that home is where he needs to be. *Home with me.*

I walk to the window at the end of the hall and gaze out, watching the golden light edging the trees as the sun starts to rise. It's that moment that my complicated feelings of seeing Jason last night submitting himself to be humiliated hits me, and for a moment I think it's more than I can handle. Maybe *he* is more than I can handle.

I can't be with him if every time he doubts me or has a bad day he puts himself on the train tracks in front of the road to total destruction. I can't walk into another dark room to find him shackled and abused. I just can't.

Sinking down into a chair facing the window, I let out a long, sad sigh. I stare up to the glowing sky framed by the window and wonder what this all means for us. Maybe I'm just exhausted and down, but I'm starting to feel like the universe is against us. Or maybe Jason needed to hit bottom to find the resolve to be stronger, and finally fight back . . . and in doing so, fight for us to have the future we deserve.

I'm not sure that I can be strong enough for the both of us, but if he can find his strength, together we may have a chance.

Jason . 56

THE NURSE IS REMOVING THE IV from my arm when the doctor approaches my bed. She studies my chart then glances up at me. Her long, dark hair has red streaks and she's wearing ethnic-looking earrings. I note a small tattoo on her wrist as she checks my heartbeat, tests my eyes, and then my reflexes. When she's done she folds her arms over her chest and her thoughtful gaze is a mix of sternness and compassion.

"So?" I ask, my stomach getting nervous.

"I'm going to release you, but I want to stress how lucky you are that you don't appear to have permanent damage from your reckless evening."

I let out a sigh of relief. "That's good to hear."

"I've seen kids that were in better shape coming in to the ER, than the shape you were in last night . . . and they end up with serious physical or mental issues. You were lucky. I hope you've learned your lesson."

"I have."

"So your friend said you were at The Man Cave. I've heard about that place. Did you understand what you were getting into?"

Getting into? I willingly chose the dark path I took last night. A moment of clarity flashes through my anguished mind reminding me that I have one journey in this life while in this body. Do I want to squander my possibilities with self-destruction, or open my mind to the very idea of who I was meant to be if I hadn't been abused?

I twist the edges of the sheets with my hands as I look up at the doctor. As drained and fuzzy-headed as I feel, I have to rally if I want to get released. I focus hard on her question, determined to sound articulate in my response even though I'm feeling anything but that.

"Did I know what I was getting into? I sort of had an idea, but I know now that it was a mistake to show up there high on something I'd never tried. Everything spiraled out of control fast. I swear I'm not doing that again. I know I've got some things to figure out."

She nods as I sign my release paperwork. "Good to hear it. I'm going to go tell your pushy friend that you're ready to go."

A roar of fear pulses through me knowing I'm not ready to get real with Dean. I haven't even figured out where I'm going to stay now that he's reunited with Julie.

I lean back, my eyes drooping shut again when I feel Dean's fingers skim my forehead. "What do you say we go home?"

My eyes pop open to see him calmly smiling. "Okay," I whisper, pushing back my fear. I slowly edge out of bed, determined to dress myself, but the moment Dean sees how unsteady I am he leads me to the chair. Rifling through my clothes, he takes my boxers and bends to hold them open so I can slip my feet through. He repeats the action with my jeans and then helps me stand so he can shimmy them up.

I pull off my hospital gown so I can zip up my fly. I'm already exhausted by this minimal effort.

Dean methodically finishes dressing me and leads me out of the room while muttering, "I hope this is the last time I see this place."

My cheeks flush from shame. "Me too."

The car ride to our apartment is quiet and tense. When I glance over at Dean he's staring out the windshield like he's expecting the road to suddenly open up and swallow us. I guess whatever he's freaking out about, he's been hiding pretty well.

When he pulls into his parking spot and turns off the ignition, he rests his hand on my arm and looks up at me concerned, realizing that I'm trembling.

"We're home," he says gently. "Come on, we need to get you upstairs."

I shake my head with the most energy I've shown since this mess started. "I can't go up there."

"Why not?"

"Is Julie upstairs?"

His eyes squint as he scowls. "No. Look, you don't understand what really happened last night."

"Are you moving in with her now?"

He rubs his hands roughly over his face in frustration. "No. I'm not moving in with her."

Why am I having trouble believing him? And speaking of other partners, another idea comes to me now that I'm feeling more lucid. "Hey, what happened to Ramon? He was supposed to take care of me last night."

His entire body tenses and his fingers curl into fists. "He left you in that goddamn club. Then he called me to fix his jacked-up decision to take you there."

His anger feels all-consuming.

"That's the last time you see that guy, do you understand me?"

"You're telling me not to see the guy who saved me after I saw you reunited with your girlfriend?"

He clasps his hands on either side of my head and scowls. "Damn it Jason!"

"Where is Julie anyway?"

"I have no idea where she is right now. I've been with you all night. And what you apparently saw outside the restaurant was me hugging her after letting her down."

I narrow my eyes, not allowing myself to believe him. "She had her hands all over you and you liked it."

"I didn't like it. It was awkward, and that's when I told her I was in another relationship and very happy."

I glance up at him, stunned. "You did?"

Dean glances at me and I can see the frustration in his dark eyes. "I did. I swear it. And then I came home to find you and you were gone. You can imagine how I felt when I got that call from your part-time lover that you were locked-up for the taking at some sleazy sex club."

Now that I know the truth my heart feels bruised when I realize how much all of this has hurt him when he didn't deserve it. Yes, from my view last night it looked bad, but I should've waited to talk to him before I wrote us off. He's sure to be done with me now. I try to swallow back my well of emotion but my mouth is parched dry.

My sorrowful gaze meets his. "This is it, isn't it? I thought I'd lost you when I saw you with her, but the truth is that I lost you when you found out what I'd done last night."

He doesn't answer right away . . . just turns away from me and keeps staring up at the sky. A minute passes before he finds his words.

"It's been a rough night. I don't know anything right now other than you need to get inside, keep staying hydrated, and get cleaned up. And then you need to sleep off your night from hell. I need to make sure you're okay."

"But—" I start to argue.

"Come on, JJ," he urges before getting out of the car, and walking around to open my door. Extending his hand to me, he looks down at me with intense sadness reflected in his eyes. I'm completely exhausted and feel like dead weight when he pulls me out of the car and waits for me to steady myself.

We feel miles apart, yet hand in hand, we silently walk up the stairs together.

Once inside, Dean parks me on the couch and then brings over a bottle of water and watches me until I down the entire thing. I let my head fall back on the couch and I close my eyes, trying to force all the memories from last night out of my head. Everything starts to fade to black until I feel a tight grip on my shoulders from being shook.

"You can't fall asleep yet," Dean urges. "You need to get in the shower."

"Too tired," I groan, pushing his hand away.

"You don't have a choice. Last night has to be washed off of you and I'm not taking no for an answer, even if I have to drag you in there."

My head falls back onto the top of the couch and I hear Dean stomp off. A minute later I realize the shower water is running and Dean returns with only a towel around his waist. I try not to look at how beautiful his body is since I'm pretty sure that he no longer belongs to me, and knowing that only makes everything worse. He grabs my arm and pulls me up again.

Next thing I know I'm in the bathroom with my clothes being peeled off my battered body. Despite my exhaustion, as I see all the marks on my skin there's a new feeling of clarity and profound regret now that the Molly effect has faded and I'm somewhere safe.

I slowly cup my fingers around my sore neck, wincing as my fingers skim the abrasions. Examining my wrists, I find marks that feel similar. The vague memory of being locked in the pillory comes back to me. *What the fuck was I thinking?* Clearly I wasn't thinking at all . . . it was absolute self-destruction.

Stepping into the shower, Dean reaches for me. I have no will to resist him. I take his hand and follow him in. He grabs the spray handle and circles it over my marked skin, slowly turning me to wet my back. A sharp pain sears across my skin.

"You have welts where they hit you," Dean says solemnly.

"Oh God." I cup my hands over my face as he slowly circles the soft spray up and down my back.

He then replaces the spray onto the shower attachment, and rubs my body wash into foam and carefully starts to wash me with gentle strokes. Every part of me stings and aches with pain. Unable to face him, I lean my forehead on his shoulder as he soaps up my front. He gently washes my cock and that only makes my pride sink lower. Was I violated there, too?

When he's done with my body he runs the spray over my head and then shampoos me while I rest my hands on his hips to keep myself steady. The way his fingers carefully massage my scalp reminds me that I don't deserve a man who would be this good to me. It's all too much, and I start to sob.

He lets me cry as he rinses my hair and then my body one more time. I'm still crying when he pulls me into his arms.

"Come on," he murmurs. "You're safe at home now."

"I'm sorry, Dean, I'm so sorry," I gasp in between sobs.

"Shhh," he whispers into my ear as he pulls me closer.

Pulling me out of the shower, he gently dries me off before helping me into a clean T-shirt and boxers and easing me into bed.

The last thing I remember is Dean pulling me close so that my cheek rests on his chest. Only then does sleep take me from my emotional journey in the waking world into the quiet void of sleep.

I have no idea how much time has passed when I open my eyes, but there's sun pouring in through the window. All I know is that I've been out a long time. I reach for Dean and all I feel are cold sheets. Blinking to clear my vision, I realize he's not in bed, but a second later I hear the squeak of a chair and realize he's sitting near the dresser watching me.

"Hey," he says, in a ragged voice.

I nod, studying him. "Did you sleep?"

"Not really."

"Head full of thoughts?" I ask, knowing how he is.

He nods. "Yeah."

"And what did you conclude?"

"Not much . . . just that there's a lot to figure out."

The drained look in his expression is stirring up a panic in my gut. Dean's never felt so far away.

"Is this it for us?" I ask, with wary eyes. Even if Julie isn't a factor, I'm pretty sure I pushed him too far.

"Is that what you want?" he asks.

My heart surges, my love for him so big that I know without a doubt that he'll always own me whether he moves on or not. "No. Never," I admit.

He stares at me silently with a fathomless expression. I see hurt and a world-weariness weighing him down, as if he aged overnight. What does this exceptional man need with screwed-up, gay me?

"Hey, you look wiped out. You need to rest." I pull back the covers on his side of the bed.

He leans forward and presses his face into his hands.

"Come on, Dean. Please come get some sleep."

He slowly rises off the chair and approaches the bed before easing down on the mattress. He stretches out awkwardly as if we're strangers. Is that what my transgressions have done to him . . . to us? I refuse to accept the idea so I pull him into my arms and stroke his back. He resists at first but eventually gives up, and he settles against me. I run my fingers through his hair over and over because I know he loves that. Soon he's asleep but I keep touching and soothing him like he did for me last night. I'm overcome with a surge of emotion for him that could melt the most frozen of hearts.

I may have ruined us, destroyed my one chance for true happiness, but I still state my truth to Dean even if he can't hear me as he sleeps. I rest my hand over where his heart beats. "I love you, Dean. I always have and I always will."

Dean . 57

IT'S LATE AFTERNOON WHEN I wake up to a weight sinking down next to me on JJ's bed. I hear a sigh and then fingers gently massage my scalp, before he softly says my name. I slowly blink until my eyes adapt, and then concentrate on Jason. I sense he's been up for a while, and he speaks up with a clear voice.

"I brought you a Coke and a roast beef sandwich. Eat it."

I give him a wary look as I fight back a smile since he's flipped the game from when I served him my half-assed version of breakfast in bed just yesterday. Yesterday morning is feeling like a lifetime ago.

"How are you doing?" I ask.

"I still feel like complete shit, so that's the end of my relationship with Ecstasy."

"Good." I nod before I sit up, slide back against the headboard, and take a big bite of the sandwich. I guess I shouldn't be surprised that I'm ravenous.

He lets out a long sigh. "I'd like to think that I wouldn't have been so stupid last night if that stuff hadn't screwed with my head."

It's good to see this more self-assured side of Jason. That's how I've always known him, so these last few weeks have been rough for me to navigate.

He sits quietly while I eat. The silence is surprisingly comfortable. It's how we always were with each other, and how I'd like it to always be. When I take the last bite of the sandwich and gulp of Coke, he leans forward, folding his hands together and leaning his elbows on his knees.

"So, I've made some decisions.

"Yeah?"

"I called one of those therapists that the law firm recommended and made an appointment. I need to start dealing with my issues."

"Wow . . . okay. I've got to say, that sounds like a better plan than whatever you were trying to do last night."

He shakes his head, his forehead furrowed. "I was trying to destroy myself last night. But then you showed up and screwed up my plans."

"Or maybe I reminded you that you're indestructible."

He gives me a sad smile. "I don't know about that. But I do know one thing, I can't keep going on like this."

"I agree." I let out a sigh of relief.

"And you'll be happy to know that I called Ted and said I'd be part of the lawsuit."

I sit up straight and pull my shoulders back. "That's great, Jason. I'm really proud of you."

"That's not all. I went on that website for survivors of abuse by priests and did some research. I think it's going to be a great resource."

"All this while I slept?"

He smiles. "I wanted you to wake up to good news for a change."

I hold out my arms. "Come here."

He sinks down alongside me so I can slide my arms around him. After I hug him I pull back and trace my fingertips along his jaw and then across his lips. "We're going to be okay."

He studies me for a long moment before a smile breaks out across his face. "I want that more than anything," he whispers, then settles back down into my embrace.

The week ahead at school is rough. After losing several days of classes and study time, we're scrambling to catch up. It feels like time is moving faster than ever, and I'm not sure where we'll end up when school is over. I just want it to stand still.

We're careful with each other . . . too careful. Although we've slept in the same bed we just hold each other. I want him so damn much, but I can sense he's still broken. I just have to be patient, trusting he'll let me know when he's ready for more.

Wednesday he comes home edgy from his first therapy session.

"So?" I ask.

"They say it will get worse before it gets better."

"Do you want to talk about it?"

"Not yet."

I'm curious but doing my best to be chill about it. "Okay, just let me know when."

Thursday night I come home to find Jason in the kitchen on the phone. From the tone of his voice it must be his mom.

"No, I didn't go to church last Sunday."

He rolls his eyes when he sees me.

"I was busy, mom. You have no idea how busy I am."

There's a long pause. "No, I still don't have a girlfriend."

Looking miserable, he shakes his head. "Ma, I've got to go. Okay, yeah, I'll think about it."

A moment later, he ends the call and sets the phone down.

I shrug off my jacket and toss it over the chair. "What was that about?"

"The usual stuff. She wanted to make sure I'm eating right, and she called the Catholic church on the edge of campus and asked for their latest mass schedule for me."

"Why can't she let it go?" I ask with a scowl.

His gaze drops to the floor and I can see he's upset. "She'll never let it go. And now she wants me to come home for my birthday next weekend. She was pushier than normal about it."

"You're not going, right?" I stop myself before I go off about his mother. Or I could tell him that I've got something special planned for his birthday so he'll cancel with her but that's not fair. His mother may be an uptight bitch, but she's still his mom.

He clutches the edge of the counter and then curves forward like he's preparing to leap over it. Instead, he lifts back up straight and pulls his shoulders back. "I'm going to go."

"All the way to Boise? What the hell kind of birthday is that?"

"I'm going to tell her I'm gay."

My mouth falls open, but I shut it quickly. "Yeah, that sounds like an awesome way to spend your birthday. She'll probably put a paper 'birthday-boy' hat on you when you arrive, and then after you lay the gay thing on her, she'll have you institutionalized. What are you really planning?"

He nods, his expression resolute. "Seriously, Dean, I'm going to tell her. If I'm going to get my life on track I need to quit hiding and pushing away what's uncomfortable."

"But your mom is crazy," I insist.

"But she's still my mom. And I can't hide who I am from her forever. If she can't accept me, so be it."

I shake my head disapprovingly.

"I'm also going to tell Mom how I feel about you . . . not just how much you've helped me through all of my shit, but how I've always felt about you."

I take a sharp breath. As much as I don't want him talking to his mom about me, I can't lose sight of the bigger issue. "Damn, Jason, are you sure you're up for all of this? You should talk to your new therapist first before you decide for sure."

I want to tell him that he's not ready yet . . . that he won't be able to handle her reaction, which is guaranteed to be awful. But he seems so determined and isn't my role to stick by his side and support him? There'll never be a good time for this reveal, so maybe he's right to get it over with.

"I'm going to leave after my last class next Friday."

"It's a four-hour drive."

"Yeah, so?" he asks with his brows knitted.

"I'm going with you. Actually, I'm going to drive."

His gaze softens. "You don't have to do that."

"Yes, I do. I'm going to be there for you."

Jason . 58

THE TRIP TO BOISE IS pretty much the drive from hell, endless vistas lining the never-ending highway, when all I can do is fixate on my fears and anxiety about how Mom will take my news. Dean remains quiet as he drives, I'm sure dealing with his own worries about me. I tried to talk him out of driving me, but he was resolute. And now, as we finally approach Boise, I feel my heartbeat speed up and I realize how grateful I am that he was so stubborn about coming along. Reaching over, I take his free hand and squeeze it. He doesn't let me go and the warmth passing between us calms me.

We agreed that he would drop me off at Mom's and he'd stay with his parents until we head back to school early Sunday. My actual birthday is Saturday night so we have plans to get together at one of our old haunts after my evening ends with Mom.

When he pulls up in front of Mom's apartment complex I have to sit in the car and get my bearings before convincing myself to go upstairs.

Dean rests his hand on my shoulder. "You don't have to do this you know."

I nod. "But I want to. It's time." I twist my hands together and then shake them loose.

"Stay strong," Dean says. "I'm only a phone call away if it gets rough."

I nod then open the door, grab my duffle bag out of the backseat and walk around to the driver's side.

He rolls down the window, his eyes watching me carefully.

"Say hi to your parents," I say. I lean down and I want to kiss him, but I'm pretty sure he wouldn't want me to kiss him out in the open here in Boise. "Thanks so much."

"Remember, JJ, I'm always with you. Call me later. Okay?"

"Deal."

After Dean drives off, I slowly ascend the stairs until I reach Mom's apartment.

"Hey, Mom," I call out as I open her front door. I'm trying to sound as upbeat as I can, considering how drained I am from worrying throughout the long drive.

She rushes out of the kitchen and gives me a big hug, but when she pulls back the corners of her mouth turn down. Placing her hands on either side of my face, she studies me. "You look anxious, Jason. What's the matter?"

Leave it to a mother's intuition.

I'm not ready to get into it with her yet so I shrug. "It's just been a hard semester."

She pats my chest as she takes my duffle bag off my shoulder. "You've got to take better care of yourself. You don't want to get sick."

"Okay, Mom."

"I'm doing roast chicken and potatoes tonight, but tomorrow for your birthday I'm making your favorite for dinner."

"Lasagna?"

"Yes, indeed. Why don't you rest from the long drive, and then you can help me with the salad."

"Sounds good. Thanks."

Lying on my childhood bed has never felt stranger. As I look around the room with posters of my favorite tennis stars from my early days playing competitively, sketches I'd done of various buildings, and the Frank Lloyd Wright poster of his epic home design, Falling Water, taped to the wall, I wonder about the boy I was back then. Knowing what my dreams had been for the future, would he be okay with the man I am now?

I'm also curious now about what Dean really thought about me back then. Did he ever feel 'more' like I did? It's upsetting to realize that we are both back in Boise but not together. All I want is to be in his arms. I finally doze off as I imagine my favorite times that we've shared since we became more than just friends.

"Jason, wake up," Mom says gently.

I slowly start to lift out of the deep fog of sleep only to see my mom and my childhood bedroom. *What's going on?* And then I remember why I'm here and my sleepy smile fades.

She smooths down my hair. "Dinner's almost ready and I was hoping you could put the salad together."

I know it'd be easier for Mom to just throw the salad together herself, but it was always part of her parenting strategy to give me jobs to do. Even if I don't agree with her conservative views, I do appreciate that she did the best she could raising me. I rise up and stumble my way to the kitchen as I slowly wake up. Mom points to the ingredients on the counter and I get to work.

As I cut up and toss together the lettuce, tomatoes, and cucumbers, she tells me about the gossip at her job and at church, the only two places she has any meaningful interaction. Is it any wonder that I couldn't wait to get out of our unremarkable life in Boise?

When we move to the table to eat, Mom surprises me by setting two wine glasses on the table along with a bottle of red wine. I glance up at her, surprised. She normally only drinks wine on special occasions.

"My boy coming home to see his mom is something to celebrate," she says with a smile. "And tomorrow I'm baking your favorite cake for your birthday."

I smile at her as I open the bottle and fill her glass but leave mine untouched. I need to keep my mind clear. Before you know it I'm on my second helping of food, and she's pushed aside what remains of her dinner and downed half the glass of wine. Maybe drinking wine has become a more regular occurrence for her.

She sways a bit as she studies me. "I was hoping you were bringing a girl home this weekend for me to meet. I've heard from Erik's mom that you're quite the rogue with women flinging themselves at you at school. Is there a particular girl you fancy?"

"No," I answer, my stomach rolling since the hard truth is now on the tip of my tongue.

"Don't you think it's time to find a nice girl and settle down? You'll be out in the working world soon and it'll be good to have a wife to look out for you."

My fingers clamp down on the handles of my chair as I nervously clear my throat.

"Besides, I don't want to wait too long for grandbabies." She winks at me as she lifts her wine glass for another sip.

My spiraling mood convinces me that this will go worse than I'd feared. It's not like the news of my sexual orientation should be a complete shock. After all, she was the one who found gay porn under my mattress and sent me to that crazy camp to straighten me out. But perhaps my college years—where she's only heard about me being popular with the girls—filled her with false hope.

I take a deep breath, trying to slow down my speeding heart. This is likely one of the hardest things I'll ever do in my life. I press my hands hard into my thighs and sit up straight as a board.

"Mom, I've got to tell you something."

She sets her wine glass down and blinks rapidly as she waits for what I'm going to say.

For a moment I feel hopeful. She's been in a good mood tonight and maybe my worst fears won't be realized. I'm the same Jason she's always loved, her only child, and if she's mellowed she'll know that my being gay isn't the end of the world. Especially once she realizes how happy I am with Dean. I give myself an inner pep-talk. *Come on, man . . . just tell her. Everything will be okay.*

"The reason I haven't brought any girls home is . . . well you see . . . it's complicated," I mumble.

Her expression is full of confusion as she waits for me to finish my thought.

Suddenly my mind is swirling into darkness, taking me back to when I was ten and first realizing that I was *different*. I can still hear my mom lecturing me to stay away from our neighbor, Bill, because he had a sick mind and preferred to lie with men instead of women. Her face twisted up with disgust before warning me that God would punish him for his filthy sins.

The recollection makes me feel like I'm ten years old again and I start to backslide, deciding it's too soon for this big confession. I'm just not ready to tell Mom that I'm like our neighbor, Bill, and face her unbending censure. But a second later that early memory links to one of Father Ryan, and the first time he threatened telling others about my sinful ways.

His hand that was resting on my shoulder suddenly tightened and his eyes narrowed to dark slits as he addressed me after I'd begged to leave his study.

"So, Jason, what would your mother and the leaders of the church think of the fact that you'd confessed to me your homosexual desires and attempted to touch me inappropriately?"

I'll never forget the terror that overtook me. I was leveled by the realization that he could make up such outrageous lies and yet everyone would believe his word over mine. I had no power, and no hope. I was nothing.

No, I insist to myself as I pull my thoughts back to the here and now. As the therapist said in our first session, the man I am now is bigger and stronger than all those memories.

Taking a deep breath, I close my eyes and see Dean's face and him telling me that he's always with me. I need to honor the painful journey that finally brought us together, and I have to be brave for both of us . . . it's now or never.

I take another deep breath and close my eyes. "Um . . . you see . . . I don't have a girlfriend because I'm gay." My whole body sags from the effort it took to put those words out there. I open my eyes and set my gaze on my plate, but I finally glance up at her.

Two big tears are running down her cheeks and her lower lip is trembling. "No," she whispers.

"Yes," I respond firmly. "I've always been, but it hasn't been easy to come to terms with . . . especially knowing how you feel about homosexuality."

"My only child," she laments, shaking her head frantically like I'd just told her I was dying or something.

My earlier hope for her being supportive is freefalling without a parachute. There will be no compassion. All I can do now is manage her disgust so I don't lose her completely. I scamper into what feels like enemy lines to do damage control.

"I'm not sick or anything, Mom. I just like men. You don't have to worry about me, or feel sad for me because when I'm true to who I am, I feel happy."

"No, no, no," she says her face twisted in anger, the intensity in her gaze fierce. "Who did this to you? Was it that nasty boy, Dean? I always knew he was trouble, getting you interested in things he shouldn't have."

"What?" I ask, my fury building at her depiction of Dean.

"Yes! I overheard him telling you about watching pornography on his computer when you were still just in middle school. It's the devil's work. I should've told you to stay away from him. If you had, none of this would've happened."

I rake my fingers through my hair as I try to get a grip on my wild thoughts. It's taking everything I have not to yell at her. Just then my phone pings and I look down to see it's from Dean. I lift it up to read the message.

Are you okay?

I feel a swell of emotion that he's reminded me how much he's with me and I wish he were here physically, too. I quickly type *"No"* and set my phone down again.

"That boy showed you those devil-worshipping videos to win you over and then lead you astray. I always thought he was vile. And to think you've been roommates all these years and he's corrupted you with his homosexuality."

A blaze is burning through me. She's clearly not ever going to listen to reason in regards to Dean. My face must be beet red with fury. "Is that really what you think?"

She folds her arms over her chest. "It's what I know."

I place my hands on the table to steady myself before I lean forward to scorch her with a glaring gaze. She may be my mom, but I can't have her vilifying Dean, the one person in my life who has walked through fire with me.

"Let me make this clear for you since you have no idea what really went on. I am the one who corrupted Dean, so in your eyes I must be the vile devil worshiper."

Mom pulls her hand over her gaping mouth and lets out a cry, before shaking her head frantically. "You're just saying this to upset me," she whispers, new tears trailing down her face.

"No I'm not. I'm telling you because you need to know the truth."

The best way I can describe Mom's expression at this point is that she must now think *I'm* the devil. Her eyes are wide and fearful, her mouth gaping and her skin pale with a sheen of perspiration.

I lower my voice and try to sound calm because otherwise I may snap. "Mom, Dean is the best person I've ever known. He just texted me to see if I was all right. He's supported me and looked out for me in ways you'll never know. I love him . . . so much."

"Oh good God," she gasps, clutching her stomach. "Both homosexuals."

"I've found love and that makes me so happy. Doesn't that mean anything to you?"

She glances up at me, her expression resolute. "It's wrong. It's unnatural. You know I can never accept this. He's not welcome here."

Every worthless feeling wells up in me. I'm shattered knowing that what I feared has come true. My mother can't love me because of who I am. My head drops, and my heart is racing so fast I can feel my pulse throb.

"So am I not welcome here either?"

She twists her hands together and bites her lip. "I don't know. I need to pray on it, Jason."

I nod, and we sit in silence for a minute, both letting the gravity of decisions being made settle over us.

"If Dean isn't welcome here, then this is no place for me anyway. I just need you to know this, Mom. He's my family, too."

"He's not family," she hisses.

"He's the essence of what family means to me."

I feel the rage bubbling up again at how wrong all of this is. I look down and realize that my hands are trembling. My mother prays and loves God, but she can't love her son because of who he loves?

"I'm going to talk to the priest after mass tomorrow." She nods her head like that's the perfect solution. It's the last straw for me.

"Yes. Talk to your priest. And while you're at it, you may want to mention that I'm not the only dark sheep that was in his fold."

"What are you talking about?"

"I'm telling you that Father Ryan sexually abused me for two years. So believe me, church doesn't hold all the answers you think it does."

She gasps and pushes her chair back with such force that she almost topples over backwards. "What are you saying?" she screeches.

I'm shocked, having never seen her react that dramatically to anything. My shaking hands curl into fists as my voice rises with equal fury.

"Father Ryan forced me to have sex with him. He was the one who bought me all that gay porn."

"No!"

"Yes, and I've just recently learned that I wasn't the only boy he did this to before they transferred him to another parish and God knows what he's done there."

"I don't believe it."

"Really? So you think I'm making that up?"

She nods her head. "You're making it up because you want to hurt me with your evil lies. You're trying to make me question my belief in my church."

I let out a groan. "That's right, because this is all about you. There's a lawsuit against him. I'm not making it up, Mom."

She stands up and smooths her skirt down, belying her frantic expression. "I'm going to my room and I'm going to pray for you,

Jason. And tomorrow at Mass I will pray for you. And I'll never give up until you're healed."

Gazing up at her, I realize that she's shut down and may never open up to me again. "I don't need healing, Mom, I just need you to love and accept me. I'm a good person and I'm in love with a good man. I hope one day you can make peace with that."

She stares at me for a few more long seconds and then turns and walks toward her bedroom. For the first time ever I hear the lock click after her door is pressed shut.

I numbly collapse over the table, resting my cheek on the wood surface with my eyes wedged shut. I wish I could at least feel relieved that I'm over the biggest hurdle of my life even if I face-planted on the way down, but instead I'm shattered. I've now been deemed unworthy of love by both of my parents. It's as if I were a tree and the very roots that held me up as I reached higher in life had been savagely cut away.

A buzz of panic starts in the tips of my fingers and then vibrates up my arms, creeping across my chest, and then clawing up my neck until I feel like I'm being choked. I feel my eyes bug out as I start gasping for air. *Oh God . . .* my mind is whirling as I try to grasp onto a solid thought but any feeling of self-control has slipped away.

I stumble over to Mom's bedroom door and yank at the handle, hoping it isn't actually locked . . . but it is. I start knocking sharply on the door, and when she doesn't respond I start banging harder. "Mom! Mom! Please talk to me! I'm freaking out!"

My entire body is shaking as I fall against the door listening for any kind of response. The dead silence pushes me over the edge. *Is she that fucking cruel?*

I'm dizzy now as my panting accelerates. "Mom, please help me! I'm having trouble breathing! This feels like more than a panic attack!" I hear my voice break, and the sob that escapes me is followed by several gasps. I slide my hand down her door. "Please, Momma . . . please!"

That single moment when I realize that she's not going to help me, and I can't catch my breath, is when I wonder if I'm about to die.

As I stumble back to the kitchen, the only thought I can grasp onto is that I need Dean. He'll know what to do. Grabbing my phone,

I drag my sleeve across my wet eyes trying to clear my vision to call him, but I notice there's another message from him that I missed. His words are a spark of light in the darkness that's descending over me.

Hold on. I'm on my way.

Dean . 59

WHEN I DROPPED JASON OFF earlier, I didn't have a good feeling as I watched him disappear into the stairwell for his mom's apartment. His duffle was sagging off his slouched shoulders and his head was down. I had to fight myself from yelling out for him and convincing him to stay with me. The odds that this was going to be anything but a shit show with his mom were very slim.

The feeling didn't subside, but when I pulled up in front of my childhood home I decided to make peace with JJ's decision to share his truth with his mom. If I ended up having to pick up the pieces if their talk didn't go well, so be it.

When I step inside our living room all is quiet until I hear a faint clicking from the dining room that my parents turned into an office. My dad looks up from his computer right as I enter the room.

"Dean!" he says as he pushes out of his chair to reach me. "You made good time!" He gives me a big hug. "I'm so glad you're here. Your mom's at the market getting stuff for dinner. Trent's coming over, too."

"Nice," I reply with a smile, settling down on the couch.

Knowing what a long drive I've just had, he goes to the kitchen and gets me a glass of water, and then pulls his desk chair over to where I am, and sits down.

As I down half the glass, my eyes scan the wood wainscoting and elaborate molding of the old house. Just sitting here brings up a warm sentimental feeling.

"So Mom said Jason drove up with you. How's he doing? She said he's been having a rough time."

"Yeah, I'm worried about him. He's going to have a big talk with his mom . . . probably tonight."

Dad looks down at his glass and swirls the water. "I see. Is this about him being gay?"

I nod. "And you know how she is. I'm really worried how he's going to take it when she doesn't accept him."

Dad shakes his head with a frown. "You know how much we love Jason. He's always been such a great kid. It hurts me to know that his only parent could reject him. Please let him know he has our support."

I look into his eyes and I'm filled with warmth knowing how lucky I am. "That will mean so much to him, Dad. Thank you."

"Of course. And I'm proud of you, son, for standing by him. You're a true friend."

It hadn't occurred to me that I'd be having this conversation with my parents, but in this moment how can I not? If Jason is telling his truth, the least I can do is tell mine.

"About that, Dad . . ."

"Being a true *friend*?" he asks, a knowing look in his expression.

"Yeah." I reply, pausing to find the right words.

"You guys are more than friends."

When I look to see if his expression tells me something his words don't, all I see is calm acceptance. "Yes, yes we are."

Leaning forward in his chair, he rests his hands on his knees. "Dean, we pretty much figured that. We'd honestly always wondered. There was just something so connected between you. But then later, when nothing seemed to come of it, we figured we may have been wrong."

"Wow. So I really was the last to know," I marvel.

He smiles. "Sometimes our minds and hearts wait until we're ready."

I look up at him, presenting the one question that's hard for me to ask. "I know how open minded you and Mom are. But I'm *your* son. Are you disappointed?" My heart is thudding as I wait for his reply.

For a moment, he casts his eyes down, rubbing his hands over his knees. "The only part of this that pains me is knowing that it isn't an easy road. Any parent who loves their child doesn't want them to suffer the cruelty and derision of others. But you're a very strong, centered young man, Dean. You're twenty-two and have lived some life and now you've chosen to be with someone we greatly admire. So no, I'm not disappointed. I'm hopeful for both of you."

He stands up and holds his arms open. Overwhelmed by his love, I step into his arms and hug him back. "You're the best, Dad. I'm so damn lucky."

"So are we, son. So are we."

Later, I end up passed out on the couch in the den while both Mom and Dad pull together dinner. Trent shows up and turns on a baseball game at a low volume, while Dad fires up the grill. I guess while I was asleep the details of Dad and my conversation was shared which spares me from having to repeat the speech twice more, and I'm grateful for it.

I know this because when I finally wake up and sit up, my gaze moves over to Trent who's watching the game. He notices I'm awake and nods to me, then the corners of his mouth turn up, and he arches his brow.

"So you and Jason, huh?"

I feel my cheeks color as I nod.

"I warned you to lock your door at night, bro," he says with a chuckle.

"Trent—" I start.

He holds up his hand. "It's cool. I'm just screwing with you. I like Jason. You know that. Besides, he's a lot better for you than that Julie you were hung up on."

I hold my breath waiting for more but he just turns back to the game.

"What's the score?" I ask.

"Four to zero, the Dodgers are ahead."

And just like that we fall into an easy silence as we watch the game.

Most of suppertime is spent with Trent talking strategy with Mom and Dad about how to handle his high-strung new boss, and Dad describing the challenges with the current book he's writing.

It's a relief to hear what other people I care about are dealing with, rather than just focusing on Jason and my struggles.

But then Mom turns to me. "How's the job search going? Has the placement office been helpful?"

"Yeah, but the market is tough. I have a number of resumes out there and plan to send more this week."

"Don't forget that Bill is still interested in talking to you about working with his team here. It may be a good stepping stone for you into a bigger firm," Dad says.

My plan was never to return to Boise, and ultimately my decision will also be affected by what happens with Jason. But when it comes right down to it I'd rather work for Bill's group than some meaningless job while I'm trying to get into a more impressive firm in another city. I assure Dad I'll consider it.

After dinner is over, Trent is clearing away the plates and I pick up and check my phone for the twentieth time.

"No word from Jason yet?" asks Mom, a worried expression on her face.

I shake my head. "And he promised he would call."

"Why don't you just text him?" Trent asks.

"I've been resisting in case they were in the middle of it, but the suspense is killing me." I quickly type out. *You okay?*

We all sit silently as I hold my phone up. I'm holding my breath to see if he answers. A few seconds later I let out the breath I've been holding as my fingers tighten over my phone. "Fuck!" I curse.

"What?" Mom asks.

Setting my phone down, I press my hands over my face. "I asked him if he was okay, and he just texted back and said 'No'."

"Oh poor Jason," Mom says with a sigh.

I stand up and take a step away from the table as I frantically try to remember where I left my keys. "Damn! I'm going over there. I knew this was a bad idea."

Mom nods, her gaze softening. "You're welcome to bring him back here to stay if they don't work it out."

"Thanks, guys. Seriously." Grabbing my jacket, I fish in the pocket and find my car keys. I make it out the door in record time.

Turning on the ignition, I pull out my phone to send one more text.

Hold on. I'm on my way.

Jason . 60

HOLD ON. I'M ON MY way.

When I realize Dean is coming for me I grab my phone to walk to the front door, desperate to reach him. However, as I head to the hallway another overwhelming wave of panic crashes over me and I'm so dizzy that I sink down to the floor. I close my eyes and begin rocking as I start repeating a prayer from Psalm thirty-four. I used to chant it over and over during the panic episodes following my times with Father Ryan.

I sought the lord and he answered me, delivering me from all my fears.

I'm still trembling and repeating the prayer as I struggle to slow down my frantic breathing when the front door swings open. The tall, broad figure is backlit from the porch light and in my stupor it takes me a moment to realize it's Dean. I see the shock on his face and for a brief moment I'm ashamed for him to see me in this state, but I'm beyond hiding anything from him.

He rushes over to me and my panic accelerates again when I glance up at his concerned expression. "What is it, JJ?" he asks after he crouches down close to me on the floor.

"She doesn't want me," I whisper.

He straightens back up abruptly, his intense gaze scanning the room. "Where is she?" he yells out before he steps back and slams the front door.

"No, Dean," I gasp. "Please!" My second plea comes out sounding like I'm a wounded animal.

He glances at me, and his expression falls when he recognizes the extent of my panicked state. "Oh, JJ," he murmurs before he pulls me up and into his arms. He rubs his large hand up and down my back. "I'm so sorry."

I soak up his tenderness because it's the only thing holding me together. He continues to embrace me, his other hand now running through my hair. "Why don't we get the fuck out of here? My parents know everything now, and they want you to come stay with us."

I press my face into his neck and let out a sob.

"Shhh," Dean murmurs.

"They do? Really?" I choke out.

"Absolutely," he replies before kissing my forehead.

I think I hear the sound of a lock turning, and a door opening, but I can't be sure. Her shrill voice comes out of nowhere, piercing the silence.

"Get away from my son, and out of my house!"

Dean and I abruptly pull apart to see Mom in her bathrobe pointing at him like he's a filthy vagrant who's broken into her home.

"Mom!" I yell out.

"This is all your fault, Dean Whitley. If you don't get out of my house, I'll call the police."

I see Dean's nostrils flare and my blood pressure soars. Dean takes a step toward her with his fists clenched. "And you call yourself a mother!" he spits out, before cursing low under his breath, "You're crazy!"

I grab onto his arm, and he doesn't shake me off. So I just hold onto him for dear life.

Dean points at her and then me. "Your son is the best man I know, despite the fact that you almost ruined him with your holier-than-thou, self-righteous bullshit. Why did you have to make his life a living hell? Are you really going to reject him . . . cast him out of your life?"

She folds her arms over her chest and gives Dean a stern look. "Until he asks for God's forgiveness and casts out the likes of you."

Lightheaded, I feel myself sway.

Dean steps back and slides his arm over my shoulder, pulling me close before addressing her again. "He deserves so much better than you. My family welcomes him with open arms."

"Is that so?" She's looking tough but I see a glimmer of raw pain born of loss in her eyes.

"Yes, and when you're old, dried up, and alone, remember tonight and the pathetic choice you made. But one day *if* you realize the mistake you've made, and you choose love instead, you know how to reach him . . . and then you can pray that it's not too late for him to care."

He nudges me. "JJ, grab your bag. Let's get out of here."

"Don't you dare go with him," she commands before turning toward Dean and thrusting her pointer finger at him. "You get out of here," she cries out.

We're both stunned but I can't stay here another minute.

It takes me a matter of seconds in my bedroom before returning with my bag slung over my shoulder and jacket in my hands.

"I'm going to call the police," she sputters.

"Mom!" I plead. "Don't do this."

She grabs her phone and before we hear whatever lame thing she's going to report, we storm out the door.

Dean . 61

ONCE WE'RE BUCKLED IN, I floor the ignition and Jason curls over so tightly that his forehead presses against his knees. "Oh my God, oh my God," he chants.

I slide my hand across his shoulder until it's cupping his neck. I'm sure it'd be safer to drive with both hands on the wheel, but I can't care about that when Jason's whole world has just exploded.

"I'm an orphan," he croaks out, sounding as pathetic as I'm sure he feels.

"No you're not," I reply with an angry tone that I hope he knows isn't about him. "*I'm* your family, my parents *are* your family. We've got your back, JJ. Always."

"What would I do without you?" he mumbles.

"You won't have to find out."

When we arrive at my parents, I tuck him under my arm as we enter the house and walk down the hall to the family room where I know everyone is watching TV while they wait for us. They all turn when we step into the room.

"He's staying here tonight," I say in a somber tone, telling them everything they need to know.

Mom gets up first and hugs Jason. "We're here for you, sweet boy. Please know that. Whatever you need . . ."

I look over to see the tears streaming down his face, and I glance up and nod at Mom in appreciation.

"Thanks, Mrs. Whitley," he whispers.

"Sarah," she reminds him with a gentle smile.

Meanwhile, Dad has gotten up and fixed drinks. He comes over and hands them to us, then pats Jason on the back. "It's strong," he says gesturing to the amber liquid. "But a night like tonight calls for it."

Jason accepts the drink and takes a large gulp, then coughs. But he still nods. "Definitely."

Trent holds out his bowl. "Popcorn?"

Jason wipes the tears off his cheeks and shakes his head. "No. But thanks, man."

Trent nods with a sympathetic gaze. "We're glad you're here."

I feel a wave of gratitude as I study my brother. Yes, he teased me endlessly when we were growing up, as big brothers do, but deep down he's a really good guy.

We settle down on the uninhabited part of the sectional, slowly sipping our whiskey and watching but not seeing whatever is on TV.

Trent is the first to leave since he has work in the morning. Mom next, and finally Dad wanders through the house, checking to make sure the doors are locked before heading upstairs. "See you in the morning. There'll be pancakes," he says.

"Thanks, Dad," I reply. After he's left I turn to Jason. "Do you want another drink before we head up?"

He shakes his head. "No." He glances over at me with a somber gaze. "They're pretty great you know."

I nod, and squeeze his hand. "They love you." Rising, I reach out for his hand. "Come on, JJ. I know tonight was hell, but tomorrow is a new day."

Jason . 62

WHEN I WAKE THE NEXT morning, Dean is still asleep so I lie in bed and reflect on these last few weeks and the emotional field of land mines I've stumbled through. There've been so many low points: imagining Dean had gone back to Julie, Dean having to rescue me from that damn sex club, all topped off by the brutal rejection by my mother. I know that I'm stunned and angry at her right now, and when it all kicks in I may regret telling her my truth. I also know that without Dean and his family's support, her rejection would've left me completely broken.

There's no doubt that I've got plenty of therapy ahead of me. At least I told my therapist that I hope to move to Seattle, and she assured me she has a couple of good referrals she'd give me when that time comes.

Each issue I've faced in the last few days is life-changing enough to knock me to my knees, yet here I lie. I'm emotionally bruised from head to toe, but with this new day I have to stand tall and walk toward the life I deserve. During the inevitable rough times, I know having Dean by my side will give me the added strength to push through.

When Dean wakes up we head downstairs to find that his mom has made my favorite breakfast—chocolate-chip pancakes—and she's put a birthday candle in my stack. They even have a card and a gift for me. It reminds me of what Dean said yesterday about his parents being my family now. I no longer have my roots from my mother securing me, but the Whitleys are the braces now holding my branches up. They are the family that knows all my issues, and they've chosen me anyway. If that isn't a blessing, I don't know what is.

When we're done with our pancakes Sarah insists on me opening my gift. It's a large, flat package and I almost hate to tear the paper off it's so beautifully wrapped with a big blue bow on top.

"Come on!" Dean says with a smile, as he waits impatiently to see my reaction.

When I finally tear the paper open, I peer down to see a framed drawing. Lifting it out of the bag, I turn it toward me. My heart skips a beat and I'm instantly overwhelmed with a rush of memories. "I remember this," I whisper.

Dean's mom grins and nods.

When we around nine or ten, Dean and I told his parents that one day we were going to open our own architectural firm.

His father challenged us by saying. "Well, if I were your client and wanted you to design us a modern house, let's see what you'd come up with."

We were both so excited by the challenge that we scrambled to their kitchen table and got to work. What we came up with looked more influenced by *The Jetsons* than anything we'd seen in books, but Dean's parents made us feel like we'd created something special. His dad had us both sign the drawing, and he dated it.

"I can't believe you guys kept it all these years," I marvel.

"I know. And look at the plaque they had the framer engrave," Dean says.

There's a brass plate secured to the matte surrounding the drawing and it says *Sorentino, Whitley & Associates*. The line just below reads, *Early Concept Drawing*.

"Pretty cool, huh?" Dean says with a grin.

"We were going to give it to you for graduation, but we thought it would cheer you up today," Dad says.

"Yes, such an awesome gift. Thank you so much," I wrap my arms around it and hold it close to my chest. I'm choked up because it's the best gift anyone has ever given me.

"Maybe it's an omen. A good luck charm for us," Dean says.

I nod my head excitedly. "Yeah!"

Dean insists on doing the dishes after breakfast and then asks me what I want to do for my birthday, since our original plans have changed. Honestly all I want to do is get the hell out of Boise but then a thought occurs to me. "Hey, let's have burgers at Big Jud's for lunch and then head back to Utah."

"Sounds good to me," Dean replies. "I'm buying."

Just past noon, after saying a heartfelt thanks to Dean's parents, we drive over to our old haunt that serves the best burgers in town. Being there feels both completely familiar and eerily foreign. The old guy that runs the place remembers us, as do a few other people who work there. Even some of the customers are familiar, including two guys that were a year behind us in high school, and what looks like their younger brothers, who appear old enough to be in high school now.

"Does it taste like you remembered?" Dean asks with a grin after I've swallowed my first big bite.

"Pretty much. And this is even the table we usually sat at."

Dean nods. "Do you ever think of coming back to live in Boise?"

I give him a look like that's a crazy question. "No, and after what happened with my mom I really don't have a reason to be here."

"But what if I were here?" Dean asks.

I can feel my smile evaporate. "But I thought you were looking for work in Seattle, like I am. I thought—"

Before I finish Dean cuts me off. "Yes, that's the dream. But let's be real for a minute. This market is brutal and my advisor warned me not to get my hopes up about Seattle. It's different for you. You've won national design awards and stuff, but I have to be realistic. And the thing is that a friend of my dad has a small firm here and they have a position open. He knew I was about to graduate and wants me to apply for it."

I'm speechless. The idea of Dean staying behind in Boise is something I never even considered. I guess I wanted us to be together in Seattle so much that I didn't think about another outcome. Staring down at the tabletop, I try to control my emotions. I can't cry again for fuck's sake. Surely my tear ducts are dry as the Sahara by now.

Dean begins to look nervous. "JJ, don't flip out. I'm just talking about a back-up plan and wanted to get your thoughts. Things could also work out where we end up in the same city, at the same firm, and living together."

I try to sound nonchalant when I ask the very question that has been haunting me. "Would you like that . . . us living together? Or do you think you'll be moving on to do your own thing once our time is up in Utah?"

Dean gives me a long look before shaking his head, grabbing our trays, and standing up abruptly. "I'm such an ass. Why the hell did I even bring that stressful shit up on your birthday? This stuff around graduation and getting jobs isn't about moving on from what we have together, but figuring out how we can make it all work. Hey, let's shelve the job talk for now, and hit the road."

I'm not ready to end this conversation but I also know he's right. "Okay," I agree as I slowly get up to follow him out to his car. I notice that table of guys from our high school are staring at us, and now I'm staring back wondering what they are finding so fascinating. *Weird.* I give them a quick nod of acknowledgement before heading outside where Dean has paused in front of the passenger door of his car.

Confused, I glance at him with a furrowed brow. "Do you want me to drive?"

Dean gets a devilish look in his eye. "No, it's just that there's another birthday gift I want to give you now."

"Really? What is it?"

"A surprise. Here, lean against the car and close your eyes."

"Yes, sir," I tease, and then do as I'm told. I'm hopeful, remembering a promise from our past.

I let out a sigh when I feel his lips skim across my lips before trailing kisses along my jaw. The pleasure pulses through me, making every part of me feel alive. He sighs as he sinks against me and takes my head in his hands, so he can kiss me deeply. My man with his heat-infused passion makes me swoon. Two more kisses follow, and I'm ready to give him everything. I love him so damn much.

"Happy Birthday, boyfriend," he whispers in my ear.

I smile and nod mutely, because at this very moment I open

my eyes and remember where we are. Is it wrong that the fact that I'm getting my promised birthday kiss out in the open, in the broad daylight of a place where people know us . . . in uptight Boise, and that's turning me on beyond anything I've ever felt?

And suddenly another thought occurs to me. Knowing that Dean worries that he may end up back in Boise, and he's still kissing me in the open like I'm all that matters, is blowing my mind. He's taking a stand for me, no matter what happens to him as a result.

"Hey!" we hear a voice call out our direction, and we both look up to see the group of guys that we'd recognized from high school. They all have looks of disgust on their faces. "Get a room, faggots," the stocky, shorter guy with bad skin yells out, throwing ice cold water on our moment. My entire body tenses as I can sense Dean's energy shift instantly from loving to lethal.

Dean whips around fast and starts storming toward the group with his hands clenched in fists, while I trail right behind him trying to hold him back. We're outnumbered but that doesn't seem to faze him since he's fueled by rage.

"You want to say that to my face, you ugly fucking troll?" he spits out, and when the guy gets a good look at Dean's size and muscular build you can see the alarm in his expression. His ugly face blushes bright red.

Two of the younger guys are already quickly backing away, while the other guy is practically dragging the troll to their truck. "You better pick up the pace, Jimmy, unless you want your face smashed in."

I watch them hustle into their truck while Dean stands his ground with his powerful arms folded over his chest. "If I you try that again, I'll beat the shit out of you, asshole!"

They burn rubber out of the parking lot, and I'm paralyzed from the whole encounter, standing with my mouth gaping open.

Dean glances back and looks at me, before returning his gaze to where the truck had exited. "I'm sorry," he says, his expression somber.

"Don't be. I don't care about them. That birthday kiss was the best present ever. Considering what your parents gave me, that's saying a lot. Believe me, Dean, you have nothing to be sorry about."

"Shall we hit the road?" he asks, looking tense, like he still wants to pound someone's face in. "I want us to get back to Salt Lake."

I nod. "I want that, too."

The entire drive back I'm touching his leg or arm, or holding his hand. The physical connection is a constant craving, and the way it calms him makes it clear that he wants it, too. Unlike the drive to Boise, this one is so much more satisfying because I know it's taking us home.

Dean . 63

WE'RE BOTH QUIET AND DEEP in thought most of the drive back to our place. The silence is a relief after all the intensity, and I realize that Jason was the only one who ever understood how much I needed to be quiet at times. When Julie was unsettled about something, she never stopped talking and it made me crazy.

I think about the public display I made kissing JJ back in Boise without freaking out or being embarrassed about gossip getting around. Even with those losers who taunted us, I have no regrets. I'm proud that I took a stand for Jason and I'm sure he feels the significance of that gesture. I'm past being afraid of people knowing how I feel about him.

When we cross from Idaho into Utah, Jason picks up his phone and checks his messages. I can feel the energy in the car shift, and when I glance up his cheeks are flushed and his eyes wide. He looks down at his messages again, then shuts his phone off and turns to look out the window.

In that moment, I have a powerful sense that everything has changed. Is this about a job? That possibility makes me want to hold onto him tighter than ever knowing that our time left to be together may be short.

Finally back in the house, I take dibs on the shower and Jason removes everything except his boxers and flops down on the bed with his phone. He's looking at his messages again and it fires up my nerves. I both want to know what's going on, and I don't want to know, as I step inside the bathroom and close the door. The hot water cascading over me loosens me up and helps me relax a little.

"The bathroom's yours if you want it," I say when I approach the bed after drying off, leaving only a towel around my waist.

He shrugs and sets his phone down. "I'm good." He holds his arm out, beckoning me, and I slide onto the bed until I'm by his side.

"Hey birthday boy," I lean over and kiss him on his cheek. "You want to go out or something?"

"No. Let's just hang here and order pizza. Okay?"

I nod and skim my fingers over his chin, down his neck where I feel him swallow back his desire, then across his chest and finally pause on his lower abs.

He leans into my hand as I skim my fingers up his toned muscles.

I hook my leg over his and kiss his shoulder, breathing him in and wondering if I'll ever get enough of him. I love him so damn much.

Taking my hand, he kisses my open palm, then presses it on his chest that's now flushed and hot to my touch. "More," he whispers.

This time I'm playful, lightly skimming my index finger across his chest like I'm drawing a design. I glance up at him and his eyes are twinkling.

"Are you really drawing something on my chest, or is this some new kind of freaky touch therapy?" he teases.

I laugh. "Nope, I'm drawing. Hold still and quit squirming, will you?"

He points to his desk. "If you really want to draw there's a pad right over there.

I shake my head. "No. I want to draw here."

His eyes narrow playfully. "I think that long drive made you screwy."

I keep skimming my fingers over his smooth skin. He sighs and slides up on the pillow a bit so he can watch me. "So what are you drawing, Picasso?"

"The future."

"Oh yeah? Is it bright?"

I nod, continuing to make little hash marks across his skin like I'm filling something in. "So damn bright."

"Are we together?" His expression shifts to something vulnerable and raw.

My finger picks up speed, pretend outlining two stick figures right over where his heart is beating fast just below my touch. "Here we're in our own firm getting ready for a meeting." I move my hand to his calf and glide it upwards. "See, here's the client in the elevator riding up to meet us."

"You drew him riding my leg up the elevator? What am I, three years old?"

"Hey, I'm being expressive and creative here. Work with me."

He laughs softly. "What are we designing for this client?"

"It's a Neutra-inspired home design, of course. It's built on levels into the hillside, overlooking Puget Sound."

"Nice. And are we a couple, or just business partners?" he inquires softly, a flash of hope in his hooded gaze.

I have to clear my gravely voice to speak. "We're together in every way."

He nods with approval. "I like it." He turns onto his hip, so we're facing each other. "Would you like that, too? I mean, I know I'm a handful. You've had to put up with a lot."

This time it's my turn to swallow down my emotion. "I'd like it. You're not so bad, you know."

He slides a little closer to me. "You're not so bad either."

I smile at him, slowly tracing my fingers over his full lips.

I've paused my hand on his hip and notice his hard cock is pressing up against the thin fabric of his boxers. It takes everything I have not to reach for his dick and wrap my fingers tightly around it. My cock throbs at the thought of it, and his eyes steal a glance down to confirm what he's feeling pressed against him.

He reaches up, takes my hand, and drags it down his body until he presses it over his erection. "I want you so damn much. Can you kiss me already?" he insists more than asks.

"So demanding," I tease as I rise over him. He shifts and returns to lying on his back, then spreads his legs so I can settle back down on top of him. I lift up on my elbows to look in his eyes. His intense gaze of longing is working me up to where my restraint is hanging by a very frail thread.

"What do you need from me?" I ask, my voice rough and heavy with desperation. Our hard cocks are pressed together and every time I shift just slightly, the sensation of our connection sends sparks shooting up my spine.

His eyes flash a bit of mischief. He's going to toy with me. I know it. "I just want another birthday kiss," he whispers, rocking his hips up. "The *complete* package kiss."

I shudder from the sexual tension vibrating from my head to my toes. "Complete package, huh? I think I can do that." I study every part of his face, which is now flushed with desire. The complete package means I'll soon be buried deep inside of him. Suddenly it feels like it's my birthday, too.

He sighs impatiently. "Well, what are you waiting for?" His pupils are dilated and he chews his lower lip, already worked up with anticipation. He helps me push his boxers off.

Hovering over him, I roll my hips so my hard cock rubs over his.

I start slow, kissing his neck, his jawline, and his temple before finally tasting his lips. He's already moaning and breathless, inspiring me to kiss him deeper.

"Oh," he gasps, "I've missed this so damn much." He winds his fingers into my hair and pulls me closer while biting my lip, and then brushing his fingers over the bite mark and kissing me again.

"I'm going to make you feel so good," I warn, "like crazy good. I need to achieve permanent status as your sex god. That way you'll never want anyone else."

He huffs and shakes his head. "Like wanting anyone else is even possible after you."

"Exactly," I moan.

I work my way down his neck and chest with hot kisses, licks, and tender bites, teasing each nipple, before trailing lower to his hipbone. He shudders when I slide my tongue along his swollen cock.

"More," he groans, so I take him in deeper, over and over until he's panting and groaning my name.

"Do you want me to fuck you?" I ask, desperate to hear him agree.

He lets out a long, low groan. "Yes . . . yes." He nods his head toward the bedside table and I quickly lean over, pull open the drawer, and grab the bottle of lube.

He spreads his legs eagerly, his heated gaze setting me on fire as I lube up and ease my finger inside of him.

"More," he begs just a minute later.

He shudders and reaches his hands up to cup my face and pulls me down into a passionate kiss. We've got each other so worked up that all he'd have to do is stroke me a few times and I'd explode. But he doesn't touch me anywhere but my face, kissing me into such a frenzy that I'm not even sure where I am. All the while I keep working him until I can feel him start to unravel.

"Please, Dean, please," he cries, his whole body trembling.

I rise up on my knees and generously lube my cock while he looks on mesmerized. Leaning over him, I scrape my teeth along his jawline and then whisper, "Are you ready?"

His eyes grow wide as his legs inch even farther apart. "I'm so ready." His voice is deep and husky and his face and chest are flushed.

I focus while I position my cock and begin pushing into him, meanwhile lowering myself so we can kiss. By the time my cock is buried deep inside, my mouth is ravaging his. I feel wild and desperate; the intensity of it is mind blowing.

I'm thrusting hard now and he's clawing at my back, his eyes half-mast with pleasure.

My gaze is tinted through a lust-filled, hazy filter as I watch him come undone. "Is this how you dreamt it would be for your birthday? I want it to be just how you imagined it."

"Even better," he gasps, as each thrust feels deeper. All the while we keep kissing like lovers reunited after a long parting. I'm a man who keeps his promises, and I promised him this.

"Oh yeah, oh God, that's it!" he cries as he starts coming, sparking every nerve in his body. His climax goes on and on and it's the hottest thing I've ever seen.

When he finally settles, I bear down, so I'm taking him with everything I have. I can see in his eyes that he loves the effect he has on me. No sex has ever come close to how I feel with this man . . . the way *he* makes me feel.

"JJ," I gasp, my heart thundering.

"Yes, baby. . . . so good." His hands grab my ass pulling me closer so I go deeper.

The next moments are so blindingly vivid in pleasure and sensation that I nearly black out. I'm on fire and breathless as I fly higher and higher until I finally let go and soar into my climax.

After my final thrust, Jason slowly straightens out his legs and pulls me down on top of him, so I can catch my breath.

"Was that—" I start to ask before he cuts me off.

"Perfect, absolutely perfect," he says with a contented sigh.

I skim kisses across his face until I feel him smile under my lips.

"A better birthday than the go-cart racing my parents took us to when you turned thirteen?" I ask.

He laughs into the crook of my neck. "Way better."

I slowly ease off of him and then lower myself down to the mattress. Taking the washcloth he left on the bedside table, I clean off his chest and abs, then mine from where I'd pressed against him.

He's watching me and I see something more in his expression: sadness, concern, uncertainty?

"Are you okay?" I ask, resting my hand on his chest as we lie together.

"Yeah."

"You sure?"

"It's just that you said you want to be a sex god so that you'll be all I ever want. Don't you know that you already *are* all I've ever wanted, Dean? You've always been all I've ever wanted."

"You're not just saying that?" I tease.

His eyes bug out like he's insulted or something. "Isn't it obvious?"

"Pretty much," I say, with a bit of uncertainty in my voice. "But there was Ramon and everything."

The corners of his mouth turn down. "He wasn't important to me and you know it. It's just been hard because I always thought that the white-picket fence and a wife and kids was your dream, and it was a dream I'd never be able to give you."

I shrug, and give him a reassuring smile. "Sometimes dreams change."

He lets out a sigh of relief. "Thank God for that. And this is exactly why I want us making our next move together. None of this, I'll think 'I'll go back to Boise' bullshit." His neck is red and his eyes are glazed like he's about to cry.

I look down at the sheets and I can feel my entire body tense up. "You got some news today, didn't you?"

He stares at me silently for several long seconds and then nods his head. "It looks like I may have an offer in Seattle . . . at Daniels, Slater and Watson. They want to fly me out so they can meet with me."

I wish he looked happy about it. Then it would be much easier to pretend that I'm happy about it. "Wow, that's great, right?" I manage to choke out.

There's no pleasure in his expression. "It really doesn't mean much to me if you aren't going to be there with me."

I shake my head. "This is your future."

"You're my future," he insists.

"I can't let you turn down something because of me. I can't."

"Then come with me, Dean."

"Move to Seattle without a job? How would that work?"

"You'd be living with me, and it'd be much easier getting a job there if you're in the city. We'll be making contacts through my work and we can focus our energy on learning all we can. You're amazing and soon you'll be meeting people and they'll see how amazing you are, too."

Now my damn eyes tear up. He wants me so bad that he'll carry me. He's not just my lover, he's still my best friend. So there's nothing to consider: a mediocre job in Boise alone, or an adventure with JJ in Seattle? I can be stupid at times, but I'm not crazy. There's no other choice.

"So you and me in Seattle, huh?"

He nods his head excitedly. "I swear you won't regret it. You'll get a great job . . . I know you will."

"And I'll be living with you? Sharing your one bedroom or single apartment? Seattle's expensive you know."

He grins. "Yeah, we share a bed, and we can do the Top Ramen and peanut butter and jelly sandwich thing until the steady paychecks kick in. It won't kill us."

"Because we'll be together."

"Yes." His eyes are shining. I've never seen him look so hopeful.

"Can we still order pizza once in a while?"

He huffs before folding his arms over his chest, full of fake bravado. "Just the one topping kind, and none of that thick-crust nonsense—that costs extra," he teases with a cocky smile.

I nod with a grin bigger than his. "Okay, you've got me, JJ, I'm all in."

"Yes!" he exclaims before reaching over and kissing me.

I flop back on my pillow and think of the wild turn my life has taken. I'm in love with my best friend, having the hottest sex of my life, and now I'm going to jump off the career cliff to be with him, hoping I'll land on both feet. Maybe I *am* fucking crazy, but I don't care. "Hey, you know what?" I ask, just as he's wound his fingers through mine.

"What?" He turns toward me and brushes my hair off my face and then kisses my cheek.

I stare up at the ceiling before glancing over at him. "I fucking love you, JJ. Yeah, I know, you're a handful and all that. But it's real and as true as it will ever be . . . I'm really *in* love with you." I squeeze his hand, tightening his fingers over mine. "So there."

Blinking at me, his face is awash with emotion as he takes a sharp breath and then blinks some more.

I squint my eyes at him. "So this is the part where you say that you fucking love me, too."

He nods, this beautiful man, the softness in his soulful gaze gutting me. I feel a tear glide down my cheek. *Stupid eyes.* But then I see one glide down JJ's cheek as well.

"I love you, Dean . . . so damn much. With all my heart, and all that stuff."

I shake my head. "Look at us crying like two twelve-year-old girls."

He laughs as he brushes his hand across my wet cheek, and then does the same to himself. "So, you hungry?"

"Always," I say. "Still want birthday pizza?"

"Yeah, but I want all the toppings tonight."

"Can we do thick-crust, too?"

He scoffs. "It's my birthday not yours."

I point at him defiantly. "You said you loved me."

He grins and his smile is everything. I look over at my man as he picks his phone up off the bedside table to call for pizza delivery. He's got the sheets gathered low on his waist and it gives me a moment to admire his perfect body—his broad, strong shoulders and perfectly defined abs and chest. My gaze then trails up to his beautiful face. He's so damn fine looking that sometimes it hurts to gaze at him because I know everyone else wants him too. But most importantly, he's smart as hell, and a good man with a loyal heart who has always watched out for me. All of that awesomeness and he's mine . . . *mine.*

He clears his throat when the pizza place rings through. "Yeah, I'd like to order a large with everything since it's my birthday. Yeah, thanks. Yup, same address. And you know what? My guy wants thick crust. So let's do that, too. Thirty minutes? Okay, thanks."

As soon he hangs up, I tackle him, pinning him to the mattress. "Thick crust? You must really love me!"

He kisses me, and then slides his lips over my cheek and sighs. "Always have, and always will."

Dean. Epilogue

"JASON," I CALL OUT, MY voice echoing through the empty space. The high ceilings and raw brick accent walls give it a loft feeling while the unexpected angled lines and strategic bold use of color keep things lively. It's the perfect melding of what JJ and I love best about architectural modernism—a little bit of Mies Van der Roe meets Frank Geary. We've come a long way from daydreaming about our future firm while living in our crap college apartment to now, where it's actually happening better than we could've dreamt. "In here," he calls back.

I walk slowly through the loft until I see him standing in front of the floor-to-ceiling window of what will eventually be our conference room. He doesn't turn, just keeps gazing out at the view with his hands resting on his hips and his shoulders pulled back. His hair is shorter now, but some longer parts fall over his forehead, adding edginess to his already striking features. His personal style has come a long way since our college days and he always looks sharp, in lean pressed jeans, fitted button-down shirts and his black cowboy boots that are worn enough to look cool. I have a tendency to put a proprietary arm around him when I notice other men and women ogling him. I like to let the world know that *he's mine*.

JJ always tries to turn the tables and say it's me the flirty ones want, so we both hold on to a visceral claim on each other, making it clear to others not to even bother.

Walking right up behind him, I rest my chin on his shoulder and wrap my arms around him. He lets out a contented sigh.

"Pretty amazing view," I murmur, taking in his scent, realizing he's wearing my favorite aftershave and his ass is looking particularly tempting in this pair of jeans. He's so damn distracting.

"It's perfect," he murmurs.

It's an exceptional day in Seattle. After a morning rain, the clouds have parted, spreading golden sunshine over the views of downtown, Elliott Bay, and the Olympic Mountains.

"I'm going to have such a hard time focusing on meetings with this scenic splendor calling out to me," I grumble.

He chuckles. "Well then I'll make you sit with your back to the window."

"Oh yeah?" I tease. "Good luck with that."

Grinning, he then returns his gaze toward the view. "You know, sometimes I can't believe this is really happening."

I nod and rest my hand on his shoulder, kneading the tight muscles. "I know there were plenty of times we almost gave up thinking we could have our own firm, JJ. Yet here we are."

"We worked hard for it," he says. I can hear the pride in his voice.

I sigh remembering all the struggles we had to overcome. "I'm proud of you for staying strong. Without that settlement money from your case it would have been years before this could've happened for us."

He nods, his expression intense as he turns back to look out the window. My man is a different person now than he was when our relationship changed our last few months of college. He was always sexy and smart as hell, but now he's also powerful and confident, the kind of man everyone notices when he walks into a room.

Still, it wasn't that easy for us after college. He got his dream job in Seattle with a great firm before graduation, and the day he got the news I was sure I was going to get lost in the shuffle. The only viable offer I had gotten was back in Boise, not at all where I hoped to work.

But JJ insisted that I that I would find a better job more easily while living in Seattle, and meanwhile we'd be together. Thank God he was right, and now here we are almost six years later totally immersed in our careers with all areas of our lives shared.

As time went on we also faced some really rough challenges, especially around the lawsuit he'd agreed to be a part of. The worst

Connect with Ruth

For book stuff:
https://www.facebook.com/RuthClampettWrites

For a more general stuff:
https://www.facebook.com/RuthClampett
http://instagram.com/Ruth_Clampett
https://twitter.com/RuthyWrites

About the Author

RUTH CLAMPETT IS A 21ST century woman aspiring to be Wonder Woman . . . now if she could only find her cape and magic lasso. Meanwhile she's juggling motherhood, a full-time job running her own fine art publishing business for Warner Bros., and writing romance late at night. Travel is her second obsession after writing, and it's enabled her to meet reader and writer friends all over the world. She's happily frazzled, and wouldn't change a thing about her crazy life.

The rooms in her home are all painted different colors and her books are equally varied, infusing humor, drama, and passion into the romantic lives of strong heroines and heroes and their worthy and determined counterparts.

Ruth has published eight books: *Animate Me, Mr. 365,* the *Work of Art Trilogy, WET, BURN* and *Unforgiven*. Three of her novels have been translated in German, French and Portuguese. She grew up and still happily resides in Los Angeles, and is heavily supervised by her teenage daughter, lovingly referred to as Snarky, who loves traveling with her mom with a sketchbook in hand.

future I can't work with anyone but her, and I assured them not to worry. She's a gem.

My cover designer, Jada D'Lee will certainly also be invited out with the boys, despite the fact that Jason resents being relegated to the back cover. But they both agree with me, that Jada made a gorgeous cover. Thank you my friend.

I am so lucky to be working with my L.A. Bestie, Jenn Watson, from Social Butterfly PR. She tackles everything with grace and humor, which is no small feat since authors go a little nutty when it's book release time and I am no exception to that rule.

Thank you Flavia Viotti of Bookcase Agency—the goddess of international book deals. I am honored by you and your team's support of my work.

Many thanks to lovely Melissa, of There For You Editing, for cleaning up the error of my ways . . . and to the delightful Christine Borgford of Type A Formatting for doing a terrific job formatting. You both are total pros.

Finally I send so much love to you, dear readers. If you have read other works of mine, I'm so pleased that you took a chance on my first M/M love story and I hope you enjoyed it. As for new readers, welcome! I hope Dean and Jason's story is one you'll hold in your heart. I love those boys, and they are forever in mine.

Thank you so much.

Acknowledgements

IN WRITING THIS BOOK I found inspiration from my gay friends who've had a significant impact on my life. The list is long from my girlfriend DW I looked up to more than anyone in high school. She modeled for me a strong, confident woman who boldly achieved her dreams. There was my prom date, guy-bestie SC who treated me like a queen, BA my beloved photography studio partner who became a second brother to me, BN the best man at my wedding, AS my inspiring boss at Warner Bros., SD my creative partner at Warner Bros., to my dear friends and staff, significant people in my life today whom I love like family. I have been so blessed to have each of them in my life. They taught me what it meant to be true to yourself so you are free to follow your heart.

Thank you to my wonderful book-community friends, who encouraged me to write this story and have cheered me on through every stage. I'm grateful to early readers Glorya Hildago, Azucena Sandoval, Lisa Fortunato, and Jenn Watson whose early feedback gave me the courage to keep going. My wonderful daughter Alex as well, who often tells me she's proud of me and is always encouraging.

I love our community of indie bloggers, authors, promoters, designers and readers, and I'm so grateful for your support of my work. Thank you!

Endless gratitude to my wonderful content editor, Angela Borda, I think Dean and Jason would like to take her out for a drink and perhaps dancing at the Abbey in West Hollywood for the firm, yet tender attention she bestowed on them. They told me that in the

Research for Unforgiven

WHILE WRITING UNFORGIVEN I DID extensive research regarding the early clerical abuse Jason suffered in his young life. I was very moved by the members of S.N.A.P. The Survivors Network of those Abused by Priests, who bravely stepped forward to tell their stories of abuse to help other victims. I was able to read and listen to recordings of many heartbreaking accounts that helped me understand Jason as his character took shape in my mind. As a survivor myself of a violent sexual attack, this is a subject I took very seriously, and hopefully you as a reader will feel that I handled the subject with sensitivity and not sensationalism.

I have learned that once abused or attacked, people are forever changed and for young people who are repeatedly abused the damage is unfathomable. I know first-hand, people whose lives were changed by such experiences.

There are great organizations where victims can reach out for help. Listed below are two that I am familiar with. I encourage anyone who has suffered to get help, even if years have passed since their abuse.

www.snapnetwork.org/
www.911rape.org/about-us/who-we-are

Also by
RUTH CLAMPETT

Burn~L.A. Untamed Series Book 2
Wet~L.A. Untamed Series Book 1
Animate Me
Mr. 365

Work of Art~Book 1 The Inspiration
Work of Art~Book 2 The Unveiling
Work of Art~Book 3 The Masterpiece
Work of Art~The Collection

Many thanks to those of you that take a moment to leave a review ~ it's much appreciated.

I sigh. "Deep down I wanted it so much, that I always believed we'd work together. I imagined it all the time. Although honestly I didn't think it would be this amazing."

"Well, it was meant to be," he says.

I glance over at our drawing remembering us as two young boys, sitting at his kitchen table taking turns sketching on his big drawing pad. By the time we were finished there were eraser crumbs all over the tabletop, the remnants of many discussions over design changes discussed and redrawn. Once satisfied, we raced to the family room, tumbling over each other to share our masterpiece with Dean's parents. We were praised, and thus inspired to never stop designing and building our skyscrapers of hopes and dreams, one floor at a time.

Little did we know back then that we already had the blueprint etched in our hearts for our future. Falling in love hadn't been in the original design, but time and experience had taught us that inspired revisions should be a gift to embrace.

So here we are. We're imperfect, yet have faith in our foundation. We've raised a roof to protect us against life's inevitable storms. There are balconies to stand and dream on, and landscaping to connect us to the earth so our feet are solidly on the ground. Like anything wonderful built over time, we are perfectly imperfect and whole.

Dean steps forward, and nudges the corner of the frame a fraction to straighten it. "Sorentino, Whitley, and Associates," he says, reading the plaque before turning back to smile at me. "Tomorrow's our first official day in business. Are you ready?"

"I'm all in," I reply, standing tall.

He slings his work satchel over his shoulder, tucks the box of champagne under his arm, and then reaches out and takes my hand. "Come on, love. Tomorrow our big, bright future begins."

"If you want it to be. Hey, there's nothing more romantic than pizza and champagne in bed with mood music playing in the background."

"No Miles Davis," I insist, rolling my eyes. For some reason he thinks Miles Davis' music is sexy.

He points his finger at me and wags it. "And no Adele."

I've been playing my Adele playlist over and over since he made my birthday wish come true and took me to her concert. It was awesome, and very cool of him since he's not really a fan.

"Actually, I'm thinking Marvin Gaye," he says with that sexy smile and determined look that he knows I can't say no to.

"Well, let's get a move on." I'm already imagining what a great evening it will be. "We need to get that champagne on ice so it'll be cold when the pizza arrives."

We've packed up our bags and are getting ready to turn off the lights when a thought occurs to me. "Hey, we forgot the most important thing of all."

His eyes widen. "What's that?"

"Do you have the hammer and a nail?" I ask.

Dean steps out of his office for a minute and then returns with a smile. It's apparent he's figured out what I'm referring to. "Where are we going to hang it?"

I scratch my chin. "How about in the hallway, on the wall between our two offices?"

He nods. "That feels right."

He holds the picture in position so I can make a marking on the wall where the nail will go. Once I've secured the nail, Dean carefully hangs up the framed drawing that we drew together twenty years ago.

We take a step back, and I pinch the bridge of my nose because I don't want to cry, even though it'd be a happy cry. I think I've shed enough tears in front of Dean for a lifetime. He deserves a break.

His gaze is warm as he pulls me into his arms and holds me close enough that I can feel his heart beating. He gently kisses me on the forehead. "Can you imagine if we'd known back then that we'd end up here?"

thinking, touchy-feely stuff, but I think they're great and I remind him often how lucky, he is . . . hell, how lucky we both are.

Opening the box, he pulls out a bottle of fancy champagne.

He makes a face. "I'd rather have beer."

I laugh. Dean will always be *that* guy—no pretensions, just true to who he is, and I love him for it.

"Hey look, here's a card." I hand it to Dean and he tears the envelope open and begins reading.

Dear Dean and Jason,

Congratulations are in order. We're so proud that you've made your dream of your own firm come true! Your future is so big and bright!

Love,

Mom and Dad

"Kind of sappy, don't you think?" Dean says, searching my expression with his intense gaze.

"I love your parents, Dean. I think they're incredible."

His gaze softens and he nods his head. "We're pretty damn lucky."

"Indeed we are," I agree, realizing that I'll always treasure having his family in our lives. I also reflect on all the struggles we fought through to get to this moment. There's so much to celebrate.

I step behind his desk and rest the edge of my ass against the one spot of the polished desktop not covered with project folders.

"What do you say we take off early tonight?" I ask.

He glances down at his watch and arches his brow. "Yeah, it's only seven."

I nod with a sigh. I can't count how many nights we've been working past midnight to make all this happen.

He rolls his chair over until he's between my legs and he rests his big hands on my hips. "Should we head home, order a pizza, and crack open that bottle? I've gotta warn you, champagne makes me really horny."

I give him a wink. "Sounds like a plan."

"You okay missing the gym?"

He shrugs. "I'll go in the morning.

"Is this going to be like a date?"

I'll ever have, and I'm grateful that they've been here for Dean and I when my mother refused to be, still desperately shaping her life from her fears rather than love. I tried on and off for a couple of years to get her to come around but finally I just had to let her go. Our relationship has now been reduced to polite greeting cards sent on birthdays and holidays. She never acknowledges Dean in the holiday cards she sends even though I always sign hers from the both of us.

I carry the package to Dean's office and pause in the doorway when I realize that he's on a business call. I can tell he's talking to the head contractor on the Newman job because he sounds all alpha, and it's hot as hell. I never get tired of seeing him in action at work. Not that I ever doubted it would be this way, but he's the perfect business partner for me . . . the perfect *everything* for me.

He still hasn't noticed that I'm standing here, and I watch his jaw tighten and he clenches his fist and releases it, all the while I'm not listening to his actual conversation but remembering him in bed last night. He was very alpha with me too, instructing how he wanted me while he slowly pulled off his shirt and slacks, the fierce gleam in his seductive eyes turning me on with such need that my thighs were spreading apart in anticipation.

He loved me passionately as I begged for it, turning me inside out with raw pleasure. When we finally collapsed onto the sheets I'm pretty sure I'd never felt more satisfied.

I've snapped out of my lusty daydream when I hear his throat clear as he sets his phone down.

"What's that?" he asks, when I place the box on his desk.

"It's from your parents." I point to the shape of the long, narrow box. "From the looks of it I'm guessing it's liquor. Don't you think? Knowing them, I bet its champagne to celebrate us finally making this crazy dream a reality. After all, they've been behind us every step of the way."

He shakes his head with a grin. I know he thinks his parents are way over the top with their 'celebrating every victory', positive

Printed in Great Britain
by Amazon